BLACK BONES RED EARTH

LEE RICHIE

Right Track Publishing
Hill Top, Australia

Lee Richie/Right Track Publishing
49 Cumberteen Street
Hill Top, NSW 2575

www.leerichie.com

This book is a work of fiction. Any references to historical events, real people, or real places are used fictitiously. Other names, characters, places and events come from the author's imagination, and any resemblance to actual events, places or people, living or dead, is purely coincidental.

Black Bones, Red Earth/Lee Richie. -- 1st ed.
ISBN 978-0-6482564-4-1 Hardcover
ISBN 978-0-6482564-3-4 Paperback
ISBN 978-0-6482564-5-8 E-Book

Author's note

In the years between 1920 and 1970, 130,000 British children were despatched to other countries, mostly Canada and Australia, under the Child Migrant Program. Government policy was facilitated and implemented by churches and charities, ostensibly to give children a better life. In reality, they were often little more than unpaid servants, labourers, and bloodstock for the colonies. They were separated from siblings, and sent to remote farms, church missions and state-run institutions, where they were often subjected to sexual and physical abuse.

Prior to and including those periods, the Australian government implemented various policies of assimilation. Indigenous Australian children were forcibly separated from their families and placed in institutions, where they were taught to reject their Aboriginal culture and adopt white culture. Speaking traditional language was forbidden.

The above practices tore families apart, destroyed communities and left a legacy of shame that affects those traumatised until this day.

For Mum, and all the other children, orphaned, sent away, separated from families, taken or abandoned, regardless of race, colour or creed.

&

For my family

Black Bones Red Earth

PART ONE

Prologue

Present day, Cumbria, England

'Forgive me, Lord, for I have sinned, but then You know that, don't You? Because You helped in the cover-up. Why then couldn't You let it be? I'm seventy-six years old, and – perhaps quite foolishly – I had thought we had come to an agreement, You and I.'

I look skyward, as heavy cloud envelops and consumes the mountains, a vanishing act only nature could conjure with such total disregard for their mighty bulk. I watch the transformation unfold from my bedroom, as a dense curtain of rain moves through the valley with astonishing speed, obliterating all things from view until only the near pasture is visible. Sheep huddle against the dry-stone wall and turn their heads from the stinging onslaught, fading from sight in the swirling deluge. The squall is at my window, spreading rivulets across the panes like fingers, testing the frame for access. The wind howls. A plastic bucket cartwheels across the lawn and the trees in the yard thrash like angry giants.

The disturbance is brief. As quickly as the downpour sweeps through the valley, the clouds lift to reveal the brooding fells once more. Light dramatically cleaves the dark grey blanket, splashing golden rays over the glistening wet peaks. The squall has ended, and calm has returned to the dales and mountains I have come to love so dearly. To the west, more dark clouds threaten; there is more rain to come. But already the storm that promises to tear me apart and expose the weathered bones of my past has begun in earnest.

Chapter 1

Orphan-Walkanya

Western New South Wales, Australia

October 1951

There had been no respite from the dry the day I arrived at Cutaway Creek. One day rolled into the next with the same oppressive heat, offering no promise of change, no chance that the day would bring the big wet to this strange and desperate land. The creek had shrunk to isolated pools of muddy brine, a dwindling lifeline for the cockatoos that had gathered in great numbers along the banks. They squawked, argued and complained, performed somersaults and hung upside down from the limbs of river gums, wings spread wide like restless albino bats. Perhaps, with their aerial contortions, they hoped to impress the rain gods, or maybe they performed for me, a grand circus greeting for the new girl with the lily-white skin, as pale as their snowy feathers. A lazy monitor tasted the air with its flicking tongue and examined a leathery carcass of hide and bones. Blowflies buzzed and harassed the lizard, persistently irritating the creature, hoping perhaps that it would lead them to food. They swarmed over the parched carcass while the lizard looked on, but not even the blowies could find nourishment on the dried-out remains. I watched as the lizard moved slowly beyond the fence line, the blowflies following. This world was as foreign to me as were the mountains of the moon.

The wind pump stood idle, stark against the azure sky, looking for all the world like a lonely black flower. Someone should paint it yellow, I thought. Father Donahue had disappeared inside the house, leaving me to wait beside his dust-covered motorcar, a blanket of russet hues covering the once-shiny black metal. Silence. I scanned the vast landscape and wondered how something so big could look and sound so empty. I traced a heart in the dirt with my fingertip and thought of Archie. 'I'll find you!' My brother's last words, called across the train station as they dragged him kicking and screaming to a different destination, a different opportunity. Three years older than me, Archie had always been there to lead the way. I tried to follow, but I had no chance, and was plucked from the ground and bundled into my carriage by an irritated woman who slapped me so hard I could hear nothing in my right ear for several hours into the journey. 'Ungrateful little bitch,' said the woman with the pig eyes and the hard slap. I didn't cry.

The Cutaway Creek homestead sat in the centre of the compound. With windows like eyes peering out beneath the low steel roof, it looked to me like a fat cat wearing a tin hat pulled snuggly over its ears. It smiled at me. Not a welcoming smile but a sly grin that said, don't even think of running away, little girl. 'Where would I run?' I asked the cat with the hat. I looked out over the parched wasteland. Red soil, a foil for the tussocks of straw-coloured grass, stretched as far as the eye could see, all the way until it melted on the horizon. *Where would I run?*

Eventually, a man emerged from the homestead, took stock of me. Unimpressed by what he saw, he shook his head and returned inside with a slam of the screen door. BAM! I cringed at the explosive sound and waited some more in the punishing heat. I sat on my brown leather suitcase with the makeshift string handle, and imagined that the case, nearly as big as me, might hide me inside, and Father Donahue would take me home to Archie without knowing I was there. But Father Donahue would notice. He saw everything.

Patiently, I waited as the sun burned my skin. I looked for the lizard, but he was well gone. I gagged and swallowed hard. My throat burned, raw and painful. They removed my tonsils the day before taking the train journey, but they gave us no ice-cream after. Lots of children had the operation on arrival from England, and none of us had ice-cream. I had joined the line of screaming, desperate kids, forcefully dragged to the surgeon's table where we were sedated by a nurse dripping dreams from a bottle onto white cotton masks, pressed hard against our tortured, terrified faces. A second nurse held our arms to stop us fighting. I remembered nothing else until I awoke on a rubber mattress, a nurse holding a bowl and saying, 'Spit, don't swallow.'

Flies buzzed my face. I waved them away, but they returned in higher numbers, settling on my eyelashes, nose and mouth. I brushed them off and waited. Father Donahue emerged from the homestead, followed by the man and a woman, who, on first sight, appeared to smile. Closer examination revealed a snarl that would rarely leave her angry face. She locked her eyes on mine as the priest took me roughly by the wrist and, with my tattered suitcase, led me to the steps of the verandah where I stood to be assessed.

'Scrawny,' said the man.

'Doesn't look like she's got a day's chores in her,' said the woman.

Father Donahue turned me like a top so they could see me all over. 'She'll grow,' he said. 'And besides, she's after a home, not a job, Mrs Stuart.'

I choked over the sweet metallic blood still burning in my throat, and spat a long, stringy trail of saliva that refused to break away. I lowered my head and spat again. Still the saliva refused to part.

'For God's sake, girl, show some decorum,' said Father Donahue, shaking me by my arm so that I had bruises the next day where his fingers had squeezed so hard. Then to the woman on the verandah. 'She's had her tonsils removed, Mrs Stuart. Nothing that a good salt rinse won't cure and she'll be right as rain by the morning.'

The priest turned back to me. 'Say hello to Mr and Mrs Stuart, Katherine.' His Irish lilt sounded almost joyful, as though we were all close friends and about to have a party. 'And thank them for their Christian charity, taking you in and giving you a new home. You're a lucky young lady.'

I didn't feel lucky, though I thanked them dutifully, despite the pain in my throat, the sounds of appreciation sounding more like the squeak of a mouse. Did mice squeak when they apologised? I wasn't sure. The pain in my throat brought a misty haze to my eyes, but I refused to let the tears run.

Father Donahue disappeared in a cloud of orange dust. I watched him for a few moments, the urge to run and catch him strong enough to make me take a step or two towards the gate. Too far to even try, I thought, and who could catch a cloud anyway?

'Bring your case,' said Mrs Stuart, as she made her way down the house steps and led me to a small timber building to the right of the farmhouse. She opened the heavy wooden door and waited while I dragged my bag across the yard, leaving a dirt furrow in my wake. 'I haven't got all bloody day,' she said. 'This is your room.'

One small window faced the yard; it had a large crack and so much grime, it let in little light. The room had a bed, a wooden bench, a shelf and a cupboard with a curtain on a wire instead of doors. A box of wax candles stood next to a crude, steel holder where wax had pooled, layer upon layer, to form a small mountain.

'Unpack your stuff and put it in the cupboard. Get your water from the kitchen to wash. There's a bowl on the bench and a bucket underneath. Breakfast is at cock's first crow. Don't be late. If you're late, you don't eat. There's a tub hanging on the wall.' She pointed to a galvanised bath the size of a large sink, hanging from a rusty nail near the door. 'You can boil a kettle in the kitchen. Laundry is Mondays. You can wash your clothes with the rest of the laundry. You'll eat dinner in the kitchen before Mr Stuart comes home for his. If he's early, you'll take a plate to your room. Any questions?' I shook my head. 'Good. I hate questions.'

Mrs Stuart closed the door and disappeared to the house, leaving me standing alone in the grim surrounds with the creepy shadows, broken by the startling brilliance of light bleeding in through the cracks in the wall. I felt trapped, a helpless bird in a dark wooden box, shafts of sunshine my only glimpse of freedom.

Unsurprisingly, I didn't sleep that first night, but lay awake to the sound of a thousand crickets. Silent by day, the sounds of night at Cutaway Creek were almost deafening. I sensed unknown creatures stirring, scurrying in the shadows, watching the new girl with glowing eyes. A skink did battle with a giant black spider in a splash of moonlight by the broken window. The little lizard took the spoils and disappeared into a dark crevice between the window frame to devour his prey.

Alone, I sat, terrified of untold horrors lurking in the dark. I imagined things that only come out at night to prey on children, little girls with no one to watch over them. Archie wouldn't have been afraid. Be strong, he would tell me. I thought of him, that last image as they dragged him to his 'opportunity', fighting all the way, until I lost him in the bustling crowd at the train station. 'He should be grateful,' said the woman with the hard slap. 'Why anyone would want you brats is beyond me,' she added.

An opportunity, the official word, repeated over and over by everyone involved in our transfer since leaving England, and we should be thankful, thankful for this opportunity. I asked Archie what it meant. He said it was their way of saying they were palming us off on someone else. I wasn't sure what palming us off meant either. I wondered often where they had taken Archie for *his* opportunity and had vowed from the start to escape and join him.

Father Donahue had accompanied six children on the train from Sydney, four of whom he delivered to waiting nuns at Orange. An older girl then alighted from the train at Parkes – she had been placed in service there – leaving Father Donahue and me to complete our journey to Broken Hill. From there we took Father's waiting car on the dusty road to our destination, a bumpy two-and-a-half-hour drive to Cutaway Creek. I wondered if I could find my way back to Sydney without having to board a train, but the idea seemed impossible, every mile looked the same as the last; I would die trying.

I heard tiny, skittering footsteps on the roof – rats, perhaps. London had lots of rats after the war. But this was not London; this was as far from that city as could be imagined. Did they have rats in Cutaway Creek? Did they have rats in Australia? I didn't know. They had kangaroos. Archie told me how they hopped on two legs and wore gloves for boxing. Boxing kangaroos, bigger than rats. Archie said they were as big as a man.

I turned my attention to my accommodation and realised that for the first time in my life I had a room of my very own, though not what I had hoped for when Archie and I dreamed of a proper home. Archie told me stories of children who had private bedrooms, well-to-do families who lived a life of luxury. When we lived in London we spent hours imagining wealthy couples who would come to claim us for adoption, rich couples with money to burn. People burned money for fun, Archie told me one day, as we watched city toffs strolling London streets in their posh suits and bright dresses. In our bedrooms, Archie said, we would have wallpaper: butterflies for me and dragons for him. I would have a bed of my own with a canopy of lace, and we would curl up under sheets of white cotton and sleep on pillows of down so soft we would have to dig ourselves out in the morning. Down was another word for feathers, Archie told me, soft feathers plucked from geese, he said.

'What would the geese do without their feathers?' I asked.

'They wouldn't need them because we'd eat them for Christmas dinner,' said Archie.

Our mother died nine months before the war ended. Hitler's unmanned flying machines saw to that; buzz bombs they called them. The bombs came day and night with only enough fuel to reach London, they dropped from the sky when the fuel ran out. I remembered that sound. Archie said it was all in my imagination, that I was too young to have memories and I merely remembered his stories and related them as my own. Either way, on nights after the war I would recall the drone of the flying bombs, then the sudden silence and the waiting, the holding of breath before the boom and destruction that followed. One of those bombs killed my mother. They may be Archie's memories, not mine, but they are as real to me as anything I recall.

A distant howl echoed eerily across the night, causing the farm dogs to bark and yelp in agitation. I trembled beneath a coarse woollen blanket and felt a sudden warmth beneath my legs. I couldn't help it, and there was no one to notice. No Sister Josephine to say God doesn't like dirty girls who wet themselves, to get angry and rip the sheets from the bed while I shivered in the cold. I squeezed my eyes tight. No one was coming to scold me or comfort me; no one cared I was alone or afraid, but I didn't cry. Ten years old and already I had no more tears to shed. Perhaps I should have saved some for later, a bucketful of tears for what was to come.

Chapter 2

Blowfly-Pulara

Four-feet, three-inches tall, skinny as a whip, but I was a fighter. Archie said I had to be tough – tough as nails, he said – if I wanted to survive. I thought I was tough until I met my new carers. In the days that followed my arrival at Cutaway Creek, I battled to show no fear, to be like Archie said I must.

The Stuarts were unimpressed by my impudent attempts at independence. Lachlan Stuart didn't say much, but his surly manner was enough to serve as a warning to stay clear. I didn't need telling. Despite my age, I recognised the distant flicker of a slow-burning fuse, and when his eyes met mine it sent a chill through my spine. Mostly he ignored me. To him, I was little more than an annoying insect he would swat if I got too close. One day he bumped into me by accident – knocking me off my feet – and carried on walking as if I wasn't there. 'Get up,' Mrs Stuart had said, as though I had deliberately thrown myself in front of her husband, 'and get on with your chores.'

Rather than pay me no heed like her husband did, Daisy Stuart chose to make my life a misery. On the first morning she spelt out my chores and responsibilities. My first good hiding came when I asked her what she would be doing while I did all the work. Daily beatings became the norm, her thrashing me for the slightest error, or just because I was within reach. Mrs Stuart made it clear there would only be one winner in our battles and the sooner I got that into my thick head, the better.

I may have been young, but Archie had taught me to stand up for myself, and so I did, usually with dire consequences.

'Expect the worst and be prepared for a beating, but don't let the buggers win,' said Archie one day. 'They're no better than Hitler's gang, and you know what trouble he caused when people let him have his way. And don't let them see you cry,' he added.

At the time, Archie was referring to the nuns who ran our orphanage. Sister Mary Agnes and Sister Josephine, known to all as the 'stinger sisters' for their habit of rapping a twelve-inch rule across the back of our legs to make them sting whenever they chose to make an example of us. 'Spare the rod, spoil the child,' Sister Mary Agnes used to say. She spared nothing, especially during spelling class.

'Spell, rabbit.'

'R-a-b-i-t, rabbit.' Whack! Ruler across my knuckles.

'Spell, donkey.'

'D-o-n-k-y, donkey.' Whack! Ruler across the knuckles. I hated spelling.

The sisters weren't always unkind, not like Mrs Daisy Stuart. I didn't understand why she was always mad at me.

Stockily built, and with arms like a man, Mrs Stuart had a dour, formidable presence, as though she were quarried from rock, and just as hard. Weathered skin, wrinkled and dry, like old leather, aged her beyond her forty-three years; hard work and too much sun had taken its toll. Bird-like eyes pierced my own as though she could see inside my head and know my secret thoughts. I found it almost impossible to look at her and tell a lie. Almost. Her blonde hair, tied always in a bun that increased the severity of her face, was almost silver in daylight. Her aggressive demeanour served as a warning to outsiders to stay away, like the snarl of a guard dog baring its teeth at the gate. It showed in the way people reacted to her, avoiding eye contact, almost cowering when in her presence. She walked with her head held skyward, as though she breathed a different air. When she passed between buildings, they seemed to lean away fearfully to let her go by. Grizzled and coarse, she had little to endear her, and though she got on with the tasks of living, she seemed forever bitter at her lot. Like Mr Stuart, she had little time for conversation; words were used sparingly in the bush, a precious resource not to be wasted on idle gossip.

Despite her harsh nature, Mrs Stuart cut a powerfully dignified figure, strong in every sense of the word. But for all her strengths, her husband was the undisputed head of the household and demanded everyone's respect. Though it seemed at times that I had been tasked with all the work around the home, in truth Daisy was far from idle and worked hard to please her husband. This she managed with no apparent signs of affection for him, but rather a keen sense of duty.

Born of Highland stock, Lachlan Stuart's great-grandfather, James, a sailor from Glasgow, had arrived from Scotland on a schooner in the year 1848, jumped ship in Albany, and worked his way across the outback. He came to Broken Hill where he took up work in the mines, toiling in the smelter's yard to earn a living. He married Jenny Frank, a convict's daughter, who gave him two daughters and a son. James died, aged fifty, from lead poisoning, after years of breathing the fumes from the smelter.

Lachlan's grandfather, also named James, had followed his father, working at the mines until, unexpectedly, he received a sizable inheritance from a deceased uncle's estate in Scotland. James purchased the 165,000-acre Cutaway Creek Station freehold, and began life as a pastoralist, paving the way for Lachlan's father, Robert, to follow in his footsteps. Robert Stuart had two sons. Lachlan's brother, Cedric, died during the first days of the Second World War. Lachlan escaped military service because, as a farmer, he claimed his work was of national importance. Even so, I later learned of the ridicule he suffered from townsfolk. When most able-bodied men had gone away to fight, Lachlan stayed home, and was branded a coward by some who thought he should have joined his brother at the front in France.

When he went into town to get supplies, Mr Stuart never missed the opportunity to spend time at the hotel, drinking at the bar with a small group of regulars, most of whom also missed the draft. They would often get drunk and fight amongst each other until someone called the police. Mr Stuart spent more than one night in lock-up. As hard as the land he toiled upon, Lachlan Stuart confronted every challenge head-on. He took setbacks on his jutting chin. Drought, flood, disease and pests, nothing seemed able to break him. He simply picked himself up, dusted himself down, and started all over again.

They may not have shared many conversations, but the Stuarts often fought, and when they did, all hell broke loose at the homestead. Blows were thrown by both husband and wife, and the verbal violence was just as damaging. Daisy's foul tongue spewed every vile insult; the Devil himself could not have cursed with such venom, and their battles left me terrified. I would run to the creek to hide until calm had been restored, expecting to find someone dead when I returned. Physically, Mrs Stuart gave as much as she got, and more, though she seemed to sense a limit, a line that if she crossed would result in frightening consequences. She could not conceal, on more than one occasion, the look of fear in her eyes before she backed off and retreated, slamming the door to her bedroom where she stayed to cool off, leaving her husband to pace the homestead looking for something to kick. I always made sure it wasn't me.

The homestead interior had wooden-clad walls that went up to and across the ceiling, in the centre of which hung a brass chandelier with four electric globes. The front parlour, as Mrs Stuart called it – even though it was an unused room at the back of the house – had two tired-looking leather armchairs and a settee in a green floral print, a table and four dining chairs, and a floor lamp with a shade the size of a dustbin. There was a solid-looking oak sideboard covered by an embroidered table runner with pink roses. The tiled fireplace had a copper screen set on the hearth and above the mantel, a painting of the Scottish Highlands. A faded photograph of a severe-looking woman, wearing a bonnet and round wire spectacles, looked down from a frame on the wall by the window. Mrs Stuart said it was her mother.

I don't remember my mother. I try hard to see her face, but I can't. Perhaps, like Archie said, I was too young when she died to remember. Neither do I know my father. Having lost his wife, he simply surrendered his children. He didn't need us anymore. Sister Josephine said one day that men didn't raise children on their own, they weren't built for it. I don't think I was built for being without a father either, or for being raised by nuns in an orphanage.

I studied the photograph on the wall. I had nothing to remember my family; no house or possessions, no pictures, no words. The bombs took them along with our mother.

'No sense in worrying,' Sister Josephine used to say. 'Lots of people lost their homes and their loved ones. We can't change what happened in the war, so there's no point in crying over spilt milk. There are folks worse off than you,' she told me. I never did understand how spilt milk fitted into the story. I wasn't even crying, and I hated milk.

Situated away from the main homestead, my new home at Cutaway Creek was more like an outhouse than a posh house. The roughly sawn slabs that formed the walls let in light through cracks during the day, and creepy crawlies by the dozen through the night. Paved with stone tiles and dirt, the floor showed signs of chicken shit when I arrived. A chicken-shit carpet, not many kids could claim such luxury. Instead of a chandelier, thick cobwebs draped and dangled from rustic wooden beams, supporting a corrugated-tin roof with dozens of tiny holes that would leak if it rained. The corrugations of the tin reminded me of seaside sand, ripples left by the waves on the outgoing tide. Lying on my back with my lumpy flock mattress atop its iron-spring base, I imagined I was on the beach at Bournemouth, making sandcastles and decorating them with seaweed and shells, then Archie carrying me piggyback into the water and threatening to drop me until I screamed.

I had only been to the seaside once. We went on a train, and all the children from the orphanage were there; I had the best time of my life. We splashed and played for hours and had sandwiches of salmon paste and bully-beef. We sat in the sand and Archie told me of faraway islands with palm trees and coconuts, a place where we would live one day. Archie said a man could live off coconuts alone. He never said which man. The following week we were all excited when told we would see the ocean once again, that we were going on a boat trip, a holiday to the Isle of Wight. We danced and screamed hysterically at the prospect – cheering children, overjoyed with the news. They lied about our destination.

Chapter 3

Rock-Karnu

If Cutaway Creek was a sheep station, where were all the sheep? We had horses, cows, dogs, pigs and chickens, all living at the homestead and adjoining paddocks, but not a single sheep to be seen. I asked Mrs Stuart.

'They're out there,' said Mrs Stuart.

'Out where?'

'Spread out across the far pastures.'

'How come?'

'They have to wander to find feed.'

'Why can't we feed them?'

'Because we can't. There're a lot of sheep and we don't have enough to feed them.'

'Why?'

'You ask a lot of questions.'

'Who looks after them?'

'They look after themselves. We make sure they have water at the pumps, but until it's time to bring them in at muster time, they're on their own.'

'How many sheep are there?'

'Not enough,' said Mrs Stuart.

She went on to say that a long drought had meant reducing sheep numbers and letting stock hands go. She said it was common for workers to come and go through the seasons, but they never had so few employed in a long time.

'There're usually eight or ten stockies here at any one time; sometimes the bunkhouse is full, twenty or more at shearing,' she said. 'Now we've got two stockmen working fence lines in the far reaches of the station, we don't see them from one week to the next. But otherwise, Lachlan has to handle the work alone. He's got no choice until things improve.'

Six weeks after my arrival, Father Donahue called in to see how I had settled, and to remind the Stuarts that I was to attend church at least once every month as part of my care agreement.

'Your church attendance is very disappointing, Mrs Stuart. I can't help wonder what the committee was thinking when they placed the child and, I'll tell you quite honestly, I voiced my concerns at the time. If you're not planning on fulfilling your obligations, I'll take a very dim view of the situation, a very dim view indeed, and I'll bring it to the committee's attention, so I will.'

'I know my obligations without having you to remind me, Father.'

'Yes, well, we'll see about that shall we?'

Father Donahue enquired about my home-school progress, to which Mrs Stuart answered, 'She's not too bright when it comes to learning. You'd be better off teaching a monkey.'

The priest shook his head and gave me a look that said he was disappointed in me. 'Nevertheless, she must do her schooling, Mrs Stuart. It's your duty to ensure she's educated.'

Mrs Stuart scowled. 'Yeah, well, I'll see she keeps at it.' Already I knew better than to speak out of turn, but as yet I hadn't done any schooling whatsoever, and by the look on Mrs Stuart's face, I doubted I ever would. 'Shouldn't we be getting some help with her schooling? An allowance or something,' she enquired.

'We'll see if we can organise some textbooks and some new exercise books,' he promised. 'I'll have them ready on Sunday, Mrs Stuart.' Mrs Stuart didn't seem impressed by the offer.

Father Donahue stood six-feet, six-inches tall and had extraordinarily large hands and feet. An imposing figure, he was intimidating in every way. Square-jawed and flat nosed, he looked like a boxer. His brogue sometimes made him difficult to understand, but he left Mrs Stuart in no doubt that he expected to see me at Mass on Sunday. Though a formidable match for the father, I knew even she had to heed his warnings.

Sunday morning came with the usual bright-blue sky and a feeling of great excitement. I wasn't sure why I was excited, only that our trip to town would give me a chance to escape the daily grind of the station. I sensed a buzz around the homestead; trips to town were rare, and Mrs Stuart seemed almost happy as she hurried through breakfast. She had dressed herself up in Sunday best and looked for all the world like a lady instead of a man, as she usually did, though it did nothing to soften her intimidating demeanour. Even Lachlan Stuart had put on a clean white shirt for the occasion, though it had a brown patch on the back in the shape of an iron.

In the weeks I had been at Cutaway Creek, I had washed myself each night with a bowl of cold water in my little outhouse bedroom – I was still afraid to boil the kettle. This Sunday was unusual, however. Mrs Stuart had prepared a bath with hot water in an iron tub in the back room of the homestead. She took to me with a washcloth, scrubbing brush, and a large block of Lifebuoy soap – soap I would later taste when punished for my filthy mouth – cleaning me from head to toes in preparation for our trip to church. I enjoyed the warmth of the water. It brought back memories of hot baths at the orphanage, where we fought to be first in the queue for the cleanest water. But Mrs Stuart's rough treatment took any other pleasure from the experience. A clean white dress had been laid out for me, and I was surprised to find it fit like a glove.

The drive into Wilcannia took forever. Not quite as forever as the train ride from Sydney, and not nearly as forever as the passage from England, but for a child, it was still an eternity. I counted the passing fence posts to have something to do, asking at intervals of one hundred posts how far it would be to the town and when would we arrive at church. It did not take long for Mrs Stuart to slap me and tell me I would be dumped at the side of the road if I asked again.

On arrival at St John the Apostle, Mr Stuart dropped us off and drove away in the truck without a word of goodbye. The church didn't look like the one I knew in London; this one had a roof and didn't have broken windows. Mrs Stuart led me to the church entrance where we were greeted by a kindly looking lady wearing bright-red lipstick and a hat of the same colour. Her exaggerated gestures and bubbly welcome seemed to have a deepening effect on Mrs Stuart's permanent frown. She explained that I was to join other children at the front of the church, leaving Mrs Stuart to find a seat at the rear. She clucked like a mother hen guiding the children into organised lines and directing us to our seats on the first pew. Like little chicks, we traipsed behind, and some of the boys tried to copy the sway of her hips, making others giggle. Once seated, I waited for the service to begin, craning my neck in search of Mrs Stuart, and wondering where Mr Stuart had gone. I eyed the other girls in their clean Sunday frocks and compared them to mine. One girl wore yellow chiffon and looked like a princess, with her matching, daisy-flower tiara.

As I looked her up and down to assess her beautiful dress, a terrible thought hit me; the realisation turned my flesh quite cold. Knickers! In my excitement when dressing, I had put on my frock first, admiring the white fabric, twirling around the room like a dancer. Mrs Stuart shouted that I should get a move on and I'd rushed out, forgetting to put on my clean knickers. I pictured them laid out on my bed. Stunned by my disaster, I wondered what I should do and who I should tell, but it was too late to do anything, and telling someone would only add to my humiliation. I squeezed my legs tight, wishing the pew would swallow me up and spit me out after everyone had gone home.

When the procession started and the congregation rose to their feet, it was all I could do not to run for the door. Father Donahue entered, dressed in his Sunday robes and finery, but I was too concerned over my error to take it all in. I signed the cross and asked the Lord to have mercy on me, but still I had no knickers. I didn't hear the words of the priest, didn't sing the Gloria or follow the words of the gospel. My head swam. Overwhelmed by fear, my thoughts leapt from one horrifying possibility to the next. What if I fell off the bench with my legs in the air? What if I tripped, making everyone point and laugh? Two nuns sat across the aisle; I felt them staring. What if they checked who had clean knickers? I glowed red hot at the thought. Father Donahue stood at the pulpit and said, 'Blah, blah, blah,' and everyone answered, 'Amen!' When we prayed, I clasped my hands together and prayed for knickers, and when I received the Eucharist, I feared that God would strike me down for showing no respect.

Finally, with Mass over, children ran to join their families. I searched for Mrs Stuart, eager to leave my embarrassment behind. I joined the slow procession of parishioners as they emerged from the chapel and gathered outside, shaking hands, laughing and smiling. I saw Father Donahue amongst the throng of people. He had pulled Mrs Stuart aside and together with another lady, who I did not know, they appeared deep in debate. Most people dispersed at a leisurely pace, the crowd dwindling until only a handful remained. I sat and waited in the dusty yard. Mr Stuart was nowhere to be seen. I later learned that he joined his mates drinking sly grog and playing two-up behind the pub. The law banned alcohol sales on Sundays, but this didn't stop some town reprobates from enjoying a schooner or two while the righteous went to church. Mr Stuart was happy to join them.

My first disastrous trip to town got even worse. I loitered around the churchyard, passing the time kicking dirt, throwing pebbles and waiting for Mrs Stuart and our ride back to the station. Father Donahue and the two nuns from the front row stood with some straggling parishioners, discussing the merits of an earlier morning Mass, while Mrs Stuart chatted with a lady in a straw hat, in what seemed to be a one-sided conversation. I wandered to the rear of the church. The sun, now high in the sky, burned my arms, forcing me to take refuge under a solitary spreading shade tree. As I stood in the shadow of the great tree, a group of children approached. Five or six in number, older and bigger than me, they circled until the tallest boy stood menacingly before me.

'Pommy bastard,' he said.

Puzzled by the comment, I didn't answer, but I had been through enough confrontations with strange kids in my short life to know that these were not friendly words and the manner of these children was meant to be threatening.

'Why don't you go back where you came from, you pommy bastard?' the big boy said, scowling like Mrs Stuart.

'Slut,' said another child. 'You're no better than an Abo, you pommy bastard.'

The tall boy pushed me, two hands on my chest. I wobbled but stood my ground, heart thumping, thinking of my knickers. What if he pushed me onto my back? I tried to walk away, but they moved to block my path.

'Pommy bastard,' came the same call from several kids now, following the tall boy's lead.

'Poms and Abos, my dad says they're all the same,' said a girl, wearing a pink floral frock that made her look like a wad of bubble gum. I didn't know what a Pom or an Abo was, but I was sure the names were meant to be cruel.

I took my chance to escape and darted past the big boy, avoiding his outstretched hand as he tried to catch my arm. I made it several yards, stooped, and picked up a rock. I turned to face the rushing mob, and with a stance that said, come and get it, I held the dogs at bay.

'Pommy bastard, pommy bastard, pommy bastard.' The chant was like a war cry as they edged towards me. I grasped the rock tightly, drew my arm in readiness, and waited. Take one more step, I thought. They came closer; I aimed and let fly.

Sometimes life goes by in an instant, sometimes in slow motion, and sometimes it stands still. My rock took an age to reach its target. Jaws dropped, eyebrows leapt high on surprise-filled faces, as the missile found its mark. Thud, blood, thud, marked the sequence of events. First, I heard the dull thud as the rock hit the tall boy's forehead. Second, I saw the fountain of blood and the splatter of droplets hang in the air like lazy rain. Third, the thud as the boy crumpled and his unconscious body hit the ground. Thud, blood, thud, followed by a moment's silence. Disbelief filled the stunned children's faces, all eyes on the unmoving, bleeding boy. Seconds passed without a sound, as though the air had been sucked from the lungs of everyone present. When the silence eventually broke, and the shock turned to reality, the scream from the bubble-gum dress came like the wail of a banshee. Ear-shattering and pitched to attract every dog in the town, she screamed as if the rock had struck her instead of him. I looked on, defiant and proud.

Moments later, Father Donahue, one of the nuns, and four adult parishioners came racing around the corner of the church to find out what had happened. The nun went straight to the boy who was now opening his eyes and beginning to cry like a girl. The other adults followed, gathering around the boy with obvious concern. A large woman in a blue bonnet held out a handkerchief for the boy's bleeding head. Father Donahue heard the accusations from the other children and followed the pointing fingers to where I stood alone. Anger turned the priest's face scarlet to match the tall boy's bloodied skull.

'Whatever were you thinking, you evil child?' said the priest.

I looked for Mrs Stuart; she wasn't there. I stood alone, unrepentant, fists on hips. 'Pommy bastard,' I said. 'He's no better than an Abo.' Archie would have been proud of me; Father Donahue wasn't.

The giant priest strode across the gap between us and slapped me hard across the face. 'How dare you,' he said.

I refused to break down and cry, meeting his fierce eyes with an obstinate glare, a smirk on my face that said I had no regrets. He slapped me again, this time with the back of his hand. I wobbled but did not fall; refused to weep, though the moisture clouded my eyes. I defied him, and he would never make me yield.

'Go to hell,' I cried

The outraged priest took me by the arm and marched to the front of the church – my feet hardly touched the ground – where he delivered me to Mrs Stuart, who by now had been joined by Mr Stuart.

'Child's play,' said Lachlan Stuart. 'Kids get into mischief.'

'There's no child's play in that filthy tongue of hers,' said the father. 'But there's an evil that needs thrashing out of her.'

'Get in the truck, Katherine,' said Mrs Stuart. I did as she asked, with one last defiant scowl. Mrs Stuart followed, leaving Mr Stuart to face the priest.

'The kid probably had it coming,' said Mr Stuart, wobbling back and forth, his weight on one leg while the other stabbed at the ground, as though he found it impossible to find a firm footing.

'Are you drunk, Lachlan Stuart?'

Mr Stuart snickered. 'Not drunk enough for a Sunday.'

'And I suppose you think that's funny? You should be in church instead of consorting with the likes of those delinquents you hang around with. Drinking on the Sabbath, you should be ashamed of yourself. You'll likely to go to Hell yourself, Lachlan Stuart, if you can't control your drinking.'

Mr Stuart didn't answer. He reeled his way to the truck and climbed in beside me. Daisy sat in the driver's seat with the motor running, and with one last glance to the watching priest, she crunched the gears, pulled away, and headed out of town.

Our return drive to Cutaway Creek passed in silence. Mr Stuart slept off his drunkenness, while Mrs Stuart concentrated on the road. I had never seen someone who had drunk too much alcohol, though I had heard talk of such behaviour. Mrs Stuart didn't seem surprised to see her husband in this shameful condition, and I later learned that he enjoyed more than the occasional binge to oblivion. I sat between them in silence, worried about the probable consequences of my actions. During the drive, I had to keep pushing Mr Stuart off me. Slumped like a sack of potatoes, he slept all the way back, snoring like a pig, his stinking breath more than I could stand.

I expected the worst when we reached home. It never came. Mrs Stuart asked why I had thrown the rock, and I told her, relaying what the children has said word for word. She gave me no beating, did not scold me as I'd expected.

'Yeah, well, don't you worry your head about them little shits,' she said. 'They can stick it up their bloody arses.' Mrs Stuart had a way with words.

Her support surprised me, and gave me a lift in spirits. 'How come you never had children of your own?' I asked.

Mrs Stuart looked me up and down, deciding if my question deserved an answer. 'I tried,' she said eventually. 'Though God knows why.'

'What happened?'

'Well, that's the point, nothing happened.'

'Why?'

'There was no reason. That's just the way it is sometimes. Some are blessed, others not. Anyway, it's water under the bridge now.'

'Does it make you sad?'

'Maybe once, not now.'

'Because you've got me, right?'

Mrs Stuart's lip curled at the edge but she didn't reply.

'What's a pommy bastard?' I asked, now we were almost pals.

She looked down on me and smirked. I heard no malice in her voice; there might even have been a hint of humour. 'You are, y'little runt,' she said.

I took the disparaging jibe without truly understanding her sarcasm. I found it hard to know what she was thinking, why she found the need to be cruel, so I didn't press the point. She told me to go change into my new dungarees – overalls her sister had made especially for me – and put my dress in the wash. I never wore that dress again. I had pants now, more suitable for the environment, and knickers. I never did tell her about my knickers.

Unable to sleep that night, I wandered out to the paddock to lay beneath the stars. The Milky Way they called it, and that's how it looked, a trillion stars smeared across the sky in a creamy swathe of light. Cutaway Creek must have more stars than any place on earth, I thought. A shooting star cut a trail across the heavens before burning up in a brilliant ball of fire. I crossed my fingers, made a wish and turned three times. That's what you had to do if the wish was to come true.

Silhouetted against the sky, the homestead crouched in darkness; the hat-wearing cat was sleeping. There were no lights to mark the lives inside, just the distant rattle of Lachlan Stuart's snores, reverberating through the open window like a stuttering motor within the shadows. The day replayed in my mind; each horror, each unkindness relived. I'd come through it bravely, but I felt lonely, and loneliness is hard to overcome when you have no one. I looked to the distance and vowed to find a real home, to leave the cruelty behind and find someone who cared. First I would find Archie, wherever he may be. Together we could escape our captors, we could make it to some faraway place where kindness grew with the flowers, and everyone had smiles made of sun. I could go now, I thought, while the Stuarts slept. I could follow the moon.

'Shall I go, Archie? Shall I leave now?'

I made up my mind to go. There's no time like the present, I remembered someone saying once. With the homestead at my back, I started to run, past the loading chute, past the barn, past the rail fence, and into the night, bare feet churning the dirt, face into the breeze to fill my lungs with the cool night air. Thirty yards. Sharp stones hurt my toes, I didn't stop. 'Ouch!' A sharp prick, a stumble. One hundred yards. I increased my speed, my chest heaved. Faster! Three hundred yards. I came to a shuddering halt, heard my steady breathing. I looked into the blackness, heard a sound, a thumping sound, a rustle in the shadows. I turned to see the homestead behind me, its windmill, black against the brilliant stars. I turned back to the night with its unknown sounds and waiting terrors. Animals. Dark shadows moving. I paused, breathing heavy, heart thumping fast. A minute passed. I listened, straining to hear what might have been a growl. I peered through the darkness and imagined strange creatures with sharp teeth, claws like knives. I thought I saw a monster, stalking beyond the fence line, a devil perhaps. The night closed in around me and a cloud passed over the moon. A distant yelp brought a prickle to my spine. At last I turned in panic, legs like jelly, sprinted, felt hot breath upon my back. I reached my room at a dash, slammed the door and jumped into bed.

'One day I'll run, I promise, Archie. One day I'll run.' I pulled the covers over my head, shaking. 'One day, one day soon, Archie. I promise.'

Chapter 4

Creek-Yalka

Weeks became months, spring turned to summer; this life was as far from my life in London as I could imagine. Cloistered from the modern world, I might well have travelled back in time fifty years or more, such was our rustic rural existence. I settled into my new home reluctantly. A constant source of annoyance to Mrs Stuart, for whatever reason, she had chosen to resent my presence. I could do no right, and she would take every opportunity to tell me so. I was a useless waste of life, she said, and of all the kids to get saddled with, I was probably the worst. 'No wonder your mother abandoned you,' she said, after I accidentally dropped a plate full of dinner, then knocked a cup to the floor as I tried to sweep up the mess. I said she was lying. I wasn't abandoned, the Germans killed my mother. But she sneered and said, 'Is that what they told you?' I flew at her with clenched fists, and she slapped me down to the floor. I didn't cry.

Isolated and alone in my remote outback prison, I prayed to go back to England. God was punishing me, and I didn't know why. Archie had said, 'Forget God, He never did anything for us.' But Father Donahue said that God sees everything, that there's nothing escapes His notice, and He brings down his judgment on us when we sin. We have to ask for forgiveness. But how can we ask if we don't know what we've done?

Each day, when my chores were complete, I walked to the creek and sat beneath the overhang of a large rock. Hidden from view, I made this place my safe place, my secret cave where I would dream and escape from the real world. I set about furnishing my cave with various objects salvaged from around the property. Two old wheel rims made the perfect table and chair. Later, I dragged up a third steel rim for Archie to sit on, just in case he decided to visit. I made curtains of brushwood and hung a drawing I'd done of Archie on the wall. I made him look older, as if he were my dad, and he was carrying a birthday present wrapped in beautiful paper and sealed with a great big ribbon tied in a bow.

I sat for hours, looking out on the creek with its green pools of slime and the dwindling trickle of water, which was all that remained of the flowing stream. River red gums flanked the far banks like twisted giants. Gnarled and defiant, these ancient trees had seen it all and lived to tell the tale. If they had survived, then maybe I could too. I gave them all names.

Mr Churchill, the largest and oldest gum tree, stood opposite my cave, stretching his wooden arms in the air, he stood tall and strong, kept away everything that was bad and warned me of danger. I felt safe while Mr Churchill looked on. In a line next to Mr Churchill, his wife, Tilly Mint, and daughter, Sweet Pea, danced and gyrated to the music of the breeze. They made for perfect companions, and I would invite them every day to tea. Tilly Mint was not fond of Mrs Stuart, and Mr Churchill thought Mr Stuart a mean man.

Cutaway Creek had twin dunnies – corrugated-tin sheds situated out the back of the main house. Mrs Stuart warned me not to put my hands under the rims of the toilet seats. 'Redbacks hide underneath the edge,' she told me. 'They'll kill a skinny snippet like you if they bite you, and I won't be running to town for help,' she said, waving a finger in my face. She never did explain that redbacks were tiny spiders, so I never knew what to avoid. I lived in mortal fear for months after her warning, conjuring all manner of red-backed monsters, little red devils lying in wait for me to go to the toilet. I would hold on to my pee for as long as I could and only braved the dunny when I had no other choice. Sometimes I would sneak off and find a quiet spot where no one could see me, and pee in the dirt.

It wasn't only the spiders of course. There was the heat like an oven inside, and the stink alone was more than good reason to stay away from the dunny. Blowflies massed in numbers, sometimes in their thousands. Mr Stuart called them dunny budgies, because they were big and green, and were as noisy as a flock of budgerigars when they took flight all together. You would open the door, and a million flies would swarm out into your face.

One of my jobs entailed tearing up newspaper for wiping our bums. I had to thread the pieces – five inches by five inches square – onto a length of string to hang on the back of the toilet door. On one occasion I accidentally dropped the newly threaded bundle into the poo pit. Angry at my clumsiness – newspapers were valuable in the bush and only available when someone went to town – Mr Stuart dangled me over the drop hole, his hands tight manacles around my skinny ankles, threatening to drop me head first into the stinking cesspool below. Dunny budgies swarmed around my face, in my eyes and mouth so that I spat and gagged. I never dropped the papers again.

Christmas came. I knew it was Christmas because the diesel man said so. During a fuel delivery, he asked if I was excited.

'It can't be Christmas,' I said. 'It's not cold.'

'It sure is Christmas. Old Father Christmas will be coming on his sleigh and bringing presents for all the good girls. Are you a good girl?'

I had to think about that one. 'Will he have reindeers?'

'No such thing,' said the man. 'He'll come with six white thumpers.'

'What's a thumper?'

'You don't know what a thumper is?' I shook my head. 'Father Christmas has six white kangaroos to pull his sleigh. We call them thumpers because they thump their feet on the ground as a warning. You be good, and if you're lucky, you may see them racing across the sky on their way to the south pole to pick up presents.'

'Father Christmas lives at the north pole,' I argued.

The man told me we had two sleeps to go, and left me to contemplate the coming festivities. The following two days went slowly. I saw nothing to indicate a celebration and assumed that the Stuarts were keeping secrets for a surprise. Christmas was my favourite time of year. The orphanage always had a tree with candles. In the days before, we would build a nativity scene using dolls from a box they kept in the attic and have straw for the baby Jesus to lay on in His cradle. We would sing carols and go to church dressed in our Sunday best, then Father Christmas would appear and give each child a gift before we all sat down for Christmas dinner, with goose and stuffing, and Christmas pudding.

Excitedly I waited. I couldn't sleep Christmas Eve, and I didn't want to rise too early in case Father Christmas hadn't finished organising the presents, and the Stuarts weren't ready to surprise me with a beautiful Christmas tree. I couldn't even smell the cooking wafting in from the kitchen. I heard the screen door slap. Footsteps. I snuggled into my blanket, pulled it tight to my chin and giggled. I was so excited that I wanted to pee. I listened, imagining the surprises that must be coming; a doll perhaps, with long blonde hair. I waited, wriggled down tight beneath the covers, expecting at any moment to hear Mrs Stuart call me to the house. I waited. A motor turned over with a hacking cough. I jumped up and peeked out the window, saw Mr Stuart's truck pulling past the yard, Mrs Stuart at the wheel. Puzzled, I watched her disappear down the drive. Mr Stuart came out of the house and went to the barn. I dressed and went to the house; everything looked normal. I sat on the verandah and waited. Mr Stuart returned to the homestead, went inside. I waited. We never did have Christmas at Cutaway Creek Station.

I struggled with the heat of that first summer. Long, energy-sapping days, endless clear skies, temperatures that could fry an egg on the hot rocks – something I tried. Most days, the wind pump watched over the homestead in silence, there not being enough wind to move the sails for weeks on end. Every so often it would creak and groan as though about to turn, but the breeze would die and so would the pump.

I found station work hard. I hadn't an ounce of fat on me, and my wrists were thin like twigs. I couldn't do the washing, though I tried, as I wasn't strong enough to haul the wet clothes out of the boiler and run them through the mangle. Instead I helped Mrs Stuart with as much as I could manage.

She told me she wanted a washing machine, but until that day came we did the laundry by hand, boiling water once a week in a large galvanised, electric tub. I got to add Surf from a colourful cardboard box to soften the water; it came out like tiny snowflakes. Cigarette in mouth, Mrs Stuart scrubbed collars and cuffs with a brush and a bar of pink carbolic soap against a washboard set over the tub. 'Look at these collars,' she would grumble. 'How does he get them so bloody grimy?'

Washing took most of the day. Mrs Stuart topped up the boiler every so often from the kettle and used the mangle to squeeze excess water back into the tub. We worked together to lug the clothes and linen in a basket to the hoist in the yard, where she would peg them out to dry in the sun. The advantage of hot summer days meant clothes were dry within minutes. By teatime, we were both exhausted, and I would feel like sleeping.

The other days were just as difficult. My jobs included: darning socks – a skill I had learned at the orphanage, and one I hated, scrubbing floors, feeding chooks and collecting eggs, milking the cows – we had two, feeding the pigs and the horses. I peeled potatoes, but Mrs Stuart would always take over; too slow to catch a cold, she would say. I prepared vegetables when they were available – mostly we ate meat, eggs and potatoes. I tried to pluck chickens, but my fingers weren't strong enough, and I learned to make bread and pastry. I also tended the kitchen garden, though with little success. The drudgery of my days seemed to me like slavery, but by late afternoon I had usually finished my work and sought escape at my hidden cave, where I was the lady of the house and I told others what to do.

Mrs Stuart would often sleep on the verandah for an hour before teatime. Alone, I would wander to the cutting and paddle in pools of mud that formed at intervals in the creek bed. Sometimes I stripped naked and immersed myself entirely in the cooling brown porridge. Then I would hide in the shade of my rock shelter and allow the mud to cake and crack on my skin, before peeling it off like great scabs. It was a ritual I found strangely satisfying.

I was at my secret cave beneath the rock when I first saw a blackfella. The sun had set in hues of purple, pink and red, and the land had turned to fire. I'd watched a mixed flock of budgerigars, galahs and cockatoos drink at the stagnant pools of the creek before taking to the air in a raucous chorus, a synchronised display of noisy, acrobatics, like warplanes in the dying light. The budgies were British Spitfires, finally winning the day to great cheers of celebration from Mr Churchill and his family of gum trees.

When the creek returned to silence, leaving me to marvel at the kaleidoscope sky, a strange figure appeared in the cutting. The banks of Cutaway Creek stood fifteen-feet high, towering over the man. He wore a black sleeveless vest, khaki daks and a wide-brimmed hat, like Mr Stuart and the cowboys pictured in Archie's comic books. The blackfella had bare feet, no boots. I watched him in silence from the safety of my shelter. Frozen in fear, I dared not blink.

He made his way along the cutting, a slow dance, stopping every few yards and freezing like a statue. His legs sank up to his ankles in the muddy creek bed; his gaze flitted from here to there and back. He made no sound as he walked, all I could hear were the chirp of crickets and a frog somewhere amongst the tree roots opposite. Mr Churchill looked on and appeared to frown as the man stalked beneath his outstretched limbs. Thirty feet from my hide, he stopped, as though he sensed some danger. He scanned the trees and banks, bent, checked the tracks left by a heron, and continued up the cut in silence.

My heart raced. I held my breath as he neared, cowering low against the rock. He drew parallel, so near I could have reached out to touch him. I heard myself breathing, chest heaving as I tried not to make a sound. He stopped. I trembled.

Without turning to see me, he said aloud, 'Makara'll be here soon.'

I shook like jelly, wanted to run, but he was too close to make my escape. He turned and looked right at me, a yard away now, and I gasped. Dark and slicked in sweat, his skin looked like chocolate, real chocolate, dark glistening chocolate. Hooded eyes disappeared almost completely beneath heavy brows; his cheeks shone with tiny beads of moisture. A mop of fuzzy black hair waved like Mr Churchill's arms in the air. Then he smiled, a grin from ear to ear, gleaming teeth, white like cockatoo feathers.

'Rain,' he said. 'Rain'll be coming.'

I glanced at the sky, not a cloud in sight.

Chapter 5

Rain-Makara

I watched the blackfella wander into the station and settle into the bunkhouse without a word to Mrs Stuart to herald his arrival. Lachlan Stuart had gone to check the flock in the far pastures, so I hurried to tell Mrs Stuart what I had seen. She dismissed my excited concern.

'That'll be Toby Wiamungu,' she said. 'Don't worry about him. The bugger comes and goes as he pleases. He's a horseman, a bloody good one, but he can't be relied on for long; he'll do odd jobs for a few bob, food, tobacco and a bed. Then he'll shoot through without a word of goodbye, gone until the next time he chooses to come calling. Couldn't have come at a better time with Lock gone; there's plenty for him to do around here.'

That night I lay awake and thought of Toby in the bunkhouse. Every little sound set my nerves jangling, and I imagined him creeping around in the dark. A mysterious fellow, he looked frightening when deep in thought, but then he would turn and smile, making me smile too. I knew then that he would never hurt me. I wanted to know more about our strange visitor with the midnight skin.

I gobbled breakfast and got straight into my chores, but I couldn't get the blackfella out of my mind, taking every opportunity to look for him in between tasks. When I could, I watched him from a distance, fixing fences, digging new pits for the workers' dunnies, cleaning up the stable. He worked in silence, pausing now and then for a smoko, hand-rolled durries from a kangaroo-skin pouch in his pocket. His body glistened with beads of sweat under the hot summer sun, and I wondered if he felt the heat like I did. Mesmerised by his appearance, I followed him everywhere, remaining at a discreet distance so he wouldn't know I was there. I slipped away from chores to sit and stare. Mrs Stuart caught me once, cracked my head with a heavy hand and sent me back to work with a mouthful of swear words, of which she knew a lot. Undeterred, I needed to learn about the blackfella and his mysterious ways.

Rain. A simple word, inadequate for what followed Toby's unlikely prediction. It came in the night, three days after his appearance at the creek, biblical in scale.

The days had been parched since I arrived at the station, with not a hint of humidity, but this summer afternoon had drained the life right from me. My clothes clung like wet rags to my body, and my hair lay limp against my skin. Chores complete, I sat on the verandah and watched Toby work to replace a rusted tin sheet on the side of the ramshackle chook shed. He worked with ease, flexing lean muscles, as the chooks looked on with interest, inspecting his work as if they had the final say in its completion.

When he stopped to take a drink from a water bottle, he pointed to the distant sky. 'Makara,' he said. That same strange word he'd used at the creek.

'Rain?' I inquired.

Toby grinned. 'That's right, rain. Makara,' he repeated.

'Makara,' I mimicked.

Restless clouds climbed on the horizon. Like glowing coals on a smouldering fire, they silently blinked and winked in shades of orange, purple and yellow, lit from within, a growing storm. Occasionally, a bright white flash of lighting would split the air and make its way to the ground, followed minutes later by low rumbles of faraway thunder. Mrs Stuart sat in her favourite old lounge chair with threadbare patches and a twisted frame at the far end of the verandah, cradling a warm beer. We didn't have one of those modern refrigerators to keep food cold; we had an icebox with no ice – Mrs Stuart said they didn't deliver ice so far from town – and a Coolgardie Safe, a cupboard with galvanised mesh sides to keep the flies out, draped with wet cloths to keep the food fresh. It was one of my jobs to make sure that the tray always had water in it to soak through the fabric.

Mrs Stuart watched the storm build with more than a casual interest, and what was almost a smile curled her lips.

'She'll be right, missus,' said Toby, following her line of sight to the horizon.

'Maybe.'

We watched the distant light show until well after dark, Mrs Stuart in her chair, me on the steps and Toby on a fence rail rolling tobacco into cigarettes. Mrs Stuart didn't roll; she smoked Senior Service cigarettes, which came in a pack of twenty with a picture of a sailing ship on the front. She smoked a lot. Even when she worked around the house, a cigarette would dangle from her lips, the ash sometimes growing to an inch or more before it fell to the floor. She coughed a lot too.

When the storm appeared to stall in the distance, Mrs Stuart said it had changed direction and would probably bloody miss us. 'All fart and no shit,' she said with a dismissive wave of her hand. 'I'm turning in for the night.'

Toby disappeared to the bunkhouse and I to my room, but there could be no sleep while the storm threatened. The rumbles grew louder over several hours, more frequent, and I watched the station light up with eerie blue splashes, counting the seconds between flashes and thunder. Archie had said each second counted for a mile. But I found it impossible to tell which flash belonged to which crash because they all seemed continuous. Moisture hung in the air like a damp blanket, my skin slicked with sweat.

I smelt it before I heard the single drops hitting the tin roof. Splat, splat, splat. Crickets sensed it too, and frogs, their chorus building to a deafening pitch. Horses whinnied, galloping around the stockyard, restless and worried by the rolling thunder crashes and lightning strikes. I heard Toby's assuring voice as he rounded them up and led them to the barn for safety. The first pitter-patter of moisture, then a few hailstones the size of marbles bounced off the roof as though fired from a cannon. I stood at the window watching; continuous flashes giving me a clear view of the yard as the hail hit the dirt, throwing up little explosions of dust and moisture. An extreme crack of thunder made me cringe and retreat to my bed, where I pulled the woollen blanket over my head and shivered. Seconds later, the rain stopped abruptly. Maybe Mrs Stuart was right, 'All fart, no shit,' I mimicked her comical expression. I listened, waited, peeked out of my blanket. Minutes passed.

A drop on the roof. Splat. Seconds later, another splat, and another; then, as if permitted to open Heaven's door, the sky unleashed its deluge with unimaginable power. I could no longer hear thunder because machine-gun rain and hail, so loud on the tin, drowned out all other sounds, even thunderclaps. Within seconds, water cascaded from the roof, spilling from the overhang in wet sheets to the ground. Rivers ran through my room, splashed through cracks, dripped from holes. The storm continued for half an hour with no let-up in intensity, and my room started to flood. Strike after strike lit my otherwise dark world, and all around me water flowed. I paddled my way to the door, opened it, closed it quickly. The homestead was barely visible across the yard, awash with waterfalls.

Before I knew it, water had reached my bed. I had to rescue my shoes as they floated away like little ships on a dark and choppy sea. A wax candle burned on a shelf; it hissed and flickered, soft wax pooled around its base. The candle hissed again, guttered and died as a leak opened up in the tin ceiling, sending a waterfall spilling from a hole in the roof. Relentlessly, the downpour intensified, pounding my little outhouse bedroom like a wild drummer gone mad with his drumsticks. Wind followed, violent wind, clawing at the roof panels so that they lifted and buckled, creaked and groaned under strain. The water rose rapidly to the level of my bed so that I feared for a moment that it would float away. I felt the soggy mattress on my bottom, jumped from the bed and fell into the water with a scream.

So much water. I started to panic, opened the door, headed for the homestead, the heavy rain slapping my skull with great splatters. Deep moving water threatened to pull me off my feet. Mrs Stuart stood at the door to the house, sheltered from the rain, waving. I crossed the yard, heard dogs barking. The station had three dogs, two kelpies and a blue heeler. The kelpies were on the verandah with Mrs Stuart, but the Heeler, named Blue, was out in the yard. A night-time wanderer, he had to be chained behind the barn after sundown each day. He had an angry and unpredictable temperament, and an intense dislike for me. I heard him yelp above the thunder crashes and knew he would be in trouble if he were not released soon. I paused, torn between safety and Blue.

Changing direction, I waded to the rear of the barn, water up to my thighs. I rounded the tall building. Lightning lit the yard in snatches, like photographs snapped with a flashbulb. Blue paddled frantically on the spot, gulping at the air, already in danger of drowning. I reached him quickly and released the chain. Blue allowed me to take his collar and we headed back towards the homestead. But now the water flowed against my path, pulling me away from the house. I struggled forward with the dog. A surge of water swept me off my feet. Blue and I clung to each other for support, paddling until we came upon the clothes hoist. I grabbed the metal pole in a desperate lunge and held us both against the current. Mrs Stuart called from the verandah.

I took a mouthful of water. Blue scratched my face in his fight to stay afloat. Lightning flashed, splitting the night, and found its mark nearby. Almost overhead, another crash of thunder; Blue yelped and my grip on his collar weakened. I would have to let him go. Another flash. I saw Toby making his way towards us, water up to his waist, arms held high. He reached us as my hands were about to give up on Blue. I wrapped my arms around Toby's neck.

'Hold tight,' said Toby.

'Makara,' I said.

Toby grinned. 'Bloody oath!'

Toby grasped Blue's collar and with the dog in tow, made his way back to the house. When we reached the verandah, Mrs Stuart took Blue to safety. Toby and I followed, taking refuge inside. The storm raged on.

The homestead sat on a rise, yet still the water rose over the verandah, eventually sweeping through the house, moving furniture as it passed through, front to back. The generator died, and Toby lit candles and placed them on the dresser. Mrs Stuart and I sat on the kitchen table and watched the water rise. Toby squatted on the kitchen bench with the three whimpering dogs at his side. Blue had his eyes on me.

'How come Blue didn't bite me?' I asked.

'Why would he bite ya?' said Toby.

'He always growls at me and shows his teeth; he always looks like he wants to bite me.'

'He knew you was helping him, I reckon. Dogs is smart like that. And you was brave for a littl'un. Don't ya reckon, missus?'

'She did alright,' said Mrs Stuart.

'Yeah, she did alright.' Toby grinned at me and ruffled the hair on Blue's head.

Hours passed and daylight came with no sign of the sun. All night, the rain had continued unabated, and now water lapped our table refuge. The front door gave way, bursting suddenly under pressure. We watched as a slow-moving river passed through the house. The water levels climbed so that we soon sat in two inches of it.

'We should head to the roof,' said Mrs Stuart.

'No worries,' said Toby. 'We'll get the nipper up first.'

Toby lifted me so that I scrambled over the eaves and onto the tin, not the easiest task with an overhanging verandah and no ladder. Mrs Stuart tried to follow.

'Give me a leg up, Tobe,' she said, grappling for the gutter. Try as she might, there seemed no way to hoist herself onto the roof, even with Toby's help. She cursed aloud, one foul word after another. 'No use, I can't do it.'

Toby grabbed the overhang and swung himself up beside me, his muscular physique making light of the challenge. He prised up the edge of the tin until he could grasp and remove the entire panel; nails popping under the brute force. Mrs Stuart stood on a chair and passed the dogs up one at a time, before taking Toby's hand to be hoisted through the gap to safety. All accounted for, we moved to a spot where the two roofs came together and where we could sit and wait for help, or for the flood to recede. If water levels continued to rise, Mrs Stuart said, we would make our way to the ridge. Thankfully, the lightning could now be heard and seen moving away in the distance. We would be safe for the time being at least, though soaked to the bone.

With a groan and a grating of steel, we watched the dunnies lurch to one side and give way to the water. The panels leaned and fell like creaking dominoes before being swept away with other storm-washed debris.

'I always wanted a flush toilet,' said Mrs Stuart without a smile.

That was the only time I ever heard her attempt a joke, and it passed without laughter. The chickens stood in a line on one of the outhouse roofs, now only five, the remainder of the flock of twenty-five having succumbed to the flood along with Bobby, the rooster. We slaughtered three pigs the previous week, fortunately, and took them to town for the butcher, but two milk cows had disappeared to a fate unknown from the paddock on the far side of the barn. We watched forlornly as a dead sheep floated by, curling lazy circles in the murk before disappearing below the surface. Hypnotised by constant flow, it had a calming effect, we sat in silence for hours, just staring at the water.

'Number One's about to go under,' said Toby, to break the trance. 'He's about to go for a cold swim. He's had a good life, ay, missus?'

'Who's Number One?' I asked.

'Down there,' said Toby, pointing to the veggie patch, where all that could be seen was the top of the scarecrow's head. The scarecrow stood on a long pole. He had a bag of straw for a head and a dusty-brown Akubra for a hat, and he was about to disappear completely if the water rose any further. 'That there's Number One. It's his job to keep the birds away.'

'Why's he called Number One?'

'Aah, that's a story an a half, ay, missus?'

'And then some,' said Mrs Stuart, curling her lip.

'See, it was couple of years back, fella came calling; smart fella he was, fancy suit and tie, polished boots and a brand-new Akubra hat; even had a feather in the band to show how fancy he was. Said he was the number-one salesman in all of Australia. He wanted to sell the boss-lady one of them noisy sucking machines to clean the house.'

'Vacuum, it was; a Eureka vacuum cleaner. Why on God's good earth would a salesman come all the way out here to try and sell me a vacuum cleaner?' said Mrs Stuart. 'He'd more chance of selling ice to Eskimos; bloody drongo.'

'That was it, a vacuum cleaner.' Toby nodded his head in agreement and laughed. 'Missus, she told him to get moving if he knew what was good for him. "Why would I want one of them when I got a broom?" she asked him.' Toby's voice went higher as he tried to sound like Mrs Stuart, making me giggle at his impersonation. 'He wouldn't go though, eh, missus? Kept on flapping his lips he did.' I watched Mrs Stuart chuckle at the memory and it made me smile. Toby went on, 'So you told him, ay, missus? "If you get Esmerelda to say yes, you got yourself a deal." Poor fella got all excited, said he never lost a sale yet.'

'Who's Esmerelda?'

Toby laughed again for several long seconds. 'Well, that's just it. The boss said Esmerelda was in the barn, and she was. 'cept this fella didn't know it, but Esmerelda was an emu, made herself at home here in the barn one day and didn't take kindly to intruders. She thought it was her special place.' Toby laughed again, making me giggle more at his antics and Mrs Stuart to crack into a smile, despite trying to keep a straight face. 'That number-one fella turned and ran to his car, stumbling and falling, crawling on all fours he was,' Toby continued. 'Esmerelda on his butt like one of those jack-hammers they use at the mine. I never laughed so much in all me life, and I'm still laughing now. That poor fella drove off without his hat and never looked back, and it's been sitting on the scarecrow's head ever since.'

'I like that story.'

'Yeah, me too,' said Toby, grinning ear to ear.

'What happened to Esmerelda?'

Toby took a few moments to answer. 'She got a call from a big male that came by the paddock one day, then off they went and we ain't seen her since.'

We settled once more into silence. From our perch we looked out on the vast expanse of water. The inland lake of milky tea, dotted with mulga stands, desert oaks and gum trees, floated peacefully across the ground like a sheet of coloured glass. Where once the creek had wound its way from north to south, only red river gums marked the course, their limbs waving at the air as if to send a signal across the flooded land. Mr Churchill and his family stood defiant. 'We will be fine,' I heard him shout to our rooftop gallery. Mrs Stuart didn't hear him, but I was sure Toby got the message when he turned and winked at me. Our little secret.

Arms wrapped around my legs, chin on my knees, I started to sing. 'Five little ducks went swimming one day, over the hills and far away. Mother duck said...'

Mrs Stuart gave me a dirty look, and I stopped halfway through the first verse. Steady rain pummelled the roof with a rat-a-tat-tat, softer now and vertical because the wind had died, but relentless. I watched the rainwater run between the valleys of the roof on its way to the eaves, and I imagined small ships sailing on the water, then dropping off the edge, like it was the end of the world and all aboard would be lost. I thought of Noah. Perhaps we should gather the animals and put them in a boat, two-by-two.

My nightdress, sodden against my body, felt heavy and cold on my skin. I squeezed the water from the hem and watched it join the rivers of rain. My hair hung heavily against my face and dripped water onto my legs. I flicked my head and a curl of water arced in the air. Mrs Stuart scowled.

My guardian appeared as wretched as me, clothes soaked, hair plastered on her head, water dripping from her nose. Waiting for the clouds to break, she gave no hints of her thoughts, except that maybe she thought I was to blame for the flood, which I decided was evident in her cold stare. Toby's hat spilt water like a tap when he tipped his head. I giggled. He turned to me, pulled a face and smiled. I laughed again. Two sulphur-crested cockatoos joined us on the roof. They opened their yellow crests as they landed, a greeting display meant to say hello and introduce themselves to the party. They examined us closely with piercing black eyes, then sidled up to each other on the far end of the ridge as if they were keeping each other warm. 'We're all in this together,' I heard one say.

A second night on the roof did nothing to raise our soggy spirits. The deluge had ceased, but the water had yet to recede. Cold and wet, I shivered until dawn, watching the sun rise slowly from the horizon with an eerie yellow glow. Fine mist floating above the water like delicate lace burned away quickly as the sun climbed high. Throughout the morning we watched the flood subside, and the earth emerge from its watery veil. By midday, it had gone completely from the rise the house sat on, leaving a slimy layer of mud to coat the station, so that it looked for all the world as if a dirty brown blanket covered the land and all its features. We climbed down to ground level and inspected the damage. Mud squelched beneath our feet. The flash flood had moved with fantastic speed through gullies, channels and creeks, unable to cope with the volume of water. Vast lakes still covered the flat lower pastures.

'The Darling burst its banks,' said Mrs Stuart, looking to the horizon. 'It's either all or nothing with that bloody river.'

Released from the barn, the horses made clear their feelings. Spooked and hyperactive, they raced around the holding yard, kicking up their heels and clods of mud to celebrate their release. I had feared for them, trapped in their stalls.

Clean-up started in earnest. Toby and Mrs Stuart took everything out of the house, washed it all down with buckets of bore water and set it to dry in the hot summer sun. I swept the mud from the house and helped scrub the floors. Mrs Stuart set to work on the furniture and bedding; the wooden furniture had buckled, joints loosened and cracked. To a more fragile woman, the sight of her life's possessions covered in mud and silt would have been heart-breaking, too much to endure, but Mrs Stuart went about the clean-up task without apparent signs of emotion, her face wearing the same scowl it always did, this latest setback just another day in her hard station life.

The flood was a turning point in our relationship, and though she never showed me affection or gave me a reason to believe that she cared for me any more than she cared for the sheep in the paddock, from that day on, she seemed more tolerant of me.

Chapter 6

Horse-Kaangkaru

After the rain, came the miracle of life. The desert flourished, transformed within days, and the once-dry earth produced incredible growth. Lachlan returned from his travels with tales of far pastures rejuvenated. He had escaped the worst of the floods but witnessed days of nourishing rain while holed up near the far corner of the station. Native grasses turned the red earth green – Mitchell grass and button grass, native clovers, saltbush, she-oak, mulga and bullock bush, everything bloomed at once in spectacular fashion. Animals appeared from nowhere – flocks of budgerigars, corellas and galahs came in their thousands. Budgies formed fast-moving clouds of synchronised flight, and the once silent pastures gave way to the songs of frogs, cicadas and crickets. Additional rain followed, though not with the same devastating consequences; days of good steady rain, much needed moisture to consolidate the break in drought. Cutaway Creek flowed steadily once more, flushed with the recent torrent. New cuts in the bank, new rocks exposed. My cave had gone, swept from existence. The rock beneath which I sheltered, the size of a motorcar, had been washed away by the force of water and deposited downstream. Mr Churchill and his family of red gums had their roots exposed.

Despite the brief and devastating effects of the flood, the resulting growth made everyone happy, and the event itself was quickly consigned to the past. The Stuarts had a noticeable lift in spirits as the land bore fruit, feed for the stock was suddenly plentiful, and life seemed bearable at last. Though we had lost many sheep to drowning, Lachlan replenished stock quickly, buying cheaply from farmers in the north who had missed the rain altogether and needed to reduce numbers from their flocks to stay in business after years of drought.

Word went out that Cutaway Creek would soon be hiring again. Toby stayed to help Lachlan restore order, and our two stockmen joined him in the bunkhouse. My fascination with the blackfella had only increased after our time together during the crisis. I watched him from the top of the water tank. From there I could see the entire homestead, and our land, out to the distant horizon on all sides of the property. From this perch, I observed Toby working with horses, training and exercising them in the yard. They would respond to his every command as if they were puppets on strings. Gentle in his methods, he never hurried a horse or got cross at them like Lachlan. Toby spoke in whispers, secret words between horse and man. Sometimes it seemed as though they could understand his language.

He always knew when I was watching. Even when I thought he couldn't see me, he did.

'Why don't ya come down and give it a go?' he said one day.

I frowned. 'Give what a go?'

'Have a ride,' said Toby. 'She's gentle.'

'I can't ride.'

'Sure ya can.' I shook my head at him. 'Got a bum don't ya?'

'Yes.'

'Then ya can ride.' Toby held the reins out and waited. Cautiously I climbed down and went to the ring. 'Climb in,' said Toby.

I climbed the rails and joined Toby and the mare in the ring. The horse seemed enormous as Toby brought her head down to meet me.

'Now give'er a blow up her nose,' said Toby. I laughed. 'Go on, it's her way of saying hello.' I did as he instructed and the mare snorted back. 'That's it, and now you're mates.'

He lifted me into the saddle and adjusted the stirrups. I sat proud, queen of the station. He led the mare around the ring and let me hold the reins.

'Not too tight now,' said Toby. I gave the horse some slack. On my third time around, I realised Mr Stuart's presence, watching from the rails. I braced for a telling off. 'She's a natural, ay, Lock?' said Toby, grinning.

He nodded. 'You'll need to learn to ride if you're going to be any use around here,' he said to my surprise. 'Toby'll teach you after chores each day.'

I couldn't sleep. The following day passed at a painful pace. I raced through chores, but Mrs Stuart kept pulling me up for being shoddy. I swept the kitchen floor three times before she let me finish. At last, I raced to the ring to meet Toby for my lesson; devastated, I found myself alone. It turned out that Toby was away fixing fences. I waited another month before my lessons began.

With grasses plentiful, life emerged from the land in not-so-welcome ways. Rabbits by the thousands, as though they had sprung from the ground like the spinifex on which they grazed, as if God had chosen to spread rabbit seed to test Mr Stuart's resilience. He provided rain to grow the grass, then rabbits to take it back. I recalled Sister Josephine's words when she said I was too old for my comfort blanket and replaced it with a prayer book. 'The Lord giveth, and the Lord taketh away,' she said, handing me the book and prying the blanket from my unwilling fingers.

Mr Stuart and Toby set to work immediately to control rabbit numbers. I thought bunnies were cute and had images of cuddly balls of fluff hopping around the property like Peter Rabbit in Mr McGregor's garden. I was horrified at the prospect of killing them. How could they be so cruel? Lachlan Stuart did not have much sympathy for my concern, and neither, to my dismay, did Toby. With such devastating numbers, it would not be long before the pastures were cleaned out, so they had to do it, he told me. I didn't understand why we couldn't just catch them.

'Rabbits came with the whitefellas,' said Toby. 'They brought them here, and now they want them gone. Clever lot, your mob.'

Shooting took place at dusk, then working through the night from the back of Mr Stuart's Austin pick-up truck, Toby and Lachlan killed everything that moved. I lay awake and listened, every shot a bullet to my heart. In the weeks that followed, rabbit carcasses piled up in the holding yard. I watched the mountain grow to over three feet in height, a rabbit massacre of immense proportions. And when the final bodies topped the pile, the heap stood well above the level of my head.

Kangaroos followed rabbits. A mob of sixty or seventy eastern greys took up residence in the pasture within sight of the homestead. Excited by their arrival – these were my first kangaroos – I couldn't wait to get up close. Fascinated, I studied the bounding marsupials at play, taking every opportunity to sit and observe from the fence line at dusk and dawn when they were most active. But like the rabbits, they were unwanted pests to pastoralists whose lives depend on the land.

'They'll eat the bloody lot,' said Mr Stuart. 'Feed's precious. If we don't eradicate them, they'll leave nothing for the stock.' I had to ask what that meant, and once again was horrified to be told of more killing.

Despite my objections – it didn't matter what I thought in the end – I had to bear the heartache for the good of the land. Like with the rabbits, they hunted at night from the pick-up truck to cull kangaroo numbers, using the headlights, which caused the kangaroos to freeze and wait to be killed. Easy targets for Mr Stuart and his .308 rifle. It didn't take long to complete the massacre. Heartbroken, I despaired at the sight of bodies piled high in the truck bed. More than this, I felt disappointed in Toby for aiding the slaughter.

It was not long after the cull that the coppers came looking for Mary. Two tall policemen arrived in a station wagon with a woman from the welfare mob. Toby had quietly slipped from sight when he saw them coming. They were looking for Mary Cobham, an Aboriginal girl, and her half-caste daughter. They questioned Mr Stuart briefly, as Mrs Stuart and I watched from the verandah steps. Mr Stuart stood with the woman while the policemen nosed around the barn.

'Got nothing better to do?' Mrs Stuart called across the yard, as they returned to the car. They didn't answer.

'What do they want?' I asked.

'They're after some kid from the mission, bloody mongrels. I don't trust coppers with them young girls, and them mission lot are even worse.'

We watched the visitors drive away. It would not be the last time they came calling. Toby didn't reappear until the following day.

When Toby finally had time to teach me to ride, we made the most of every opportunity. Once begun, nothing could stop my progress. Toby taught well, me a quick learner, and between us we accomplished my initial tuition in a matter of weeks.

'You were born in the saddle,' he said, encouraging my new-found passion.

I felt as if this was true, that I belonged on a horse. But I wasn't satisfied with my accomplishments, I wanted to be an expert like Toby. With Mr Stuart's approval, we kept up lessons in the months that followed, riding out to far pastures at dusk each day. To my surprise, and despite Daisy's objections, Lachlan Stuart permitted me to ride the bore line with Toby, leaving her to tend to chores alone at the homestead, thus creating a foul mood for my every return. She even argued that I should be doing schooling instead of riding out with Toby, despite having shown no interest in my education before. When a Catholic-schools inspector had arrived at the homestead one day, little had come of the visit. My books had barely been touched since.

'Don't need no reading and writing if ya can fix a buggered bucket,' said Toby.

Following well-worn trails to the bores dotted throughout the station, we checked them daily for maintenance, Toby showing me how to fix a blocked valve, and grease up the cog-wheels.

'Where did we get water before the bores were drilled?' I asked.

'The creeks and billabongs,' said Toby. 'But the whitefellas brought their sheep and cattle, they let them drink at the billabongs, waterholes we'd used for a thousand years. But they was too many and they shit in the water, poisoned it. Soon was no good for anything, no sheep, no cattle, no kangaroo or wallaby, no blackfella, no nothing. So they drilled bores to the water under the earth. I reckon, if they could shit down them bore holes, they'd bugger them up too.'

During our rides, Toby would teach me about plants and animals, the birds and trees, which plants I could eat and which I could not, how to survive off the land if I had to. Toby said you could live off bush tucker, and his mob had been doing it for thousands and thousands of years.

'Your mob must be very old,' I said.

'Yeah, I reckon we've been around a while. My ancestors walked these lands when food was plenty enough for all. We respected country; there was no sheep, no cattle, no fences. Each mob knew the boundaries and knew each other's land. Each mob was the keeper of their own country and stories.'

'Do you know lots of stories?'

'I know some, but whitefellas don't want us keeping up the traditional ways and passing on yarns and songs, so a lot's been forgotten. There are still old fellas and elders that know all the stories; some of the men went through the initiation when they were young men.'

'What's an initiation?'

Toby smiled. 'Big word ay? Initiation is secret men's business. When a boy becomes a man.'

'Did you have one?'

'Nah. But I do remember some traditional things from when I was a nipper, being taken to ceremonies by me uncles, and stuff like that. We would gather around the fire and men painted their faces and danced through the night. We called them corroborees,' Toby said. 'But they don't happen around here no more. There's an old bloke who lives here on the station with his granddaughter. He knows a lot about the old ways.'

I asked Daisy Stuart about the old man. She said he lived in a humpy – a makeshift shanty – with his family beyond the far paddock by the creek. He used to work for Lachlan Stuart's father as a drover in the early days.

'He's old,' said Daisy. 'The old man reckons he's a right to be there on our property. Doesn't pay any bloody rent, mind. I wouldn't give the bludger the time of day, but Lachlan says they're all good.'

'What's a bludger?'

'A lazy bastard,' said Daisy.

Not everywhere was flat across the station. Toby and I would sometimes ride out to rock outcrops, some several-hundred-feet high, made up of exposed yellow, orange and red rock, weathered and worn by a million years of storms and wind.

'Why is the dirt red?'

Toby glanced at the ground, then at the rock face; it appeared quite scarlet against the deep-blue sky. 'Kupaar. That means red earth in our lingo. But it depends on the light, especially in the early morning or late afternoon. Sometimes it's red, but sometimes it's yellow. I've even seen it look blue like the sky, and sometimes the colour disappears altogether, like it's been spirited away. Whitefellas say it's minerals.'

'What's minerals?'

'Iron in the soil so it goes rusty.'

I laugh. 'Soil can't go rusty, Toby.'

'Well that's what I think too, but them whitefellas are supposed to be smart.'

'What do blackfellas say?'

'We say it's red because it was made that way. But maybe it's red because it's stained with blood.'

'What blood?'

'The blood of our ancestors. And when the colour disappears altogether, it will be because our tears have washed it away.'

We said nothing more and I followed Toby through a gully, deep in thought, the cliffs towering up on both sides as we passed through the narrow gap. Toby stopped suddenly, confronted by a snake, which reared up on the trail, rolling its head from side to side and hissing menacingly. Usually, Toby said, a snake like that would hear us coming and slither on out of the way before we even saw it, but this one was not about to let us pass unchallenged.

'He's an angry bugger,' said Toby.

'What shall we do?'

'Just wait awhile and see if he wants to slide away somewhere safe.'

'What if it doesn't?'

Seven- or eight-feet long, Toby said it was a mulga snake. 'Whitefellas call them king browns,' he said. 'This one's not going anywhere in a hurry.'

Rather than move off, the snake wound its way towards us, agitated and ready to strike.

'I think it's time to let him have his way,' said Toby, pulling on the reins and backing his horse slowly towards me. 'Just back her up real slow and easy.'

I tried to do likewise, but either my horse didn't understand, or I was doing it all wrong, because it reared up. I felt as if I would fall, and thought of the snake in terror. I managed to hold on, but the incident left me shaken. Toby said I had done a great job of staying in the saddle. Soon after he gave me lessons on backing up a horse the right way.

On these rides, I gained an appreciation for the size of the station, and realised why Lachlan and the stockmen were away so much of the time. Toby and I sometimes rode out to the north and joined the Darling River, a jade-coloured waterway where boats could navigate to and from towns along the way.

Toby said its real name, before the white man, was the Baaka, and it went all the way to join the mighty Murray.

Of all the things I liked to do most, a gallop topped my list. We would ride across the salt pans and dried-up lakes where the earth would crinkle and craze in patterns of red, yellow and white. The flat terrain allowed us to gallop at full speed. Sometimes Toby would set out markers through which we would slalom, racing against each other to reach the end. Most occasions, he won, but as time went by, I managed some victories myself.

Toby insisted that this was all training for the work of a stockman, but, training or otherwise, I loved every minute spent riding with him and learning from his experience of the land. I looked forward each day to our meeting. So it was with a heavy heart that one morning I went to the bunkhouse to find Toby's swag gone. Mrs Stuart said he'd gone walkabout. We would not see him again for almost a year.

After Toby's departure, Lachlan Stuart hired an overseer named Johnson Milne. A half-caste, he was almost as white as me. Good-natured and patient, he partially filled the space in my life vacated by Toby, and continued to develop my knowledge of horses.

Life was changing slowly; I began to feel as if I could belong at Cutaway Creek. I was happier, and Daisy and Lachlan Stuart seemed kinder, or more tolerant at least. Before I knew it, thoughts of escape no longer came to mind. I still thought of Archie, but with each passing day I began to accept that he was gone and might never return to find me.

My first experience of muster came later that year when Cutaway Creek became a community like no other. Spirits ran high after more weeks of good rain, and the desert had come alive once again with good fodder for the animals. All manner of unusual characters came to help; old friends and new, men hard like Lachlan Stuart, born to the land.

I had soon learned that farm workers were called stockmen, and drovers were responsible for driving flocks from pasture to pasture. Drovers also took stock to transport centres, to be loaded onto trains bound for Goulburn, Sydney and Adelaide. The stockmen came from the far reaches of the state and beyond, itinerant workers who drifted from station to station and found work when available.

Stockmen arrived in numbers to the station as if answering an invisible call. They came unannounced, some in pick-up trucks with motorbikes in the trays, some on foot, some with horse trailers. A group of ringers – cowboys – from a cattle station on the South Australian border, arrived on horseback. Daisy said there wasn't work for everyone, but most found a job if they didn't ask for too much pay, and some even worked for food and tobacco. She said they arrived every year around muster time.

'It's the bush telegraph,' Daisy said, 'that's how they heard we're hiring.'

In the weeks of muster that followed, Lachlan Stuart seemed a different man. He walked with a bounce, laughed and joked with the workers, who called him Lock or Lockie, never Lachlan, and appeared to enjoy the annual gathering. Most of the stockmen were mixed blood – half-castes as we knew them then – part black, part white. Two of the ringers said they were pure-blood Aboriginals, but Johnson said that he had doubts and that they were no more Aboriginal than he. He told me he didn't like to be called half-caste.

'It makes me feel like I don't belong anywhere,' Johnson said. 'I'm Wadigali, no matter what colour me skin.'

Only two stockmen were white like me, and one man, who they called the Afghan, looked different to everyone else. Someone asked him where he left his camel, and everyone laughed when he told them to leave his wife out of it. I didn't understand.

On arrival at the station, the workers gathered and swapped stories, catching up on the news and renewing acquaintances. They lit a massive cooking fire every night in the yard, and Cutaway Creek came alive to the sounds of laughter and lively conversation; excitement filled the air. I longed to join the men on the muster, but Lachlan Stuart said no, it was men's work and no place for a sheila. It didn't stop me hanging around the camp.

Muster lasted two whole months. Shearers arrived days after the stockmen and set up shop beneath enormous tarpaulin covers stretched over poles to protect them from the sun. Sheep were driven to the homestead in batches so as not to overcrowd the yards, but I had never seen so many woolly animals in one place at the same time. Once shorn, sheep were inspected and dipped, and young males were castrated – a process that left me distraught – before being released for another year into the outback pastures. Everyone knew their role without the need for orders from the boss.

In the years to come I would earn my place amongst the stockmen, even if it wasn't women's work. I would see these same men come and go as the seasons passed, and get to know them well. I was growing in strength, and my character with it.

Chapter 7

Elder-Wirtuulu

Ten turned to eleven, eleven became twelve, and before I knew it I approached my thirteenth birthday. Cutaway Creek had gradually become my home, despite the lack of affection shown to me by the Stuarts, who I now addressed as Daisy and Lachlan. I found solace in a life on the land, the vast country of which I was now a part. I had always been self-reliant; even when Archie watched over me, I knew I was capable of fighting my own battles and winning. In the years since arriving in Australia I had hardened that resilient streak, that edge that gave me an air of defiance, though I'm sure to some I was still just an insolent child. Nevertheless, this was now my place in the world. I had survived the worst and life looked brighter, or so I thought.

Two days before my thirteenth birthday, I received word that Archie had died in an industrial accident while working at the steelworks in Port Kembla. The news came in a letter addressed to Miss Katherine Bower, C/O Mrs Daisy Stuart, Cutaway Creek Station, Wilcannia, NSW. Archie J. Bower was sixteen years old when he died. I tried not to cry at his passing, Archie would have said I was weak to do so, but in the end I sobbed my heart out. I remembered his promise to come for me, his assurance that we would be together again one day, promises he could not keep. Had he tried? I would never know. But I like to think he would have come one day, when he was rich perhaps, wealthy enough to care for us both in a big house by the sea.

On my birthday, Lachlan Stuart astonished me by letting me choose a stock horse from the mob to call my own. I chose a beautiful two-year-old bay gelding with white socks, a white nose, and a blonde mane and tail. I called him Jack, my brother's middle name, and we instantly became the best of friends. That afternoon, I was in the barn, having just filled Jack's trough with oats. I was leaning on the door of his stall, admiring my new love as he chomped on feed, his coat shining under a shaft of light, glowing gold. I turned, suddenly aware I was not alone. Lachlan stood behind me, so close that he startled me. I started to laugh off my shock, but I saw a look in his eyes that both confused and frightened me. An awkward silence followed where we just stared at one another, before I pushed past him and headed for the yard, trying to understand what had just happened. I glanced back and saw him standing in a trance, as though he hadn't realised I was no longer standing there before him.

That night I had a dream. I was running through the orphanage in London, searching for Archie and the other children. But each time I entered a room there was no one there, just empty space. In a panic, I raced from room to room – they were endless – calling out for Archie. I turned and saw Lachlan; Daisy stood behind him. I looked down at my arms, but they were not my arms, they were covered in fur and I had paws instead of hands. I felt my face. Something wasn't right. I realised I was a dingo. I stood before Lachlan and tried to tell him it was me, not a dingo, but I couldn't find my voice, just a terrified wheeze as I tried desperately to speak. Lachlan raised a gun and pointed the barrel at my head. 'Go on, end it,' said Daisy. 'Put it out of its misery.' *No, no,* I wanted to say. *It's me, Katherine.* But I couldn't. 'End it,' said Daisy. And then I awoke to the thumping of my heart. And though it was just a dream, I couldn't help but feel dread at what lay ahead in my future.

On days when I could be alone, I rode Jack to a bend in the creek known as Drover's Elbow, where I would sit in silence and daydream while Jack nibbled saltbush in the shade. The elbow in the stream was a special place.

'See the way the water bends like a thurru through the grass?' Toby said one day.

'Thurru?'

'Snake,' said Toby. 'This is Ngatyi yapara, home of the Rainbow Serpent. When the creek is full and the sun hits the water at certain times of the year, some say you can catch a glimpse of Ngatyi, gliding through the water.'

'Did you ever see him?'

'Nah, but I know he's there in the creeks and the billabongs, the rivers and lakes.'

'Did you come here when you were a boy?'

'Came here a lot with me brothers, just to sit and watch the water, looking for Ngatyi, listening to the grass swaying gently in the wind, whispering all the old yarns.'

Drover's Elbow was a place of long grass, swathes of it close to the creek banks. Toby said it grew there because of an underground spring, which made the grass grow tall.

'When the breeze comes in from the west, you can hear whispering spirits, dancing amongst the leaves. Listen,' said Toby.

'I hear them. What are they saying?'

Toby thought about it for a long moment. 'Well, that's between you and them,' he said eventually.

I thought a lot about Toby when he wasn't around. He came and went as years passed by, just as Daisy Stuart had said he would. And though I knew we were friends, he never said when he would next appear, or told me when he would leave.

Mobs of kangaroos, eastern greys, often joined me at Drover's Elbow. They seemed to accept my presence without any sign of fear. I called them the Bludger Mob on account of them spending most of the day laid out under desert oaks in lazy poses, scratching and preening in between carefree naps. Joeys stayed close to mothers but seemed particularly interested in Jack, approaching him curiously, and then taking off in alarm to their mum's pouch every time Jack flicked his tail, or snorted. I got to know the Bludgers well, and named them for their unique characteristics. Scar, the big male, watched over everyone like a king. He had a scar like a lightning blaze cut diagonally across his face. Red, a female with an unusually red coat, stood out from the others, and Patch, a male with one eye, kept himself to himself. Dopey, my favourite young joey, did silly things, falling over his feet, or being frightened by his own tail, and would leave me crying with laughter.

For some time, Lachlan Stuart had acknowledged my usefulness around the station and accepted that I had more to offer than household chores. I had taken part in the last two musters and shown that my riding skills were as good as anyone's. One day while we were in Broken Hill, he took me into the gun shop.

'Pick a rifle,' he said.

'Why?'

'Time you learned to shoot.'

'I don't want to shoot. What if I killed something?'

Lachlan laughed. 'That's the idea, ya daft bugger. Who's going to protect the stock when I'm away?'

By then I understood that pests must die for the survival of the station. Wild dogs and dingoes were a problem, as they could take many sheep, while foxes came to the chook house almost nightly. Lachlan and Johnson shot and killed many predators, hanging their carcasses on fences to serve as a warning to other dogs who might take a fancy to easy prey. These hunters were particularly active during lambing season.

Lachlan selected three guns and laid them out before me. I picked a Marlin twenty-two calibre because I liked the name.

'That one,' I said, running my hand over the shiny wooden stock. Lachlan and the man behind the counter smiled.

Johnson taught me to shoot, and I soon became proficient. A long time passed before I killed something, but when my first deadly encounter came, it turned out to be traumatic and led to a frank conversation with Daisy.

One night, while Lachlan was away, a fox came to the homestead to raid the chook house. I heard the chooks squawking and carrying on, and knew from previous raids we had trouble.

'Fox at the chook house!' cried Daisy.

I took my rifle and loaded the magazine. Daisy grabbed the torch, and together we sneaked out so as not to warn the thief. Daisy had to stifle a cough; she had begun to struggle with her lungs and the night air had set her off.

'You stay here,' I whispered. 'Turn on the light when I shout.'

I crept forward while the chooks continued their cackling alarm. I gave the signal; Daisy aimed the beam and switched on the torch, catching a big red fox in the light. Like glowing pearls in the summer sun, his eyes stood out in the dark. I didn't hesitate, took aim and fired, killing the animal with my first shot to the head. I checked the dead creature, running my hand along its soft fur and wishing he had stayed away, and that I hadn't needed to take his life.

'That'll teach the bugger,' said Daisy, returning inside.

As the warmth ebbed from the animal's body, I felt sick, the guilt almost making me weep. I lay awake long into that evening, thinking of the beautiful fox and wishing I had missed on purpose and let him run away. I dreamt about it later that night, and woke in a fright, sweat covering my body, pangs of regret tormenting my mind. Sleep came fitfully, and I eventually went to the kitchen for a drink of water. Daisy startled me, sitting in the dark.

'You couldn't sleep?' I asked, lighting a paraffin lamp – we didn't run the generator through the night. Daisy sat on a ladder-back chair, staring blankly into space. 'Are you alright?'

'Life wasn't meant to be like this,' said Daisy absently. 'One minute you've got plans for the future, next you've got no future at all.'

I didn't know how to respond. Daisy never talked about her thoughts or feelings; it took an effort for her to speak at all unless it was to curse and scold. Our conversations usually centred on practical things, day-to-day chores, stock issues, the weather and the seasons.

'What do you mean?' I asked.

Daisy turned to me as if she had only just noticed my presence. Her lips curled into an ironic smile. She shook a cigarette from a pack, lit it with a match, took a long drag, and coughed at the effort. 'I had ambitions,' she said eventually. 'I could have been an air stewardess, you know; had an interview, everything.' She gazed into space, as though she were seeing her past unravel before her eyes. 'I could have travelled the world, Singapore, America, even got to see your bloody mob in England. I was a finalist out of all the applicants; hundreds applied. It was every girl's dream. I thought I was in for sure, got my weight down to what they wanted, I wasn't too tall, and I passed the medical exam.' Daisy took another drag, producing the anticipated coughing fit.

'What happened?'

'I had a boy and we planned to get married, but at the final interview they said I had to choose, because you can't be a stewardess and be married. One or the other, the manager said, rules are rules. I told him I had made my decision and I was getting married. Bastard told me it was no problem, I wasn't pretty enough anyway.'

'So you married Lachlan.'

Daisy scoffed. 'It wasn't Lock I was going to marry. His name was Gordo, and he buggered off with a tart from Wagga, before I'd even got home from the interview. I met Lock later. Lucky bloody me, eh?' She looked me up and down, assessing me, but finding only the object of her contempt. 'You'd have been pretty enough,' she said, unable to hide her resentment.

'I can't imagine flying.'

'Everyone's flying around now. Ordinary people, if you can afford the tickets that is. You can leave Melbourne and be in London in four days. It's marvellous how quick they are. I would have liked to go. To London, I mean.' Her lip quivered, almost imperceptible in the dim light.

I couldn't help feeling moved by Daisy's revelation. It stirred in me the realisation that I didn't know her at all. As I stared at her, she must have seen something in my expression, and she reacted.

'Don't you dare pity me,' she said, stubbing out her cigarette in the ashtray, as though she was trying to kill it.

I didn't respond. We sat in silence. Daisy lighting another cigarette and staring into the shadows while I looked away and tried to hide my irritation at her sudden backlash. Her contempt for me seemed to have no bounds; she showed it in every barbed comment, every glance and curl of her lips, making me weary of her abusive remarks. There had been moments over the years, conversations that had taken a lighter tone, periods when she almost seemed happy and we might even have been friends if she'd lowered her guard further. But they were rare and never lasted, and her demeanour always returned to the sharp-tongued, bitter woman I saw before me. From our very first meeting she had treated me like an unwanted stray, as though it was my choice to arrive at her door. I had never understood her spiteful attitude towards me.

'Why did you take me in?' I asked.

'What are you on about?'

'Why did you give me a home when you never showed the slightest interest in me? Why bother at all if you didn't want me?'

'What's got into your knickers?'

I didn't answer. We sat in silence again, and just as I was about to return to bed, she spoke.

'It was Lock's idea,' she said, a hint of shame in her eyes as she tried to avoid mine. 'Others had done it, stepped forward and volunteered when the call came to provide homes for the Pommy kids. His mate, Shane, had a place on the committee and pestered Lock to jump on the bandwagon. Free labour, that was what Shane said. That bugger never missed a chance to feather his own nest. When he and his missus took in two strapping boys, both thirteen years old and on the verge of being useful, he was adamant that Lock should follow suit, kept spruiking all the advantages.' Daisy paused, struggling to catch her breath. This happened regularly with any kind of exertion or stress. 'We were... We were supposed to get your brother, and you were to come along as part of the deal,' she continued. 'Shane said he was a big lad, your brother, and good with his hands, did a real sales job, did Shane.' Daisy paused to clear her throat. 'Lock was keen for the lad. Then it all went to shit. A misunderstanding, they told us. The lad had been allocated to a mission home on the south coast and you were to be sent here alone. Shane washed his hands of the whole thing and Lock was seething. He didn't want you and neither did I, but what the hell were we supposed to do when they put us on the spot? Lock wanted no part of the deal after instigating it, but I felt guilty and agreed to take you. More fool me for giving in.' Daisy finally looked me full in the face. 'And haven't we been just the best of pals since?' she said with a dry smile.

'You should have said no. It would have been better for all of us.'

Daisy scoffed. 'Bloody oath I should have.'

I spent the rest of the night thinking about Daisy's revelations. I wasn't angry or upset. I pitied her, trapped in a life she did not want; hateful and embittered. I had glimpsed a dark and desolate soul beneath her stoic mask, and despite her loathing, it saddened me. That particular lowering of her guard was never repeated, and we never again discussed the past.

Life took a turn for the better when the Stuarts hired Ellin Cobham, an Aboriginal woman, to cook and help with the housework. Daisy had become frail, forcing me to take on her share of the chores. It was only when Ellin arrived that Daisy revealed that she had been hiding a serious illness. Diagnosed with lung cancer, she refused all but the necessary medical assistance. She would have no fussing over her, she told us. Despite her condition, she continued to smoke heavily and wouldn't hear of quitting.

'It's the only pleasure left to me,' she said, choking.

'You'll die if you don't stop,' I told her.

'I'll die anyway,' she snapped, 'and it won't be a moment too bloody soon.'

Chapter 8

Snake-Thurru

Thirty-five years old with a friendly, caring disposition, Ellin lived with her mother and her grandparents, in a tin shanty near the creek on the far side of the northern pasture. The grandfather turned out to be the old man Toby had once described, the one with knowledge of traditional ways. Intrigued to learn more about Ellin's family, I asked about her grandfather.

'Do you know Toby?' We were pinning washing to the clothesline, a strong wind causing the items to fly horizontally from the line.

'Toby Wiamungu? I know of him.'

'He told me about your grandfather. He said he was a big fella.'

Ellin laughed. 'He's an elder if that's what you mean.'

'Like an Indian chief?'

'Kind of. Grandad is a tribal elder. He's more like a teacher than a chief. They pass on the knowledge to the mob.'

'Who's mob?'

'His. Ours.'

'You live with a mob?'

'Just Grandma and Grandad, my mum and my cousin. The rest are all over.'

'All over where?'

'Scattered. Some on reserves, missions. Stock-workers go where the jobs are, living on stations right across country.' Ellin's mouth hardened. 'Our mob lived all the way from Queensland to South Australia once. Our camp at the creek was home to a mob of eighty or ninety Koori people. Not anymore.'

'You're angry.'

Ellin paused and sighed, then turned to me and smiled. 'Not at you, tidda. But sometimes I just...'

'Just what?'

A gust of wind took one of Lachlan's undershirts off the line, and we watched as it tumbled off across the paddock.

'Like our mob,' said Ellin, sadly watching the laundry disappear in the distance.

'Tell me more about your grandad,' I said.

'Uncle Charlie Cobham,' said Ellin. 'That's his name. He was one of the last men in the mob to go through.'

'Go through?'

'He became a man during an initiation ceremony. The Milia, they called it.'

'Toby told me it was secret men's business.'

'That's right. Hey, you and me got secret women's business,' said Ellin.

'We do?'

'Sure do. Like not telling Daisy we lost one of Lock's shirts.'

Ellin and I soon became friends. She took everything in her stride and was the only person I had ever seen who could take on Daisy Stuart and somehow defuse her volatile nature. Daisy groaned, grumbled and complained, cursed Ellin like she cursed me, but Ellin simply smiled as though she didn't hear the insults. She cared for Daisy's needs, only to be abused for her efforts, yet she never stopped smiling.

'It would take more than Daisy Stuart to spoil my day,' she would say.

Ellin and I were in the veggie patch when the welfare lot came calling again. Two policemen and a man and women dressed in city clothes. They parked up close to the homestead, getting out as the dust slowly dissipated. The man taking out a cigarette and lighting it. They stood for a moment, assessing the yard, before the man and woman approached us.

'Hello, Ellin,' said the woman.

Ellin mumbled beneath her breath. They were obviously acquainted with each other.

'Where is she?'

'Who?' said Ellin.

'You know very well who,' said the woman. 'She can't keep doing this.'

I looked to Ellin for a response, but she said nothing in reply.

The man spoke. 'What is it about you mob that doesn't get it?'

'I get it mister. You want to lock her up in that mission. What *you* don't get is that she don't want to be there.'

'Show some respect, girl,' said the man. 'You're not talking to some blackfella now.'

'It's for her own good,' said the woman. 'She belongs there and so do her children.'

'Where's Mary?' said the man, impatiently.

'Well she ain't here, go look for yourself.'

At that moment Daisy came to the door, but before she could speak, she erupted in a full-blown coughing fit. Everyone stood and waited for her to compose herself. When she spoke, she was adamant. 'You heard the girl, don't waste your time looking here. Why you can't leave them be... And you coppers should be ashamed of yourselves, dogs the lot of you. If the bloody people don't want to be there, why the hell do you have to go chasing them down and dragging them back?'

'It's the law, Mrs Stuart,' said the woman.

'Law my arse. Get the hell off my property and do something worthwhile, like shooting yourself in the head,' she snapped.

The visitors stood speechless for a while. Eventually, the man shook his head, stubbed his cigarette beneath his foot, and returned to the vehicle, followed by the uniformed policemen, who seemed bored by the exercise. The woman paused to issue a warning.

'The law says Mary and her girl should be on the mission. If it turns out your concealing information that may lead to her apprehension…'

'I'm quaking in my boots,' said Daisy.

Daisy returned to the house as the car disappeared. We watched them go.

'Who's Mary?' I asked Ellin.

'No one for you to worry about, tidda.'

When we were alone, Ellin told me stories, funny stories that made me laugh aloud, something I'd rarely done since leaving England. She called me 'tidda' and said it meant girlfriend, we shared confidences and personal news. She quipped and joked, celebrated life, and said she was blessed to be alive. She talked freely about most things, but when I asked her about her simple life in the ramshackle humpy, she was cautious, changing the subject to distract me.

'You don't want to know about that old place,' she said when I pressed her.

'But I do.'

'Why?'

'Because.'

'That's not a reason, tidda.'

I had known about Ellin's shanty for some time before she took up work at the homestead. Daisy called her camp the Abo's humpy, but said in all her years at the station she had never been out to see for herself.

'I've got no interest in going to see a bunch of blackfellas, squatting on our land,' said Daisy one day. 'If it was up to me I'd send them packing. But Lachlan thinks they're fine where they are, so I suppose that's where they'll stay. As long as they don't knock off the stock and keep to themselves, and Lachlan doesn't have a problem, then neither do I.'

I wondered what Daisy would have thought if she had known back then that one of those blackfellas would be caring for her personal needs. Perhaps she would have been more sympathetic, but I doubted it. When out riding alone I would sometimes pass Ellin's little settlement. I'd stop at a distance and watch the smoke from cooking fires, see the family come and go, and wonder what kind of life they lived amongst the jumble of tin and timber. I continued to ask her about her life in the camp, until she finally relented and told me to come and see for myself.

Little more than a collection of temporary shelters, corrugated tin nailed and wired to rough wood skeletons, Ellin's home seemed vastly inadequate for a family. The main living area had a dirt floor and crude furniture, some of it salvaged from the rubbish tip. My first impulse was to feel pity, even anger. I wanted to help in some way, to make their life more comfortable. My own accommodation at Cutaway Creek had improved somewhat since my early days in Australia. I had eventually moved into a bedroom annexe at the rear of the homestead, leaving my lean-to outhouse to the chickens, who reclaimed it quickly by installing a brand-new chicken-shit carpet. But even by those early standards, Ellin's humpy sitting beside the creek seemed dismal and depressing.

A dump had been created by the Stuarts to discourage the Aboriginal settlement, but it had not stopped them setting up home there. Various rusting wrecks had found a final resting place amongst the tussocks and trees. A tractor with steel wheels, a Morris flat-bed truck with no motor and rotten tyres, a decaying water tank – they stood like ghosts of the past, brown monsters inhabited by weeds and scrub. Broken bottles littered the ground along with broken pottery, rusted tins and assorted rubbish, tipped by the Stuarts over years of occupation. Agricultural iron, mechanisms of unknown function, grew from the ground like pieces of sculpture and mounds of rubble reminded me of London in the aftermath of the war.

On my first visit I found Ellin cooking over a fire pit, as her family had done over generations before her. Her mother, Colleen, a woman in her sixties, smiled a toothless grin, called me 'sunshine' and made me feel welcome. Lean and bony, she sat mending a pair of worn daks, sewing a patch of material over a hole in the bum. As worn as the weathered earth, she looked like she belonged in the desert landscape, unlike me, though my skin had taken on a golden hue and my hair had turned quite blonde. I glanced through the lopsided door, into one of the structures. Ellin's grandfather lay on a low bed, smoking a cigarette, staring at the roof. He took a long drag on his durry, the smoke emerging from his mouth in rings. I could see two more beds inside the shack, but there was little else to make it a home as I would know one.

Ellin's grandmother emerged from a shack on the far side of camp, and I was surprised to see a younger woman, a teenager, sitting in an old armchair under a nearby river gum, and nursing an infant that she cradled under her arm. I was even more surprised to learn this was Mary, Ellin's cousin. The same Mary sought by the welfare people when they came to the homestead with the policemen.

'Mary's been in and out of the mission her whole life just about,' said Ellin. 'That there's her third baby. She lost the other two to the welfare.'

'But she's so young. Where's the baby's father?'

'Oh, there ain't no father, least none we can name. Mary's not the brightest girl I know. She has a way of hooking up with the wrong sort of fellas, and there's always enough, black or white, who see she's easy pickings. She came here a few weeks ago, running from the coppers again, but this is not the place for her to hide.'

'How can you live like this?' I said, surveying the camp with pity.

Ellin reacted. 'Well, it's not much, I'll give you that, but our palace is being fixed right now, and our other home is full of house guests.

'I'm sorry. I didn't mean...'

Ellin smiled, and her mother shook her head. 'That's okay, tidda.'

We sat in silence for a long time, watching Mary feed her child, before Ellin spoke. 'The welfare mob will come for her again; they won't rest until they have her back on the mission.'

'Why do they want her to stay there?'

'They want all the half-caste kids in the missions, and everyone else on reserves. They say it's to protect us.'

'Protect you from what?'

'Ourselves, tidda. They say we need to learn the modern ways for the good of our children. We can't teach them schooling so they'll do it for us. Granddad says they want to breed us out. We just have to take it while my kids will never know me; they'll grow up thinking I didn't want them.'

'You have children too?'

'I've got two littl'uns, a boy and a girl, both taken, like Mary's.'

'Taken?'

Mary, had joined us. 'Took my first two, just like Ellin's.'

'Taken by the protection mob,' said Ellin. 'I don't know where they are now. Some years ago, when they was just babes, one and three years old, they came without warning and stole my babies. They said it was best for them to be with whitefellas who could teach them better ways.'

'They can't just take your babies.' I was astonished.

'They can. They did. The Aboriginal welfare mob can do what they want, tidda. They came for mine; they came for Mary's. They said it was for their own good. Now they want this little mite and Mary too.'

'Ain't having her,' said Mary, holding the child close to her breast.

'I don't see how you're going to stop them, baby,' said Ellin. 'They'll find you sooner or later, like they always do.'

Charlie appeared at the door and chipped in. He had been listening. 'That was a bloody caper,' he said, joining us at the fire. 'They came for my grandchildren; damn them to hell, four or five coppers and a white woman from the authority. I said bugger off, I'm not having that caper from your mob. But the coppers stood between us, and I'm not the man I was who could stop them. They pushed me aside and took them off to the mission. We're not good enough to raise our own children, can't even teach them our own lingo.'

'Isn't there anything you can do?' I asked.

'The authority sets the rules,' said Ellin. 'They won't change their minds. All half-caste kids got to be in the settlements and missions.'

'They want to turn them bloody white,' said Charlie.

'Charlie was a top stockman,' said Ellin's mum, suddenly changing the subject.

'Still would be if someone would give me a horse,' said the old man. 'I could make a horse dance,' he said, a sparkle in his eyes.

Mary laughed. 'You would fall off a rocking horse,' she mocked.

I saw how hurt he was by the comment and before he could respond, I jumped in. 'I bet you were a wonderful rider.'

I could imagine Charlie Cobham had been an imposing man in his heyday, driving stock high in the saddle and surrounded by clouds of dust and dirt. Like many of his occupation, the hard-working life had been etched in his weary features. Shaded beneath the wide brim of his stockman's hat, the old man pointed to the east, as though he could see his past on the horizon.

'That's where I lived, that's me home,' he said. 'Wherever there's a tree to hang me hat, that's my place. I've worked all over, every station north to south, east to west. This land is mine, no matter what the whitefella says.'

We sat by the creek and the old man, eager to talk, shared his experiences driving sheep and cattle on the old stock routes from the south across eastern Australia, all the way to Cape York. Charlie had lost none of his mental capacity, with every name of friends and acquaintances remembered. At eighty-eight years of age, he was still as sharp as a prickly pear. He took off his shirt and showed me the marks on his back.

'Me father put me through the initiation,' he said, displaying short parallel rows of scars that formed a pattern on his skin. 'Wiljaru,' he said, proudly.

'Ellin told me there are lots of different tribes all over Australia.'

Charlie put his shirt back on, struggling with a sleeve until I helped him sort out the tangle. He settled and drew a map in the dirt with his wizened finger. 'This here's Barkindji, Wiljakali, Danggali here, Maliangaba over there.' I watched as the old man rattled off clan after clan. 'Some are gone now,' he said, shaking his head. 'Ellin's mum comes from the Poolamacca mob. They were a big mob, two hundred or more out beyond the Corner. And me father married a Danggali woman.'

'How many in your clan?' I asked.

'Not many left around here now, they've all gone, mixed with other mobs and moved on to find work. Some settled in Tibooburra; they was a big mob too, and after me dad died, me mum remarried a Tibooburra fella. I had half-brothers and sisters there, nephews and nieces. That was before the Protection Board moved them down to Brewarrina. Mum and her bloke stayed in the settlement there a couple of weeks and then moved up to Queensland.

'These whitefellas don't trust us with our own lives,' the old man said, his face hardening. 'but no one in our mob does anything about it. We allow them whitefellas to take our kids, break up our families. Where's our pride?' he asked no one in particular. 'Young fellas should be raging about it, but they're all too busy kissing the whitefellas thithi. No one has any respect for the old ways now,' he said sadly.

'The young ones aren't interested in the old ways, Grandad, why would they be? We need jobs, not dances and face paint,' said Ellin, pitching in from across the yard.

Charlie scowled, the muscles in his jaw tense as he clenched his teeth and barked, 'I'm not talking about dances and paint, damn it, I'm talking about pride in our people. Buggers all want to be whitefellas,' said the old man. 'But they can't be. One day they'll understand we need respect. I was respected.'

'Do you miss being a stockman?' I said, trying to calm him down.

'There used to be a day when I was a big fella around these parts,' he said. 'Station managers called for me by name. They used to say, "there's no one works a stock horse like Charlie Cobham".'

'I bet they still talk about you.'

'Nah, nobody remembers, there are too many blokes looking for work now, willing to work for tobacco and grog. Whitefellas get picked first, even when they don't know the front end of a horse from the backside. We're treated like dirt. Fellas from our mob signed up for the war, to fight for the king, now they won't even let them inside the bar for a drink,' Charlie said, his voice raised. 'I used to drink at the bar in the old days, alongside them whitefellas, bought me grog they did, said I was a good bloke. "Good ol' Charlie Cobham," they would say. There wasn't a man who would refuse me a schooner or two back in them days, white or black. Now look at us, can't piss without a whitefella telling us how.'

Along with the anger, there were tears and heartache in his eyes. Minutes passed in silence as we sat watching the sun dip below the horizon and thinking of how it had once been. I shouldered the guilt of my white heritage as though it were my own.

Chapter 9

Sick-Kalhika

Daisy Stuart's health deteriorated slowly over the following two years. With the steady decline came the need for almost constant care, and Ellin spent more and more time at the homestead. I was now fifteen years old, and we had become the best of friends. She had changed the way I looked at the world; cynically in some ways, but positive in others. I was confident in my abilities and self-worth – though Ellin joked I was just cocky and full of myself. To my delight, she moved into my old room in the outhouse. My happiness increased as Daisy's health grew worse, not because I wished her ill, but because it meant spending more time with Ellin.

'You need hospital care,' said Doctor Forsyth. Daisy stubbornly refused. 'Without specialist care, there's nothing I can do, other than to make you as comfortable as possible.'

'Is that what you're doing?' Daisy scoffed. 'I won't have any more doctors pawing all over me like I'm a piece of meat,' she said.

'Old goat meat maybe,' whispered Ellin, making me giggle, so that I had to turn away and hide my face.

Just as she had been in health, Daisy was miserable in pain and suffering. She served up a constant tirade of abuse, delivered between desperate breaths and bouts of coughing. She did not confine her slurs to Ellin and me, or Lachlan, who would stay away from the firing line, using any excuse to be absent from the homestead. Even Doctor Forsyth, the town practitioner, had to warn her that he would never return if she continued to insult him during his visits.

'There are new treatments for cancer,' Forsyth told Daisy one day. 'New drugs and radiation therapy have shown great promise of success in other parts of the world, when used together.'

Daisy wouldn't hear of it. 'How's it possible to cure someone with radiation when the Americans have just killed millions of Japs with the very same thing? You must think I'm stupid, Forsyth.'

'I'll admit it does sound contradictory,' said the doctor. 'But many feel radiation could be the cure-all for this kind of disease, that we could see the end of cancer altogether within one or two years.'

'That's probably why the Brits are testing all those bombs in South Australia then,' she said with a sneer. 'So they can cure everybody once and for all, and good riddance to the lot of us.'

With Daisy confined to her bed, the way was paved for an unpleasant encounter, one that made me realise I was growing up fast. At fifteen years of age I had led a sheltered, uneducated life. I knew little of the world beyond the towns of Broken Hill and Wilcannia; my early years in London were already faded memories. The Darling River had been the boundary of my range since arriving from England, and my home-schooling had virtually ended where it began, with unopened textbooks. Father Donahue had left the parish before my first Christmas. A new priest had made an impromptu visit on his arrival to the area, only to be given short shrift by Daisy, and we never saw him at the homestead again. A school inspector came once, and after that, no one followed my progress. Our rare trips to church lapsed completely and I fell through the cracks, just like the dust on our verandah decking.

My education in all things at the hands of Daisy Stuart had been minimal. Even when it came to feminine subjects, Daisy seemed somewhat negligent in her approach. She broached the topic with all the sensitivity of a rutting bull. I had just turned thirteen at the time, faced with the first horrifying sight of blood in my knickers. I imagined every strange ailment that might have caused the flow. I was convinced I would die young, drained of my lifeblood one terrifying drop at a time. Eventually, I plucked up the courage to tell Daisy. Nothing could have prepared me for her response.

'You're on the rags,' she said crudely. 'Every damn month you'll bleed. It's just another burden we women must bear. It's how we know God's a bloody man, His idea of a joke. The day you don't bleed, you'll know you're damn pregnant.'

She said this without compassion or thought for how this must have sounded to a scared child. She disappeared, while I sat stunned by her explanation, and came back with a length of terry towelling, instructing me to cut the cloth into squares to be folded and tucked into my underwear. These 'rags' I was to wash for reuse the following month.

'But not in with the rest of the laundry,' Daisy said sharply. 'I don't want your filth in with the wash.'

These instructions ended our discussion and with it my sex education. Daisy never told me how I would get pregnant. I assume she thought I would figure it out by watching the animals. She taught me nothing of men, nor warned me of their intentions.

Despite my worldly ignorance, I had developed a good sense of character. I knew who I liked and who I didn't. So when Lachlan hired McEwen, a 'mate from the old days', I knew instantly to be wary of him. He spent more time at the homestead than out in the pastures and followed me about through the day, making rude comments and slapping my backside. He wouldn't have dared set foot in the house if Daisy had not been confined to bed.

One day he cornered me in the kitchen, his hands all over my body. 'Pretty little thing like you needs a man who can take care of her,' said McEwen.

I pushed him away. 'I don't need anyone to take care of me. I've been doing it all my life.'

'You know what I mean,' he said, following me around the kitchen as if he was waiting for scraps from the cooking. He tried to kiss me and I instinctively kneed him in the balls. I shouldn't have laughed when he doubled over in pain.

McEwen became furious, grabbed my neck and squeezed. 'Why you—'

The screen door slammed, and Ellin came in from the yard in time to intervene. McEwen dropped his hand and backed away, seething.

'Time for you to get out of my kitchen,' said Ellin.

'Your kitchen?' said McEwen. 'This isn't your kitchen, and if I'm not mistaken—'

'Get!' said Ellin, holding the door ajar.

McEwen strolled to the door. 'Filthy black whore.'

Ellin laughed. 'You should know, because your mother's one.'

'Was that wise?' I asked, as we watched McEwen slink away to the barn.

'Probably not. But there's not much fellas like him can do to me that hasn't already been done.'

'He wanted to kiss me.'

'Yeah, well you be careful, tidda, you're no nipper no more.'

McEwen didn't last long because Lachlan didn't like bludgers. He gave him the flick after catching him sleeping in the bunkhouse when he should have been working.

I knew Daisy was dying, and though I had sympathy for her desperate battle, especially when she fought for breath, I couldn't help feeling relieved that I would soon be free of her tyranny. Incapacitated almost entirely now, and bedridden, Daisy's hold over me no longer had power. She complained from her bed, cursed my existence, but she could not dampen my growing good spirits. I have to admit, shamefully, looking back, that I felt she had it coming, that she was getting what she deserved for her life of misery and that of mine. I enjoyed her inability to make demands and influence my behaviour.

It may sound harsh now, that while Daisy came to terms with her last days on earth, I had only feelings of joy and an unmistakable belief that my life was about to get better. Was I heartless? Yes. I took advantage of the new order, but I would eventually pay dearly.

When Lachlan left us to the homestead, which was more often than not since Daisy's diagnosis, Ellin would tune the wireless to shows like ABC's *Top Forty,* and in between chores we would dance in the parlour, causing Daisy to complain about the noise. I discovered the new sounds of rock-and-roll and tried to learn the words to every song. When Paul Anka sang 'Diana', I pretended he was singing about me, and Ellin said she had hopes of marrying a boy named Elvis.

During these final months of Daisy's life, I noticed a change in Lachlan's attitude towards me. I found him staring a lot, as though he had only then become aware of my presence. He kept thanking me for my help with Daisy, saying I was a godsend to him.

'I don't know what I'd have done without you,' said Lachlan.

'Ellin does most of the work,' I said, embarrassed.

'You've become a woman before my eyes.'

I blushed. 'I'm not a woman.'

Lachlan continued to act strangely and make odd gestures, like opening the door for me or offering to carry stuff. Since my arrival at Cutaway Creek, he had cared little for my existence. I usually annoyed him. Things had improved since I became able to help with the stock work. I rode well and held my own at muster, but even then Lachlan paid me little notice. He would show his appreciation as he did with all the hands, with little more than a nod of the head and a tip of the hat that said, 'Good job, well done.'

I found it unnerving when I suddenly became the focus of his attention. He went out of his way to be pleasant, smiling whenever he caught my eye. I worried that I had done something to encourage this behaviour. Aware of the changes to my body and the way men looked at me, I knew I was attractive to the opposite sex, but Lachlan was Lachlan, and he'd never once given my appearance a second thought. Until then.

On the day Daisy died, we stood in her bedroom. Lachlan put his arms around me and embraced me, I thought to comfort me, though it was unexpected. Ellin stood at the side of the bed, having just closed Daisy's eyes. She watched Lachlan's actions and by the look of her expression shared my surprise. Not usually a man to show his emotions, I thought Lachlan was about to cry. I wrapped my arms around his shoulders and hugged him. Ellin's surprised expression turned to a frown behind his back, and I sensed a warning in her look. I signalled that I didn't know what else to do.

'I'm sorry,' I said to Lachlan.

'Yeah, well these things happen,' he replied, and that was all he could put into words.

We buried Daisy four days later at the Wilcannia cemetery, on a rare, drizzly day – damp and dismal, a suitable send-off. She would have approved. Lachlan, Ellin, myself and Daisy's sister were in attendance, but no one else came to pay their respects. The local priest conducted the ceremony while we stood in silence at the graveside. We had no church service, according to Daisy's wishes. I watched the coffin be lowered into the dirt, but could summon no grief at her passing.

As the days went by, it became clear there was more to Lachlan's odd behaviour than any feelings of loss. I began to see him in a new light; this was not the Lachlan Stuart I had come to know and often fear. He was kind, thoughtful even. Perhaps Daisy's death had somehow set free the real Lachlan, allowed him to emerge from her shadow. I wanted to believe it to be true.

I responded to the new personality, making the most of Lachlan's change in attitude. He spent time around the house, finding excuses to be there, making long-overdue repairs, and I would encourage him, thanking him profusely, as though he were doing them solely for me. He joked and flirted, and I flirted back. There was no mistaking what he wanted. He wanted me and, unexpectedly, I liked it.

Chapter 10

Shame-Palta

Three months short of my sixteenth birthday, I became Mrs Katherine Stuart, wife to the widower Lachlan Robert Stuart at a registry office in Broken Hill. My date of birth had been conveniently altered on the paperwork to reflect the requirements of state law, making my legal age sixteen. No one asked for my birth certificate, evidence of my age or objected to the marriage out of concern for my wellbeing. The Justice of the Peace, a novice, had been paid by Lachlan to ignore the lack of documentation. He performed the short ceremony in front of three witnesses, Ellin Cobham, Johnson Milne and a city clerk. We had no grand ceremony, no happy congregation to sing in celebration.

Ellin wasn't happy. She had said as much in the weeks leading up to the wedding, but I was determined to ignore her comments, even putting them down to jealousy, though I knew she didn't like Lachlan. On reflection, I realise she was only trying to help, but her repeated warnings only increased my determination to marry him. Perhaps it was childish for me to yearn to be the woman of the house, to succeed Daisy Stuart and take my place in the world as an adult, but isn't that every child's dream, to be one of the grown-ups?

The homestead fell eerily silent on our wedding night. Crickets didn't sing, frogs didn't chirp, the wireless sat on the sideboard, silent, condemning, its twin rotary dials like dark eyes watching my every move. I passed through the parlour, surveying my new domain with enthusiastic satisfaction, opening drawers and checking the contents, seeing the room in a new light. Was I an interloper in Daisy's house? I didn't care. Now it was mine, and I wanted to enjoy the moment. I stood at the window and watched the fading light over the blackness of the land, which somehow emphasised our isolation from the world, and at the same time focused the nearness of Lachlan and I, so that I felt the electricity between us, the anticipation almost palpable.

Lachlan had left the generator turned off when we got home, lighting candles and paraffin lamps instead. An attempt at romance, perhaps. I wandered the room as if for the first time, observing every detail. I assessed the leafy-patterned wallpaper behind the fireplace, green and dismal, a reflection of Daisy's life in that old house. I would have it changed to a bright new pattern. I walked to the hearth where the fire never burned and wondered if it had ever been lit. Perhaps we would light a fire on a cold winter night, and I would curl up with

Lachlan and we would watch the flames, wrapped in a blanket, drinking hot cocoa together. I opened a sideboard drawer and ran my hand over an unused linen tablecloth. Another held tarnished cutlery with fine bone handles. A mirror picked up the light from a candle, sparkling with the flicker of orange flame, Lachlan caught in the reflection, watching me with quiet amusement.

'It's all yours now.' I didn't answer. 'So when ya finished checking for hidden treasure,' he said, mocking me, 'we'll drink to our future.' Lachlan gave me a glass of sweet yellow wine and proposed a toast. I didn't wait for speeches, drinking the whole glass down like water. Lachlan laughed. 'You're supposed to sip it, ya galah.'

I didn't like the taste, though alcohol was not entirely new to me. I had drunk beers several times while sitting over a campfire with stockmen during muster, and the sickly wine tasted no better. An awkward silence filled the space between us, as I twirled my empty glass. Lachlan filled it. This time I didn't scull.

'Bloody nice ceremony,' he said, eventually, even though it wasn't.

'Yes,' I lied. 'Pity—'

'Yeah,' he said before I could finish. 'Best we didn't make too much of a fuss though, eh?'

'Probably.'

A distant dingo howled. 'Bloody dingoes, probably after our sheep,' said Lachlan, though I knew it was small talk.

Until that point, I had given little serious thought to what would happen next. In the past, Ellin had shared stories, raunchy stories about girls and boys, causing fits of laughter between us as we went about our chores. She told of what went on between men and women and made terrible jokes about it. I refused to believe some of her tales, too bizarre to take seriously and far too gross to think couples did such things, even in private. In recent days, however, Ellin's tone had changed, and she no longer seemed to think it was funny. She gave me advice, tried to tell me what to expect, and how I should handle the experience. Her explanations were awkward and grave, but I couldn't help giggling. In the end she'd become annoyed, said that I wasn't taking it seriously and dropped the motherly advice altogether. 'Don't worry,' I said, smugly. 'I'll have *Lachlan* – I emphasised his name to show we were on new personal terms – eating out of my hand before he knows it.' Ellin wasn't amused, and my own sense of humour disappeared quickly when Lachlan now led me by the hand to the bedroom.

Daisy's presence lingered in the room, an almost physical remnant of her being. The bed where she had lain for so much of her final years of life, seemed ominously large and brooding. I heard her coughing and struggling for breath, a ghostly echo off the walls that enclosed us. The dresser, where once Daisy's medications and personal effects had been arrayed, now appeared startlingly empty. The room itself had an ugly presence, stark and lifeless. Sage-green paint covered tongue-and-groove wall and ceiling panels. It had an oppressive effect, enclosing the space like a coffin. The smell of gum turpentine, sweet and piney, could not disguise the underlying odours of sickness and ill health; it seeped from every crevice like death itself.

'Katherine! Katherine, you bludger! Where the hell's Ellin? Get me a bedpan! I need a drink, you worthless little shit! Katherine! Katherine! Where's Lachlan?'

He's here. We're both here, Daisy.

Lachlan took my shoulders in his hands, jolting me from my reverie. He lifted my hair and kissed my neck. I shivered. In all my years of life, I never had, until that moment, felt the affectionate caress of another human being. Archie had sometimes offered a shoulder, a supporting hand, but he had little tenderness to give. Archie believed in staying tough. 'Only the weak show signs of love,' he would say. Lachlan worked his lips gently down to my shoulder. I closed my eyes, acknowledged the pleasure of his gentle touch. At last, someone cared for me. I wanted so desperately to be loved, and I didn't care what Archie would have thought. A candle guttered, like a little cough, and I instinctively looked to the bed for Daisy. Was she watching? I shook the idea quickly from my mind.

Tender was not a word I would have used to describe Lachlan Stuart, though I had known he was capable of love. I had seen him show such affection for Hero, his stock horse, on more than one occasion; a gentle kiss on the animal's nose, the love returned in a nuzzle, a nodding head and the flick of a mane. Calloused hands brushed my skin like sandpaper. He unbuttoned my dress, stumbling because of his thick fingers. I trembled. The garment dropped to the floor and I stood in my underwear at the foot of the bed, embarrassed, humiliated. I felt my face flush. I was no longer sure. My chest tightened. I wanted this to be right but I felt only terror at the unknown – fragile and exposed. Lachlan had seen me naked before, on more than one occasion as I bathed as a child, but I had blossomed since into the full flower of young womanhood, and I could see the excitement evident in his wide eyes as he completed my undress, kissing my body so that I quivered and quaked nervously at his touch. My heart raced, a captive animal, fight or flight? Was this love, this fear inside me, or something else entirely? The spectre of Daisy appeared in my mind again. I forced it out. I would find tenderness where she couldn't, love where she found pain. Lachlan pushed me gently to the bed so that I lay on my back, waiting, trembling. He stood over me, a dark colossus, seeming to fill the room and block out the light. I tried not to be afraid. This was what I had been missing since birth, the cold emptiness inside me now to be filled at last with warmth and affection.

My fleeting euphoria disappeared in the blur of what followed. Lachlan traced my body with the palms of his hands and squeezed.

'Ow! You're hurting me,' I said, suddenly confused.

His hands ran down my hips, over my belly, down my thighs and legs. I gasped, shook uncontrollably, took a deep breath, tried to stay calm, but his hands were rough and forceful.

'That hurts,' I said again, though I was afraid to upset him.

Lachlan ignored my calls for care, a new look in his eyes; instead of tenderness, I saw hunger, wild and urgent, cold and loveless. He stood back and undressed quickly, popping buttons, almost ripping the shirt from his back. I panicked. Had I done something wrong to spark this change? I tried to slow him, but he was on me before I knew it, heavy, breathing hard.

'No, please, please be careful.'

Sweating profusely now, he groaned, sliding against me like an oily fish. I smelt his odour; thick, musky, confused by other smells, none pleasant.

'No, Lachlan, stop it. I don't want to do it anymore.' This felt so wrong.

Then came sudden pain, a knife within me, my terror reflected in his eyes. What was happening? I fought, but it happened too quickly, too soon and I couldn't adjust. He gripped my wrists. I twisted beneath him. Strong hands, tender hands only minutes before, held my wrists rigid. He pushed his face to mine so I could smell his sour breath. I struggled beneath his weight.

'Lachlan,' I croaked, as the room shuddered around me. I couldn't focus.

His mouth covered mine but did not kiss me, just gaped, making me spit and struggle to be free.

'You're hurting me, stop.'

But he didn't stop. The bed shook violently beneath us. I closed my eyes and tasted tears, sobbed silently into the bristling hair of his face, scratching my skin so that it grazed and burned. I suffered the brutal jolts, a pounding rhythm, like the slam of the screen door, sending shock waves through me, punishing me. Then there was the smell, that awful smell. A strange mix of odours, turpentine oil, alcohol, Lachlan's bad breath, his sweat covered body. I wanted to be sick. But there was something else, something worse that soured my senses. The smell of Daisy Stuart. I caught it in the sheets and bedding where she once lay, a lingering reminder, her last word to spite me.

I prayed for my ordeal to end and slipped into a trance, an out-of-body state to distance myself from what was happening. He held me tight against my struggle, and all I could do was endure the humiliation, submit to his power over me, and wait for it to be finished.

'Argh!' Lachlan cried out as if he had been stabbed with my pain.

Seconds later, he slipped from me with a mighty sigh, lay on his back, arms out wide. The only sound now, our heavy breathing. I dared not move for fear it would start again. I closed my eyes tight, fought the impulse to scream or sob, held my arms close to my chest to shield me from the horror, and waited.

Without a word, he rose from the bed, pulled on his trousers, threw on a shirt and left the room. BAM! The screen door slammed. I lay rigid, stunned and silent. I heard the truck start up and pull away with a growl of gravel. I listened, unmoving until it faded into the night. I tried to comprehend, to make sense of what had happened. My lip quivered. I didn't cry. My chest heaved, shoulders jerked, I suppressed the sobs. It had not taken long for Lachlan Stuart to destroy my innocence, my naïve sense that my world was getting better, though it had seemed an eternity at the time. No longer a child, I blamed myself. After all, I had what I wanted. I was now the lady of the house. But I had paid a heavy price.

I didn't sleep, but lay there in pain and shame, feeling dirty, thinking, replaying, fighting tears. I felt Daisy Stuart look on and gloat, thought I heard her laughing. 'Everyone gets what they deserve, eventually,' she said from her grave.

After a while, the candles died, the sun rose, filtering in through the window to the east, throwing a long wedge of light across the room. I suddenly tensed to the sound of Lachlan's truck, a slow approach until it slewed to a halt in the yard. My heart quickened. I heard him go to the barn, its doors creaking, listened to the sound of horses, then nothing for a long while. I didn't move. The screen door opened and slammed. I listened to the sound of footsteps through the homestead. I waited.

'He's gone,' Ellin said, startling me. She stood in the doorway, arms folded across her chest, her face unsympathetic, somehow accusing, as though this were my own fault and I deserved whatever I got. 'Took his swag and left for the Corner.' I didn't move, didn't say a word. 'He said he's hooking up with Jack Sweeny from Yandinnia Station to help move stock down to the Adelaide Hills. Said he'd be back in a fortnight.' Still, I did not speak. Ellin turned and disappeared into the kitchen. I heard her clattering pots and dishes.

Chapter 11

Angry-Kurlika

I should have left there and then, got in the truck and driven to the nearest train station, never looked back. But I didn't. I had experienced the full gamut of emotions, lying on that bed through the night. Pain, self-pity, denial, despair, guilt, regret. Now I felt only anger; anger at myself, at Lachlan, at Ellin. Anger at Archie, the nuns, Father Donahue, my mother, my father, the world. I felt a rage swell within me and told myself never again, never again would I be used and abused, or taken for granted by anyone, ever.

With new resolve, I rose from the bed, pulled the sheets, blankets, dress, underwear, everything into a pile with the pillows and hauled them to the yard. Ellin came out to watch. I returned to the bedroom, strong, determined, I dragged the mattress from the frame, pulled, pushed and manipulated it through the house, stumbling, picking myself up, going again, fighting it all the way to the door. Ellin stood by without saying a word, unhelpful, arms folded as I heaved, humped and manhandled the mattress to the yard and dumped it on the pile. I strode to the barn, filled a can from the diesel drum, returned and doused the bedding. I didn't have a match. Ellin shook her head. I returned to the house, took a box of matches and went back to the yard. Standing in the dirt, naked as the day I was born, I lit Daisy Stuart's pyre, thereby cleansing myself of her spirit, and setting my marker for all to see from that day forth.

Life was never the same after that; I was never the same. Part of me had died, replaced by something new. I was stronger, adamant to show my self-reliance, to show that no man nor woman had claim to me. Lachlan Stuart had brutally taken my innocence, and I would make him pay.

The day he returned home from Yandinnia Station, he came back to a different woman. He must have seen it in my eyes. I threw my arms around his neck, causing him to flinch as though he expected to receive a blow. But I smiled instead and told him slowly, as if I were talking to a child, if he ever hurt me again I would kill him. I knew from the look on his face that he did not doubt me for a minute.

He returned to his bedroom willingly, the room where he had spent the years while married to Daisy. Perhaps it was guilt, or maybe he'd had his moment and was no longer interested in me. I didn't know what he thought, or particularly care. I demanded things of him and got them. My new bed arrived directly from Hordern's Palace Emporium, Sydney's finest store, complete with spring mattress and plush new bedding. I had a new septic pit installed and connected to an indoor flushing toilet. Cutaway Creek was moving into the twentieth century. The Bendix washing machine that Daisy dreamed of arrived the same week as a President Industries electric refrigerator. 'Because you love beautiful things,' said the brochure.

Lachlan didn't give in to my demands without some resistance. After the first few weeks when he had seemed to be confused by my intentions, he tried to put his foot down and reassert his dominance, but it was too late, the horse had bolted. We fought constantly about every little thing, just as he and Daisy had done, but he always backed off and conceded defeat. The more I asserted myself, the more he bowed to my wishes, as though giving in to me was the only way to get himself peace. Life in the Stuart house would be different now, whether he liked it or not, and I told him as much at every opportunity. I had a new sense of my identity, and Lachlan had his hands full as a result. Music, once almost absent, played on the wireless during every waking hour. I demanded and received a gramophone on which I played the latest records by Johnny O'Keefe, Cliff Richard, Connie Francis and the sensational Drifters. He grumbled but complied with my whims and wishes, indulging me for reasons only he could know, but he made it clear that everything would have a price. A husband had rights, he told me. I answered that I had rights too, and if we were to ever return to my bed, it would be on my terms and my terms only. I wasn't yet ready, and only time would tell if I could ever trust him again.

In the midst of all this, my relationship with Ellin suffered. She must have seen the change in me and backed off warily, unable to reconcile the new Katherine with the old. I sensed that she didn't like what she saw, but I didn't care. Her obvious disapproval only served to make me cool towards her in return. I was the lady of the house and she the hired help. I pulled her aside one day and made it clear that I expected a good day's work in exchange for her pay. What a pompous idiot I was. She responded respectfully, though I could not miss the disappointment in her eyes. She said she knew where she stood and if that was how I wanted it, that was how it would be. Afterwards, I regretted the tone of my words, regretted everything about the exchange. I almost went to her to apologise. Almost, but I didn't, and a door closed between us.

I took to going into Broken Hill on my own, buying clothes that I thought swish. I picked out the latest swing dresses with layers of petticoats made of chiffon and silk. Satin scarfs added the rock-n-roll look. I wore hoop skirts in garishly bright colours, and Bermuda shorts, cigarette pants and shoes with high heels. I paraded around the homestead like a film star, and I started smoking stylish tipped cigarettes. It was all a childish game, but Lachlan said little in protest. I could tell from his expression that he liked how I looked.

Despite my attempts to be fashionable and aloof, I soon became bored with my new toys and bored with Lachlan too. Always in the back of my mind was the wedding night, and no matter how many gifts he gave to seduce me, or how considerate his attempts to gain my favour, the fear inside me remained, and I dreaded the day when I would have to succumb to his wishes.

It wasn't long before I craved to go riding. Jack had been acting up, irked by my lack of attention perhaps and he was determined to let me know he wasn't happy about the situation. We made up with a little display of horsey banter, and I promised to be more attentive. I started to ride out each day, alone, and soon felt the pleasure of my old life returning. Our daily sorties could last until dark, and I wandered for hours, just to feel the sun on my skin. My constant absence from the homestead irritated Lachlan.

'Where the hell do you go each day?' he raged.

'Riding,' my curt reply.

'I know bloody riding. Where riding, why?'

'Because I like riding. Anyway, it's none of your business where I go.'

I could see these confrontations were building rage in Lachlan, a frustration bottled up and ready to explode, yet I didn't care; I was determined to be strong.

One late morning, I saddled Jack and rode out to the bore line, reaching the first bore at a canter, where Jack pulled up lame. I dismounted and checked his foreleg, bending over the hoof to find a large splinter of wood in the frog of his foot. I removed the shard, causing Jack to whinny and rear up in protest.

'Now then, now then, who's a big baby?'

As I calmed him down, I sensed someone watching from a stand of desert oaks. Shading my eyes from the sun's glare, I picked out a young man, lean and dark, waving to get my attention. His horse, a chestnut gelding, stood passively in the shade of the tree. A small fire burned in a circle of rocks, and a billycan sat over the flames. Long curls of smoke climbed into the still air, dissipating in the leaves and branches of the oak. I remounted and sauntered over to where the man stood, slouched in a lazy, cocky pose against the trunk of the tree. A wide-brim stockman's hat – leather with a fancy pattern embossed on the crown and a band of snakeskin for decoration – threw a shadow on his face. His eyes and smile were bright and alive within the shadow, and his mouth twisted into a grin, like a letter 'S' laying on its side. When I got close up, his almond-shaped eyes were the green of deep water. I wanted him from the moment I saw him, he was beyond beautiful.

'G'day,' he said, a slow drawl that seemed as casual as it was friendly. He removed his hat, causing long black curls to fall over his forehead. He brushed them aside and waved away a fly before replacing the hat on his head.

'G'day,' I responded. 'Where are you headed?'

'Over yonder,' he said, waving casually in no particular direction. 'How about you?'

'I live here.'

'That right? Lockie's kid?'

'Lockie's wife,' I said, dismounting.

The lazy S curled across his face. Flashing the white of his teeth, he chuckled. 'You're looking good since the last time I saw you then, Mrs Stuart. Looking younger.'

'Daisy's dead,' I said, realising that he thought I was lying. 'Lachlan and I were married. I'm Katherine.'

He squinted and took a moment to consider this, gauging the words to see if I was trying to be funny. 'Pleased to meet you, Kate. I'm Lou,' he said eventually, removing his hat once again in a gesture of introduction. I found it unnerving that he wouldn't stop smiling, like he found it all a big joke.

He asked me to join him, and we sat silently for a while as the billy boiled and Lou made us black tea. 'This is the real stuff,' he said at length, sprinkling loose leaves into the billy to steep. 'Charlie the chink brings it all the way from China. He gave me a bag when we was working together in Silverton.'

'Charlie the chink?'

'Charlie the Chinaman. That's not his real name, but everyone knows him as Charlie.'

'Like Charlie Chan,' I said. 'On the wireless.'

'Don't have a wireless,' he said. 'Ever wonder why it's called a wireless?'

'No.'

'Do you have one?'

'Yes.'

'Does it have a wire where you plug it in the wall?'

'Yes.'

'Then it's not wireless. Anyway, I never had one, and I never been to China neither. Charlie says it's the centre of civilisation.'

We watched as Jack sidled up to Lou's stock horse, nuzzling and snorting a friendly welcome. 'That's Smokey,' said Lou, pointing to his horse. 'He gets along with just about anyone.'

'Looks like they're going to be mates,' I said. The swag cinched up behind Smokey's saddle and the ageing leather saddlebags slung over his rump told me Lou was a drover. 'Where's over yonder?' I asked.

'I just come up from Clifton Hills Station to pick up a mob of bullocks at Durham Downs. Then I'll bring them down to White Cliffs. I've got a few weeks to kill in between times. Maybe Lockie's got some work for me?'

'Maybe, though he just hired a couple of young blokes with trail bikes.'

Lou nodded sadly. 'Yep, most of the young blokes are working on bikes these days.'

'You're not exactly an old bloke yourself.'

'True, but I live like the old fellas. Bikes are okay for mustering, but you still need a horse and a dog for drovin'.'

I looked around for the dog and saw a kelpie lying silently beside a rock in the shade. 'What's her name?'

'Dog,' said Lou.

'Is she friendly?'

'*He* is, but don't move a muscle,' said Lou. 'There's a deadly snake heading your way, and *he* don't look too friendly.'

I had already seen the red-bellied black snake sliding our way out of the corner of my eye. Toby had taught me a lot about snakes. 'It's just a red belly,' I said, as casually as I could. 'They're more scared of us than us of them.' On cue, the snake sensed our presence and turned away, disappearing quickly amongst the rocks.

Lou grinned, caught out in a yarn. 'Darn! I was about to save your life,' he said. 'Impress the hell out of you, I would.'

'When you said snake, I thought you meant the taipan by your arm.'

Lou jumped to his feet, stumbled backwards and almost fell in the fire. I laughed until I almost cried. 'Got me, ya bugger,' he said and joined in the laughter.

We settled down and chatted about snakes and spiders, drinking Chinese tea, which was bitter and strong. I tipped mine out when I thought Lou wasn't looking, but he caught me in the act.

'Crikey,' he said. 'Charlie'd turn in his grave if he saw you wasting his tea. I take it you didn't like it?'

I poked out my tongue and grimaced. 'Charlie can take it back to China.'

We sat in silence for a while, watching the flames crackle. 'You look a bit young to be Lockie's missus if you don't mind me saying,' Lou said at length.

'It's a long story,' I said, keen to avoid the subject. 'I'm riding out to check the bores if you want to come along.'

Lou doused the fire and packed his billy. Smokey and Jack plodded side by side like old friends while Dog followed behind. We chatted easily along the way, although Lou did most of the talking.

On our return to the homestead, Lachlan promptly hired Lou to strain a new line of fence wire around the paddock and help with other jobs around the yard.

'If he works out, I've got a permanent place for him.'

'Isn't he a bit young?' I asked, trying to conceal my excitement.

'Give the lad a chance,' said Lachlan. 'Young blood might be what we need around here. Maybe he'll inject a bit of life into this place.'

If only Lachlan knew how right he would be.

Chapter 12

Run-Kalya

Inspired perhaps by my modernising changes to the homestead, Lachlan had his own priorities in mind for improvements to the station. He decided to build a new, permanent woolshed.

'It'll be complete with sorting pens, wool racks, shearing platform, and I've ordered three Wolsey shearing machines from Mellor in Adelaide. They've imported them from England.' Lachlan showed me the plans, unable to hide his excitement.

Timber came by the truckload from Oberon, dressed iron bark for the framing and cladding, and shiny new corrugated sheets of tin arrived by train from Sydney to clad the roof.

'If we start before the end of the month, we can have it built in time for muster. I reckon it'll take three weeks if we get the right crew.'

News spread fast, and every available itinerant worker came to find a job. Soon Cutaway Creek took on a carnival atmosphere, as twenty-odd hired hands set to work. I got caught up in the excitement, helping Lachlan with the organisation. Putting our difficulties aside, we cooperated like proper partners, husband and wife. Everyone wore a smile, including Lachlan and me.

Lou proved to be a hard worker. I couldn't help searching him out whenever I came on site. 'G'day, Kate,' he would call across the yard, and I would ignore him. Our eyes kept meeting, though not accidentally, so that I blushed every time I saw him smile. For smoko and lunch the crew sat at oversized trestle tables, catching up on the news from other stations. Popular amongst the other workers, Lou always had something to say and made jokes out of every discussion. I made it my business to sit in on these breaks; I wanted to watch his every move.

'Hey, Lou,' said one of the hired hands. 'I heard you met a breeder who tried to sell you a talking horse. That right?'

Everyone fell silent.

'It's true. You wouldn't believe it, when I got there, I was surprised to find that the horse really could talk.'

Everyone laughed. 'What did it say?' asked the hand who began the conversation.

'Well,' said Lou. 'I asked the horse where he learned to talk. He said he learned when he worked in a circus and it was a monkey who showed him how. He said he got better at talking when he spent three months crossing the outback with a camel driver who taught him Arabic. He finally perfected his speech while he served in the cavalry during the war in Europe, picking up German and French along the way.'

'That's amazing,' said the hand, laughing. 'Why did the breeder want to sell such an incredible horse?'

Lou paused while everyone waited for his answer. 'He said he was selling it because the horse was a liar, the horse had never worked in a circus.'

The camp erupted in laughter. I had never heard anyone tell such a joke before and I was spellbound. Lou revelled in being the centre of attention and looked to see if I was also laughing. I was. Lucky for me that Lachlan had so much on his plate he didn't notice the energy between us, but it was clear to anyone interested that Lou and I had more than construction on our minds.

With enough stockmen already on hand, the muster started immediately after the build. I rode out each day with the men, always keeping Lou in view. He was an amazing horseman, even by Toby's standards. With every day that passed, my obsession grew, until I ached for his attention.

Muster came and went, the shearing done, the new shed worked out brilliantly. Lachlan stayed on a high, and our relationship mellowed. Happy to see me acting normally, Lachlan took it as a sign that things had settled down between us. We argued less, and I encouraged Lachlan's good mood, hoping, I suppose, that he would be less likely to notice my infatuation. Then one day I looked for Lou, only to find he had gone without saying goodbye.

'He's overdue for a job up north,' said Lachlan when I casually asked Lou's whereabouts.

'He didn't say he was going.'

'Why would he tell *you*?' said Lachlan. I didn't answer.

Furious, I wondered what it was about some men that made them come and go so easily without telling anyone. Lou's sudden departure shook me badly. He'd left that morning, telling Lachlan he would return when he got the chance. I rode out on Jack, hoping perhaps that I'd catch up with Lou on the trail.

I kicked the horse into a gallop, raising a long plume of dust in my wake, and made my way past the bores and out to the far pastures and fence line. I turned west at the Darling in full gallop and maintained my adrenalin-fuelled charge. A mob of kangaroos scattered, momentarily joining my race into thc wind before peeling off to watch me go by. Jack thundered over the ground, skilfully avoiding mulga thickets and dodging boulders. We leapt dry creek beds, churning sand under his powerful hooves.

Eventually, we slowed to a walk and came to a standstill where the stream took a sharp turn to skirt a high outcrop of orange rock. Marked on the station's map as 'The Bluff', it was known to all as an important waterhole, where, on the far side, two separate natural springs emerged to form deep rock pools beneath the cliff face. Toby had said that his ancestors had used the site, not only to find water, but to make tools by grinding stones against the rock. He showed me the grooves worn by years of grinding, and said he knew the place as Yalta Maku, Koori for grinding stone. The highest point on the station, from the bluff you could see the world turn from above, and imagine the world beyond the far horizon, feel it live beneath your feet. Toby said that all the corners of the world came together to meet at this place. No wonder the blackfellas thought it was special.

A small mob of rock wallabies disappeared into cover on our arrival. I dismounted, leaving Jack to drink at the high spring. I had ridden him hard, and he had sweated up badly. I felt guilty. Rocks crunched and rolled underfoot, tumbling and echoing down to the gully where the creek ran deepest. I climbed the steep slope, past the deep-red slash in the rock that looked like a bloodied scar, and scrambled to the summit.

Yalta Maku had three large rock carvings on the bare plateau. I traced one of them, the outline of a fish, with the tip of my finger and imagined the carver. Who was he, long ago when the land belonged indisputably to the blackfellas, and white men had not yet come to their shores? Was he celebrating his catch when he chiselled the image? Perhaps it was Toby or Ellin's ancestors who had toiled away at the rocks.

A twinge of guilt passed through me when I thought of Ellin. She deserved more from me. I thought of her broken family, dispersed across the country, her children gone, her clan scattered to the four winds. I thought of my family, just as broken. Perhaps we had more in common than I had imagined. I resolved to ask for her forgiveness, in the hopes that she could still be my friend.

Looking towards the distant haze, I saw no sign of life. I wondered where Lou would be by now. Had he tried to catch me before he rode out? I doubted it and cursed myself for wanting him and feeling dejected that he left without me. He can't have felt the same way, or he wouldn't have gone.

A wedgetail eagle circled overhead, joined by another in broad sweeps of the sky. A mated pair, I guessed. Toby said they mate for life. Perhaps that was now my fate, mated for life to a man I despised. Which one, I wondered, was the male? And did he go off for weeks on end in search of food? Such was the life of a stockman. Even station owners like Lachlan spent many lonely nights away from home, camped out under the stars. No doubt sometimes they preferred it that way. I know I certainly did when it came to Lachlan's absence.

The sun was very strong and the rock shimmered in the heat. Sweat glistened on my skin. I scanned the land to the east until it dissolved in a watery kuurlurku. Kuurlurku, the Paakantyi word for mirage, ever present during the hot summer months and looking, as they always did, like vast lakes of water. The wedgetails turned and headed east. A mob of red kangaroos kicked up dust and disappeared in the same direction, thirty or more, bounding at speed.

I looked down to where Jack stood tied beneath the shade of a tall acacia. He pricked his ears and shifted nervously from one foot to the other. Something had spooked him, a snake perhaps. I looked to the west, trying to make out the strange cloud formation climbing in the sky. A bank of storm clouds had formed in a band across the land. *Rain?* We hadn't had rain in months and were heading into one of the worst droughts in the state's history. The ABC had said nothing of rain. The ground had become so dry and weathered that it had turned almost entirely to bulldust, so fine it became powder. I watched in wonder as the formation quickly changed, so that the clouds appeared as a thick bank of dark brown fog. I watched two more roos racing east. I looked back to the skyline. *Fire?* Nothing to burn. Then I remembered what Toby had said one day when the winds whipped up dust in an unexpected whirlwind, and we'd had to take cover in the barn.

'This land is dangerous for those who don't pay it enough respect,' said Toby. 'Kariputu – great dust storms – strike without warning, swallowing everything in their path. They can be deadly if you're caught in one.'

Toby's words came back startlingly as I took in the spectacle. Already the murky storm had risen in height and closed in on the bluff. Spurred at last into action, I ran, tumbled and stumbled from rock to rock in my dash for Jack, who by now was highly agitated, pulling at the reins and ready to run. Quickly I untied him, but panicked, knotting the lead on the tree branch. I told myself to stay calm, undid the tangle and mounted quickly, sending Jack into a canter through the rocky terrain to the trail below. Sure-footed, Jack picked his way safely through the gorge until we reached the creek. But now the wind was on us, dust flying with stinging force. I stopped, turned and looked to the west. The dust plume, miles wide, had risen like a giant ocean wave above me. Rolling from the crest, dust tumbled forward in an avalanche of coffee-coloured dirt, threatening to engulf all before it.

Toby's voice came back to me. 'Cover your mouth, eyes and ears.'

What with? I took off my shirt, soaked it with water from my canteen, and tied it around my head, leaving only a slit for my eyes. Anxious to move on, Jack flared his nostrils, his eyes grew wide and wild, frightened by the imminent threat, he reared and bucked. I reset myself in the saddle and kicked him into a full gallop, but the storm was already on our backs.

Visibility deteriorated within seconds. I prayed that Jack would know instinctively which direction to run, and that his eyes could withstand the onslaught. I held on tight, knuckles white on the reins, while he dodged the scrub, changing direction with each encountered obstacle. I gave him his rein, and he responded, churning the dirt with powerful strides. I closed my eyes against the grit, allowed Jack to take control. The sharp sting of wind-driven sand tore at my bare skin. Could we find shelter?

More of Toby's instructions came to mind. 'Find high ground and shelter on the leeward side, avoid the creek beds and gullies where you can be buried alive.'

I had left the highest point on the station thinking we could outrun the storm. *Idiot!* Too late, we pressed on. Our only chance was for Jack to outrun the storm to the homestead.

Visibility nil, the dark centre of the cloud had overtaken us in an eerie, swirling, disorientating shroud, leaving us floundering in circles. The ghostly shapes of trees loomed large. Jack reared up, galloped into a stand of oaks, reared again in fright and threw me from the saddle. Jack, panicking, reared again, striking me on the head with his foreleg. Then there was only blackness.

Chapter 13

Bone-PiRnha

How long had I lain unconscious? I couldn't be sure. I awoke to a cloudless sky, uncurling slowly from a thick layer of dirt. I removed the wet shirt from my head, unwrapping it like a turban, wincing at the pain in my skull as I got to my feet, a headache so intense that I thought I would faint.

West, east, north, south, the land looked empty and still. On the horizon, the earth shimmered. No sign of Jack, no hint of the storm, no landmarks to give me bearings. I saw the nightmarish visions of Jack rearing above me in terror, the storm enveloping us. I shook the memory from my mind.

By my reckoning, it was between three and four o'clock. I had probably been out for two hours or more. I took stock and plotted a rough course north-east and prayed it would take me towards home. My hat was gone and I had no shade or water. Painfully, I set out walking.

It didn't take long for the conditions to take a toll on my already battered body. One can travel miles in the outback without seeing scrub, but fate conspired to place a thick band of acacia bushes to bar my way. Stripped of leaves by the dust storm, they offered no shade but scratched and scraped my already bleeding body as I picked my way through the tightly knit branches. Beyond the bushes, the land stretched out before me, an endless barren landscape of nothingness beneath a cloudless sky. I struggled on for the best part of an hour, hoping for a sign of life, and came to a dry creek bed, five feet deep. Toby had said it was possible to find water below the surface of a creek, even when dry. I climbed down, dropped to my knees and scrapped the dirt with my hands to form a bowl, two feet deep. Nothing! I was exhausted at the effort, the heat making me sick to my stomach, dizzy and dazed. Perhaps this was God's way of punishing me for thinking of Lou, for wishing I were free of Lachlan, for being happy that Daisy had died, for turning my back on Ellin. Without water, I would surely die. I slumped to the ground.

Get up, you weakling! I can't. *You must.*

I rose to my feet and willed myself forward, clambering out of the creek bed, desperately looking for strength to haul myself back to ground level. I found a tree root, pulled, but it came away in my hand and I realised it wasn't a root, but a bone. The crumbling bank had more bones, emerging from the earth like sprouting flowers.

I tried to make sense of the jumble of half-buried objects, but when the realisation struck, the shock threw me onto my back. I saw a whole ribcage, white against the vivid soil, bleached by exposure to the sun. The bones of a hand gripped the ground, fingers wrapped bizarrely around a rock, as though it were clinging on to prevent the arm from slipping down the bank to the creek below. I recognised the top of a human skull and then a second, much smaller. Bones lay scattered for several feet in either direction. Suddenly aware of the leg bone in my hand, I threw it quickly to the ground. A skull toppled loose and rolled to my feet, a hole the size of a penny in the crown. What hell was this?

Confused by the macabre scene, I stumbled along the creek bed for several minutes before attempting to climb again. I thought of the bones and laughed hysterically. Would that be my fate, dingo dinner? I laughed again, but didn't know why. What was so funny? Dingo dinner? Laughter turned to tears. I didn't want to die.

Making little progress, I pressed on. I wanted to lie down. I wanted to sleep, but a voice inside my head said I couldn't. Archie said I couldn't. I staggered forward, dropped to the ground, picked myself up and fell again. I thought of Archie fighting a big boy who had called him names.

'I can't remember the big boy's name.' I spoke the words aloud.

'Does it matter?' Archie's voice.

'Where have you been, Archie? You said you would come for me.'

'Karl! The big boy's name was Karl. Keep going, Katherine.'

Archie never gave up, no matter how big the challenge. I saw a lake in the distance. Water.

'It's a mirage,' said Archie.

'It's a kuurlurku,' I said, correcting him. My bloodied skin had dried, sticking to my shirt in a crusty coat that drew blowflies by the dozen. 'Why didn't the storm drive the flies away, Archie?'

'How many legs do flies have?'

I couldn't remember. 'Six? Is it six?' I stumbled on. 'Come on, Archie, give me a clue.'

I reached a clump of saltbush and crawled into its shade. My lips and tongue were swollen and cracked, I dreamed of water.

I thought I was still dreaming when I awoke to a full moon, a billion stars and a chilly night breeze. Such beauty defied description, such vastness beyond scale. I shivered. The air had turned inside out, hot to cold. I shook like jelly. If I walked now, I could make headway before sunrise and the return of searing heat. I wouldn't last another day in the sun. I thought of Lou and wondered if he had made it through the storm, then cursed myself for thinking about him.

'Dear God, please help me find my way.'

Silver and blue, the earth stretched before me, a monotone moonscape of eerie shapes and shadows. I had little sense of direction, but found the southern cross and traced a path to the two stars that would mark the way south. Toby had taught me how to read the sky, but I was confused. I remembered talk of emus and seven sisters. Which ones were they, and would they lead me east or west? I picked out the south star and guessed the rest. Though a fog remained to cloud my brain, the delirium I had experienced during the hot afternoon had cleared with sleep, and with renewed energy, refreshed by the cold, I set out again, determined to survive. Several bores lay between the bluff and Cutaway Creek. If I could reach one, I could still get through this ordeal.

I walked steadily, willing myself to stay positive, humming the tune to 'Mack the Knife' – a new song I had heard on the wireless. It had stuck in my head for days. I tried to remember the words, the distraction helping as I picked up the pace. I could see a long way ahead in the moonlight, but time was not on my side. 'One two three, one two three.' I counted my steps to a rhythm and watched my shadow grow longer as the moon dropped behind me. It would soon disappear below the horizon. In the waning light, the landscape had a ghostly glow, surreal and dreamlike. I wondered if Aboriginal Dreamtime stories had originated on such nights. Did spirits once dance beneath these very stars?

Dark shadows cast by low scrub, dotted the landscape ahead. But something didn't look right about these mounds of vegetation. As I came closer, I saw that it wasn't scrub at all, but sheep lying dead, victims of the dust storm. Moving slowly through the mob, I saw twenty or thirty, all dead. Like budgerigars I had seen earlier, the flock had suffocated. I slumped to the ground in despair as the moon made its final dip from the sky.

'I can't go on.'

'You must. You must go on,' said Archie.

'Why?'

'Because.'

'That's not a reason, Archie. And anyway, you gave up. You gave up on *me*.' I heard a faint bleat of distress. 'Did you hear that Archie?' I got to my feet, the effort almost beyond me. I found the animal amongst the carcasses, barely alive.

'Nothing you can do to help.'

'We have to help, Archie, we have to.'

'Leave it.'

And so I left it, left it to die.

I soon stumbled upon more sheep, checked them one by one, but they were all dead. My legs began to buckle, the weight of anguish too much to bear, my spirit broken. I heard a snort from deep in the shadows, stopped and listened. I screwed my eyes in an effort to see through the darkness, making out a large mound, twenty feet ahead. Tentatively, I moved closer. Ten more feet. It was an animal, it was too dark to make out the detail, but already I knew. I came up close, a whimper escaped my dry throat. Jack lay wide-eyed and dying. He tried to lift his head as I approached but was too weak to do more. I knelt at his side, cradled his head in my arms and said that I loved him. I talked to him gently, stroking his neck and whispering in his ear.

'Who's my beautiful boy?' I thought of all the days I had left him in the stable while I played my selfish games. 'I'm so sorry, my lovely, sorry I left you. When we get home, I'll make it up to you, I'll give you a nice soak and feed you those oats you so love.' I bent and kissed him. 'I promise I'll never neglect you again.' I started to sing to him, softly, my voice barely a murmur, half breaking under the strain of grief. 'All things bright and beautiful, all creatures great and small...' I brushed the sand from his coat and wept. 'All things... All things wise and wonderful... the Lord God... made them all.' Dear Jack gave one last snort, then gave up living.

Morning came with a soft pink sky. I sipped from the canteen that had been strapped to Jack's saddle, keeping what I could for later, but knowing it wasn't enough to save me from the coming day. I didn't want to leave Jack, but I had no choice. I said my last goodbyes and walked on again.

I had three hours at most before the sun got too hot and then, inevitably, I would succumb to heatstroke and die. I set out fast but quickly slowed to a crawl. Already I felt hot and tired. I thought of Jack and how I had let him down. It was all my fault; everything was my fault. I stopped and looked to the sky.

'God, if you can hear me, I'll change. I promise I'll change.'

A solitary desert oak. Had I been here before? Was I going around in circles? I squinted at the sun, looked to the horizon. A shape, I couldn't make it out at first. I felt a rush of excitement, burst out laughing, half sobbing. A mirage? No, the sails of a wind pump. Could it be? I headed for the landmark and soon I saw the bore tank. I laughed.

It took me another twenty minutes to struggle to the bore where I ducked my head beneath the water and drank my fill. Station bores were all marked with numbers. This bore was the nearest to the homestead and only a few miles to safety. I filled my canteen and checked my position, climbing the windmill and scanning the landscape. My heart leapt. Riders on trailbikes cut a track in the distance, wending their way across the land, one after the other. I waved my arms like a mad woman. I tried to call but the sound was weak, my throat too raw. I waved again desperately. I was terrified that they would miss me. The first rider swerved towards me, followed by the second.

I looked once more to Heaven. 'Thank You.'

Chapter 14

Hurt-Nkalka

In the days that followed, I brooded and slept in equal measure. Lachlan avoided me almost entirely. Perhaps he sensed my fragile state of mind and didn't know how to deal with it, or maybe he was sorry to see me home. Either way, I was glad he stayed away. Lachlan and the stock hands had begun a search when I failed to return home, joined later by others from Wilcannia, they searched through the night. I hadn't told anyone where I was going – a mistake I would not repeat in a hurry – so they didn't know where to look. Lachlan was angry, cursing my stupidity and the trouble my disappearance had caused. When he talked of stock losses, it was almost as though he were blaming me for the tragedy.

'What were you thinking? Never, ever, go off again without telling someone. Do you know how many sheep we lost? I had enough to worry about without having you getting all the bloody attention.'

I had no energy to defend myself, and maybe he was right. Perhaps I *was* at fault for everything. Despite my survival, I felt in such a desperately depressed state of mind, largely because of Jack. Looking back, I think the death of Jack was my first real loss. Even my separation from Archie and his passing did not have the same devastating effect as Jack's cruel end. To this day, I hear the last breath expelled from his body. I console myself that I was with him in his final moments and that he was not alone.

Kind and caring, Ellin bathed my skin gently each day and applied a salve of melaleuca leaves, crushed to a paste, to soothe and prevent infection. Her tenderness seemed underserved. She cared for me like a mother. It was a kindness I needed so badly.

'I've done a lot of thinking,' I said one day, as Ellin combed my hair. 'And I want to say I'm sorry. I've been unkind since...'

Ellin paused in her task, waiting for me to continue. 'Since the wedding,' she eventually finished for me.

'Yes, since the wedding.'

'That was a long time ago, and I got the message. Anyway, you're the lady of the house now,' she said, returning to brush out the knots. 'You can treat me how you want.' She could not disguise the hurt still evident in her voice.

'No I can't, and it wasn't that I was trying to be like Daisy... Well, maybe I was. I...' My wedding night flashed through my mind, causing a flush of anger, the event still raw. 'I thought you were mad at me, disappointed in me for marrying Lachlan, so I tried to show I didn't care what you thought. Then after the wedding night... I didn't want to hear you gloating, saying I told you so.'

Ellin took time to answer. When she did, her voice was soft and sympathetic. She came around to face me. 'Disappointed in you? Oh, tidda, I was angry when you went ahead and married him, but only because I knew what you was in for. Disappointed *for* you maybe, that you couldn't see what you was doing. I wept all night thinking about you, almost came here to drag you away from him.'

'I never imagined it would be like that. It was nothing like your funny stories. I didn't expect... You have no idea what I went through.'

'Do you think you're the first person to be raped?'

'Raped? *I wasn't raped.*'

'Call it what you like, little sister, but you're still a child. And just because you don't resist doesn't mean... Anyway, I know Lachlan and I know what he's done. Men like him never change their ways. When he—'

'When he what? What do you mean, *you know what he's done*?'

I had sensed something more in Ellin's comments. She hesitated, reluctant to say more.

'Ellin?'

'Do you really think a woman like Daisy Stuart would put up with that nonsense? A man like Lock has certain needs and if he can't have them satisfied by his wife... You know what I'm saying?'

Stunned, it took me a moment to take it in. 'Lachlan and you?' Ellin looked guilty now. 'When?'

'I've said too much.'

'*When?*' I demanded.

Ellin avoided my eyes; instead, she looked out the window. 'It started the week before he married Daisy,' she whispered. 'I was fourteen – Lock likes them young.' A feeble smile played across her face, then quickly transformed to a look of shame. 'He came to the humpy while Mum and Gramps was in town. Grandma wasn't well and was sleeping in her hut. I was on my own preparing food for dinner and he came on real nice and friendly like he was just going to come inside to see what our home was like. He kissed me, said I was pretty.' Ellin paused. 'I'm not sure I should be telling you this, tidda. I don't see what it's going to do to—'

'It's too late for that now. I want to know everything.'

'He undressed me,' she said, reluctantly. 'All gentle and caring like, telling me he wanted to show me what it was like to be loved by a whitefella. I was trembling, said I was scared and he told me not to be silly.' Tears tumbled down her cheeks as she recalled the humiliation. 'Terrified of what he might do if I kicked up a fuss, I let him kiss me. I prayed that Grandma wouldn't hear and that Grandad wouldn't come home and start trying to fight him. I thought if I just let him do what he wanted I would be fine and it would be over and he would go away. Then he got rough,' she sobbed. 'Throwing me about and being all wild-eyed and cruel, like he almost enjoyed hurting me. I didn't scream because I didn't want anyone to know. I was ashamed. I knew it was wrong, but he was a whitefella. It didn't last long, but the pain did,' she said, wiping her eyes. 'I told my mum I fell out of a tree. Lock came back whenever the opportunity was right, or he'd find me out bush somewhere and want more of the same. He was never that cruel again. Like he'd shown who was boss and was satisfied that I knew my place. I got used to it, decided that he wasn't going to kill me, that if I shut up and endured whatever it was he wanted, he would quickly go away and I could pretend it never happened.'

'You never told anyone?'

Ellin laughed at the idea, as if to even contemplate telling was foolish. 'Never,' she said after a long pause. 'Lock stopped coming around after a while. A few years passed. I married a stockman from Echuca. But Larry, my man, didn't hang around much. He went where he could find work and didn't need me trailing along after him. Lock started coming back when Larry was gone, and I got pregnant. A little boy. I didn't know whose child it was. Larry stayed for a while and worked here on the station. I became pregnant again. That's when Larry took off for good. He didn't care much for being a daddy the first time, let alone when the second came along. I looked after them on my own until the protection mob came with the Silverton Police and took both my kids away. We heard they was taken to a mission in Cootamundra, but no one would tell us anything official. Lock stopped coming after that. Maybe he found someone else, someone younger.'

I struggled to find the right words. 'I don't know what to say. You should have gone to someone for help.'

Ellin gave out a short ironic laugh. 'You really don't get it, do you? Who would I go to for help, tidda, who? Whitefellas have been taking what they want since they arrived in our country.'

We sat in silence while I considered Ellin's story. 'How can you work here?' I said eventually. 'After all that, how can you bear to be near him?'

'What doesn't kill you makes you stronger. I want him to see me and know that he hasn't broken me, that I still hold my head high.'

I had no answer.

'I'm sorry for what happened to you, tidda, but it's just the way it is with people like Lachlan. The only surprise is that you ain't black.'

Chapter 15

Who?-Wintyika

After three weeks, my mental state had returned to near normal, and my body had healed enough to function without pain. I felt ready to start again, but I wasn't sure how. During the darkest moments of my days in peril, lost and alone, I had prayed, calling on God to save my life and He had answered my call. But if I had found religion, my faith lay shrouded in doubt. It had always been that way. Even as a small child I had questioned the existence of God. Archie's influence no doubt. He said that church had more devils than Hell. He defied the nuns who ran our orphanage, asking unwanted questions and disputing their teachings, infuriating them with outrageous statements during religious classes.

'If God is real, then why did He kill our mother?'

I thought it was a good question and deserved a good answer, but all Sister Josephine could say was that it was God's will.

'Well if it was God's will, I hate Him,' said Archie. 'It was Hitler's will too when my mother died, what makes God's will any different? Hitler and God, in it together, *murdering allies,*' he screamed.

He received a severe thrashing for his outburst, but it didn't stop him challenging the nuns and priests at every opportunity. In secret, we talked about God and the Devil. Archie said if there was a real devil, then he came in the form of a Mother Superior. I believed him.

Yet it had been to God I turned for help when all seemed lost, and I felt I must pay for my survival by keeping the promises I had made. Alone in the wilderness, I had confessed my sins to God. Desperate for salvation, I had shown remorse for losing my mother, for driving my father away. I had said I was sorry for wishing Daisy dead and had asked for forgiveness for my transgressions. I had accepted that I was responsible for Lachlan's abuse, that I had brought it on myself with my immoral conduct and my arrogance. I deserved to be abandoned for wanting Lou and neglecting my marriage, but had asked to be spared. I understood that I had needed to be punished. I had to atone for my sins, just as the good book said; just as they taught us in class back in England. If God chose to forgive me, to give me another chance, I had promised Him I would make up for my deeds. I would show more kindness to others, work hard. I would pray each day. And despite Ellin's revelations, I would change my attitude towards Lachlan and become a dutiful, obedient wife; this would be my penance.

Things got better for a while. Ellin and I were friends once again, though never quite like before. Lachlan responded to the change in me, he seemed satisfied that life was somewhat normal and routines ruled our days. We had to spend more than we wanted on rebuilding the stock, having lost a third of our sheep to the storm. A short period of rain lifted our spirits but did little to fill the dams and billabongs. I didn't venture from the homestead except to drive into town for supplies. Ellin often joined me if I made the trek to Broken Hill. We would browse the clothes stores, but my shopping days were over and we never stopped to buy. Always in the back of my mind were the promises I had made to a god I did not believe in, despite my best efforts. My rampant spending and devil-may-care attitude had come to an end. But I was restless.

Lachlan, encouraged by my new more subservient ways, attempted to stamp his authority on all things marital. But I made excuses and asked that we take things slowly until I had fully recovered from my ordeal. We argued less, and I usually gave him the last word, though it sometimes tore me apart to do so. I tried to be wifely, making sure he had good food and fresh clothes. However, I could not return to the bedroom.

'You have to give me time,' I told Lachlan.

'How much bloody time do you need? It's not like you were badly injured, or suffered some terrible deformity.'

That night I had another nightmare, they'd had a recurring theme since the dust storm. I stood in church beneath a brilliant white light, surrounded by towering, hooded figures, dressed in black flowing robes. They pointed at me with wizened fingers and talon-like claws, chanting in foreign tongues to a rhythm played out on an enormous pipe organ. The organist had too many hands. His fingers raced across the keys like frantic spiders, picking out the notes with unbelievable speed.

'Promises are easily broken.' A booming voice.

'What promises?' I looked into the light but my eyes burned in the glare and I had to turn away to shield my sight.

'Time to pay the piper.' Boom! A thunderous blast from the organ pipes.

'I don't understand,' I said, dropping to my knees, cowering in fear.

'I think you understand very well,' said the booming voice.

The organist turned away from the organ, yet his fingers remained on the keyboard, playing without pause. I felt his steely gaze as the circle closed in with a rush and they grabbed me all at once. That's when I awoke, covered in sweat, shaking and begging for mercy. Throughout the day I could still feel their icy fingers clawing at my skin.

'I think God is watching me, Ellin,' I said to her the following morning.

'That's a good thing for your mob, right?'

'No. I mean He's watching me to see if I keep my promises.'

Ellin stopped what she was doing and listened patiently while I explained my pact with Heaven, and my pledge to be a good wife if God would forgive me.

'Well, I never did take your god for the forgiving kind of fella. It seems to me it's all hell and damnation, and unless they was some kind of perfect angel, I don't know who could live up to them high and mighty standards He sets. What made you go promising stuff you can't deliver anyway?'

'You don't understand, I had to. And I'm trying as hard as I can to do the right thing.'

'Okay, okay, don't get your knickers knotted. I'm just saying, is all.'

'I just don't see how I can... *be* with Lachlan again, after what he did, after what he did to you.'

Ellin took her time to answer. 'You know, sometimes you just have to close your eyes and suck it up, do what you have to. And if God thinks that you owe Him... Well, you know what I'm saying. There ain't nobody but you can decide what to do, tidda.'

I allowed the thoughts to slide from my mind. But I knew that I was only putting off what I thought was my inevitable duty.

I attended to all the regular chores around the homestead, with Ellin's help of course, and tried to be the wife Lachlan needed, taking an interest in all aspects of the station. For the first time, we sat together to do the bookkeeping, and

I quickly learned to balance the ledger, though the sums themselves took forever to complete. Financially we were in reasonable shape. The Stuarts never borrowed money like other pastoralists; they owned everything. If they could not afford to buy something outright, they went without until they could.

'Cash is king,' said Lachlan. 'While all them other galahs are up to their necks with the banks, we're not beholden to anyone.'

'But what if we need to buy something important and don't have the money?'

'We don't buy no matter how important it may seem. There's always going to be a good reason to spend money, but you're just kidding yourself if you can't afford it. We save, then we buy. Simple.'

'Is the money safe here in the house?'

'Safer than with them shonky bankers.'

Yes, cash was king, and we kept it in a secret hiding place in the roof. Sometimes our reserves amounted to more than a thousand pounds: before the stock losses, over three and a half thousand.

Pressure had been building in Lachlan. He became agitated easily, raising the subject of a wife's duty to her man on a regular basis. When he'd been drinking too much, he would come home from the bar in good humour, laughing and joking with me. But his attempts at jest always seemed just a comment away from a simmering rage that lay beneath the surface, and any chance of intimacy was quickly banished when he tried to force the issue. Despite these moments of volatility, we managed to get through our days without any serious conflict. But I knew it could not last forever and I would have to accede to his wishes.

When Lachlan had his way, it came out of the blue. And though I had been the one to set the train of events in motion, I had no control over what eventually happened. Lachlan had returned from riding the fence line, dusty and tired, smelling like rotten mutton. It had been a good day for me, my mood was light. I drew him a bath, hot and steaming, adding rose-smelling bath salts to the water.

'I'll smell like a bloody poof!' he complained.

'Oh, and you're such a blokey fella, tough as a mallee bull, and you stink like one too.'

'Bloody hell, can't a bloke have a bath in peace?' he said, feigning anger, the corner of his mouth curled.

It was an impulse, perhaps pressure from above, but I knelt beside the tub and took the washcloth, gently sponging his dusty back, pushing memories from my mind and trying to see him in a good light. He looked old, worn in many ways. His leathery skin felt burned and dry, rough to the touch, his hair bleached grey by the sun. His muscles, though taut and hard, were aged beyond his years. Several white scars ran like ribbons across his back and upper arms. I touched them with the tip of my finger.

'Barbed wire,' he said. 'Fell from me bloody horse at full gallop when I was a nipper.'

'I doubt you were ever a nipper.'

The room went quiet as I washed him, the only sound the trickle of water as it ran from the washcloth in my hand to the tub. Neither of us spoke, but the anticipation could not have been louder. My heart thumped as I willed myself to be strong. I let tension linger between us, only our breathing breaking the silence. Sponging the grime slowly from his body, I allowed my hand to dip into the water each time, so that I brushed the inside of his thigh. Could this really be what God wanted from me? Lachlan turned his head. I looked into his eyes and saw the monster lurking within those dark pools, staring back with an intensity that brought instant fear. I had an immediate reaction and panicked, suddenly ready to flee, rising quickly to my feet, but he grasped my wrist firmly and pulled me into the tub, slopping water to the floor in a sudden surge that spread a great foaming pool across the floorboards. I screamed in fright as the water drenched my clothes. Lachlan pulled the plug, and I no longer resisted. I closed my eyes and prayed for it to be quick.

I tried to be congenial, to hide my dread and do what was expected of a wife. In the end it was neither violent nor passionate, just an awkward kind of lust, restrained by memories and fear, thoughts of my wedding night, of what he had done to Ellin. Lachlan didn't seem to notice my frigid compliance, the rigidity of my body. He even tried to be affectionate, whispering something about *beauty* in my ear, no doubt resisting the brutish urge within him. Nevertheless, his efforts were clumsy and insincere and did little to ease my terror. Repulsed by the images in my head, it was all I could do to conceal my disgust long enough for him to finish.

Duty done, Lachlan seemed happy at last. It showed in his conversation, him babbling on like an excited child after consuming too much sugar. We ate together, and I pretended to listen with interest, but I was consumed by feelings of loathing.

'We're going to add to the flock,' he said. 'And we'll improve the quality of wool by putting in a wash station. Wool's fetching top prices at the moment...'

His words faded into background chatter. I smouldered. If my penance meant more copulation, I was doomed to fail.

'Oh, by the way, that young blackfella's back,' said Lachlan. 'The one who followed you back to the homestead. Remember? And guess who came walking in with him, you'll never guess. Bloody Toby! I hired them both on the spot. Well, if I'm going to be away, you'll need someone around, and I could use a hand with the new wash station.'

It took me a moment to register what Lachlan was saying. Toby, he had said, but had I heard right?

'I'm sorry, Toby and who?' My heart had already doubled its beat.

'That young black kid, Lou. Bloody hard worker and can ride like a champion. It's hard to find kids like that anymore.'

To say that I had slipped into a state of shock was an understatement. I tried to act casually, but couldn't think a coherent thought.

Chapter 16

Firewood-Kunika

I avoided all contact with Lou, choosing instead to spring-clean the house, a distraction to keep me busy and out of his way. Ellin and I set to work until the house took on a sparkle it had not seen in years. I cooked up a whole mess of treats and pastries, something rarely seen in the kitchen. Lachlan, still in a state of euphoria since our unexpected bath, had been amused by the sudden activity.

'It's good to have the old you back,' said Lachlan, eating a slice of freshly baked pie.

'What do you mean?'

'I mean, having you concentrating on your chores instead of traipsing off somewhere. Things are going to be different around the place now that we have things straight. The future's bright,' he said, 'as long as you know your place and I take care of business.'

I didn't answer. Instead, I let him enjoy the fantasy while it lasted.

Unavoidably, I kept getting glimpses of Lou as he went about his work. I wasn't sure if it was my feelings of anger at his sudden departure or my new-found need for salvation that kept me from him, but I was determined to stay clear at all costs.

Toby, on the other hand, was a welcome sight. He came to the house to yarn, and we sat and drank tea in the kitchen while he told of his travels. He had hurt his back after falling from his horse and had plans to stay around for a while. I told him of the dust storm and how Jack had died so tragically. He told me Jack lived on in the Dreaming and would one day return to finish his journey. I asked him if he believed in God.

'God? You mean your god, like the one in church?' I nodded. 'Nah, He's too much of a government man for me. You can't have a god that only looks after some of the people.'

'I've seen blackfellas go to church. Don't they believe in God?'

'Yeah, but they got to thinking they was going to be part of the whitefella world, where God is the boss man. Sometimes, they forget their own stories.'

'Like the Dreamtime stories?'

'That's right. You got your god, and you got your heaven. In the blackfella's culture, we got the Dreamtime, the Dreaming.'

Toby had taught me stories about his ancestors, how they had come down from the sky and created the land, the sacred places and the people. About how the Rainbow Serpent had brought water so that plants and animals could live.

'Isn't that kind of the same thing?'

Toby put his hand to his chin and frowned. 'Maybe I do believe in God, but my God lives in everything, everyone, and leaves no one on the outside.'

'Do you pray?'

Toby laughed, but he wasn't mocking me. 'I speak to the earth and the stars, the trees, sometimes. I talk to me ancestors who live in the Dreaming, ask they look kind on me.'

I told Toby of my prayers and my obligation to God. 'I thought I would die. I knew I'd been evil and God was punishing me, so I asked Him to forgive me and made promises if He let me live. I was scared, Toby.'

'We all say things we don't mean when we get scared.'

'Do you think I'll go to hell if I don't keep my promises?'

Toby smiled. 'I don't know a lot of things, but I know you're not evil. If your god thinks you need punishing, I'd tell him to bugger off.'

We sat in silence for a while. I wondered if God would be angry at Toby for not believing in Him, for being disrespectful.

Toby broke the silence. 'I went to church when I was a nipper.'

'You did? But I thought...'

Toby reached into his bulging shirt pocket and pulled out a bundle of dog eared papers. Amongst the collection was a photograph. Creased and cracked, the faded sepia image had a torn corner and had been folded in half. Toby laid it on the table and pointed. 'That's me.'

Ten or twelve people stood outside what looked to be a chapel – there was a cross at the apex of the roof. The indigenous men, women and children depicted in the picture, paraded before the camera, alongside a white priest. A little boy clung to his mother's skirt on the far end of the gathering.

'Me mum was a devout Christian. Went to the Methodist church in Yass every Sunday, and I went with her. Went to school too.'

'You never told me that before. Where's she now, your mum?'

'Died of the flu when I was four or five. Me Uncle Jarra took me in.' Toby tucked the photograph back inside the bundle and returned it to his pocket. 'She liked church, my mum. Liked singing hymns and dressing up for it. I never took to it, and me uncle never had time for it. He was a bushman. We lived on station camps and he taught me horses, and our ancestors ways of living. That was my school after mum died.'

We didn't say any more, finishing our tea in silence. I stood a while on the verandah, and watched as Toby joined Lachlan and Lou, wondering what God really wanted from me, and why He had sent Lou back to test me. Lou had seemed to sense my coldness towards him and had made himself scarce. When he did try to engage me, I was brusque and gave him no encouragement. He kept a respectful distance, but I could see the hurt in his eyes whenever I turned my back on him without speaking. I tried to convince myself it was for the best, that I owed it to God, but the want was relentless.

Cutaway Creek needed to rebuild, and Lachlan's plans for expansion had taken a setback when our station manager, Johnson, had up and left after the storm, taking a job at the mine where they paid double. Two permanent stockmen followed, leaving us shorthanded, so it was fortunate to have Lou and Toby arrive out of nowhere. Lou took on the role of top hand, even though we had no one left to supervise. Toby couldn't do any of the hard labour and couldn't ride well enough to wrangle because of his back. But Lachlan wanted him for his experience and promised to hire more workers just as soon as conditions allowed.

Livestock sales up north, provided the opportunity for Lachlan to buy in breeding stock to strengthen the flock. He left with Toby in the truck, for Cunnamulla, a purse full of cash and high hopes for a good deal on some breeding ewes at auction. Lou and I were left to watch over the homestead and wait for their return. Cunnamulla would take a day and a half to reach if the old Ford held out. She had been overheating, and Lachlan was unsure of the problem. They would stay in town, attend the sales and head straight home, arriving two days later with a full load of ewes. All in all, it would take five days to complete the trip.

The day of their departure, Ellin's mum became unwell. We had the household chores in hand, so we agreed that she would stay home for several days and care for her. I set about making myself busy and decided to clean out the chook shed. Forking out the soiled bedding, I barrowed the waste to a compost heap near the barn. The girls followed my every move with the usual curiosity of chickens, pecking around my feet and waiting for scraps and bugs to fall to the ground where they were quickly dispatched. I cleaned the roosts and dragged out the nesting boxes so I could scrub them down properly. Ivan, the rooster, stood imperiously on a pole nearby. More intelligent than previous roosters, Ivan had the usual protective instincts of his predecessors, but with a cruel streak that manifested in sneak attacks on animals and humans alike. He waited until I had my back turned before making his move, attacking me from behind, wings aflutter and spurs drawing blood from my calves within seconds. I kicked and screamed, but he kept on coming, intent on doing me harm, oblivious to the heft of my boots. The girls scattered into a circle, distressed by the commotion, squawking like cockatoos, the scene like a schoolyard fight with the classroom bully. Lou came running. He grabbed the broom from the stoop, took a wild swing, clipping Ivan and sending him for cover beneath a shower of floating feathers and bruised pride. With the skirmish over, Lou helped me replace the nest boxes and pitch in fresh straw.

'Here,' said Lou, taking a bandanna from his pocket as I sat on the verandah steps, nursing my cuts and bruises. He crouched at my feet, took my legs and dabbed the bloodied wounds gently. I studied the top of his head, the sheen of his coal-black curls, puckered my lips and puffed like a tyre deflating. He looked up with those deep-water eyes, smiled his lazy S, and all the knots I had so carefully avoided began to twist and tie inside.

'You should put something on it,' he said, cradling one of my legs like a baby.

Time stood still. We held each other's stare, and I knew I was lost. I shook the feeling, pulled away quickly and ran to the house where I stayed until the sun had set. I dared not look out of the windows. I wished for Ellin to keep me grounded, sat in a corner and huddled from sight, listening for signs of life, and hoping they would not come.

Night fell slowly. I shivered. Autumn nights are cold without a stove, and with no wood in the basket, I had to go outside if I wanted to light one. Reluctant to venture from the house in case I ran into Lou, I checked the area through a crack in the door. Nothing. I told myself Lou would be in the bunkhouse by now, and I would have a clear run to the woodpile, then I told myself it was crazy to be so obsessed. Despite feeling foolish, I reached the pile at a dash and loaded my basket, hesitating when I saw the flickering glow of fire, reflected against the barn wall. Lou had lit the fire pit.

Chapter 17

Blood-KaantaRa

I returned to the house with an armful of chopped wood and kindling, thankful I hadn't bumped into Lou in the process. Hide and go seek, the game seemed absurd. Why should I be hiding in my own home? I made my way to the kitchen. It felt dismal and cold, ominously empty. I opened the stove door, the squeal of cast-iron hinges echoing off the walls, and prepared to set a fire within. My gaze roved the gloomy room, fell on a plate of meat, sitting on the bench. I had prepared two beef steaks earlier, two out of habit. I stared at them, thought of Lou outside alone, and asked myself if I had subconsciously put two pieces of meat aside in hope. After fretting for at least five minutes, I gave in to temptation and carried the steaks out to the barn with two plates, cutlery and

two large unpeeled potatoes, telling myself it was an innocent act of consideration.
Lou sat on a stump, poking logs with an iron, sending sparks into the air where they danced in the night sky. He looked contemplative in the orange glow of the fire, lost in thought, but serene and peaceful. He reacted with surprise when he saw me.

Lou made people smile, feel safe, feel good about themselves, even when they didn't want to. He had a power over me that wouldn't let me be, and despite my attempts to be cool and aloof, it didn't take long to fall back into our easy ways of conversation. The steaks sizzled over hot coals, delicious smells of which filled the air. We chatted over dinner as though the last months had never happened, and he had never been away. Eventually, I asked him why he went without a word.

'I met a German fella once. Big bloke he was, said he came to Australia after the war in search of a peaceful life. He was looking for opals near White Cliffs when I come across him, and we yarned for a while – he did at least – and he told me of all the places he'd been and seen. I always thought Germans were scary people. I'd never met one, mind. Half-expected him to have two heads and a tail, but he was a nice sort of fella, not a bit like the stories I'd heard from the blokes who'd been to war. When it came to leaving, he said you should never say goodbye, and he taught me the words to say in his own lingo. Auf Wiedersehen. It means until we meet again. I didn't say goodbye to you, Kate, because I knew we'd be catching up again soon enough.'

'What if I'd died while you were gone, died in the dust storm?'

'You wouldn't have.'

'How do you know?'

'Because it was written in the stars. Don't you see it?' Lou pointed to the sky. 'Right there above the Emu. Do you see it?'

I smiled. 'I see it, right next to the one that says never trust a blackfella with your heart.'

'Oh, that's cruel.'

We sat in silence for a while, watching the fire and feeling its heat on our faces. 'I came after you,' I said eventually.

'I didn't know.'

'That day of the dust storm, I came hoping to find you. Daft, eh?'

'I'd of waited if I'd known.' Lou poked the fire, causing it to crackle and pop. 'Toby said you got caught up in the storm, said you was banged up pretty bad. Sorry about Jack, he was a good horse.'

I closed my eyes. 'He was my best friend.'

Lou nodded, he had no words to comfort me.

'When I was lost,' I said after letting the heartache pass. 'I stumbled across human remains half-buried in a creek bed, somewhere between the bluff and the eastern bore. I saw three skulls, and there may have been more.'

'Black bones,' said Lou.

'No, white,' I said stupidly.

Lou smiled. 'Blackfella's bones,' he said by way of explanation. 'Our mob've been burying our dead out here for thousands of years. On the edge of the old camps, you'll usually find burials, but there's lots of remote sites too, like the one you found. The old mob didn't have graveyards like you white blokes, with stones and crosses. There's nothing to mark our graves. But bones get exposed by storms, flash floods, animals, bone collectors.'

'Bone collectors?'

'Whitefellas looking for bones to sell.'

It took me a few moments to understand. 'Sell to who?'

Lou took his time to answer. 'Your mob, whitefellas, see us as curiosities, like roos and wallabies. They collect specimens for museums and private collections, souvenirs to ship home to Europe.'

'They don't,' I said laughing.

'*They do* , seriously. There's a fella named George Black. The old folks say he's the Devil himself, travels the back country digging up remains and carting them away to the cities. They say he can smell a grave site before he can see it.'

'You're not serious.'

'I saw him once at the Corner, Maliangaba territory. He looked at me like he was looking at a new hat in a shop window, sizing me up I reckon.' Lou paused. 'Toby says they used to have a blackfella's bones on the wall, right here above the fireplace, set out like the bloody Jolly Roger.'

Horrified, I sat in silence, picturing the creek burial site. 'All three skulls had holes in them, like those I've seen in kangaroo skulls after the hunt.'

Lou shrugged. 'Probably shot.'

'Shot? Shot by who?'

'There were run-ins between settlers and the local mobs, back when they started moving in sheep and cattle. The blackfellas would knock off a sheep, and the settlers didn't like it. They would confront the mob. Sometimes they got more than they bargained for. There'd be some spearing, and a couple of whitefellas would get wounded. Then the settlers would come back with policemen and sort it out.'

'Sort it out?'

'Shoot them. Shoot them all. Of course, these are yarns passed down through word of mouth, don't know if they're all true. But it happened to the Wiradjuri on the Turon River, that much I do know, Wiradjuri women and children butchered along with their men.' Lou sat in silence for a while. I had no words to say in reply. 'One thing's for sure,' Lou said at length. 'lots of blackfellas got killed for no good reason and no whitefellas got held to account.'

'That's so awful,' I murmured.

We sat in contemplation as the fire crackled and Lou set fresh logs to burn. 'Do you hate the whitefellas for what they've done?' I asked eventually.

As though I had said something funny, Lou chuckled. 'Hate? Nah, I don't hate anyone me. Besides, I've got enough white in me to take some of the blame. Me mum's half-caste, me dad's a whitefella. Me mum's mum is full-blood, and her dad's brother was a half-caste. It gets complicated pretty quickly.'

'But you think of yourself as an Aboriginal.'

'Why wouldn't I? You can't cut me veins open and separate the parts that are white from the ones that are black. This here's my ancestral home and I'm proud of it, proud to be black. I have white blood too, but that doesn't stop me being a blackfella.'

'I didn't mean to upset you,' I said.

'I know that, but it does hurt to be asked if I'm a real Aboriginal.' Lou hesitated. 'It's not only you whitefellas that give me a hard time over me colour. Some darkies don't think I'm black *enough*, not worthy of calling myself a blackfella, like I've let the side down in some way by being too white.'

I laughed. 'But you're as dark as—'

'Don't say it!'

'Say what?'

Lou smiled. 'I don't know, but it can't have been good.'

'You're making fun of me.'

'Maybe. But as me mum used to say, "If you can't have fun, don't go out in the sun.".'

I giggled. 'That's silly. Your mum sounds like she had a great sense of humour.'

'Yep, she had that alright.'

Can you play the didgeridoo?' I asked, wanting to keep the mood light.

'What, you think all Abos can play the didge and throw a boomerang? Talk about prejudiced,' he said, feigning disgust. Then his smile lit his face like the flames lit the fire. 'Well, it just so happens I've got one in me swag.'

'You don't.'

'Do.'

Lou disappeared, returning with his hands clasped behind his back, as though he were hiding a great surprise.

'Where is it?' I asked like an excited child.

Lou opened his hand to reveal a strange curl of metal.

'It's me didge,' he said. 'You don't like it?' Lou sat and placed the object between his teeth. Cupping his hands around his mouth, he strummed a metal spring with his thumb, manipulating his lips and cheeks, and imitating the vibrating sounds of a didgeridoo. He stamped his foot in the dirt to the rhythm.

I laughed aloud and clapped along until he had finished. 'Let me have a go,' I said, taking the instrument and trying to copy with no success whatsoever. I sounded like a cat being strangled. Lou wrapped his arms around me, placing his hands over mine and positioned the device.

'Now strum it with your thumb,' he said, laughing.

'I am!'

'*You're not.* You're all thumbs and no rhythm,' he said, and we tumbled to the ground in a heap of giddiness. I wanted to hold him there and never let him go. We paused for too long before I pulled away and returned to my seat at the fire.

'Maybe you need a real didge,' he said, tucking the instrument back into his pocket.

'Where did you get that thing anyway?' I said, for want of something to say, while I cooled my thoughts and lowered my pulse.

'That *thing*, I'll have you know, is a jew's harp,' he said. 'Someone gave it to me when I was young; me mum reckoned it was me dad, and he left it for me before he disappeared for good.'

'Your dad was a Jew?' I asked innocently.

Lou laughed. 'No,' he said. 'It's called a jew's harp but it's got nothing to do with Jews. Some bloke told me it was originally called a jaw harp. Mum said me dad used to play it for me whenever he came home, but I was too young to remember.'

'Still, that makes it very special,' I said.

A cloud passed over his expression, and for once Lou seemed sad. 'Yeah, that fella made sure I had everything I needed in life.'

A tense silence followed Lou's sarcasm. I pushed a stick into the flames, making it crackle and spark, allowing him time with his thoughts.

At last, Lou jumped to his feet, smiling again. 'Time for a karka-maarni,' he said.

'What's karka-maarni?'

'You don't know karka-maarni? Well, shame on you.'

'It sounds rude.'

'Rude? It's you who's got a rude mind. I said let's dance.'

'We can't dance,' I said. 'Where's the music?'

'Ah! That's where you have to use your imagination. But first,' he said, taking charred coal from the fire pit, 'we need a little decoration, and then we'll have us a little corroboree.' Using the charcoal with his fingers, he painted two lines across my cheeks, and dabbed my nose, making me cross-eyed. 'There,' he said. 'Now you look like a real Abo.'

Lou removed his shirt and began to dance in the light of the fire, the flames licking the night, flickering on his waving arms and glistening off his skin, his body gilded by the glow. Spellbound, I watched his wide-eyed portrayals of kangaroos, jabirus and Dreamtime spirits. 'Come on, shake a leg,' he said each time he circled the fire pit.

Resisting his attempts to coax me to my feet, I watched him move with quiet pleasure. It didn't seem right to join him. This was his world where only he and his people belonged to dance beneath the stars. Content to be his audience, I didn't follow his lead, and he soon forgot my presence, lost in his own realm of spirits, a trance like state as he reeled around the fire, intent on his performance, his depictions of the characters set in folklore over centuries past. Mesmerised, I followed his fluid movements, graceful, full of mystic meaning and soul. I saw in him then, the spirits of his ancestors, the Aboriginal blood that coursed through his veins. Perhaps it was the firelight, or the beers we had drunk, maybe it was the chill night air, but I suspect it was his life force I found so intoxicating. It left me so emotional, I thought I would cry.

Eventually, Lou ran out of steam. He replaced his shirt and joined me at the fire, where we watched it collapse into flickering coals. I could still see him dancing amongst the red hot embers, and in my mind's eye I imagined the dancers who had gone before him.

'Do you want a blanket?' Lou said, snapping me out of my thoughts. 'You look cold.'

Before I could answer, he was on his way to the bunkhouse to get one. I rose and followed, standing in the doorway while he stripped a blanket from the bed. He turned, startled, placing a hand over his heart.

'Who did you think it was,' I said with a chuckle. 'The bone collector?'

'Yeah, laugh all you want. If you keep sneaking up on a fella like that, I'll end up having a heart attack, and then Mr Black will have me bones for good.'

'These are your worldly possessions?' I said, scanning the contents of his swag strewn across an adjoining bed.

'Everything I need.'

I smiled and considered the surprisingly large number of items spread out before me. A knife, billycan and mugs, frying pan, water canteen. A bedroll, tobacco pouch, lighter and box of matches. His leather hat, a pair of long-neck spurs, a box of ammunition. A razor and strop, a cake of soap and a tin of dental powder. He had a rifle and a gun-cleaning kit, an oilskin coat, a neatly folded tarpaulin, and various leather straps and ties: whips, snare lines and bandannas.

'Everything?' I asked, meeting his eyes in an exchange we both recognised for what it was.

He moved up close, blanket in hand. I closed my eyes and waited. Lou leaned in and kissed my lips gently. Softly he said, 'Are you sure about this?'

I nodded my assent without opening my eyes, and he kissed me again. I thought of Lachlan and our wedding night. Briefly, I allowed fear to return but pushed the thought from my mind as I responded to Lou's touch. I told myself this was not Lachlan, and it would not be the same. A single lightbulb dangled on a long wire from the rafters, throwing a subdued yellow glow over the bunkhouse. The bulb swayed gently to and fro, casting shadows that gave the otherwise stark room a warm, romantic feel. I heard the distant hum of the main generator, the only sound to break the silence. We undressed, each helping the other out of our clothes, slowly appreciating the moment, and trembling with anticipation. Lou's dog watched, making me feel self-conscious. Lou noticed my unease and smiled.

'Get, Dog.' Dog, as though he understood the need for privacy, headed for the door. 'He's just jealous,' said Lou.

The room felt chilled but his body warm. He wrapped me in his arms and held me close, pulling the blanket over us, so that I felt safe and protected. I sensed no urgency in his actions, just the gentle awareness of my needs, as though his only intention was to care for me, to cherish me. His lips brushed my skin, delicately working his way down my neck to the hollow of my shoulder. I felt an excited tickle of blood, and the hairs stand on my flesh. My breath quickened, soft gasps, as he kissed my eyelids tenderly. My senses seemed heightened, blood tingling through my body. I felt the silky skin of his back beneath my fingers, traced the contours of his body and pulled him tightly to my own. I allowed myself to ask if love was real this time, if this feeling of love could last and my world was not about to be shattered. A sliver of doubt crossed my mind; should I stop before the dream ends? He touched me and I winced in fear. He assured me and I relaxed again, encouraging him to go on. Lou took his time, teasing me with his delicate touch, his slow, sweet affection. His mouth continued to graze my body, causing me to squirm at the sensations. I gasped aloud, could bear it no longer, pulling him up to my face so that we breathed the same air. I felt the warmth of him inside me, two souls entwined at last.

Chapter 18

Lover-Nganpa

We awoke to the cockerel's crow and the first dawn light, made love again, then lay lazily, wrapped in each other's arms.

'I don't want this to end,' I said at length.

'It has to end, I've got work to do. I have to check the bore line, or Lockie will have me guts for garters.' We lay a while longer. 'Why don't you come with me?' Lou said eventually.

I hesitated. 'I haven't ridden since...'

Lou kissed me and smiled. 'You can ride Smokey; I'll pick out another horse.'

Before I could argue, Lou was dressed and on his way to the stables. I dragged myself from the bed, pulled my clothes together and paused to reflect on the night. Dog lay on the floor, his chin resting on his paws, eyes fixed on mine.

'What? Don't look at me like that, Dog.'

I had no regrets. The night had progressed as if I had no control at all. But underneath my impulsive behaviour, I knew there was retribution. I couldn't help feeling that with Lou's affection, I was getting what I deserved, but so was Lachlan.

Smokey, every bit the horse I imagined, lived up to his reputation. Responsive to every subtle instruction, he could almost read my mind. Some of the best stock horses behave for only one rider, they get to know their ways and don't feel comfortable with a stranger. The great ones like Smokey are good with anyone on their backs; they know the job regardless of rider.

Lou gave me time to put my fears aside and adjust to the ride, our slow progress adding to the pleasure of his company as we sauntered out to the far pastures joined in easy conversation. We checked three bores, making sure that the water ran clean and the tanks were full. Sheep gathered in numbers nearby, a sure sign that fresh forage was in short supply. Mid-day came and Lou said we should take a break at Yalta Maku. I suspected this was his way of having me confront all that happened that day. We reached the bluff with the sun high in the sky, coming to rest at the welcoming oasis, where natural springs spilled into aqua rock basins, fifteen feet deep in the shadow of rocks and trees. We tied the horses loosely in the shade of river red gums, where they could drink from pools that nestled under the rock shelf, and climbed the winding path to the top of the cliff. We found a spot overlooking the horses and sat quietly together, a tickle of a breeze on our faces.

'Do you feel it, Kate?'

'The breeze?'

'The earth. Do you feel the earth?'

I brushed my hand across the rock surface, felt the warmth of the sun on my fingers.

'Me uncle Mick, me mum's brother, brought me here when I was a young boy. He used to say I had to understand where I came from, so I'd know where I was going. I didn't know what he was going on about. We'd sit here for hours, him with his eyes closed, me, watching him and wondering what he was thinking. When I asked him, he said he was just being.'

'Being what?'

'That's what I wanted to know. Just being, he said. I still didn't understand. He said being was connecting, connecting to the land, to the earth, to our ancestors. He could feel life all around us, he said. Said if I closed my eyes, I'd feel it too in the rocks beneath me feet, in the soil, the trees, the air. If I listened, he said, I'd hear the earth speak.'

'Did you hear it?'

'Not then, not right away.'

'But you did eventually?'

'Uncle Mick talked in riddles sometimes. He said I had to listen to the land because it had lots to say. I thought maybe he was a bit doolally – whoever heard of a talking earth – so I asked me mum. She said what he meant was: the land is a living thing, just like us, we're made up of the same thing, dust, me mum said. We come from the land, and when we're done we all go back there. If we don't respect the earth, then we have no respect for ourselves.'

Respect the earth, it lives and breathes. Toby had taught me much the same thing. It seemed to me that the Aboriginal way of looking at the earth was a sure way to protect it from harm. And according to Uncle Mick, by protecting the earth you protect yourself and all things. 'I like your Uncle Mick,' I said, deep in thought, my palm pressed flat against the ground.

'I am the earth, the earth is me,' said Lou, placing his hand on mine.

'Do you think we'll live forever in the rocks and the land?'

'Forever and a day,' said Lou. 'Forever and a day.'

Suddenly fearful of the future, I wondered how things might unfold, now that we had given in to our feelings. We talked about forever, but that moment, us, there together, seemed fragile, as though a strong enough breeze would carry our hopes and dreams away and we would wake to the past, locked in all our yesterdays. Panicked by the thought, I reached out for Lou to hold me, rested my head on his shoulder and took his hands in mine. His reassuring embrace brought down my pulse, and I snuggled in beside him, comforted by his nearness. I pushed the questions from my mind and tried to enjoy the moment of tranquillity.

Situated at intervals around the bluff, several large rocks stood alone, as though keeping guard over Yalta Maku. 'I want you to bury me bones out there,' Lou said softly, pointing to the strange arrangement of boulders. 'Right down there beneath that big old rock so that Mr Black can't find me.'

'I don't want to bury you anywhere,' I retorted. 'When we die, we'll die together. Someone else can bury us.' Lou smiled and pulled me in tight. We allowed the silence to hang in the air. But Lou's words had brought back worries. 'Let's make a pact,' I said eventually, 'that we'll live to an old age and our bones will lay forever together, in life and death.'

Lou smiled, ruefully. 'As long as we're not lying side by side in a cardboard box on some museum shelf, I'll drink to that.' But I saw a shadow of sadness pass over his face like a cloud across the sun, and I knew he was thinking of Lachlan. We sat some more, pressed up close without speaking. For then at least, nothing could take him from me.

After a time, we clambered down the slope to a rock shelf overlooking the deepest pool. From a height, its turquoise looked clear and tempting. Lou stripped to his glistening bronze skin, and I marvelled at the defined, muscular lines of his body. I watched him step forward, toes curled around the rock ledge, knees bent. Then with a loud whoop, he leapt, sent a wave of water into the air, and disappeared below the surface. In the crystal-clear water, he covered the bottom of the pool like a fish in a smooth glide.

'Come on in,' he called.

'I can't swim.'

'*What?* Everyone can swim.'

'I can't.' I watched Lou for a while, then climbed the rocks to ground level.

'Come on, I'll teach you.' Doubtful, I shook my head. 'Trust me,' he said, treading water.

Reluctantly, I slipped out of my clothes and stepped into the water. 'It's freezing!'

I moved in up to my knees, wobbling on the rocky bottom so that I almost fell. Lou came across and took me gently by the hands, steering me into deeper water.

'Turn around and let yourself float.'

'I can't.'

'You can.'

'I'm scared.'

'Turn around,' Lou insisted.

Despite my fear, I did as he said. I felt my feet leave the bottom of the pool, panicked momentarily, but felt Lou behind me, taking my weight and giving me enough confidence to go with his body. He took me on his chest, kicking back across the water in a gentle drift. The tension slowly left my rigid body, and I relaxed enough to place my trust in him entirely. As we floated, I gazed at the sky and allowed calm to take over. Returning to the shore, we climbed to a flat rock and embraced, shamelessly, under the drifting clouds.

Early that evening I spoke to Lachlan on the shortwave radio. They had made good time but couldn't find a room, so were going to sleep in the truck. I told him that everything was fine at the station and wished him good luck. Already, guilt played on my mind.

Lou spent that night in my bed. We made love and talked, talked and made love, alternating between the two until we fell asleep near dawn. The third day we rode out again, following the creek and taking a gallop over a large salt pan unencumbered by scrub, pushing the horses to their limits. Exhilarated, we arrived back at the homestead by late afternoon, and I prepared roasted lamb, which we ate at the kitchen table by candlelight. Lachlan radioed to say they had finished at the auction and had successfully acquired the stock he wanted. Lou stood at my side as Lachlan spoke, making the guilt even more palpable. After dinner, we lit a fire in the hearth and snuggled, listening to a Glen Miller special on the wireless and wondering what it would be like to see a big band in real life.

'Let's go to the picture house tomorrow,' I said. 'There's a new film called *South Pacific*. Ellin heard it was supposed to be fabulous, full of music, and I've never been to a picture show.'

'Fabulous? What might not be fabulous is if someone saw us together.'

'We could go to Silverton. Oh, please...'

The following day, we lazed and chatted, making the most of our time together, pushing the consequences from our minds as if we had no cares in the world. But our night at the pictures turned out to be a disaster. *South Pacific* wasn't running until the following week, and we might have gone in to see *Dracula* with Christopher Lee, but a horrible woman at the ticket office put us off altogether, saying Lou had to sit with the other blackfellas if he wanted to come into the theatre. Instead, we returned home to the comfort of my bed.

In the late hours of what was to be our final day, the shortwave crackled to life in the back room of the homestead. Lachlan's voice came across with a distant echo from a petrol station near Cobar.

'The truck's blown a head gasket,' said Lachlan. 'We won't make it back until late tomorrow night at best.'

'Well, don't worry,' I said, watching Lou across the room. 'There's no rush.'

'Luckily we found a local bloke with a holding paddock for the stock.'

'That's good.'

'Yeah. We're about to have a schooner and a bite to eat, then I'm off to sleep. I'm buggered, I've got to tell you.'

'Stay safe. Tell Toby I said hello.'

As it turned out, Lachlan and Toby spent two more days waiting for a gasket to come from Sydney. Toby said later that they had spent their time at the pub, where Lachlan had a run-in with local copper miners – Lachlan and miners did not mix well. Someone called the police. Toby said he feared for Lachlan's life until they were well clear of the town.

Lou and I spent those extra days in isolated bliss. We lived in the moment with no thought for what would come next, blocking the world and the future from our minds. I think we were in a state of denial. Ellin came back to work, and we were careful not to flaunt our relationship, but in the end, I couldn't help but tell her everything. Of course, Ellin already knew what was going on.

'You have to be careful, tidda. You and I both know what Lock's capable of. I'm not scolding you or saying you shouldn't do what you're doing, but it's a dangerous game you playing.'

I knew all too well what might happen, but I couldn't see a life without Lou now, even if I had no idea how to get it. 'I love him, Ellin.'

'I know you do, tidda. You two belong together. I just don't see how you're going to find a way to be with him.'

I had more than Lachlan to worry about. I also knew that as soon as I let Him into my head, God would have a lot to say about the situation.

When Lachlan finally came home I found it difficult to act normally. I wandered about the homestead in a dreamlike state, deep in thought at any one moment, trying to find answers for what I should do next, and finding none. The happiness I had experienced lingered giddily for a while. I could no longer function as usual for thinking about our days together. Desperate to be with Lou at any opportunity, I took chances to snatch a word or a kiss. My actions were dangerous and often careless. Lachlan almost caught us out near the barn, yet all I could do was giggle at the near miss. It wasn't fair to Lou, who appeared terrified at times when I took such risks.

Eventually, I came down to earth. If Lou and I were to be together, sooner or later I would have to tell Lachlan I was leaving him, and I imagined every reaction and dire consequence as a result. Hidden within him, a violent streak festered, which I had witnessed first-hand. It was foolish to think I could tell him the truth and just walk away from our marriage.

'How am I going to tell him, Ellin?'

'Bake him a cake and tell him when his mouth's full.'

'Seriously?'

'Maybe you should both just run away.'

'Maybe we will.'

'Just make sure you run far enough, tidda, or he'll find you.'

After the euphoria of our time alone together, I suppose it was inevitable that reality would soon take hold. The more I thought of telling Lachlan, the more terrified I became at the prospect. Lou kept saying he would take whatever came if Lachlan became violent, but I could see in his eyes that he shared my fear. As a result, nothing changed. Weeks passed, and the naïve belief that things would turn out for the best faded to a point where I wasn't sure of anything anymore. With the delay, our passions cooled. We saw less and less of each other in private moments, and it seemed the world was determined to keep us apart. When we did get to talk, we went over and over the same ground, worrying about the fallout but lacking the strength to confront it. My determination shaken,

I was reluctant to be the one to say 'let's go', and when Lou made no move to resolve the stalemate, I started to question his willingness to commit. With everything still up in the air, I was mortified when Lou joined Lachlan on a trip to the border to pick up some rams from Finnis Springs.

Two weeks later, they were back. The time had come to muster the stock and bring them down to the homestead paddocks for dowsing before breeding began. Now I worried over our lack of plans, and I found myself contemplating a life unchanged with Lachlan. When muster finished, Lou offered to help up at Yandinnia Station where they were short of a stringer. He would be gone a further six weeks.

Chapter 19

Father-Kampitya

In the years that followed my first period, it had fluctuated wildly. I would often be late, and I once went almost two months without one. Sometimes they were light, other times I thought I would die from the blood loss. Over time I came to accept that this was the way it was supposed to be. So in my naïveté, I had taken little notice at my apparent lack of a period. It came as something of a surprise when Ellin pointed out the swelling around my tummy, accompanied by nauseous mornings, tender breasts and a sudden dislike for cheese. At first I scoffed at the idea of being pregnant, laughing and telling Ellin I had just been overeating, hoping perhaps that it would all go away. But as time went on, it became clear that nature had a hand in my changing body.

Lachlan and Daisy did not have children, though it was common knowledge that they had tried, and most thought the fault lay with Daisy. When Ellin gave birth to her first child, rumours pointed to Lachlan being the father, adding weight to the theory that it was Daisy who could not conceive. According to Ellin, Lachlan was probably the father of at least two bastard children, and possibly three. Therefore, I had no way of knowing whose child I was bearing; it could have been Lachlan's or Lou's.

I lived in a trance-like state as life went on around me. Wrapped in my own little head-space, I didn't feel part of the broader world. Lou had cooled his attention and accepted that things had returned to normal, while I came to grips with ever-changing moods that played havoc with my mind.

'They could almost be mates,' said Ellin.

We stood side by side at the kitchen sink and looked out to where Lachlan and Lou were replacing rails on the sheep-loading chute. Lachlan held the timber in place while Lou drove the nails, and Lou must have said something that made Lachlan laugh.

'How could I have been so stupid? I never once gave a thought to getting pregnant.'

'Young ones never do think about consequences. It's too late when they realise.'

'I think he would kill me if he knew.'

'You can't hide it forever,' said Ellin.

'I don't know what to do. How can I be sure who's the father?'

'You can't.' We stood in silence, watching the two men work. 'Look at them, happy as Larry. They have no idea you're about to drop a bomb on them.' I didn't answer. 'You know there are people who can fix it for you.'

'Fix it?'

'There's a Ngangkari woman who might be able to help, a healer. She lives in a camp out past the Corner. Maybe she can fix it so you don't have the baby.'

'But how?'

I had no idea she was talking about killing my child. Ellin explained, leaving the idea to hang horribly in the air for me to consider. Perhaps it was a reflection of my uncertainty that I considered the possibility, though only for a moment. While a baby was an unexpected complication, I had an overwhelming sense of motherhood, and already felt protective of my unborn child.

'I couldn't do that,' I said.

'Think about it,' said Ellin.

I said nothing in reply, but I knew I had to do something. If only I knew whose child it was, I might be able to make a decision. If it was Lachlan's child, would it inherit his sullen, domineering personality, would it bear the same nasty streak? At least with Lachlan the child would have security, a roof over its head and a guaranteed future. And what about Lou, should I confide in him, would he stick around long enough to be a father?

Eventually, I told Lachlan. We were in the barn together and I was cleaning tack, the air thick with the smell of saddle soap and leather. He remarked on my belly, catching me off guard, and I blurted it out and told him he was going to be a father. I wasn't prepared for the reaction.

'I'm going to be a father? Me?' For a moment I thought he was about to explode. In the dim light of the barn I mistook his expression for anger. He said nothing for one whole minute, before erupting in laughter and whoops of joy. He picked me up, hugged me, spun three-sixty degrees so that I felt dizzy and screamed. Never had I seen such a display of happiness from this man.

'You're certain?'

'Yes.'

'How? When? What will...?' Lachlan whooped again and threw his hat in the air. 'You bloody ripper!' he shouted to the rafters. The horses whinnied and pricked their ears, alert to the excitement. I couldn't help but smile. He grabbed my hand and raced me to the yard, where Lou and Toby came out of the woolshed to see what the commotion was all about. 'Grab a couple of coldies, Tobe. I'm going to be a bloody father. Woohoo!'

Ellin stood on the verandah watching. I turned to her. The slightest knowing, ironic smile played on her lips, but her expression was also tinged with worry. I could barely look at Lou. When I did, he smiled sadly and congratulated us both.

Lou avoided me altogether after that, though I wanted to explain, to talk through my feelings and find out how he felt. He used any excuse to disappear for days on end, tending fence lines, checking the bores, running stock. It annoyed me that he never made the effort to talk and I began to think it was all for the best. Fate seemed to have taken a hand and had steered me to Lachlan, who could not have been more pleased. I saw a different man in him, a proud man. He treated me with consideration, which was unnerving yet reassuring. I felt relieved by the change I saw in him.

The months passed slowly and Lachlan continued his thoughtful ways. But with time on my hands, my thoughts soon returned to Lou and what might have been. A yearning swelled in me, along with my stomach. Though Lou tried his best to avoid me, each meeting proved awkward and heart-wrenching, and we never spoke beyond idle exchange.

I was eight months into my pregnancy before circumstances conspired to bring us together alone, when Lachlan asked Lou to drive me into town for my doctor's appointment. The uncomfortable Land Rover rattled over the ruts in the dirt road, each bump making me feel dizzy and sick. We hit a pothole, causing the car to jump and lurch to the shoulder.

'Sorry,' said Lou.

'For what?'

'I didn't see that pothole.'

A few minutes passed in silence. I was brooding, and his closeness added to my emotional state. 'I thought for a minute you were apologising for abandoning me,' I said tersely.

Lou looked puzzled. 'I don't understand.'

It was an unnecessary gibe. After all, it was me who had chosen Lachlan to be the father, me who had turned my back. 'I waited for you to ask.'

'Ask?'

'Ask if the baby was yours.'

Lou pulled off to the side of the road.

'Is it?'

'How do I know, Lou? You tell me, how do I know?'

Poor Lou looked totally baffled, as though he were trying to work out the possibilities and figure out the odds. He looked like a child, trying to do sums that were beyond his capabilities.

'I thought it was Lockie's,' he said at last. 'Why else would you announce it like you did if it wasn't?'

'I didn't *announce* it, Lou. At least, I didn't mean to. I didn't mean for it to happen like it did. I wasn't ready when Lachlan confronted me and I had no choice but to tell him. There seemed no point in denying it, he was going to find out sooner or later. I didn't think he'd go shouting it from the rooftops. After that... Well, after that there was no turning back. You seemed uninterested and I didn't know what to do. I wanted to talk to you about it, but...'

'Do *you* think it's his?'

'I honestly don't know.'

'But all this time...' Lou hesitated. 'All this time I thought it must have been *his*. You seemed happy. I thought you *were* happy.'

'You're such a dope at times.' I wiped my face on my sleeve. 'I wanted to tell you first, but it came out before I could stop it. Lachlan's reaction took me by surprise. I don't know what I expected, but I thought he would be angry, not elated. Who could have predicted that he would be so excited?' I pictured Lachlan in the days after he heard the news. He walked around the homestead with a permanent grin, saying how good it would be to have a boy about the place. I told him it might be a girl and he dismissed the possibility with a laugh, as though it could never happen. 'You weren't around to talk it through, and I thought you didn't care when you took off all over the country. I told myself you were probably relieved.'

'Relieved? I felt like my world had come to an end.'

'Then why didn't you say so? Why didn't you fight for me?'

Lou said nothing, and silence followed. I thought about the months that had passed, the anxiety about my future and wishing Lou were with me every minute of every day. I imagined what Lachlan would be like after the birth of his child, after the novelty had worn off. I knew he could never change his ways. I wanted Lou, but I had ruined everything.

'It doesn't matter now, anyway. It's too late,' I said at last.

'What do you mean, too late?'

'I'm almost due, Lou. How can I tell Lachlan now?' I waited for Lou to say something, but he just sat there, stunned. 'Perhaps it's all for the best.'

Lou reacted as though he'd been given an electric shock. '*No*. I don't believe that. How can it be for the best? Do you love him?'

'You know I don't. How can you ask such a stupid thing?'

'I may be stupid, Kate. I know I'm not the sharpest tool in the shed, but I love you, and he doesn't. It can't be too late to put things right. You want me to fight for you? Well, I'm ready to take him on. I'm not afraid to fight him. I'll do whatever it takes if you still want me.'

Sweet Lou, so gallant. I had to smile, and for the first time in months, I was sure that I still loved him, nothing had changed. 'Of course I still want you, but I didn't mean for you to start brawling with Lachlan. I just want to know that *you* want *me*, that's all.'

'Then we'll go away without telling him, just like we said we would. Only now there'll be three of us. We can go up north to Queensland, or down to Adelaide, out west. You name it, and we'll go there. We'll go now while he's busy.'

'What about the baby, what if it *is* his?'

'I don't care. It's yours, isn't it? That much is certain, and if it's yours, I want it.'

'But you wouldn't mind? You wouldn't mind if it were his?'

'I want it to be mine, but I've got no say in it now. Let's keep driving, Kate, never look back.'

'No. We need a proper plan. We've waited this long, a few more weeks won't hurt.'

'Who needs a plan? We can head south and make our way from there.'

'I think we should wait until the baby's born,' I said eventually.

'But...'

'No buts, Lou. It's too close now, too dangerous. I don't want to be running from town to town carrying this,' I said, two hands on my belly. 'We'll wait until after the birth and it'll give us time to decide where we'll go.'

'If you think that's best.'

'It's kicking. Here, give me your hand.'

I placed Lou's hand on my belly, just in time for one almighty kick as the baby shifted to one side. Lou jumped in surprise, his eyes sparkling with delight. 'He's a strong little bugger.'

'He?'

'If it's a boy, it's definitely mine,' he said, his cocky grin making me smile too. Lou leaned in and kissed me, a gentle kiss that said how much he cared, and I was finally satisfied that we wanted the same thing for our future.

A sudden scrunch of gravel accompanied a Holden wagon as it slid to a stop beside us. We had been too preoccupied to notice its approach. Lou quickly took his arm from my shoulder and wound down the window. Dmitry Anastas, the water carrier, did likewise and smiled.

'G'day. You two need any help?'

'No, we're fine,' said Lou. 'Mrs Stuart just felt a little car sick. I had to pull over for a minute.'

Anastas looked across Lou to me. I smiled. 'I'll be right as rain in a minute. Thank you, Mr Anastas.'

'Right then, if you're sure there's nothing I can do.' One more knowing glance from me to Lou and back to me. A smirk. 'I'll be on my way then if there's nothing...'

'We're fine, really,' I said. 'Thank you for stopping.'

Anastas drove on. Lou put the Land Rover in gear and followed, tracking the Holden all the way into Wilcannia. Anastas waved out of the window as he peeled off on a side road.

'Do you think he saw us?' I said.

'Nah, she'll be right.'

Doctor Forsyth gave me the all clear, saying everything seemed fine. Though he had noticed a slight irregularity in the heartbeat, he assured me it was nothing to be concerned over. He sat behind his desk, a highly ornate piece of furniture that seemed at odds with everything else in his shabby surgery, while I adjusted my clothes and prepared to leave.

'He's a big fellow,' said Forsyth, lighting up a cigarette.

'He?' I said, recalling Lou's confident prediction. Was this a sign it was truly Lou's child?

'Lachlan says he's sure it's a boy,' said Forsyth, spoiling my train of thought. 'Can't disappoint him now, can we, little lady?'

I slumped at the mention of Lachlan, and I didn't feel so little, looking down at my ballooning body. 'We wouldn't want to do that,' I replied. He didn't hear my sarcasm.

'I understand that Ellin is going to act as midwife.'

'Yes.'

'You're going to be in good hands,' said the doctor. 'She'll probably add some traditional touches, but don't let that scare you, there's nothing that will harm you or the baby.'

'I'm not scared. Ellin is marvellous and I have every faith in her.'

'And she's had two children of her own by the way, so she knows what you'll be going through.'

A sudden flush of hot blood surged in my temples. 'And had them taken away,' I retorted, opening the door to leave.

Doctor Forsyth took a long drag on his cigarette. 'Yes, sad business that.'

Chapter 20

Mother-Ngamaka

I reached full-term, believing I would spend my future with Lou, no matter what the consequences. We would face whatever came our way, together. The final weeks had been hard, knowing that Lou felt the way he did, watching Lachlan's growing excitement and wondering how it would be when we told him – if we told him. I still hadn't decided if we should tell him, or just run. Lou had been happier, stealing quick kisses when Lachlan wasn't looking, holding my hand for brief moments when alone, and promising me things would work out just fine. Blind youth, young love; it seems childish now looking back, but I really believed he was right.

January came with a series of strong southerly winds, cooling the air to a comfortable seventy-three degrees, for which I was grateful. The summer months had been trying, with temperatures soaring well above one hundred. I felt drained of all energy, so when my labour began, I was relieved, but concerned for the storm that would follow. It must have been an omen when the pains suddenly stopped. Perhaps I knew what was in store for me.

Three days later, the pains began again. The first came early morning, mild to start with, and I decided to bake some bread to take my mind off the coming ordeal. I lit the Aga stove, stoking it with lumps of hardwood, and began making dough. Ellin joined me in the kitchen, having spent the last three nights in the lean-to, her support for me seemed total. We spent the morning laughing and joking, but I could not stem the worrying thoughts.

'Are you angry with that dough?' said Ellin. 'Only you're going to knead the life out of it pretty soon, tidda.'

I realised I was thinking about Lachlan. He was a puzzle, a changed man since hearing of a child. His mood around me was always now bright, and I saw in him a glimmer of goodness, a side of him previously locked behind the dark and moody façade. When he walked into the kitchen from the yard, he looked almost childlike. I reflected on Lou, he had a similar sparkle in his eyes that brought out the boy in him.

'Should you be doing that?'

'What, baking bread? I'm not an invalid, Lachlan.'

'No, but...'

He loitered through the morning, trying to make himself busy with trivial things, mumbling to himself incoherently, and rubbing his head like he had a migraine. Eventually, Ellin had had enough of his pacing back and forth from room to room, as if he was expecting something to happen at any moment.

'Time for you to run along, Lock. Can't have you hanging around here like you've lost your bottle of beer. This is women's business, and you ain't no woman, last time I looked. Scoot,' she said, ushering him to the door, shooing him now, as if he was being sent out to play. Lachlan took a bottle of whiskey from the kitchen cupboard. 'I'll send for you when it's done,' said Ellin, eager for him to leave.

Lachlan paused at the threshold. 'I'll... Well then... Right, I'll be off then.' One last anxious glance and the screen door slammed shut. Ellin turned to me and smiled.

'I think he's pooping his pants,' she said, and we both burst out laughing. But we knew Lachlan was a bubble waiting to explode, and if it did, it would do so with devastating force.

By late afternoon, the pains were more frequent. Ellin had only just urged me to lie down when my water broke.

'Don't look so terrified.' She laughed. 'It's supposed to happen.'

'I thought I peed myself.' I looked down at the puddle with disgust.

'All it means is that you're close now and the baby is on its way. Now you go lie down and make yourself comfortable while I clean up here.'

'Comfortable? You are joking?'

I lay on the bed as instructed, staring at the ceiling fan, watching the blades endless sweep. It had a calming effect, like the sound of crickets on a warm summer night. The sun had dipped below the horizon and with it any hope of a timely delivery. Ellin's soft voice helped soothe my fears as she reeled off a litany of stories meant to distract me. Time passed, the pain level increased, yet still I had no urge to push.

'Something's not right,' I said. 'A mother knows these things.'

'Oh, so now you're the voice of experience? *A mother knows*. Maybe next time you can talk with authority, until then let Ellin do the worrying.'

'Something's wrong, I know it. It's been hours.'

'Nonsense, tidda, nothing's wrong. Some littl'uns come into the world like they can't wait to be here, others take their time like your baby. I tell you, I might be a bit shy too if I knew what I was in for.'

The night passed in a hazy, dreamlike state. My bedroom became a surreal world of shadows and sounds. I existed between sleep and consciousness, dozing into a half-sleep and then waking abruptly in pain. The ceiling fan with its endless beat, hypnotic in its rhythm, seemed to count the minutes with no end in sight. Ellin talked a stream of background chatter that made no sense at all. The pains came and went. Sometimes unbearable, sometimes it seemed as if they were hardly pains at all, and that I might have to wait another day. Through the window, I saw the sky take on the early glow of daylight, and I wished for my ordeal to be over.

'Oooh, that was a big one,' I said, suddenly feeling the urge to push.

Ellin made ready by placing a cooking pot on the dresser and setting a tiny fire in it, using dried grasses and eucalyptus leaves. Smoke filled the room with a thin blue haze.

'What's that for?'

'Oh, I'm just going to cook you up some breakfast.'

I must have looked horrified.

' *I'm kidding, tidda* . It will help ease the pain and encourage the baby to come quicker. My mother burned them for me just like I'm doing for you. Women's business is passed down from generations, from the old people and elders. In the old days in my mob, we'd go away from the men, give birth on country in a specially made humpy.'

I screamed in pain during a prolonged contraction, and Ellin said it was time.

'You going to lay there with your legs in the air like a dead wombat?' She wiped the sweat from my face. 'White women always want to be on their backs. It'll be easier if you get on your knees and hold the bed head, tidda.'

I followed Ellin's instructions and prepared to push. She started to sing and I found the sound soothing. 'What does it mean?'

'It means we welcome the child to country, and we promise to keep the baby safe and acknowledge its place in the world. Do you have a favourite tree, tidda?'

'A favourite what?'

'Tree! You know, big trunk, branches, leaves.'

'Yes, I know what a... Oooh,' I groaned.

'We need to bury the baby's puru.'

'I don't understand.'

'Puru, afterbirth. We need to bury it. It's important for the child's life journey. Pick a favourite tree or plant and I'll bury it near the roots.'

I told Ellin of Mr Churchill, on the banks of Cutaway Creek. 'Mr Churchill's like family,' I said, with a grimace.

'Grandma said we should smoke you after we done, cover the baby in goanna fat and ashes. I laughed and said, "Grandma, they don't do things like that anymore, not with no whitefellas anyway." But maybe we give you a little bit of smoking to keep you both healthy and encourage your milk, what do you think?'

'I think it's coming.'

I stared at the crucifix hanging above my bed, and I wondered if God was watching, if He cared. I prayed for a safe delivery and followed the impulse to push. I could hardly bear the agony now. My teeth threatened to shatter as I ground out the pain, my jaw set rigid at the effort. Sweat seeped into my eyes, making them sting, and dripped off my nose like a tap. I screamed, a guttural howl from somewhere deep inside. Heard myself squeal like a slaughtered sow. I thought I would tear apart, the pain was so great.

'Push.'

'*Aargh*. I can't do this, Ellin.'

'You can. Push now. You can do it. Push.'

'What do you think I'm doing?' I pushed through the searing pain. Short breaths followed by intense effort, my knuckles white on the bed frame. 'Please,' I said between bursts of agony. 'I can't do this. I can't.'

'You can. You are. I see the baby's head. Come on, tidda, push, push some more now.'

I shrieked like the devil as, with one almighty heave, the baby slid from my body into Ellin's waiting hands.

'Oh, my goodness, it's a boy, Katherine. You have a beautiful white boy.'

The word 'white' was not lost on me, though when I looked, he appeared more red than white. Exhausted, I slumped to the mattress. It's hard to describe the feeling, the relief, the joy, the overwhelming sense of completeness when I cradled him in my arms. He opened his lungs in a high-pitched wail, and I laughed at the strength of his voice.

'Did you hear him cry, Ellin? He's so strong. You're so strong, yes.' He crinkled his nose, making me giggle. 'He's the colour of the outback. I'm going to call him Kooper, like your word for red earth.'

My joy was short-lived. The pain returned, filling me with terror.

'Breathe deep, tidda.'

'Ellin, what is it? Somethings wrong, something's wrong!'

'There you go again with your, *something's wrong*. I swear... It's just the puru still inside you, don't be concerned, you'll upset the baby. Give me one last push and it will all be over. Come on now, let's get this finished so you can relax.'

Three more times I heaved until I felt the release of pressure, my body purged, and a sudden end to the pain. I gasped and laughed, relieved at last. 'I thought for a...' My heart sank. 'What! Ellin, what is it?'

Then I heard it, the faintest whimper. I strained to listen, confused. Then another whimper, a cry. I looked. A second little boy, not even half the size of his older brother. Feeble and weak, like he was hardly a baby at all. Through the howls of my first son, demanding my attention, all I could do was focus on the boy in Ellin's arms. She brought him slowly to me, to lay alongside his brother.

'Oh, tidda, we got a lot of trouble now, darlin'.'

Stunned, my heart twisted. Two babies: one white and robust, the other like ebony, barely strong enough to live. If God had answered my prayers, He had done so with such cruel humour.

'Lachlan! If he sees the baby, he'll... Ellin, what will I do?'

I must have sounded hysterical because Ellin fixed me with a stare and told me to get a grip. 'We have to think,' she said, 'and it won't help if you're going to carry on like a cackling kookaburra. We got no time for fussing now, so let me work.'

Ellin cut the cords and quickly cleaned the babies of blood. She gathered the afterbirth and put it into a bowl, then pulled the bloodied sheets into a bundle on the floor.

'Ellin, the baby's not breathing.'

'He's breathing,' she said, 'just very weak. Here, let me take him.'

Ellin took my son and swaddled him in a blanket. My first-born stopped crying, gurgled and opened his eyes. 'It's okay, Mummy's here.'

'Katherine, this little one is so weak. I don't think he'll make it. I'm no doctor, but I've seen stronger mites go back.'

'Go back?'

'I think he might die, tidda.'

'He'll be alright. I know he will.'

'Think about this for a minute,' Ellin said, cradling the infant. 'Lock will come home soon. He'll realise what's going on as soon as he sees this babe. Then there'll be hell to pay.' She hesitated. 'There's an opportunity to make this right before Lock finds out.'

'I don't understand. What do you mean?'

'I mean, let this little one go.'

I could barely contain a scream. 'My God! What are you saying? Never! Never!' I started to climb from my bed. 'Give him to me, Ellin. Give him.'

Ellin stepped back. 'Katherine, please, consider them both. This little mite got barely a pulse. He's not going to make it through the day. If he's gone before Lock comes home, he'll be none the wiser.'

'I won't hear of it.'

'I'm not saying to do him harm, tidda. I'm saying let me take him away until we know he'll survive. There are healers, Ngangkari women who can care for him.'

'You already told me about Ngangkari women, and I won't have my baby killed.'

'It's not like that, tidda. They're healers. They can save him. If he pulls through, you can decide what to do, we'll face it together when you're stronger. If he don't make it, Lock will never know a thing about it, and you and your white baby will be safe to do what you want.'

'But I can't just let him go away. I... I don't know what to do.'

I thought of Lachlan, his reaction. If I did as Ellin said and let her take the baby, I could go to him later with Lou, then we would leave with both our sons, and Lachlan wouldn't have a chance to stop us. But what if the baby died and I wasn't there with him? I was confused, terrified.

'We don't have much time, tidda, for you or the babies. Let me take him away before Lock comes, please. It will give us time to think. It's only for a while.'

Desperate to do what was right, I nodded my agreement.

'We must do right for both children,' said Ellin. 'Things will work out, you'll see.'

'Take him.'

I couldn't look as she rushed from the room, her hurried steps across the wooden floor, the slam of the screen door as she fled to the yard, but she had only just made it off the verandah when Lachlan appeared.

Chapter 21

Gun-Markara

Lock, wait. It's not what you think,' Ellin said, loud enough to warn me.

I struggled from the bed, leaving my son in his cradle where I thought he'd be safe, and staggered through the house to the yard, my legs like lead, my head dizzy with fear. Ellin held my baby tight against her body, a protective embrace to shield him from Lachlan, who stood ten feet away, motionless.

I arrived at the door, slamming it back on its hinges so that Lachlan turned at the sound. 'Lachlan, let me explain.'

He looked puzzled by the unfolding scene, his head snapping back and forth between me and Ellin. He held out a hand for me to stay put, and stepped cautiously towards Ellin, afraid of what he might see perhaps. Ellin flinched as he took the edge of the blanket and peeled it back slowly. I waited for him to erupt, but he didn't. Instead, he paused a long moment, turned and walked calmly to the barn.

'Lachlan,' I croaked after him.

The barn doors clattered against the siding as he disappeared and I imagined him heartbroken inside. But I felt relieved. It was done. No tantrums, no yelling and screaming. He had turned his back on me, unable to confront the truth. He wanted no part of me. I would leave with Lou and both my sons and he'd be glad to see my back. We should go quickly, I thought, before he had time to think about it. I almost smiled. Moments later, Ellin screamed. Lachlan had returned with a rifle.

'Put the baby on the ground, Ellin.' Lachlan raised the gun and engaged the magazine. Ellin shook her head. Defiant. 'Lay the baby on the ground, or I'll shoot you too, you know I will,' Lachlan said with chilling calm.

'Don't! Lachlan, please, put the gun away, it's me you're angry with.'

To know the terror I felt at that moment is to know what it's like to face losing a child – there is no greater fear. I would gladly have given my life for his.

'Go back inside, Katherine,' Lachlan said, circling Ellin until he stood between us. *'I said go inside .'* His eyes fixed on Ellin.

Lou must have heard the commotion and came running. Lachlan fired into the air, bringing him to an abrupt halt. I heard myself shriek.

'Everyone stay where you are.' Lachlan fired again.

Lou raised his hands. 'What's going on, Lockie? Don't want no one to get hurt now, do we?'

'Is it yours?' said Lachlan. 'Is the kid yours, Lou?' Lou didn't respond. He looked to me, then back to Lachlan. 'I said, is it yours?'

'We can talk about this if you'll just put the gun down,' said Lou.

'Only one way this is going to end, Lou, and it's not with talking.'

A cry came from the bedroom. Lachlan looked puzzled and so did Lou. He took a step forward, causing Lachlan to shoot at the ground.

Another cry from the bedroom. I turned and ran, ignored the bedroom and rushed to the kitchen, where I grabbed my rifle and raced back to the yard, emerging with the gun cocked and ready to fire.

'Stop! Drop the gun, Lachlan, please.' I wept aloud now. 'I'm sorry,' I pleaded. 'I'm sorry for everything.'

'Sorry?' said Lachlan. 'You're sorry?' He shook his head slowly, keeping the rifle braced against his shoulder and wavering it between Ellin and Lou. 'I thought it was too good to be true. All I ever wanted was a son. More fool me for thinking you had given me one.'

'There is a son, Lachlan. Inside, you *have* a son,' I sobbed, desperate to bring him to his senses. I would say anything now to save my children. Kooper cried out again.

'What are you saying, Katherine?' Lachlan looked totally confused now. His lip quivered and a tear swelled in his eye.

'You have a son,' I whispered, my voice cracking. 'Please, Lachlan, please don't do this.'

'A son?'

'I'll explain if you'll put down the gun.'

He seemed incapable of rationalising, his face contorting through a range of emotions. Two births – was his mind playing tricks on him? For a moment I thought he would crumble, that he would relent and listen, but it wasn't to be.

'You're trying to fool me. I don't know what's going on, but it won't work.' Anger replaced that brief display of confusion and weakness, and I saw the man I recognised behind the trigger, the one I knew and feared. 'Is this your child? Yes or no, Katherine? Yes, or no?'

I hesitated. 'Yes,' I whispered. 'But—'

'I knew it.'

'I can't change what's happened, Lachlan. I've betrayed you, I know that, but what's done is done and I can't—'

'Oh, we're not done by a long shot.'

Lachlan swivelled quickly. I fired. There was a moment when nothing seemed to happen. He looked surprised, and I half-expected him to charge across the yard and knock me to the ground in anger. But he didn't. Instead he dropped slowly to his knees. The firearm slipped through his hands, coming to rest in the dirt, blood spreading across his chest like a blossoming flower. He died on his haunches.

We all stood motionless, the acrid smell of gunpowder burning my nostrils, a wisp of smoke dissipating slowly in the thin morning air, the echo of the gunshot ringing in my ears, then the silence, more deafening. Eventually, Lou approached Lachlan and checked for life. He shook his head.

'I couldn't let him do it, Lou. He would have...'

Lou came to me and removed the rifle from my trembling hands. I heard Kooper crying in the bedroom, turned, and walked inside. I was in shock. Ellin had Kooper's little brother in her arms, yet I never gave him a thought. He was suddenly invisible to me. Perhaps I had already given him up for dead, or I didn't want to face more heartache when he did die. Maybe I was simply too overwhelmed by the terrible sequence of events to think rationally. I don't really know why I ignored my child and left him with Ellin.

I heard Ellin and Lou in the parlour; sometimes their voices were raised, sometimes they whispered. They were joined shortly by Ellin's cousin Mary, who sounded almost hysterical, arguing with Ellin, though I could make out little of their exchange. I sang Kooper a little rhyme to drown out the conversation, rocking him, swaddled tightly in blankets, not giving a thought for Lachlan lying outside in a pool of blood. In those moments I believed I could shut out everything, that somehow if I didn't let the thoughts persist, then none of it was real.

At length, Ellin and Lou came to the bedroom. Mary had left with Kooper's brother.

'Lou is going to drive to town and hand himself into the police,' Ellin said. I didn't answer. 'Katherine, are you listening?'

I smiled. 'Yes,' I said. 'I'm fine.'

Lou and Ellin exchanged a worried glance. 'It was self-defence, we all saw it,' she continued. 'Lock came home drunk to find he was the father of a newborn son. But whiskey had soured his brain, he became agitated, said he no longer wanted a child. He was abusive, cursing and threatening the baby. Everyone knows he can get like that.'

Lou stood in silence, watching me, waiting for a response.

'You told him that you would not stay in the same house if he didn't calm down,' Ellin went on, 'and when he became even angrier, you took the baby and fled to the yard.'

I ignored Ellin's story, rocking Kooper and cooing at his tiny face. 'Did you see him look at me just then? I think he knows I'm here, knows I'm his mummy,' I said, smiling. But the trauma was building inside me.

'Katherine, do you understand what I'm saying?' I didn't answer. 'Lock followed you to the yard,' she continued. 'He had his gun and threatened to kill you and the baby. He was drunk and pointed the rifle and started to shoot, luckily missing you both because he was so out of it. Lou came running. He had been shooting rabbits in the paddock and heard the commotion. When he saw Lock aim again, he shot him in your defence.'

They stood in silence and waited.

'Katherine, do you hear me?'

'But why...?'

Ellin approached the bed and sat beside me. 'You do understand, don't you? We have to make this believable for all our sakes. Lock was going to kill your son.'

Dazed, I shook my head. 'No. What are you saying? Lachlan wouldn't shoot my baby, ask him.'

Ellin placed an arm around my shoulder, pulling me in tight. I started to shake violently. 'Lock's dead, tidda, not nothing going to bring him back.'

My eyes filled until I could no longer see. 'No, I don't want him to be.'

Ellin hugged me. 'Darlin' Katherine, none of us want this to be, but it is, and there's nothing we can do but to make sure you and your children are safe.'

I could no longer shut out the vision of Lachlan's face, the blood oozing from the wound in his chest. Anguished sobs emerged from my throat, thumping spasms of grief and despair. 'What have I done, Ellin? Dear Lord, what have I done?'

'You did what you had to, tidda, we know that,' said Ellin eventually. 'Your first boy is white, thank heavens. Everyone will assume that he's Lock's son. If they thought you had Lou's children, they would never believe this was self-defence. They would say you and Lou meant to kill him. It's better if Lou takes the blame and we back him up. It will be more believable.'

'But...' I tried to clear my head and reason, but I couldn't think rationally.

'Shush now, you listen to me. We will both tell the police that Lou killed Lock, but he did it to save you and the baby. Lou wants it that way. Isn't that right, Lou?'

'It's for the best, Kate,' said Lou.

The world passed around me in a blur. I existed in a twilight state of reality, as police officers arrived in numbers to the homestead. I heard voices do battle to be heard, but they were distant and mumbled. Policemen walked the yard, pointing and discussing the scene. The coroner came from Broken Hill and examined Lachlan's body, making meticulous notes as I watched from the window, Kooper cradled in my arms.

Lou returned in the back of a police car. My heart leaped as he stepped out and I saw the handcuffs on his wrists. I felt numb. When Bert Middleton, a detective from Broken Hill, arrived to conduct the investigation, he took Lou by the arm and led him to a spot near the barn. There they stood together, gesticulating, as though they were discussing the chain of events from outside the scene, Lou nodding his head as the policeman asked questions. Then they would move to another location and repeat the process.

I don't know how many times I relived the morning, how many times I saw Lachlan die, but each time was worse than the last. Full of regrets, I dreamed I might wake and find it was a nightmare, to live the day again and stop Lachlan from dying. But I knew the outcome would be the same, I had set the course of events in motion long before that day had started.

I suddenly became aware that someone was speaking. 'Mrs Stuart, did you hear what I said?'

Bert Middleton stood behind me, his voice slowly materialising and bringing me back to the moment.

'I'm sorry?' I said.

'I said, do you feel alright? Would you like a glass of water?'

'No, I'm fine.'

'I need to ask you some questions. Just a few while everything is fresh in your mind, if that's ok?'

'Yes. Please take a seat,' I said, waving an invitation vaguely in no particular direction.

We took a seat in the parlour. Middleton took a pen from his pocket and prepared to write in a notebook. He offered his condolences and added his congratulations on the birth of my son, which seemed odd under the circumstances, a bizarre conflict of concerned expressions. He seemed a kindly type, good-humoured but sensitive to the situation. A round looking man, he had a voluminous walrus moustache that seemed to make up for the lack of hair on his head. I couldn't help noticing the sprouting tufts in his ears, and wondered bizarrely if he ever trimmed them. Such a trivial thought given the gravity of the situation. He interviewed me without pressure, allowing me to relate the story as Ellin had instructed. But my account was hesitant and full of gaps; I couldn't remember all the details and worried about the consequences. Beneath the surface, my heart was breaking and my mind was failing.

'It's okay to be confused,' said Middleton. 'It's understandable given the trauma you've experienced. Maybe you'll remember more clearly later. I'll come back, and we can talk some more.'

I couldn't help thinking that Bert Middleton knew I was lying. He kept glancing at the infant, and I was sure he detected something amiss. He would look into my nervous eyes as I answered his questions, searching for the truth no doubt, and finding my lies. Ellin told her version of events to Middleton at the kitchen table.

'Lock's been acting up over the baby for weeks,' she told him. 'I knew he didn't really want the child. He didn't want the responsibility of a young one, not at his age.'

'And he told you this?'

'Not straight out, but he grumbled about having another mouth to feed, the kid getting in the way and such. I knew from his manner he didn't want it.'

Eventually, Middleton said he had no further questions.

'It's a sorry turn of events,' he said on his way to the door. 'We'll get Mr Stuart back to town now, and you'll hear from us soon. I'm sorry for your loss, Mrs Stuart.'

'What about Lou?' I asked, a little too eagerly.

Middleton's face drew into a squint. 'Let's just see where the investigation takes us shall we?'

'Investigation? But we told you already what happened. It was self-defence.' I looked to Ellin for support, but she looked uneasy and turned away without speaking. 'Lachlan would have killed—'

'That may be, Mrs Stuart, but that's for the courts to decide. It's my job to get to the truth and discover the facts, nothing more.' Seeing my alarm, Middleton added, 'Now I'm not saying you haven't told me everything, but I need to be sure I'm not missing something before I present my case. You'll hear from me after we've had a chance to interview Lou more thoroughly. If there's a case to answer, Lou will be charged accordingly.'

'Charged?'

'Mrs Stuart, your husband is dead. One way or the other, the court will have to decide if the killing was justified.'

Lachlan's body had already been transferred to the coroner's van when Middleton made his way out. Lou sat in the back of a police car. He gave us a wave and a smile before the car pulled away and we watched him disappear from view. We stood on the steps until all we could see was the dust from their tyres, drifting in the air over the horizon.

'Something tells me that detective is going to give us a lot of trouble, tidda.'

Chapter 22

Robin-Kityiri

Mr Churchill towered over us, abnormally large and twisted against the backdrop of azure sky. 'Where?' I asked.

'Anywhere,' said Father Donahue.

I began to dig. The shovel was dull, the earth hard and dry.

'Keep digging,' said the priest.

I toiled at the earth until I had dug a hole deep enough so that the ground was above my head. I looked up at the priest, silhouetted now. 'Who is that beside you?' I asked, squinting against the light.

'This is Mr Black,' said Father Donahue. 'He's come for the bones. Keep digging, girl, or you'll feel the back of my hand, so you will.'

I couldn't see Mr Black's face. He wore a big hat, and the wide brim concealed his features. The sides of the hole were steep and covered in tree roots. Worms, millipedes and spiders squirmed from holes in the earth and dropped to my feet. I started to dig again, but now I was on my knees and using my hands. My fingers grasped the dirt and pulled it aside. I sensed something there in the soil. I clawed frantically at the earth until my fingernails broke and my fingers bled. Eventually I found them, covered in earth. A head, a skull, bones. I lifted them out and looked to the priest.

'Give them to Mr Black now,' said the priest.

I observed my hands and saw my baby laid out on my palms, my second-born son. He was covered in ash, goanna fat and red dirt. I shook my head. 'This is my baby,' I said, laughing. 'I found my baby.'

'Give him here now, Katherine. Give him to Mr Black.'

'NO!' I screamed, but the priest's hand reached down and took him. 'He needs his mummy, he's crying.'

'No, he's not, Katherine. Look, he can't cry anymore. He's just bones.' Father Donahue turned and handed my baby to Mr Black.

I called out, 'My baby!'

I woke to my desperate screams, reaching for a child that was not there. Ellin rushed in to see what was wrong as the nightmare melted.

'You're shaking like a leaf,' she said.

'I need my son.'

'He's right there sleeping. Look.'

'My other son. Where is he?'

Ellin hesitated. 'Now, you don't want to be thinking about that,' she said. 'You need your rest. I'm going to look after you till you're strong, so you stop worrying and fix on getting better.'

I pushed her away. 'I want my son.' Now it was all coming back to me and my insides twisted. I had a second son and I'd let him go. What kind of a mother was I? Why wasn't he with me? 'Ellin?'

Ellin's frown deepened. 'If anyone knew you had Lou's babies, they would say Lock didn't die the way we said he did. You have to forget that child.'

'I don't care what people will say. You took my baby. I want him.'

'So what's brought this on all of a sudden? I thought we agreed.'

'Ellin, I want my baby.'

'And what you going to do when you're in the lock-up and your baby is taken from you, both babies taken away? What you going to do then?'

'Mary took him away. Where?' I asked, determined to get an answer.

'She took him to Aunty Martha.'

'I want to see him.'

Ellin said nothing. After a moment, she rose from the bed and went to the cradle where Kooper lay sleeping. She stood in silence for a moment, then spoke softly. 'I didn't want to tell you, but your baby is gone back, tidda. He passed.'

It took a moment for the words to register. Unable to look at me, Ellin turned away and put her face in her hands. She sighed and turned to speak, but hesitated when she saw my horrified expression.

'You... You knew he was... You knew he was dead but you didn't tell me?'

Ellin returned to my side and pulled me close. She wrapped her arms around me, kissing my forehead, my eyes, my hair. I buried my head in her shoulder, trying to come to terms with the news, the realisation that my baby was gone. I pushed her away.

'Why didn't you tell me?'

'My poor darlin',' she said eventually. 'I wanted to, but you had enough trouble to think about. I didn't want you to know while you was dealing with so much already.'

'You let him die without giving me a chance...'

'He was too weak to survive, tidda, you saw that. There wasn't a chance, *he* didn't have a chance. Aunty Martha couldn't save him, no one could. He's with the Dreaming now. Aunty Martha and Mary, they taking care of the sorry business, so you don't have to worry, just get strong and know he's in good hands.'

'I need to see him,' I said flatly.

'You know that's not possible, tidda.'

'I don't care what's possible, I want to see him.'

'See that little boy over there sleeping? See him? He's going to need a mama that boy. He's going to need all your strength and attention. It's going to do him no good if his mama is in prison, so you got to focus on that, give him all your love and get through this for him.' Ellin paused. 'Listen, I don't much believe in a Christian god, tidda, but maybe this is his way of making sure you and at least one of your babies survive this terrible time. You don't want him taken by the authority like the other half-castes do you? Like my children? That's what will happen if anyone finds the truth.'

Ellin's words were meant to console me. I was expected to find comfort in God's ways, but I hated Him. I hated myself for letting my son go. I'd messed up everything because of my own selfish ways. My chest tightened, my stomach sickened. I couldn't take any more. Then, as if my soul had finally surrendered, broken and desperate, a primal howl emerged from my throat, a wail of anguish, darkly mournful and wretched in my despair. Inconsolable, I purged myself of all the pent-up feelings. Every tear not shed through childhood, every scream of pain bottled up inside, now let loose, my soul exposed and bleeding. I don't know how long my outpouring of grief lasted. By the time I had finished, cradled in Ellin's arms, I had nothing more to give. My baby was gone.

'How can this empty feeling be so heavy?'

'I don't know, tidda, but it is. It's like there's a space that's filled with so much grief, it weighs more than anything one person should ever have to carry, especially one so young.'

'I don't know what to call him,' I said eventually. 'I didn't have a chance to name him.'

'You can still give him a name, tidda. Everyone needs a name, even in the Dreaming.'

'He was here and gone so quickly.' A wave of fear swept over me. 'I don't see his face. Ellin, I can't remember.' I desperately searched for an image, panicked by the thought.

Ellin held me tight to her breast. 'Shush now. Take a breath, and you'll remember. Close your eyes. Now, see his sweet little face and button nose, those dark little eyes? It's there if you try. You can remember, can't you?'

'I see him,' I said at last. 'My tiny bird, fallen from the nest, too weak to fly.'

'You fix that picture in your head and never let it go. What you going to call him?'

I thought for a minute, looking through my memories for inspiration. 'When I was little,' I said, 'we had to move out of the old convent and into a big house nearby, while repairs were carried out to the damaged building. The house stood alone in the street, everything else had been demolished. There were few trees, and even the birds had left the neighbourhood. We had a crab-apple in the backyard. It blossomed in spring, attracting a tiny bird to its boughs. I thought it was injured at first because it had red all down its breast. I remember running to Sister Josephine for help.

'"Don't be concerned, child, he's in good health," she told me. We watched the bird flit from branch to branch. "The red colour is just his breast feathers," she said. "Some say he was a brown bird until he touched the blood of Christ while trying to pluck a thorn from His crown on the cross, and it turned his feathers red forever." I thought it was wonderful that a bird so little could be so brave. Sister Josephine called it a robin and said its appearance was a sign of rebirth. Do you think my baby was brave, Ellin?'

'I know he was, tidda.'

'Then I'll call him Robin.'

'I like that,' said Ellin. 'Robin sounds like a good name.'

Chapter 23

Imprison-Nhapa

To my horror, Lou was remanded to stand trial for murder. His lawyer, Mr Tupper, an educated young man from Melbourne, insisted that charges would quickly be reduced to manslaughter, and on the basis of our eyewitness testimony, Lou would be exonerated on the grounds of self-defence.

'It's all for show,' said Tupper. 'They need to go through the motions so they can be seen to carry out justice. No need to worry, they'll never convict him of murder.'

Easy for him to say, but we put our faith in him and trusted that he knew best. Lou had been in lock-up for two months when I finally saw him. Against Ellin's advice, I visited him in the Wilcannia gaol where he had been held since his arrest. I found the prison a dismal place, but Lou appeared in good spirits.

We settled into awkward conversation, aware that someone might be listening. Eventually, I plucked up the courage to tell Lou we had lost our little child.

'I'm so sorry, Kate.'

'I wanted to tell you sooner, but Ellin said it was dangerous to come here.'

'It would have been wiser to stay away.' Lou took time to comfort me over the baby, telling me to be strong, to have faith. 'Don't think of him as gone forever.'

'What do you mean? He's dead. How can I think of him any other way?'

'He's in the Dreaming, Kate, still with us really.'

'I'd like to think that's true.'

'It is, Kate. Our loved ones live on in the Dreaming, even in death. It's like they're still alive, but they're in a place we can't see. Like they've gone away to a different town. We can't see them, but we know they're there and may come back one day. We still grieve our loss, carry on the sorry business and share the loss with others, but our mob believes that their spirits are always with us.'

'Do you believe it, that he's still with us?'

Lou looked hard into my eyes to reassure me. 'You'll see he is. Have faith, Kate,' he said again.

I told Lou the names I had chosen for both our sons, and it made him smile.

'Robin and Kooper,' repeated Lou approvingly. 'Kuparr means red earth in our lingo.'

'I know it does. That's how he looked at first, he was red like the soil at sunset.'

'How about Robin, where'd that name come from?'

I told Lou the story of the bird, and he liked it, said it was fitting. Visiting time disappeared quickly. I had to leave.

'You shouldn't come again,' said Lou.

'Why? I want to come.'

'Because if certain people see you here, they may get the wrong idea.'

'But it's not the wrong idea. I love you.'

Lou sighed, looking over his shoulder in case someone was listening. 'And I love you,' he whispered. 'But we have to stick to the story, and that means you're the boss and I'm the hired help. Nothing more. If they're going to believe us, we can't be seen to be anything else.'

'I know. I'll be careful, but I can't wait for this to be over. Mr Tupper said the trial will be quick.'

'Let's hope so. Promise me you'll play your part and won't say anything silly.'

'I promise.'

Broken Hill courthouse had an impressive two-story façade of stucco bricks and rendered blocks. A long verandah roof, supported by twin wood columns, ran across the entire front of the building, and a line of waiting public stood beneath it out of the sun. I thought the building looked grand and formal. A colourful coat of arms featuring a lion and a unicorn caught my eye above the entrance. The lion looked ferocious and ready to eat the poor unicorn.

People milled about in little groups, laughing and chatting like they had a day at the fair. The air was filled with cigarette smoke and casual banter. I recognised some of the townspeople and some stock workers who acknowledged me with a nod of the head. No one came to speak or offer condolences. Toby had my arm, and I held Kooper close to my chest in a blanket. My arrival attracted the attention of newspaper reporters, most of whom had come from out of town. They hassled me all the way to the courtroom, but Toby kept them from getting too close. He had been quiet since the shooting. Away in the pastures at the time, he knew nothing of the tragedy until two days later. I worried that he would see through my lies – Toby had a way of seeing through anything – but if he suspected foul play he didn't let on. I knew I could count on him regardless, though I felt ashamed having to lie to him. Ellin said it was better for him that he didn't know what really happened.

The main courtroom, a high-ceilinged, open structure, would have been considered substantial if it were not for the number of people packing every inch of available floor space. Court officials tried desperately to maintain order and to supervise seating. An usher led Toby and me to the rear of the courtroom and asked us to be seated. The benches were hard and uncomfortable, built from wood like the pews in church and without any padding. Reporters gathered together, jostling for places in a separate section. They babbled with excitement. Dressed in crumpled suits, with collared shirts and ties, they sweated profusely, even though it was a midwinter day, fanning their faces with notebooks.

When eventually they led Lou into court, I almost cried out to him. He appeared demoralised and wilted. Had guards mistreated him, dishing out their own brand of justice to blackfellas who kill whites? I had heard stories of cruelty and crimes committed against blacks in custody; the thought turned my stomach. Blackfellas were sometimes known to grow desperate in lock-up. They felt terror at being confined and some took their own lives rather than be trapped inside like animals in cages. Lou assured me he didn't fear prison, but I wasn't convinced for a minute. He seemed to have aged in the weeks since my visit to Wilcannia gaol, a shadow of the bright, joyful man he was to me. He appeared startled by the packed courtroom, turning his eyes to the floor as the guard led him handcuffed to the dock. I prayed that his ordeal would soon be over. Journalists scribbled furiously in their notebooks as Lou settled in place.

Mr Tupper wore a black robe and a grey wig that made him look much older than he was. He shuffled papers on a low desk, acknowledging Lou with a brief smile as he waited for the judge to appear. Edward Klein, the barrister leading the prosecution, was portly and bespectacled, with a beard the same silver colour as his somewhat tatty old wig – it looked as though it had been stitched together from dags of wool picked from barbed-wire fences. But I thought he looked kind, like a good-natured Father Christmas. I imagined him at home during the festive season, having a jolly old time with his family, and it made me feel better in some small way. Perhaps, I thought, he would be fair and compassionate. Finally, a harassed-looking clerk asked everyone to stand, and Judge Jerimiah Lawrence entered the room, causing a respectful silence to fall upon the court. He wore a red robe and a wig that appeared quite white. To my dismay, there followed a lengthy period of activity between lawyers and judge, where paperwork was offered, exchanged and entered into evidence. Debates between council were mediated by Judge Lawrence, but it was impossible to hear what was said, and everyone became fidgety and bored by the lack of progress. Mr Tupper referred to the delay as housekeeping, and it lasted for half of the morning.

At last, proceedings commenced. The court clerk called once more for silence, and Judge Lawrence spoke aloud for the first time. I struggled to hear the charges: 'Murder in the first degree'. That's when I almost fainted. My heart raced and I suddenly felt short of breath. Kooper, as though sensing my discomfort, started to niggle. I had been instructed by the bailiff to leave the courtroom if the baby caused any disruption, so I tucked the blanket tightly around his little body to make him feel secure and told myself to be calm. Thankfully Kooper settled and so did I.

Klein rose to his feet, bowed to the judge and took his place before the jury. I had to lean forward to get a better view of the twelve gentlemen jurors, all of whom were white. Ranging in age from what looked like thirty to sixty and older, they appeared a random mix of characters. By their clothes I guessed they were ordinary working men, miners and stockmen, shopkeepers and office workers. Klein steepled his hands, taking his time to begin, as though he were trying to find the right words with which to address the jury. He kept changing his mind as he was about to speak.

'If it please the court,' he said at last. 'Over the course of this trial, I will prove to you fine gentlemen of the jury, that a most heinous crime has been committed. A premeditated, cold-blooded murder, in which the perpetrator was assisted and perhaps even cajoled into its execution. I say execution because that's exactly what Oogoola Holston did when he killed Lachlan Stuart, in front of his own, innocent, newborn child. I will bring before you witnesses to show how this honest, hard-working husband tragically came to lose his life at a time when he thought his lifelong dream of fatherhood had been realised, a time when he thought the world had finally been kind to a true-blue Aussie battler and had given him a good break. For once, in his hard and often sad life, Lachlan Stuart thought he had something to sing about. That song, gentlemen of the jury, turned out to be a funeral dirge.'

Klein turned to look at Lou, then he walked to Tupper's desk, holding his hand to present the defence counsel to the jury. 'Gentlemen of the jury, Mr Tupper here will no doubt have you believe this is an open-and-shut case of self-defence. Nothing could be further from the truth. I will demonstrate how Lachlan Stuart was lured to the yard where his killer waited, armed with the murder weapon, took aim at a standing target and blasted a hole in Lachlan Stuart's heart. Mr Stuart never stood a chance. To a man with shooting skills like Oogoola Holston, it was like shooting fish in a barrel.' Klein paused. 'Gentlemen, I want you to close your eyes for a moment. *Go on, close them.*' The jury complied. 'Now imagine if you will, a man in his late forties, a man who had come to believe he would never be a father, suddenly blessed with the son for which he so desperately longed, a son to continue his legacy and that of his forebears. Imagine the joy he must have been feeling on that day when he heard his baby cry for the first time. New life. His son's new life. Now imagine his final moments after the bullet tore open his chest, blood draining the life from his body. He crumbles to the ground within eyesight of his newborn son, he holds out a hand to reach him, but he can't because he's dying. It's the last thing he sees, gentlemen of the jury, the very last thing before his eyes close and he dies, dies without even the chance to touch his precious new son.'

Klein allowed the statement to hang in the air. I felt dizzy. I saw again Lachlan's face, the look of confusion, the resignation as he fell to his knees, the blood as it spread through the fabric of his shirt. But it was not Lou who looked on holding the gun; it was me. I felt the heavy burden of guilt. I wanted to jump up and defend Lou, felt the urge to confess the truth before there could be any more lies.

'As for motive,' Klein continued, snapping me back to the moment. 'I'm sure Mr Tupper will deny the existence. But I will provide testimony that proves not only motive, but that Holston and the, *so-called,* defence witnesses, conspired to kill Mr Stuart. Each had their own motive for wanting him dead, none more potent than the illicit love shared by Holston and Katherine Stuart, the victim's wife.'

My blood ran cold. *Illicit love shared by...* My chest heaved, short of breath, my stomach rolled. Klein knew! How could he know? Several jurors were shaking their heads and frowning, clearly disgusted by the accusation. They looked at me with contempt.

'Think again, gentlemen, of those final moments.' Klein's words echoed in my head. 'Don't let them out of your mind during this trial. Think of Lachlan Stuart reaching out for his son, seeing him in the arms of his mother. It should have been a happy sight. But what he saw instead, was Katherine Stuart standing beside her lover, the man who fired the fatal shot. Were they smiling as Lachlan closed his eyes and died? We will never know for sure.'

Klein returned to his seat, his final words lingering in the silence as all eyes turned to me. It was all I could do not to jump up and say what really happened. I killed Lachlan, yes, but how could he say that I smiled, how could he think that I planned it? I felt sick.

When silence finally broke, whispers rippled through the courtroom. Judge Lawrence looked over his glasses from the bench, owl-like and stern, waiting for Mr Tupper's response. I glanced at Lou. He stared at the floor.

Tupper took his time getting to his feet. He approached the jury, stopped, scratched his head, then returned to his desk and sat down. Someone coughed in the gallery. Everyone waited.

'Mr Tupper?' Judge Lawrence queried.

'I'm sorry, your honour,' Tupper said. 'I was just preparing to write Mr Holston's obituary. Mr Klein has painted such a tragic picture of Lachlan Stuart's last moments that I feel compelled to weep. It's like one of those Doris Day motion pictures. How can I compete with that? He has my client already convicted and hanged from the gallows.'

I turned to Toby horrified. 'They're going to hang him?'

Everyone watched the judge and waited for his response. Judge Lawrence shook his head wearily.

'As everyone knows, we no longer hang people in New South Wales, Mr Tupper, and we have not done so since 1939. Now, enough of the theatrics. Get on with it, please.'

I exhaled, relieved. Toby squeezed my hand.

Tupper smirked, took to the floor at the judge's invitation and sauntered into the centre of the courtroom, where he waved his hands dramatically, as though he were conjuring something from the air. 'Smoke and mirrors,' he said, smiling. 'Smoke and mirrors. That's what Mr Klein is doing by having you focus on the infant child. Mr Klein says the child is *innocent*.' Tupper paused for effect, mopping his brow with a handkerchief. 'Well, that's a relief.' He turned to the prosecution's desk. 'Thank you for clearing that up, Mr Klein, for a moment I thought you were going to accuse the child of being an accomplice to his father's murder.'

A ripple of laughter ran through the courtroom. Judge Lawrence called for order. 'Your banter is doing little for your client, Mr Tupper. Move on, please.'

'Gentlemen of the jury,' Tupper continued when the room settled. 'I'll keep this brief because I expect this trial to be brief. We all have homes to go to and better things to do with our time, am I right?' Tupper chuckled, and one or two jurors followed suit, nodding their heads in agreement. 'Oogoola Holston, commonly known to many here simply as Lou, is on trial today because he came to the defence of two vulnerable women and a helpless newborn baby. I do wonder, had he not been of Aboriginal blood, if this case would even have come to trial.'

Klein rose to his feet. 'Objection, your honour. The question of race does not come into this matter.'

'Sustained,' said the judge.

Tupper turned his attention to where I sat cradling Kooper. He waited until all eyes were fixed on me.

'Just like Katherine Stuart's beautiful baby over there, Lou Holston *is* innocent. When faced with the prospect of watching Lachlan Stuart gun down his wife and family, Oogoola's only course of action as a brave and caring human being, was to come between the drunken husband, armed with a rifle, and his desperate wife and baby. Indeed, Mrs Stuart attests to that fact in her eyewitness account of the tragedy. She states clearly that she feared for their lives. She knew what her husband was capable of, and I will provide testimony proving Mr Stuart's propensity to violent behaviour.

'Let me make it clear, gentlemen, no one disputes that Oogoola shot and killed Mr Stuart. What you must do is decide on the justification for such killing. The prosecution must prove beyond any reasonable doubt that Mr Holston not only intended to kill Mr Stuart, but that his actions were not justified. There are two kinds of evidence in a criminal trial. Direct evidence and circumstantial evidence. I am confident that you, as intelligent men, will conclude that the prosecution's case rests solely on circumstantial evidence, the kind that proves absolutely nothing. Furthermore, you will conclude that the evidence to be submitted as motive must be dismissed as hearsay, rumour and innuendo. What is not circumstantial evidence, is the eyewitness testimony of Mrs Stuart and her housekeeper and midwife, Ellin Cobham. They will give *direct* evidence of Mr Oogoola's actions in preventing a double tragedy. If not for those very actions, it would be Lachlan Stuart sitting here in this dock to face justice, instead of an innocent man. Mr Holston's bravery must be celebrated, not demonised.'

Tupper studied the faces of the jurors one by one. 'You would have done the same,' he said. 'You, you, you and you.' Tupper pointed out each juror in turn. 'You would have done the same. Good people do such things when called upon to protect the weak, don't they? Look me in the eye, gentlemen, and tell me you wouldn't have done the same.' Some of the jurors shuffled in their seats as though they found the thought uncomfortable, some nodded in agreement. 'It was the right thing to do, gentlemen, and I say once again, you would have done the same. This case should never have come to trial. A hero does not deserve to have his name dragged through the mud. So now it's your turn to be brave, to do the right thing and put an end to his trauma. Set Mr Holston free where he belongs, so that we might herald him as the hero he undoubtedly is.'

Mr Tupper returned to his seat, and I detected an almost imperceptible smirk cross his face as the judge called a recess. It made him look smug. I hoped that the jury didn't notice.

Chapter 24

Drunkard-Maata

The afternoon session commenced with the prosecution calling their first witness. City Coroner Fred Holloway had the air of a schoolteacher. Heavy, black-rimmed glasses repeatedly slipped to one side on his bulbous nose, and he continually used his forefinger to push them back into place. His thinning hair needed cutting at the collar and his stained and crumpled suit appeared two sizes too big. He took the stand, identified himself as Fredrick Holloway PhD, and swore to the truth on a worn Bible. Mr Klein stood and approached the witness box. He wasted no time in getting right to the point.

'On February thirtieth, 1959, you attended Cutaway Creek Station, at the request of Detective Sergeant Albert Middleton, to examine the body of the deceased Lachlan Stuart. Can you tell us what you found, please?'

Holloway answered confidently, taking time to phrase his observations in simple terms. He had obviously done this many times before. 'I found the deceased in the centre of the yard, slumped to his left side, but not prone completely, as though he was resting on his haunches. His shirt and pants were red with dried blood. The ground around showed signs of blood also, but it had soaked completely into the dirt and dried. Closer examination revealed a single bullet wound to the chest. I later determined that to be the cause of death, the bullet pierced the victim's heart.'

'You conducted an autopsy?'

'I did, sir.'

'And during the autopsy, did you determine that the victim had been drinking?'

'Yes, sir. Blood-alcohol tests showed concentrations of point seven milligrams per one hundred milligrams of blood.'

'And in layman's terms, what does that mean?'

'For a man of his size and weight, I would say he was moderately intoxicated.'

'Moderately?'

'Everyone reacts to alcohol differently. Body mass and gender have a significant role in how intoxicated a person might appear. In this case, I would expect the subject to be a little jolly, no more. He would probably have been able to drive a motor car quite easily, for example, without having an accident.'

Tupper sprang to his feet. 'Objection, your honour. The witness cannot speak as to the victim's state of mind, jolly or angry, or indeed if he was capable of avoiding an accident while driving.'

'Sustained. Keep to the verifiable facts please, Mr Holloway.'

'Yes, your honour.' Holloway removed his glasses and cleaned them with a cotton handkerchief from his pocket.

Klein scratched his beard. 'Then let me put it another way. In your professional opinion, Mr Holloway, taking into consideration, as you said, his body mass and gender, would the victim have been so intoxicated that he would lose all sense of reason and attempt to kill his wife and newborn son?'

'Objection, same question, different phrasing,' said Tupper.

'Sustained. Move on Mr Klein.'

Klein fingered his beard and thought for a long moment. 'One last time, if you'll indulge me, your honour. In your expert opinion, Mr Holloway, again, taking into consideration Mr Stuart's body mass and gender,' he repeated a third time, 'would Mr Stuart have been capable of rational thought?'

'Yes. In my opinion, he would have been capable of reason. It's my considered view that the level of alcohol in the victim's system was not enough so that he didn't know what he was doing.'

'Thank you. So he wasn't blind drunk, just blind to what Lou Holston was about to do to him.' Klein's comment was not a question but a statement.

'Objection!'

'Sustained. The jury will disregard Mr Klein's comments.'

Klein took the witness through various aspects of the autopsy for almost an hour. The tedious details only served to disgust those listening but seemed to have no bearing on the matter of guilt or innocence. 'Did you determine the distance between the shooter and the victim?' Klein asked eventually.

'Yes. I estimated that the shot came from immediately in front of the victim from a range of fifteen feet.' Holloway removed his glasses and cleaned them again.

'Fifteen feet. And after examining the murder weapon, what would you say is the effective range of that weapon?'

'The weapon in question is a bolt-action Marlin M80C. It's an eight-shot repeater and fires Remington .22 calibre rounds of which seven were in the magazine. The fatal round had been fired from the chamber. That model of a rifle has an effective range of about a hundred yards when hunting rabbits.'

'Hunting rabbits?'

'The .22 long rifle is known as the varmint gun.'

'And can you tell me who this rifle belonged to?'

'It belongs to Mrs Stuart.'

Another rumble of low whispers rippled through the court. All heads turned in my direction.

'Mrs Stuart, not Oogoola Holston?'

'No, sir. The gun was registered to Mrs Stuart.'

'And did you examine the rifle found next to the deceased?'

'I did. It was a Remington model 34 long .22 calibre conventional bolt-action, tube fed rifle.'

'So similar to the murder weapon?'

'Objection, your honour. The prosecution keeps referring to the 'murder weapon', when surely that is why we are here, to determine if a murder was committed.'

'Sustained. You will refer to the firearm as the gun that killed Mr Stuart,' Judge Lawrence instructed.

'Very well, your honour. Was the weapon found next to Mr Stuart similar to the gun that killed him?'

'Similar, yes.'

'And had it been fired?'

'Yes. We found three spent cartridges by Mr Stuart's body. We later matched them to his rifle.'

'But no one else was hurt?'

'I'm not aware of anyone.'

'You found no evidence that Mr Stuart had used his rifle to try and kill his wife and child?'

'No, sir.'

'Is it possible someone else fired the weapon, dispensing three cartridges to make it appear Mr Stuart fired the gun?'

'Mr Stuart had gunpowder residue on his hands, but I have no way of telling if this resulted pre or post mortem, staged by someone else, or if he got it from shooting the weapon as described by the witnesses.'

'Thank you, Mr Holloway, I have no more questions.'

Klein took his seat as Mr Tupper approached the witness. Tupper took a few moments to look confused, saying nothing but gesturing like an actor on stage. I could tell by the expressions on jurors' faces that his performance did little to gain their favour. Lou watched him intently and I knew he would be thinking the same, he did not suffer fools easily.

'Would you say the Marlin M80C was an effective weapon of choice for pre-meditated murder, given that, as you said, it's a gun for hunting rabbits?'

'Not particularly, no.'

'And if someone were to attempt such pre-meditated murder with this *rabbit* gun, what in your estimation would be the chances of success?'

'At point-blank range—'

'At fifteen feet,' Tupper interrupted.

'For a long rifle such as this, fifteen feet *is* pretty much point-blank range. To answer your question, better than fifty-fifty.'

'And yet I'm told that many a rabbit, having been shot with a .22 rifle, simply runs away wounded.'

Holloway considered the statement. His lip curled into a slight grin. 'True. But it's that very issue that makes the .22 potentially lethal for a human.'

'How so?'

'Well, the .22 round in question is made of a soft form of lead. A rabbit is tiny and offers little resistance. Because of that, the bullet passes through the flesh without distortion and exits easily. If it doesn't hit any important organs on the way through, the animal is able to run away and usually dies later from infection or blood loss. But when it strikes a man, the effect can be very different. At the velocity in question it would enter the chest cavity, distorting on impact. It would also lose enough momentum needed to exit the chest through the rear wall. Conversely, it would retain enough velocity to ricochet off ribs and other bones around the chest cavity, piercing soft tissue such as the lungs, liver, vital organs and, in this case, the heart. Bigger bullets, such as .380 or larger, are more likely to pass through the body of a man or large animal, causing catastrophic damage to bone, tissue and organs, and leaving an exit wound.' Holloway looked pleased with his explanation.

Tupper took a few moments to consider. 'I take your point, Mr Holloway. But given the fact that there is ready access to a range of weapons at Cutaway Creek, .380 rifles they use for kangaroos, shotguns and even a .44 calibre hand-gun, wouldn't you say that the .22 rabbit gun was a strange choice of weapon if someone planned to murder a large man?'

Holloway conceded. 'I would choose one of the other available weapons if I were going to kill someone, yes.'

'Thank you.' Tupper paced back and forth, making the court wait as he pondered his next question. Judge Lawrence exhaled impatiently. 'Do you take a drink, Mr Holloway?' he asked eventually. 'A whiskey on a Saturday night perhaps?'

'Yes, sir. I like a drink. Fine scotch is my poison, if you're offering.' Everyone chuckled, causing Holloway to look pleased and Tupper to smile.

'And how many glasses of scotch would it take to make you feel drunk?'

'Quite a few, I've been drinking scotch for many years, and I don't mind saying I can hold my liquor.'

'And you're a big man like Mr Stuart, so that would help too, I suppose, adding to your resistance?'

Holloway narrowed his eyes. He knew Tupper was going to make a point, but he wasn't sure what it would be. 'As I said previously, the effects of alcohol on a person varies, depending on body mass, gender, age and even what they have been eating. No two people react in the same way.'

'And if you've "been drinking for years", that affects how much alcohol is in your blood, is that right?'

'No, I didn't say that.' Holloway removed his glasses and cleaned them, a nervous habit. 'It will not change the blood-alcohol level, but how one reacts to the alcohol could differ depending on your usual consumption. Someone who never drinks might have a much bigger reaction than someone who drinks all the time. Regular drinkers build up a tolerance.'

'Regular drinkers, like yourself?'

'Objection! The witness is not on trial here.'

'But the witness's testimony is crucial to someone who is,' Tupper said. 'Mr Holloway has indicated that he is an accomplished drinker. Furthermore, by his statement, he is implying that he and Lachlan Stuart were similar in that regard. By highlighting these facts, the prosecution witness seems to be implying that a regular drinker like Lachlan Stuart could not have been so drunk that he would react violently towards his wife because of it.'

'I'll allow it,' said Judge Lawrence. 'Make your point, Mr Tupper.'

'Have you ever been so drunk that you could not carry out your duties, Mr Holloway, or so drunk you picked a fight with an innocent person?'

'No!'

'And yet you recently did just that at your daughter's wedding, did you not? Drunk to the point where you assaulted the best man's father before passing out unconscious on the floor. How many whiskies did it take, Mr Holloway?'

The court erupted. The judge called for order several times before silence returned.

'Objection, your honour. This is an outrageous invasion of the witness's personal life!'

'What is your point, Mr Tupper?' asked Judge Lawrence.

'My point, your honour, is that just because one is an accomplished drinker, does not mean that one cannot end up drunk and out of control. Even if one is normally a well-respected member of the community like Mr Holloway. I want to ask the witness if he remembers the events of his daughter's wedding, or if he knew what he was doing when he assaulted the other man.'

'I'll allow it. Answer the question, Mr Holloway, please.'

'No,' said Holloway, embarrassed by the revelation.

'No, you don't remember, or no you won't answer the question?'

'No, I don't remember. But it was a celebration, and I hadn't eaten, that's why I ended up out of control. It must have gone straight to my head. I'm not usually like that. Ask anyone. A man's daughter only gets married once.'

Klein placed a hand on his forehead and looked down at his desk, dejected.

'Yes indeed, Mr Holloway,' Tupper continued. 'and there's not a man in this courtroom who doesn't understand the excuse for your uncharacteristic behaviour. You were, after all, celebrating a special day, just like Lachlan Stuart was celebrating the birth of his first child.'

'You've made your point, Mr Tupper, move on,' said the judge.

Tupper bowed to the judge. 'Thank you, your honour. Mr Holloway, from your investigation of the scene and your examination of the deceased, do you have any evidence to suggest that Lachlan Stuart did *not* turn his gun on his wife and son?'

Holloway hesitated, clearly shaken by Tupper's attack. 'No, but—'

'Yes or no will do, Mr Holloway.'

'No direct evidence, no.'

'Did you find any evidence to suggest that Mr Stuart's gun had been fired after his death and not as the witnesses have testified?'

'No.'

'And one final question. From your investigation of the scene and your examination of the deceased, do you have any evidence to suggest that Oogoola Holston did *not* fire his rifle in defence of Mrs Stuart and her newborn son?'

'No, sir.'

'No more questions, your honour.'

Tupper sat. Holloway rose to leave the witness box when Klein stood and halted him with a wave of his hand. 'Before you go, Mr Holloway. Just so there's no misunderstanding. Had you been drinking at any time during your duties regarding this investigation?'

'Absolutely not.'

Chapter 25

Ignorant-Mangu

Judge Lawrence called a recess for the day, and I watched as the court emptied. A police officer led Lou from the dock amid the rush for the exits. I'd been told he would be kept in Broken Hill lock-up now until the trial was over. He caught my eye, smiled and winked as he passed, trying to put on a brave face. I knew he was hurting though. I went to reach out and touch him, but Tupper grabbed my arm, pulled me aside and guided me to a seat where we could talk. Toby took Kooper outside to wait.

'It went well today.'

I had to agree with Mr Tupper, he had done an excellent job in cross-examination, but Mr Klein's opening statement still played on my mind. 'How could he say all those things about us? And how could he imagine that we planned it?'

'It's his job to think that way. He has to prove Lou committed pre-meditated murder, that he intended for Lachlan to die.

How he accomplishes that is all a matter of persuasion. He'll say whatever he can to convince the jury of Lou's guilt. Don't worry, my dear, a verdict of murder is almost impossible with what they've got. It's all circumstantial evidence and I doubt they can prove otherwise. Manslaughter is the most the prosecution can realistically hope for, and even that seems unlikely given the lack of direct evidence. Even if convicted of manslaughter, Lou will face a few short years of incarceration and be out before you can say, Jack Robinson.'

'Jack Robinson?' I couldn't believe his casual attitude. 'I don't know who Jack Robinson is.'

'Just a turn of phrase, my dear.'

'What was all that about conspiring and cajoling Lou into murder?'

'It's a concern. The prosecution must prove motive if they are to convict Lou of murder. By raising the possibility of a secret affair, it not only provides that motive, but destroys your own credibility as a defence witness. After reviewing the statements by prosecution witnesses, I do believe that the prosecutor intends to paint a picture of conspiracy to murder.'

'I don't understand.'

'I'm afraid Mr Klein is going to portray you as the instigator, Mrs Stuart. He's going to show that you conspired with Lou to kill your husband.'

'Conspired?'

'Planned to kill your husband. Klein's a canny bastard,' Tupper said, with a hint of admiration. 'I read his witness statements, and I see that he's going down the same path that I would have gone. He's going to portray you as the scheming young wife, with a young lover at your beck and call, intent on gaining her husband's property, Lou Holston the ready agent to do your dirty work. He's not your lover, is he? That would put a different complexion on things.'

'Of course not,' I said, flushing.

'Good. I wouldn't want to find myself suddenly on the back foot because you withheld vital information.'

I groaned involuntarily.

'Don't worry, I'm one step ahead of Klein, and it could play in our favour; it's all hearsay and innuendo. There is no real evidence for such a plot. It's not like someone overheard you planning your husband's death. Just leave the worrying to me, Mrs Stuart,' said Tupper, unconvincingly.

'The court calls Bertha Barton,' said the bailiff, as the room settled down to silence.

Klein took his place on the floor. 'Mrs Barton, you are employed as an usherette at the Silver City Movie Theatre, is that correct?'

Bertha Barton, a chubby-faced woman in her early forties, pushed her bouffant hair into place as she answered. Her garish floral frock seemed more appropriate to the dancefloor than the witness stand.

'Yes, your grace, that is correct as per your observations.' Bertha Barton obviously thought she should present herself as the professional kind of witness. I wondered if she'd been practising.

'You can address me as "Mr Klein" and Judge Lawrence as "your honour", if you will.'

'Yes, your grace,' said Bertha to a ripple of laughter.

Klein smiled. 'Were you on duty at the theatre between May six and fourteen of last year?'

'I was, yes.'

'Please tell the court in what capacity you were employed that day and what you encountered during the course of your duties.'

Bertha pushed back her shoulders, sitting tall as she spoke. 'The capacity of which I was employed at, was that of issuing tickets for the evening show, a Christopher Lee film called *Dracula*. I was going about my duties when to my observations, I witnessed the accused,' Bertha pointed dramatically across the courtroom to Lou, 'with a young and pretty white girl.' Again, Bertha pointed with a dramatic flourish, this time her finger aimed squarely at me. All heads turned in my direction. 'They tried to buy tickets with the intent of entering the theatre together to watch the film, *Dracula*.'

'And what did you think?'

'Oh, it was very frightening,' said Bertha with an exaggerated shiver.

Klein looked confused. 'Frightening? Oogoola Holston and his companion frightened you?'

'No, not them, that *Dracula* film. It was frightening. That's why everyone wanted to see it. Christopher Lee plays that part so well, you'd think it was all real. Him being a vampire I mean.'

The courtroom erupted in laughter. Bertha looked confused and embarrassed. After the judge called for silence, the room settled once more.

'I meant, what did you think when it appeared these two young people wanted to enter the theatre together?' Klein asked.

Self-conscious of the snickering, Bertha dropped the police notebook tone of her testimony and reverted to her usual way of speaking. 'I told them they couldn't. I said they could watch the film, but the black boy had to sit down the front with the rest of the blackfellas.'

'And did they respond?'

'Yes, sir. The girl argued, said it wasn't right and that they were going to sit together whether I liked it or not. I said no they weren't and she gave me a mouthful she did.'

'What exactly did she say?'

'She called me a stupid fat cow,'– ripples of laughter – 'and said he had more right than me to see a film on his own country.'

'And by that, she meant that as an Aborigine he had more rights than whites to watch the film?'

'Objection! The witness cannot speak as to what the girl meant to imply.'

'Sustained.'

'What happened next?' said Klein.

'I said, right then, no one's coming in, and shut my trap.' Everyone in the courtroom giggled. 'I mean, I shut my window so they couldn't get tickets. I watched them walk away, and the blackfella put his arm around her like they was lovers.'

'Objection!'

'No more questions, your honour.'

Tupper rose to his feet. 'Is it common practice for you to refuse entry to blacks, Mrs Barton?'

'Sometimes, not always. If they come drunk, I do.'

'And was the defendant drunk on the evening in question?'

'No, I don't think so. But he was abusive.'

'Abusive? What did he say?'

Bertha hesitated. 'Well, it wasn't him so much as her, she did the talking, and he was with her.'

'So he wasn't abusive?'

Bertha squirmed. 'No.' She paused to think. 'But they wanted to sit together so they could kiss and cuddle. I wasn't having that, not in my cinema, not black and white.'

'Are you referring to the movie, Mrs Barton? That too was black and white.' A ripple of laughter. 'Did either the defendant or his companion, Mrs Stuart, tell you they intended to kiss and cuddle?'

'No, but I can pick 'em out straight away. We get plenty of young courting couples come to the evening shows and spend the whole time stuck to each other's mouths like leeches in the dark. I don't mind that so much, but never mixed race, we don't allow that. All the good blackfellas know they should sit down the front, and if they want to hold hands with another black girl, then that's okay. As long as they don't go getting too frisky,' Bertha added. 'I make sure I keep an eye on them.'

'So, "the good blackfellas" do as they're told, do they?'

'Usually, yes. But you've got to watch them all.'

'Have you ever refused entry to whites at your theatre?'

'No. Whites aren't a problem.'

'But blacks are?'

'Sometimes,' Bertha said, sheepishly.

'You don't particularly like blackfellas do you, Mrs Barton?'

'As long as they keep to their own, I don't have a problem.'

'Is that why you decided to come forward with your make-believe story, because a blackfella had the gall to be seen with a white woman, even if they were doing something as innocuous as going to see a motion picture?'

'It's not make-believe. It happened.'

'Mrs Stuart came to the theatre in Silverton, accompanied by a trusted employee, so that she could reward his good work with a ticket to see a film at your picture house. It was a treat for the young man. I put it to you that at no time did they ask to be seated together, that at no time did they give you any indication that they wanted anything more than tickets to the show. Furthermore, I suggest that you took it on yourself to assume they were lovers and refused them entry even before they could make their intentions known. Is that not true, Mrs Barton? In fact, you appointed yourself as the Gestapo!'

'Objection!'

Before Bertha could answer, Tupper continued his aggressive approach. 'Are you not a bigoted woman who thinks she is the law when it comes to the Silver City Theatre? You play God when it comes to who might gain entry, am I right?' Bertha mumbled. 'I put it to you, Mrs Barton,' Tupper continued, 'that you refused Mrs Stuart and her employee entry on the basis of your own prejudice, and not content with that, when you heard of the case against this young man, you fabricated a story to further punish him for having the audacity to enter your domain and expect entry.'

'Objection, your honour, Mr Tupper is badgering the witness.'

'Sustained. Do you have any more questions, Mr Tupper?'

Chapter 26

Policeman-Muni-Muni

I didn't hear the next three witnesses give evidence. I found it impossible to keep Kooper in court without disturbing proceedings. He was unsettled. He kept wriggling and crying out just as someone would start to speak. I walked the pavements outside, strolling back and forth up the main street, stewing on Bertha Barton's testimony and wishing I'd punched her on the nose that night at the theatre. Klein followed Barton with others who had seen Lou and me together, each implying a closer than appropriate relationship. The most damning evidence came from Dmitry Anastas who claimed to have caught Lou and I cuddling in a parked car at the side of the road only weeks before the killing. Tupper cross-examined but failed to put a dent in Anastas' testimony.

Toby took Kooper while I returned to court as Bert Middleton took the stand; the last witness for the day. He retold events in his usual methodical way. As a veteran police officer, he had made notes on everything and left nothing to chance.

'Detective Middleton, how did Oogoola Holston appear when you first met him at the police station in Wilcannia? What was his demeanour?' asked Klein.

'He was calm, almost matter of fact.'

'No panic?'

'No, sir.'

'And can you please tell the court what Mr Holston said when he turned himself in?'

'It's all in the case notes. He told the desk sergeant he had killed Lachlan Stuart, and he wanted to give himself up.'

'You arrived on the scene when?'

'The sergeant at Wilcannia called Broken Hill, and I was assigned the investigation immediately. It was probably two to three hours after Holston came into Wilcannia that I got to interview him.'

'So, taking into account Mr Holston's journey to Wilcannia from the homestead, you spoke to him four or five hours after the killing?'

'That's correct.'

'And what did Mr Holston tell you?'

'He said he had shot Mr Stuart. He said Stuart was drunk and had threatened to kill his wife and son. He said Stuart fired wildly, missing everyone with his first three rounds, but that he couldn't take a chance on him getting lucky with his next shot, so he, Lou Holston, fired first and killed him.'

'And did Holston say he intended to kill Mr Stuart?'

'No, sir, he said he intended to stop him by whatever means.'

'And by whatever means meant a single, well-aimed bullet to the heart, is that correct?'

'I believe that's what killed him, yes. Lou Holston surrendered the gun to the desk sergeant and told him it was what he had used. He had been shooting rabbits in the paddock when he heard the commotion and came running with the gun still in his hands.'

'A fully loaded gun?'

'Correct.'

Klein stroked his beard between his forefinger and thumb, a tendency he had between questions. 'Did you ascertain the time of the shooting?'

'Yes, sir, it's in the report. According to the eyewitness accounts, Mr Stuart died at approximately 11.45 in the morning.'

I recalled the scene as Middleton gave his account, daylight barely having broken the horizon when Lachlan fell. Lou decided we should adjust the time to avoid having to explain the delay in going for help.

'By eyewitness accounts, you mean Mrs Stuart, Ellin Cobham and Oogoola Holston?'

'Correct.'

'Isn't 11.45 an unusual time to be hunting rabbits?'

Middleton didn't answer straight away. He frowned. 'Yes, it is. It's more normal to go out after sunset when they're active. The way rabbits have been this year, they're out in their hundreds at night, and you could expect to shoot to your heart's content.'

'Did Holston say why he was out hunting rabbits in the midday sun, and why he was using Mrs Stuart's gun?'

'Yes, sir. He said the rabbits had just got so brazen, like they were taunting station owners to come get them. He said Mrs Stuart's gun was just one of many they might use for killing pests. As far as he was concerned, all guns were station property and available for general use.'

'Were you convinced of his story?'

'Not entirely. It still seemed odd to be shooting rabbits at midday. I saw no evidence to support his story, no dead rabbits. On my return to the station, two days later, I didn't observe any rabbits running out in the paddock during those midday hours.'

'Does Mr Holston own a gun of his own?'

'Yes, sir. He's the licenced owner of a Lee-Enfield .22 calibre long arm, which we also took into custody.'

'Isn't it unusual for an Aborigine to own a licenced weapon?'

'Kind of, but not unheard of. While few firearms licences are issued to Aborigines, the Protection Board allows some Aboriginal stockmen to own guns for pest control, and they can be revoked at any time by the protector or the police.'

'And for those of us unfamiliar with weapons, is the Lee-Enfield similar to the murder weapon – sorry – the weapon that killed Mr Stuart?'

'Yes, sir.'

'Did you find it strange that Mr Holston would choose to use someone else's gun, rather than his own when hunting rabbits?'

'Yes, sir.'

Klein let the last answer hang in the air while he returned to his desk and shuffled some papers.

'Mr Holston claimed to have seen Lachlan Stuart fire three times wildly. Did you recover the bullets?'

'No, sir. But we found three spent cartridges near Mr Stuart's body. They were fired from Mr Stuart's gun.'

'You didn't recover the bullets though. So when Lachlan Stuart fired, he could have been firing harmlessly into the air?'

'Correct.'

'Like someone does when they are celebrating. Celebrating the birth of their child perhaps?'

'Objection! That goes to speculation on what Mr Stuart was thinking when he fired the weapon.'

'Sustained.'

'You interviewed Mrs Stuart?'

'Yes, sir.'

'Did she seem distraught?'

'Yes, sir. She appeared dazed. I would say she was deeply in shock.'

'Was she able to confirm Mr Holston's story?'

'Yes, sir. Though her recollections were far from clear. She seemed confused. But in the end, she did give a similar account of the events leading to Mr Stuart's death.'

'Did you interview Mrs Stuart again, when she was more coherent?'

'Yes, sir. Her account was more detailed and confirmed Mr Holston's version of events.'

'After she'd had time to confer with the other witnesses?'

'Objection.'

'I am merely asking the witness if Mrs Stuart had time to confer with other witnesses, your honour. It seems to me a fair question.'

'It wasn't a question, your honour, it was an inference.'

'Overruled. But let's move on, Mr Klein.'

'Thank you, your honour. Detective, you also interviewed Ellin Cobham, present as the acting midwife for the birth of Mrs Stuart's son, did you not?'

'Correct.'

'She saw the whole thing?'

'Yes, sir. Cobham told the same story. She witnessed Mr Stuart's aggression and his attempt to shoot his wife and child.'

'Ellin Cobham is a half-caste servant of the Stuarts, correct?'

'Correct. She has worked on and off for the family since she was a teenager.'

'So she would be beholden to Mrs Stuart, her employer, unwilling to speak the truth in case she lost her employment?'

Tupper jumped to his feet. 'Objection. Speculative.'

'I'll withdraw that remark. Detective, did Cobham appear to have been coached?'

'She seemed clear on the details, the same details told by Holston and Mrs Stuart. The only thing I might say is that all three accounts were almost identically worded.'

'Meaning that they could have coordinated their testimony?'

'Objection.'

'Sustained.'

Klein thought for a moment, stroking his beard. 'Are you aware of the rumours concerning Ellin Cobham and Lachlan Stuart?'

'By rumours, you mean her having his children?'

'Those rumours.'

'Yes, sir. During my investigation, several people raised the issue. They said Lachlan Stuart had several Aborigines who would take care of his needs, some had children by him.'

'By that you mean several Aborigines he took for his own pleasure?' Klein didn't wait for an answer. 'Do you think Ellin Cobham acquiesced to such a liaison?'

'Acquie-what?'

'Acquiesced. Do you think she consented to Lachlan Stuart's advances, or was she forced?'

'Objection! The witness cannot possibly know that.'

'Sustained. You're treading a fine line, Mr Klein.'

Klein paused, staring down at the paper in his hand. After a moment he continued: 'In your professional opinion, Detective, had Ellin Cobham been forced by Stuart, would she then have reason to conspire with Mrs Stuart and Oogoola Holston to kill Lachlan Stuart?'

'Objection!'

The courtroom erupted.

'That will be your final warning, Mr Klein. *The jury will disregard the last comments,'* Judge Lawrence had to bellow his instructions above the pandemonium.

Klein bowed to the bench and withdrew his question as the court settled. He then spent another forty minutes probing Middleton on his investigation, but finding little to use against Lou. Klein returned to his seat, glancing at Tupper as he passed by his desk, satisfied no doubt that he had scored some cheap points against him.

Tupper stood to cross-examine, shaking his head at the prosecution's display.

'Detective Middleton, can we get back to facts here, not speculation? Do you own a vehicle?'

Middleton cocked an eyebrow. 'Yes, sir. I own a Holden FX.'

'And do you use that car in the execution of your duties?'

'No, sir. I drive a government-owned Ford shooting brake.'

'Why? Isn't that a little strange?'

Middleton looked confused. 'No. If I used my own motorcar, it would get worn out too quickly. And anyway, the force insists I drive an official vehicle.'

'And do you use your own firearm or one issued by the force?'

'I use several firearms during my duties, all government issue.'

'Do you also own a gun, Detective Middleton?'

'I do. I own a fully registered twelve-gauge shotgun.'

'So you use your employer's tools of the trade and don't think it's odd, and yet when Lou Holston does the same, you say it's strange behaviour.'

'I never thought of it like that,' Middleton admitted.

'So now, do you still think it strange that Mr Holston was using a gun registered to his employer, rather than his own?'

'I suppose you could see it that way.'

'See it as normal behaviour, not strange as you previously stated?'

Middleton shrugged. 'I guess.' Tupper waited. 'Yes,' Middleton finally agreed.

'Thank you.' Tupper paced back and forth without speaking for a moment. 'When you looked for the bullets dispensed from Lachlan Stuart's rifle, did you look out in the paddocks, the pastures?'

Middleton smiled. 'No, sir.'

'An impossible task, right? So the fact you never found the bullets, but found shell casings only confirms that the gun was fired wildly by the deceased, just as the witnesses have stated. The bullets could have gone anywhere, including the paddocks. Is that correct?'

'Correct.'

'When you trained as a police officer, you had weapons training. Were you trained to stop an armed assailant by shooting him in the leg, an arm perhaps, or shooting the weapon out of his hand like we've seen them do in Westerns?'

'Certainly not. We are taught to aim for the body mass where there is less chance of missing. It's too difficult to attempt otherwise.'

'The body mass, meaning the chest?'

'Correct.'

'And can you tell us where a man's heart is located, please?'

Middleton smiled. 'The chest.'

'So when the prosecution talks about a single well-aimed shot to the heart, what they're really confirming is that Lou Holston's shot to the chest was a logical way to stop him. It wouldn't mean he intended to kill him?'

'Correct.'

'You stated that all three eyewitness accounts were almost identically worded and that made you a little suspicious.'

'Correct.'

'Do you pride yourself on observation, Detective?'

'I like to think I'm thorough.'

'I want you to watch me very carefully for a moment.'

Mr Tupper walked away to his desk, scratched his head, then took a pen and wrote on a piece of paper. He folded the paper twice and placed it in his pocket, beneath his robe, before walking around his desk three times and returning to the witness stand.

'Can you please describe to the court what you just witnessed, please?'

Middleton hesitated, looking for help from the judge before proceeding.

'Go ahead, Detective Middleton,' said Judge Lawrence.

'You walked to your desk, scratched your head, wrote something on a piece of paper, then folded it twice, lifted your robe and put the paper in your pocket before circling your desk three times and coming back here to the witness stand.'

'Very good, Detective. You're obviously good at your job.' Tupper removed the folded paper from his pocket and handed it to Middleton. 'Now, please read what's written on that paper, if you will.'

'It says, defence council walked over to his desk, scratched his head, wrote... It says exactly what I've already stated.'

'Using remarkably similar words, if I'm not mistaken. Correct?'

'Almost exactly,' said Middleton.

'In fact, this little demonstration goes to show that in all probability, when independent witnesses submit the same story, the likelihood is that they agree to the facts, wouldn't you say, Detective Middleton?'

Middleton nodded in agreement while I noticed Klein smile to concede the point.

'Did you ask Lou Holston about the absence of rabbits, dead or alive?'

'I did.'

'And did he account for the lack thereof?'

'He said he'd had no luck.'

'And did you find any evidence to dispute his statement?'

'I found no proof one way or the other.'

'Finally, Detective, during the course of your investigation, did you find any evidence to suggest that events did *not* take place as the witnesses have testified?'

'No, sir, I didn't.'

Chapter 27

Galah-Kilampa

The mood outside the courthouse had changed when we emerged to a waiting crowd of bystanders. News of the prosecution's courtroom accusations had circulated beyond the courthouse walls. Numbers had swelled and they jeered and cursed as we pushed our way through. Women, strangers to me, hurled abuse and jostled us as we made our exit. Overwhelmed by the aggression, I tried to shield Kooper from the barrage of hostility, covering his head with the shawl so that he wouldn't hear the hateful taunts. Journalists shouted questions, came up close so that their faces were in mine. *Did you have an affair with the accused? Did you plan the murder of your husband?* A woman in a blue dress came at me and spat in my face, and Toby was pushed to the ground in the commotion. Kooper began to scream. I heard angry shouts of slut and whore, from people who didn't know anything about me. My mind conjured visions from the past, children in a ring.

Pommy bastard. No better than an Abo! Encircled and separated from Toby, the enraged crowd had me backed against a wall of granite, a plinth on which a bronze soldier stood, his arm outstretched as if he were trying to defend me against the angry mob. Sounds merged as one, Kooper's cries, the crowd's angry calls, the reporter's endless questions, a wall of noise that numbed my brain. I cowered against the statue.

'Get back, get back!' A voice I recognised above the bedlam. 'You should be ashamed of yourselves, ya bloody mongrels. *This woman has a child, for Christ's sake.*'

Bert Middleton pushed his way through the mob to my side, took my arm, and fending with his outstretched hand, lead us through the unruly rabble to safety. I felt him pull back on my arm as I reached for the vehicle door, and he apologised for the crowd's behaviour. Toby joined us, climbing into the driver's seat. I passed in Kooper and tried to follow, but Middleton kept a firm grip as I attempted to get in. I turned to thank him. But when his eyes met mine, there was a moment between us. He fixed me with a look that said: *I'm being kind to you, but don't get me wrong, I know the truth. I know what you've done. You don't fool me for a minute.* I gently removed the detective's grip and climbed into the Land Rover. Trembling, I closed the door on the man who had saved me, aware of his continuing stare, rattled by the unnerving exchange. Bert Middleton stood and watched from the sidewalk, as Toby put the car in gear and pulled away. I felt his eyes still on me as we rounded the corner, but I never looked back.

Still shaking from the unpleasant encounter with the mob, we drove back to the homestead in silence, me in the back seat with Kooper, Toby driving. Had I imagined Middleton's silent accusation? Surely yes. But I couldn't get the thought out of my mind. Guilt played heavily in my thoughts, and each encounter with someone new, brought a renewed sense of shame. I couldn't look anyone in the eye without squirming. Every so often, I caught Toby staring at me in the rear-view mirror. Withdrawn since Lachlan's death, Toby had hardly said a word about the trial. Each day he had brought me to town and sat with me through testimony, taking Kooper away when I needed a break, or when Kooper became restless and fidgety. There had been no conversation between us. He was brooding, and I couldn't tell if he was worried or angry. Was he missing Lachlan, or was he disappointed in me?

'Are you mad at me?' I asked.

Toby took a moment to answer. 'Why would I be mad?'

'I don't know, but you've hardly said a word.' Toby didn't answer. 'Do you believe what they're saying about me, about Lou?'

'I believe you're a good person.'

'That's not what I asked.'

'You and Lou know the truth, that's all that matters. I got no business thinking any different.'

We drove on without further discussion. Since his first arrival at the homestead, Toby had become my mentor, the nearest thing to a father for me. We talked a lot about the world around us, and his comments always made me feel better, no matter what troubles I had before we started. His sudden reluctance to talk left me devastated.

How could I know that my nightmare was about to get worse, that the sky would fall, and tomorrow would bring me once again to my knees?

Kooper's cries woke me from a restless sleep. Exhausted, I brought him to my side and hoped he would sleep a little longer so I could rest. I had no motivation to rise, and the thought of another day in court made me anxious and sick. In the end, Kooper could not be mollified. Chilled by the morning air, I rekindled the stove and fed him in the kitchen as the sun broke the horizon to mark another day of agonising testimony. I prayed that Lou's court case would soon be over, and that the day might bring a more favourable hearing. I'd felt the pressure building with each new witness, fearing that the next would be the one to bring me undone completely. The toll on me was bad enough, I couldn't imagine what Lou was going through. I thought of him locked away in his cell, and felt the heavy weight of guilt press my chest. How could I allow him to go through so much for me?

I watched Kooper chattering contentedly, propped against a cushion on the floor, his lips turned up in a smile. I dropped down beside him, closed my eyes, and smelt his sweet scent, pure and untainted. I traced the contours of his face, allowed my finger to tickle his nose, felt the softness of his lips. He raised his hands above his head and bellowed, a declaration only he could understand. I laughed and brought my lips to his skin, breathed in his essence. How could I live now, without this tiny human? I couldn't. He was the reason for my being, and I'd do anything to keep him. Bam! The screen door slammed. It was a sound that never ceased to startle me, even after all the years.

Ellin came straight to the kitchen, stopped in the doorway and smiled. 'You two look perfect.'

'One of us is,' I said.

'Where's Toby? I didn't see the Land Rover, checked the bunkhouse, but his bed's not been slept in.'

'I don't know,' I said, puzzled. 'He dropped me off yesterday, said he had to go into Wilcannia. I haven't seen him since. I just assumed he came home late after I was asleep. We had a terrible time leaving the courthouse. I think it shook him up badly.'

We waited as long as we could for Toby to arrive before taking the utility truck and making our way to Broken Hill for the morning session. I drove, dwelling on Toby's whereabouts, while Ellin held Kooper on her lap at my side.

This was to be the last day of testimony before the weekend recess, and the Crown had three more witnesses before they rested their case. If time permitted, I was informed, I would take the stand in Lou's defence. Due to Toby's disappearance and our late arrival, two Crown witnesses had already given evidence when we took our seats after morning tea.

Thankfully, our tardy appearance allowed us to slip into court without confrontation. Two people had testified to Lachlan's demeanour in the days leading up to his death, speaking of Lachlan's happiness and his enthusiasm for fatherhood. The third such witness, and the last before lunch, was Lachlan's drinking mate, Titus Brambly. Though Lachlan had no real friends to speak of, Titus was the closest thing.

'What kind of man was Lachlan Stuart?' asked Klein as the session began.

'A cracking bloke. He was the kind of bloke to give you the shirt off his back.' Brambly paused. 'As long as you bought him a new one,' he added, to great hilarity amongst his friends in the public gallery. Brambly was a balding, ruddy-faced man. A single buck tooth protruded from under his top lip, sitting over the lower and causing him to screw up his nose, so that he resembled a fat rat who'd just encountered a bad smell.

Klein indulged Brambly's attempt at humour while the courtroom settled. 'I understand you shared a beer or two with Mr Stuart?'

'Shared? Not bloody likely, he could buy his own.' More laughter. 'If you mean, did we share each other's company, then yes, we had a beer or two now and then, a few whiskeys too. Lockie wasn't what you'd call a regular at the bar, but when he did come for a few grogs, we'd close the place together.'

'Would you say Lachlan Stuart was a big drinker? By that I mean, could he hold his liquor?'

'He could hold his liquor till he passed out like a sheila.' Once more the court erupted. Brambly surveyed the chuckling faces; he was enjoying his new-found celebrity. His mates in the gallery were having a fine time goading him on with their laughter.

'Meaning?'

'Lockie was the kind of bloke who drank and drank without showing any signs of being drunk until he'd had enough, which was usually well after closing. The locals called him Skittle because he'd be standing one minute, steady as a rock, then suddenly drop and roll over on the floor, oblivious to the bloody world. Yep, Lockie was either sober or unconscious, nothing in between.'

'Was Lachlan a violent man?'

'I thought you said violet there for a minute. Lockie wasn't much of a pansy.'

I couldn't believe my eyes as I scanned the faces around me, adorned with smiles and laughter, as though this were all a funny joke, as though a man's life was not on the line, Lou's life. The all-male jury looked particularly pleased to have the monotony broken. They chuckled and commented amongst themselves over Brambly's comedy routine. Judge Lawrence called for order, silencing the court.

'Answer the question, Mr Brambly,' said the judge.

'No, Lockie wasn't that kind of bloke. He wasn't shy of a fight, mind, but he'd never pick one.'

'Did Lockie have trouble with Aborigines?'

'Trouble?'

'Would you call him a racist?'

'A racist? No. Lockie never went to the races. He liked cards, mind.' More laughter.

Judge Lawrence had had enough. 'If you cannot control your witness, Mr Klein, I will have him removed from the court and have his testimony struck from the record. Furthermore, any more nonsense from the gallery and we will conduct proceedings behind closed doors.'

Brambly pursed his lips, raised his eyebrows, and made a *whoops* face, but his smirk showed his contempt for the trial and the seriousness of the case.

'Let me put it another way. Did you ever witness Lachlan Stuart show prejudice towards blacks?' said Klein, after quiet was restored.

'No, sir. Lockie liked them blackfellas. He employed them all the time, ask anyone. In fact, there was a couple of whitefellas came into the bar complaining that they couldn't get a fair shake because Lockie only hired blackfellas and half-castes.'

'Your honour, is there any point to this line of questioning? We've already heard ad-infinitum what a wonderful caring human being Mr Stuart was. All irrelevant to the case at hand.'

'Are you going somewhere with this witness, Mr Klein?'

'Yes, your honour. If you'll allow me.'

'Very well.'

Klein moved on quickly. 'How did Lockie take the news that he was finally to become a father?'

'He thought it was bloody ripper. Never seen a man so chuffed. It was the only time he dipped in his daks to buy the pub a round.' Brambly paused and looked sheepishly at the judge, checking to see if he had overstepped the mark with the comment. 'Lockie thought he'd never have kids,' he continued.

'Objection. Hearsay.'

'Sustained. Rephrase the question, Mr Klein. The witness cannot know what the deceased was thinking.'

'Thank you, your honour. Mr Brambly, what did Mr Stuart tell you personally about his wish to become a father?'

'He said he was over the moon because he didn't think he was able to have them.'

'But wasn't it common knowledge that Lachlan had fathered several illegitimate children, children of Aboriginal mothers?'

'Nah, that's all a load of bullshit, probably started by Lockie himself. Lockie liked a bit on the side, but he never had no half-castes, least none that I know of.'

'Objection. Hearsay.'

'Sustained.'

'Did Mr Stuart tell you specifically that he had no illegitimate children and that he wanted a child of his own?'

'He did, sir. He was desperate for a boy to carry on the family name. I used to rib him about it, told him he shot blanks. I said I'd do it for him when he married the pretty kid.' Brambly nodded in my direction and smiled, making me shiver, repulsed by the thought. 'Anyway, when she got up the duff, he was bloody stoked.' Muffled chuckles. 'He said he was the happiest man alive.'

'And did his delight in being a father carry on throughout the term of Mrs Stuart's pregnancy, or did the novelty wear off?'

Brambly turned to look at me. 'Nah, he was proper chuffed right to the end. Said he couldn't wait to have a little anklebiter around the place. When he came into the bar a couple of days before he died, he was nervous as hell. He said he didn't want anything to go wrong. He said he wanted a boy real bad, but he was shitting bricks that he'd have another sheila about the place. Scuse me French, your honour,' Brambly added, turning to the judge. 'I said boys was special and it took a certain kind of man to deliver one. Like my old dad used to say, anyone can kick a hole in a teapot, but it takes a craftsman to put a spout on it.' Brambly turned to the judge. 'I've got four boys meself, your honour. Master craftsman, that's me.'

Ripples of laughter followed, but most in the court appeared unwilling to test the judge's patience by giving Brambly his full moment of glory. Klein moved quickly to add that he had no further questions.

Tupper began his cross-examination with a veiled rebuke. 'You consider yourself to be something of a larrikin, Mr Brambly. Were you ever on stage?'

Brambly glanced at Klein as if for guidance. 'I was on a landing stage once. Didn't catch any fish.'

'Very good, Mr Brambly. I'm glad you find Mr Holston's trial a suitable venue for your wit.'

Brambly squirmed. 'Just trying to lighten things up, all the glum faces...' Brambly looked once more for support, but Klein was looking at his desktop. 'Sorry. It's a serious matter what happened to Lockie.'

'You're sorry,' Tupper repeated. 'Tell me, Mr Brambly, are you acquainted with a Bertha Barton?' Brambly snickered but didn't answer. 'Bertha Barton, Mr Brambly, she took the stand two days ago to give evidence about the accused.'

'I know who she is,' said Brambly, irritated by the question. 'She's me sister-in-law.'

'Your sister-in-law? When did you last see her?'

'What's that got to do with anything?'

'Answer the question, Mr Brambly,' said the judge.

'Last night.'

'Did you discuss the case?'

Brambly, serious now. 'We couldn't very well not, we're family. Who wouldn't?'

'Did you compare notes, coordinate your testimony, figure out ways to make the prosecution's case?'

'Objection!'

'Overruled.'

'Did you compare notes?'

Brambly forced a smile. 'Not exactly. We didn't need bloody notes to know Lockie would never try to harm is own boy.'

'You said Mr Stuart was nervous as the birth approached because he wanted a boy. Could it be that he was not worried about the sex of his child, but having second thoughts about having a child in the first place? Perhaps he thought he was now too old to start raising a family and the responsibility had now dawned on him. Could it be that you mistook Lachlan Stuart's nervousness for growing anxiety and that the thought of a baby terrified him?'

'Nah, you're barking up the wrong tree, mate. Lockie was the happiest fella I ever saw. He couldn't bloody wait for his kid to arrive, he told me so. He never would've harmed his boy or his missus, never in a million years.'

'Were you there when Lachlan Stuart died?'

'Of course not, what kind of question's that?'

'It's a simple question, Mr Brambly. If you were not at the scene, then how could you possibly know if he would have hurt his wife and son. How could you know he wasn't about to kill them in a drunken rage?'

'You can twist me words all you want, but the fact is, Lockie was a happy man. I knew him well enough to know he wouldn't hurt them.'

'Oh, I'm not surprised he was happy when the two of you were always blind drunk and out of control, making fun of every poor soul, I imagine, if your conduct in court today is anything to go by. Perhaps Bertha Barton joined you in your fun and games.'

'Objection, your honour. Where is this leading?'

'I'll withdraw those remarks,' Tupper said to the judge before he could be reprimanded.

I watched the jurors faces filled with contempt for Tupper; they seemed offended by his attacks on Brambly, by his demeanour and his smug remarks. I could see they disliked him, the gallery disliked him, the reporters, the judge disliked him, I disliked him. He was just too pompous for the locals, a slick talker come to show the country bumpkins how it was done by the professionals from the city.

'Was Lachlan Stuart a jealous man?'

Brambly creased his eyes and squinted. 'I know where you're going with that. He never knew his missus was fooling around, if that's what you mean.'

'But if he had harboured that suspicion, what sort of action do you suppose he would have taken?'

'Objection. The witness cannot possibly know what Mr Stuart would have done.'

'Sustained.'

'Well, he wouldn't have stood any nonsense,' Brambly said before he could be silenced. 'But he wouldn't hurt her. I reckon he'd have booted her out, given her the marching orders.'

'Marching orders? He wouldn't get angry, physically violent?'

'Objection!'

'Nah, Lockie was a lover not a fighter.'

'Move on, Mr Tupper.'

'Do you remember December twenty-fourth of last year?'

'I don't remember last week,' said Brambly, chuckling.

'December twenty-fourth last year, you and Lockie ended up in lock-up after brawling in the Federal Hotel with four mine workers. Charges were dropped, but Lachlan Stuart sent a man to hospital, is that not so?'

Brambly smiled triumphantly. 'That was no brawl, mate, that was a dead-set massacre. Lockie and me ripped them all a new one.'

'You bashed them?'

'Bloody oath!' Brambly seemed to realise too late that he had gone against his own testimony. 'Look, we was bloody pissed at the time,' he said, digging himself in deeper. 'You know what mine workers are like and it was Christmas for crying out loud.'

'Yet another example of how overindulgent celebrations can have unintended consequences. Tell me, Mr Brambly, wouldn't most men feel justified in taking matters into their own hands if they found their wife fooling around, especially when fuelled by too much alcohol? If you thought your wife was fooling around, wouldn't you get angry too?'

'Objection!'

Brambly looked at the judge, then the jury, then back to Tupper; he couldn't help himself. 'If I found a man fooling with me missus, I reckon I'd give the bugger a fiver and a big kiss, wish him well, and tell him to take her as far away as possible. I'd pay for the bloody train fare.' The courtroom erupted once more. 'He'd be more of a man than me, mate,' Brambly added above the uproar.

Chapter 28

Stop!-Kinurta

With the prosecution's case concluded, the morning session had ended for lunch. It now resumed in an unmistakably festive mood. I heard chuckles and comments about Brambly's earlier comedic performance. Most seemed to have enjoyed the light relief, settling into their seats with high hopes, perhaps, for more of the same. I wondered if they would still be laughing if it was one of their family members or friends in the dock.

By the time I took the stand, I had worked myself into a manic state of fear. All I had to do, Tupper said, was to repeat my police statement, stick to my story and don't stray from the facts. 'The least said the better and don't try to elaborate,' he told me. Easier said than done. I'd thought about it for weeks, what I might say that would convince them of Lou's innocence. But all the time I knew that the only sure way to clear his name was to admit my own guilt.

Filled with dread, at last I took the stand. I had a better view of the jury now, but it did nothing to ease my fears. Twelve men with their eyes fixed on me, each thinking the worst no doubt. I felt exposed and vulnerable under the intense scrutiny, but I was determined not to let Lou down by breaking apart under questioning. Ellin had left the court with Kooper so as not to distract me. I was sure I would make a mistake and ruin everything. I had seen the way the prosecutor had bullied other witnesses in order to throw them off guard. I was already trembling at the thought of being next.

I swore to tell the truth, and silently prayed for my soul. Tupper led the way and guided me gently through the retelling of events, nothing new, no difficult questions. I told the story as instructed, focusing entirely on him, shutting out everyone else in the courtroom. Tupper made it easy, just as he said he would, and by the time I reached the end of my testimony, my heart rate had slowed to a more normal rhythm.

'Did you have any indication that your husband was about to turn violent, prior to the birth of your child?'

'No, sir.'

'Finally, Mrs Stuart, in your opinion, did the defendant have any other choice but to come to your rescue, shooting his rifle in the course of defending yourself and your baby, or is he guilty of murder as charged by the Crown?'

Lou looked so sad as they waited for my answer. I wanted to run across the courtroom and hold him, tell him I was sorry for putting him through hell and that I loved him deeply.

'Lou could never commit murder,' I said firmly. 'I owe him my baby's life.' This was practically the only truth I had told since taking the stand.

Klein took a long time to organise his papers before coming to the stand to cross-examine me. He smiled warmly, and I saw genuine kindness in his eyes. It didn't stop him getting straight to the point. 'Did you have an affair with the defendant, Mrs Stuart?'

I wanted to say yes, I love him. 'No,' I said, barely a whisper.

'Speak up, please.'

'No, sir.'

'How would you describe your relationship?'

I imagined the jury could see my heart beating fast beneath my breast, that they heard my thoughts. 'I... Lou is...'

'Lou is?'

'Lou is our top hand,' I said.

'But I asked about your relationship, not his position of employment.'

'We get on well together. Because we're close in age, I suppose. I don't deny we've become friends.'

'Friends, not lovers?'

'Good friends.'

'If I can take you back to the incident at the Silver City Theatre. Mrs Barton testified that you and Mr Holston were arm in arm, 'like lovers'. Is that true?'

'He may have given me his arm, like a gentleman. Nothing more than that.'

'Like a gentleman, not a lover?'

'Yes. Like a gentleman.'

'Did you ask for seats so that you could sit together?'

'I don't recall.'

'But you wanted to?'

'I had no reason... I would have sat next to Lou if she hadn't stopped us, but we never asked for any particular seats.'

'She being Mrs Barton?'

'Yes.'

'Are you aware that it's customary for blacks to sit at the front of the theatre and whites to the rear?'

'I've never been to a picture house before.'

'But you took exception to being refused a seat next to Oogoola Holston?'

I hesitated, all I could do not to rage about the injustice. 'I saw no reason for us to sit separately.'

'So you could cuddle?'

'No. So we could watch the film together, like any other normal people.'

'But normal people don't sit arm in arm, white and black, married and unmarried in the back row of the picture house, do they, Mrs Stuart?' Murmurs rumbled from around the room. I didn't answer. 'Where was your husband,' Klein continued, 'while you were about town with the defendant?'

'He was away buying stock. We lost a lot of the flock when the dust storm came through, and we needed to replenish the breeders.'

'Was he aware that you had gone for a night on the town with a young man he employed as a stockman?'

I hesitated. Cursed myself for doing so. 'No.'

'But you told him on his return?'

'No.'

'Would you say that the loss of stock due to the storm was devastating to the station?'

'Yes. Lachlan was afraid it would ruin us.'

'And yet, while your husband was away trying to *save* the farm, you were gallivanting about with his employee. What do you think he would have said if he had known?'

'It wasn't like that. I didn't tell him because it wasn't important. Lachlan wouldn't have cared. He wouldn't want to take me to the picture house, he wasn't interested in things like that. He'd have said, go by all means, as long as he didn't have to take me himself.'

There followed an agonising pause during which all eyes fixed on me. Mr Klein let it linger. 'Let's talk about your son, Mrs Stuart,' he said after making me wait. 'Does he have his father's eyes?'

'What do you mean?'

'It's a simple question, Mrs Stuart. Does the child resemble his father?'

Panic gripped my heart. 'He... He's got my eyes.'

'Yours.' Klein smiled. 'Mrs Barton gave us a fairly precise timeframe during which the incident at the theatre occurred. The picture, Dracula, ran for two weeks in May. That makes it almost exactly nine months before the birth of your son and the killing of your husband. Quite a coincidence, wouldn't you say, Mrs Stuart?'

I didn't answer; I couldn't. Why hadn't I thought of this? Trembling I turned to Lou, back to Klein. The jurors smirked, whispers in the gallery, reporters jotting notes. My head ready to burst, palms hot and sweating, heart thumping.

'We'll come back to that, shall we?' I didn't answer. 'Are you acquainted with Mr Anastas, the water carrier?'

'Yes.'

'He told us earlier of an incident on the road to Wilcannia, in which he surprised both you and the defendant who were parked at the side of the road, cuddling and kissing. Do you recall such an event?'

'He's mistaken.'

'Mistaken? It wasn't you and Lou Holston at the side of the road?'

'We weren't kissing and cuddling. Lou was driving me to the doctor. I felt car sick. He pulled off the road in case I had to vomit.'

'So Mr Anastas is lying when he says Lou had his arm around you, that he saw you kissing?'

'I told you, I felt sick. Maybe Lou was trying to comfort me.'

'By kissing you?'

'No! By... I don't know, by being kind.'

'Kind, is that what they call it? Always the gentleman your young blackfella.' Chuckles from the gallery. 'Let's return to the day Lachlan died, shall we. You gave the court an extremely measured account of the incident. Mr Tupper almost put the words in your mouth.'

'Objection!'

'Sustained. The jury will disregard the comment.'

'You said you were in bed with your newborn son, only minutes after giving birth. You heard a commotion outside, your husband's voice, loud and threatening. He staggered into the bedroom, followed by Ellin Cobham, who tried to restrain him, and told you he no longer wanted to be a father. Is that right so far?'

I nodded cautiously.

'That must have been quite a shock.'

'He was drunk.'

'Yes, so you say. So your husband stormed in and said he no longer wanted a child, you told him he was drunk and that he should go sleep it off, at which point he lashed out at you, with what, his fists?'

'I don't remember. Ellin was holding him back.'

'You climbed from the bed,' Klein continued, 'having only just given birth, took your child and ran to the yard. That must have been hard, given your condition. And we have to admire the strength of your housekeeper, holding back your husband, a man of fifteen stone, six-feet, three-inches tall, all muscle. She must be a strong woman.'

'She is.'

'Very strong.' I didn't answer. 'So, according to your statement, once you've slipped out of the house, Lachlan manages to shake loose of your powerful Aboriginal and follow you to the yard.'

'Ellin is not my Aboriginal, she's my friend.'

'I'm sorry. I correct myself. Lachlan shakes loose of your *loyal friend Ellin,* taking a detour en route to retrieve his rifle from the barn. He comes back to the yard, takes aim, and proclaims that he's ready to shoot this tiny helpless child because he's *changed his mind* about being a father. That's quite a change of mind, wouldn't you say, Mrs Stuart?' I did not answer. 'Why did you wait in the yard, why not keep running?'

'I don't know, there was nowhere to run.'

Klein paused, stroked his beard. 'See, I have a number of problems with your account. For a start, I find it hard to imagine a man so affected by alcohol – and we've already heard how accomplished he was at drinking whiskey – that he suddenly, out of the blue, contrary to everything that had gone before, wants to kill his new son, a son he has longed for all his life. A son he told all who would listen, was the pride of his loins and his legacy to the world. A man would have to be more than intoxicated for such a change of mind, wouldn't you agree?'

'Intoxicated?'

'Blind drunk, smashed, sozzled. He would need to be out of his mind.'

'Yes; that's exactly what he was.'

'Yet this same man you claim is crazed with alcohol to the point of insanity, is cognizant enough to go find his rifle in the barn, find suitable ammunition amongst a variety of calibres, load the weapon with a full magazine – perhaps he cleaned the barrel with an oil-cloth too, follows you to the yard where he finds you waiting quite patiently for his return, arrives in the yard, without falling over I might add, takes aim at the baby and pulls the trigger three times. It just doesn't ring true, does it, Mrs Stuart?'

'He wanted to kill my baby. He would have shot him. Don't you see?' I wept out the last words, the terror building inside me, the room closing in, faces in the gallery snarling like dogs, Klein leading the pack. I couldn't breathe, a clamp around my chest. I wanted to turn and run. In my mind I saw pictures of Lachlan, pointing his rifle, threatening, distraught at his discovery. Of course he had a right to be angry, what man wouldn't be. He was just reacting to the pain I had caused. It was all my fault. He died because of me. He died by my hand. My head swam.

Klein paced the floor as he spoke and showed no sympathy for my obvious distress. 'You know,' he said, suddenly, putting a hand to his chin and holding up the other as though to call a halt to proceedings. 'I've been looking at this from the wrong angle. I do apologise, Mrs Stuart. I may have misunderstood and, come to think of it, now I do believe Lachlan Stuart did indeed storm into that bedroom and ask himself the question, *Do I want this child?* Like the rest of us here in this courtroom,'

Klein went on, aggressively, 'your husband put two and two together and made three – you, Lou Holston and your baby. I think he gave in to the rumours after hearing the stories being circulated in town about you and his lead hand. He challenged you, didn't he, Mrs Stuart? And when you couldn't deny it, he told you to leave. Just as his good friend Titus Brambly said he might, he gave you your marching orders. Am I getting warm, Mrs Stuart?'

I shook my head. 'It's not true.'

'He literally chased you from the house to the yard, that much may be true, but he was not armed, and what he wasn't banking on was that Lou Holston would be waiting for him with the intention of ending his life. You lured him to his death, didn't you, Mrs Stuart?'

'No!'

'Is it not also true that after seeing off Daisy Stuart and taking her place as Lachlan Stuart's wife, you stood to inherit everything? Why else would an attractive girl marry a man three times her age? And with your husband gone, you were free to take up with Lou Holston and his bastard child.'

I could no longer see faces. Tears blurred my vision, a swirling haze as I sank beneath the weight of words. 'It's not true. I...'

'I think it is very true, Mrs Stuart. I think Oogoola Holston killed your husband, Lachlan Stuart, in cold blood while you watched from the verandah of your home. He then took Lachlan's gun, fired three shots into the air so that it would match your account. Did he place Lachlan's finger on the trigger when he fired, to make it look authentic?'

'No, I...' I couldn't think.

Klein went on with his attack; I was helpless. 'You concocted your story either before or after the shooting, with the aid of Ellin Cobham, your *loyal friend*, her knowing that she would be rewarded for her service after you took control of your husband's estate, and you knowing that she hated Lachlan for the indiscretions of his youth.'

'Indiscretions?!' I screamed, no longer able to maintain control. The judge called for order. The courtroom was chaotic. 'He raped her! He beat her and raped her. *He raped me!*'

The noise that followed bounced from the walls like thunderclaps, voices shouting one above the other to be heard. The earth moved beneath my feet, a spinning confusion of accusing, whirling faces, angry words and screaming obscenities from the gallery. I buried my head in my hands, placed them over my ears, looked for an escape. I slumped under the barrage and slipped from consciousness. 'Order! Order!' the last sound I heard as the darkness descended.

Chapter 29

Fly away-Wampi-nya

As if waking from a bad dream, I awoke in a room at the rear of the courthouse. A doctor stood over me. He had a stethoscope slung around his neck, and held a light to my eyes. 'You'll be fine,' he said. 'Your faint was probably the result of stress and anxiety. My name is Doctor Arkwright. I want you to take these,' he said, presenting two tablets in the palm of his hand.

'What are they?'

'Phenobarbital,' said Arkwright. 'They will help you sleep and help you to cope with the news.'

Confused, my head cleared slowly. I scanned the surroundings and began to remember where I was. Klein's bullying accusations came back to mind with a sickening roll of my insides. I recalled the courtroom in chaos and tried to remember what had led to my ultimate loss of consciousness. The doctor had said there was news, but my mind was still fogged and I couldn't understand what he was saying. Ellin stood in a corner of the room, holding Kooper. She had been crying. I saw on her face a new source of distress.

'Help me cope with the news, what news?' I closed my eyes to try and focus. Had the trial finished while I was unconscious? Was Lou convicted already? I looked from Ellin to the doctor and back to Ellin. 'What is it? What news?'

'Take these first,' said Arkwright.

'Tell me!' I demanded.

The doctor turned to Ellin and sighed.

'It's Toby,' she said.

How much heartache can one young soul take? The news that Toby had died should have come as the final blow, but I just felt numb. I reacted without tears, without any show of emotion. I conceded victory. Australia had beaten me. I listened to Ellin's account, detached, her voice a distant echo.

'Toby went to the pub in Wilcannia,' said Ellin, tears returning to her eyes. 'He had a few schooners and left at closing time with a bottle of grog. Some blokes said they saw him sitting with his grog under a tree near the bridge. Kids found his body floating in the river this morning. He fell in and drowned, tidda.'

We drove home in silence. Ellin tried to fuss but I shunned her efforts. I sat on the verandah, cradling Kooper and rocking him gently. I stared out across the land, and scanned my surroundings with new loathing. I understood Daisy now.

She'd been poisoned, cursed by this place, by the isolation, the hardship, so that she turned bitter and full of regret until she died.

'What now?' said Ellin, bringing me out of my thoughts.

'I have to see Lou.'

'They won't let you. Not now the trial is on, and you still have to return to the witness stand.'

'Mr Tupper could arrange it,' I said. 'I need to tell Lou...' I looked down at Kooper, sleeping, and I knew what I must do.

'Tupper says they're going to convict him. You didn't do him any favours today. The jury thinks he's guilty, and us along with him.' Ellin came to sit beside me, stroking Kooper's hand with her finger. 'He's a strong boy,' she said.

'He takes after his father.'

'You can't let Lou go to gaol, you know that, don't you?'

'He won't go to gaol.'

'He will if you don't do something to stop it.'

Ellin was right. Only I could prevent him from being convicted. But that would mean losing Kooper, and I wasn't going to let that happen either.

'This whole thing was a bad idea,' she said.

'This whole thing?'

'Lou taking the blame for something he had no hand in. It was stupid.'

I thought about the confusion that accompanied the decision. I wasn't capable of seeing the consequences. 'It wasn't my idea, as I recall,' I said, but I wasn't being reproachful.

'I know, tidda, I'm not saying it was. We thought it would be simpler that way. It seemed the right thing at the time. But things have changed. Lou doesn't deserve to go to prison for this, he's a good man.'

'He won't. I just need time to think.'

'Lou doesn't have time.'

I didn't sleep that night. Morning came, and with it the tell-tale plume of dust on the long track into Cutaway Creek that signalled a visitor. Fifteen minutes later, Tupper's sedan arrived in the yard. He looked like a clay man, covered from head to toe in red dust that had leaked into his car through a faulty vent hose. He wasn't happy.

'I'm afraid there's little doubt they're going to find Lou guilty,' he said bluntly. I felt cold. 'I did what I could, Mrs Stuart, but Klein seems to have the jury in his pocket.'

I let the statement rest for a long moment before answering. 'You said they had nothing, no evidence against him, you said. Circumstantial, you said, hearsay. You made out as if it was a formality. We had three witnesses to say what happened. We couldn't lose, you said.'

Tupper flinched. 'I know that's how it may have seemed to you, Mrs Stuart.'

'That's how it was,' I snapped. 'You said they would believe our testimony.'

'Well, that's the trouble, they don't believe your testimony, Mrs Stuart. It's clear to anyone watching the trial that they believe you and Lou were lovers and that your baby is the fruit of that liaison. They think you conspired with Lou to kill your husband and that Ellin had reason to support your story. Your own testimony confirmed Ellin's motives. You said Lachlan raped her, and that he raped you. That only strengthens the prosecution case. When a black man kills a white man, there's often only one outcome, but when he does it at the behest of an adulterous white wife, well, that's a crime most whitefellas can't forgive. I did everything I could to throw doubt into their minds, but in my opinion, they surely think there's fire where there's smoke. I wish you had told me everything, and I wish you hadn't attacked Lachlan on the stand in that way.'

I had nothing to say. Tupper was right, the jury thought Lou was guilty and that I was to blame. Why didn't I keep my mouth shut? Why accuse Lachlan of rape? Ellin's words, not mine. Nobody believes that a husband can rape his wife. And if he was so abusive, then why did I stay, why didn't I tell someone?

'That's not the worst of it I'm afraid,' Tupper continued. 'There's a chance that if Lou is convicted, a warrant could be issued for your arrest too. You could end up standing trial for conspiracy to murder your husband.'

My reaction must have looked odd to Tupper. I had already made my plans so that Lou would go free. I calmly asked if he would be heading back to Adelaide after the trial.

'Yes, I'll be heading home as soon as the trial is over. I have a new case to prepare.' Tupper smiled. 'Look, it's not over yet,

I may be completely wrong about the jury and I'm sorry if I was brusque with you. We'll fight to the end, no matter what. It's best you know the worst-case scenario so you can prepare yourself. In the meantime, we still have time to turn things in our favour. Klein will pick up where he left off. You must remain calm and answer his questions confidently. No more outbursts. It's exactly what he wants. And we still have Ellin's testimony to come, even if her credibility as an impartial witness may have diminished.' Tupper let a long silence hang in the air until he spoke again. 'My condolences on hearing the news of your new loss, by the way. I understand that Toby was a close friend.'

I nodded. 'Yes, he was.'

We sat silently for what seemed an eternity. 'Do you mind if I ask you a question?' said Tupper at length. 'How old are you, Katherine?'

'Just turned eighteen.'

Tupper cocked an eyebrow. 'Why did you marry Lachlan, given your age difference, and given that he mistreated you?'

It took me a while to answer. 'I wanted to be loved.'

We sat a while longer, contemplating my simple answer. 'Try to stay positive, Mrs Stuart. We live in hope,' he said unconvincingly, rising to leave. He searched his inside jacket pocket and came out with an envelope. 'Lou asked me to give you this letter.'

I finished reading as Tupper's car melted into the horizon. The letter, dictated by Lou, had been written in Tupper's hand.

Dear Kate,

I asked Mr Tupper to write this letter. He's a lot better with writing than me.

I know what you must be thinking but don't, I beg you. I want you to stay strong and do what's best for the baby. Kooper is our most important consideration now, and his future is what counts, nothing else. I don't mind if the judge says I have to go to gaol, as long as I know you are both safe and well.

Don't say or do anything stupid, please.

Yours truly,

Lou

A dozen sheep grazed lazily near the holding paddock. Otherwise, the station was desolate and without life. I scanned the parched earth out to the west; a single white cloud floated above the horizon. To the south I saw Mr Churchill and his ageless family of river gums, gnarled and defiant against the drought-ridden pastures beyond. The creek, after months without rain, contained nothing of worth to call water. This land had beaten me, though I fought valiantly. Life here belonged to the strong; anything short brought only grief and defeat. Lou's letter waved in a sudden gust of wind. I clasped it but lost my grip and watched it disappear across the paddock, dancing on the wind like a child's kite. I knew what I had to do, but first, I had my own letter to write. If I could remember how to wield a pen.

To who it conserns,

I Katherine Stuart do herby confes to killing Lachlan Stuart my husband after he thretund the life of my baby. I took aim and shot him with my rifle. No one else is to blame. Lou is trying to take the blame himself even tho he had nothing to do with it. I forced Ellin to stick to my story that Lou had done the shooting becus I was scared. I'm sorry for all the trouble I caused and espeshuly for blaming Lou when he was compleetly inosent. I cannot stick around and wait to go to prison. I cannot bear the thort of losing my baby. So I'm going away to start a new life. Please don't try to find me.

Yours truly,

Katherine Stuart

Chapter 30

Hide-Maan.ga

I packed what I could in one large case, the same tatty piece of luggage I brought to Cutaway Creek as a child, and hauled it to the utility truck, making sure I had everything I needed for the baby, and little else. I left the letter on the kitchen table for Ellin to find. I had agonised over telling her in person, but in the end I decided I could not face her with the news I was running. It was a cowardly act, and one I would regret forever. I left instructions for her to deliver the letter – my confession – to Mr Klein at the courthouse when the trial resumed on Tuesday morning, Monday being a rest day. I hoped that the weekend and the extra day would give me enough time to disappear before a search could be organised to find me.

I felt strangely sad now that the time had come to leave. Instantly the house filled with memories. Voices echoed in the empty rooms, smells lingered in the abandoned kitchen.

I walked through every door, looked out through every window, saw every face in the yard by the fire. Not the home of my choosing, yet as I said goodbye, I knew I would miss the homestead until the day I died. As I drove out, a family of emus caused me to slow down and stop. I turned one last time, saw the sails of the wind pump, then never looked back again.

At Broken Hill, I headed straight for the train station, avoiding Argent Street and the courthouse. Every head seemed to turn in my direction; every face an accusing stare. A black shooting brake slowed as I passed – Bert Middleton drove one just like it – but its driver was a stranger to me. Circling the block three times, I came to a stop and parked on a quiet street not far from the station. A black sedan rolled by, it slowed down and pulled up to the curb, fifty feet away. I put the truck in gear, did a U-turn and drove away, watching my mirror for followers, then saw the driver get out of the sedan and go into a warehouse. I cursed myself for being foolish, circled the block again, came to a junction, and had to stop before turning. Pedestrians filled the busy street. Several faces turned to me as they crossed the road, and a woman appeared to be staring at me from a doorway. My face flushed, my hands clammy. I put the car in gear, but missed the clutch. Gears crunched. Heads turned. I tried again. First gear, but stalled as I tried to pull away. A truck behind me honked the horn. Everyone seemed to be watching. Panicked, I tried again. More crunched gears, but this time I moved on without stalling, turned the corner, and came to a stop at the side of the road. I waited several minutes, my legs shaking, my hands gripping the wheel so tight my knuckles were white. I took deep breaths and told myself to calm down. Kooper babbled contentedly, oblivious to my stress.

'Your mother has lost her mind,' I said. Kooper chuckled.

I told myself to be strong for him, but my anxiety could not be controlled so easily. Leaving the truck where it was, I lugged everything towards the station, terrified at every turned head, every knowing glance. In my effort to cope with my baggage, I held Kooper too tight. He squirmed in protest. It was a struggle to hold him, his bassinet and the suitcase, all at the same time. A man startled me, stepping out of a doorway and stopping me in my tracks. My heart raced. 'I got it,' he said, taking my case and helping me across the road and to the ticket office. It was all I could do to speak and thank him. I settled at the far end of the platform, cowering from sight as I waited. From there I could see the town. Lou sat in his cell not half a mile from me. I could see the courthouse roof. I imagined him there, almost within touching distance, and felt the heavy weight of my decision bear down on my heart. I loved him. I would always love him.

After an agonising wait on the platform, the train finally arrived. I hesitated, looked across towards the courthouse one last time. *I'm sorry, Lou.* We boarded in haste, almost running for the cover it gave us.

A uniformed guard looked through the window and smiled a toothy grin as I took my seat. He turned to check the platform and called out, 'All aboard.' I settled down with Kooper at my side, closed my eyes and prayed for the train to move out quickly. I heard a shrill whistle. My fists balled in terror, my eyes clenched tight.

Finally, with a sudden jolt and a whoosh of steam, we pulled away. I opened my eyes, saw a black sedan pull up to the station. My stomach twisted. I couldn't see the driver. The scene receded as a man stepped out of the vehicle, quickly lost from view along with the town, the mine head and all signs of life.

I had gone to great lengths to cover our tracks, purchasing a ticket at Broken Hill, boarding a train to Adelaide, alighting at the first stop in Cockburn, buying there a ticket for Sydney and doubling back the way we had come through Broken Hill. I cowered in my carriage as the train passed through the station, virtually laying with Kooper on the floor to avoid detection. Expecting the worst at every stop, we made our escape to Sydney. But no one waylaid us, there was no police presence to drag us from the train, just the boarding and alighting of anonymous passengers en route to unknown destinations.

I remembered my first journey to Broken Hill seven years before and the fear I felt then, a bewildered child. Afraid coming, afraid going – I had come full circle. At each stop, the guard called to signal our departure. There then followed the shush, shush, shush of the engine as it built up steam, the train whistle, the rat-tat-tat of steel wheels as they passed over the joints in the tracks. At each and every stop, I felt the terror of being caught.

Kooper, sedated by the gentle rocking of the carriage, slept peacefully, waking only to feed and be changed into fresh nappies. I tried not to think of Lou, determined not to look back. Barren plains retreated as the hours passed, giving way to scrub and trees as we climbed into the Blue Mountains. Magnificent red cliffs towered over the valleys below, and, forgetting my plight briefly, I marvelled at the sight. The train stopped at Medlow Bath, where several finely dressed passengers boarded with baggage, filling the otherwise empty carriage. Hotel porters from the Hydro Majestic hotel assisted with their luggage. They all looked very grand.

A young woman came and sat opposite, accompanied by her son. She smiled and peeked into Kooper's bassinet.

'How old?' she asked.

'Six months.' I didn't want to start a conversation.

'He's gorgeous. What's his name?'

I suddenly felt panicked. 'Oscar,' I lied, stupidly. 'We're heading home to see his father in Sydney.'

'Where in Sydney?'

Terror. I didn't know anywhere in Sydney. At that moment, the young boy – he wore a cowboy outfit with guns and a black mask to cover his face – made a loud, 'bang, bang' sound. I turned to him quickly.

'My, you nearly gave me a heart attack. Did you shoot some Indians?'

The little boy didn't answer, retreating shyly to the far corner of the carriage and averting his eyes.

'He's the Lone Ranger,' said his mother.

I smiled and quickly closed my eyes, making out that I wanted to sleep, thus avoiding any more questions.

I felt both lost and relieved when we finally reached Central Station and the harbour city of Sydney. I'd expected to find a police welcoming party on my arrival, but there was nothing to indicate that anyone knew who I was or that I was fleeing from the law. Anonymous amongst the crowds, I asked for directions and immediately made my way to the Orient Steam Navigation Company where I attempted to book passage on the first available ship to England. My passport, unused since my arrival in 1951, stated my name as Katherine Bower. Issued on the sixth of December 1950, it carried a photograph of a little girl I no longer knew. Had I changed so much in so few years?

Too many questions by the nosey booking clerk and the need to provide papers for the baby caused me to rethink my plans. I trekked on foot to a boarding house in Kings Cross, a bawdy district not far from the city centre. With lots of temporary accommodation – no one asked questions – I soon found a room. Kings Cross attracted large numbers of new immigrants, many unable to speak English and we soon became lost amongst the nameless faces.

Alone and frightened, I found Sydney a daunting place. Dwarfed by the downtown buildings – many of which towered spectacularly skyward for ten floors and more – I felt like a mouse in a labyrinth of noisy streets, mousetraps waiting for me at every turn. A haven for sailors on shore leave, Kings Cross was a vibrant mix of nationalities. They spent most of their time drinking in hotels, accompanied by ladies who flocked to the sailors in numbers. With money to spend, it seemed these seagoing men had no shortage of admirers.

With so many world travellers at hand, I risked enquiring about passage to England, hoping that someone could advise me on the best way to go about it. It didn't take long before I had offers of help from shady characters of every description, all wanting to know how much I could pay, in cash or in kind.

I let the offers of assistance slide, though I had more than enough money to pay our way after emptying Lachlan's cash box. As his legitimate spouse, I had no qualms about taking everything. Though quite vulnerable, I was not entirely naïve. I knew enough to be cautious and told no one of the extent of my funds. In the privacy of our room, I separated the bulk of our money so that when negotiating a price for our passage, I would only have enough for the fare, and little to spare. I hid the remainder under the mattress of Kooper's bassinet.

Dark and dingy, our room looked out on a brick wall and drainpipe. Set on the third floor, the steps to and from seemed always filled with desperate, homeless people. Women of low repute had rooms next door to ours, and I heard them plying their trade through the night. When I awoke in the morning, I had insect bites all over my legs and arms, and Kooper had welts on his face. Cockroaches swarmed from cracks and crevices each evening as the sun went down, making it impossible to sleep until daylight, when we walked to a park and slept under the trees. Mould and water stains from the leaking roof, patterned the walls and ceiling. I had to share a bathroom down the hall with everyone else on the floor. The porcelain sink had a crack that leaked water, and a flushing toilet stank almost as much as our old dunny.

Days passed. I lay awake at night, looking for solutions and worrying over my lack of progress. The search for me would be well underway, and I shrank at every footfall in the hallway, expecting a knock on the door at any minute. Unaccustomed to sounds in the night that weren't animals or insects, I listened to the noise of the city. Traffic, car horns, voices and music, the bells of a fire engine, an ambulance as it sped through the streets. After my years in the bush I found it difficult to sleep without virtual silence.

Despite my caution, I eventually placed my trust in the wrong man. His name was Dirk and he convinced me he worked as a shipping clerk where he could purchase tickets on our behalf, without the usual questions. I should have been warned by the filth of his clothes, or the stink of his breath. I paid him one hundred pounds and never saw him again.

Distraught by the deceit, I was reluctant to trust anyone further and I feared we would never leave the city safely. I spent my days walking, becoming familiar with the long trek down William Street, gazing in store windows, dreaming of a better life somewhere far away. As time passed, depression set in. I wondered what Lou would be doing. He would be free now; probably off to some remote station looking for work. Perhaps he'd already put the events behind him, glad to be free of the whole sorry drama. Would he remember us in years to come? I couldn't bear the thought he wouldn't.

Kooper's little expressions reminded me of the first time I met Lou. He had a twist in his smile, just like his father's, a trait that would forever remind me of Lou and our days in the sun. I watched Kooper play. Developing quickly now, he was sitting up on his own. His hair had gone darker, and even his eyes had changed colour; they were now almost grey with flecks of yellow. He clutched a wooden rattle in his tiny hand, striking himself on the head as he waved it back and forth, so that he cried real tears, and turned down his lip in a terrible pout that melted my heart. It pained me that Lou would never get to witness such moments, his milestones, causing me to ask if I could live with such guilt. I told myself that I was doing it all for Kooper, that his future was at stake, yet still I had doubts about my decision to run and leave Lou behind.

After three weeks, I decided to go down to the wharves on the far side of town. I wasn't sure what I could accomplish, but I had no other ideas. The sight of the Harbour Bridge up close took my breath away. A steel monster that crossed the water like a great grey rainbow.

'It is awe-inspiring, no?'

The man had a familiar face, and I remembered seeing him at the boarding house. I tightened my grip on Kooper.

'It is, yes.'

'I have seen you at the house, no? We are neighbours.'

The man had a foreign accent but spoke excellent English. He had an olive complexion and grey hair beneath a navy cloth cap. I remembered that he had held a door open for me to pass through once. 'Yes. Not for too long though, I hope.'

'Oh, you break my heart. You do not like having me for your next door?'

'No,' I said, quickly. 'I didn't mean it like that. It's just that I...'

'Just what?'

'Just I need to find a way to England, and it's not going very well. I had a bit of misfortune.'

We chatted for a while, and he introduced himself as Alonso, a Panamanian sailor. We walked together to Pyrmont where he pointed out his ship, telling me it was a cargo vessel about to leave for Europe via South America.

'You have money left to buy ticket?'

Instantly I became guarded. I'd told him of my stupidity in already parting with my money and trusting a stranger.

'I still have funds, but I have no papers for my baby. I don't know who to trust.'

'You think I will cheat you like this bad man, no? You think Alonso is like same?'

'I'm sorry, it's just...'

'No, don't be sorry. I understand, but I am afraid for you. If my daughter is in trouble in far land, I would want someone to help her.'

Alonso had a kindly face and talked like a father might. He showed me pictures of his family as proof of his intentions, and I could see he was a good family man, proud of his wife and daughter. When he offered to help, I placed our safety in his hands. Trusting Alonso was a desperate leap of faith and my last throw of the dice. He promised to talk to the captain and meet me later. I had an anxious wait.

'I have good news.' We sat in a café and watched two policemen pass the window. Alonso saw the apprehension on my face. 'Hey, don't worry, those policemen are not looking for you, they are busy enough.'

'Good news?' I asked.

Alonso smiled at Kooper who was bouncing up and down in my lap. 'He is like kangaroo. Bounce, bounce, bounce. I have something for him.' Alonso presented Kooper with a rubber-faced monkey dressed in a bright coloured fur coat. 'His name is coco,' said Alonso to Kooper, as if he could understand.

'You said you had news.'

'Good news, yes. My captain, who is also my brother-in-law, a good man, will give you and your bambino passage. But this will be a long voyage, my dear. First, we must sail to Argentina. There we unload some cargo and pick up freight for Spain and England. You will be at sea for many weeks.'

'I understand, and I don't care, Alonso. We must leave Australia.'

I negotiated a price of one hundred and twenty-five pounds to be paid half on boarding the ship in Sydney, and the other half on departure from South America. Two days later, we boarded the Panamanian cargo vessel for the long voyage across the sea to Buenos Aries. Despite my fears at travelling on a cargo boat, we had a comfortable cabin and free run of the ship. I felt no joy at leaving, only relief that my nightmare might soon be over. My optimism was short-lived.

We had settled into our accommodation when the ship's horn blasted across the harbour to signal our imminent departure. Hurrying to the deck to observe our farewell, I couldn't help feeling buoyant, anxious to see us on our way at last. After emerging on deck, I looked over the railings, surprised to see the massive ropes tied taught to the wharf. Like the threads of a gigantic spider's web, they held us like prey against the dock wall. We waited in place while five minutes passed. Ten minutes passed, and before long, we had stood a further fifteen minutes without moving. Kooper focused on the cranes, having a one-sided conversation that only he could fathom. My attention had been drawn to a huddle of activity on the wharf. I took a sharp intake of breath, as the gangway rolled back into place at the gunnels, and a group of men boarded the ship, uniformed officers in heated discussion with the captain and crew.

'Don't worry, my dear.' Alonso came and stood behind me. 'They are looking for a missing crewman. It seems he drank too much, got drunk and did not return to the ship. We will soon be on our way.'

No sooner had Alonso assured me, the men disembarked, signing off on paperwork and allowing the gangway to be returned to the shore. Five minutes later, the lines were removed, engines rumbled, vibrating through the decks to my feet, and a tugboat guided us out of the dock and into the harbour proper. We left Cockle Bay, passed under the great bridge, slipped past a construction site on which Alonso said they would build an opera house, and crossed the harbour, causing ferries and smaller vessels to hurry out of our way. I watched the bridge recede from view, as we passed through the heads and out to sea, seagulls diving in our wake.

PART TWO

Chapter 31

Lake-Thiltakara

Present day, Cumbria, England

Kooper's Range Rover pulls into the drive to the crunch of loose gravel. He's lucky to arrive in between cloudbursts. He glances up and sees me at the bedroom window; his face is a scowl, he's angry. He'll have been bottling it up since leaving Buckinghamshire. Corina is at his side, nattering in his ear as always, barbed instructions no doubt as to how he should handle the situation, goading him and feeding his silent rage. How he puts up with her constant whining is beyond me. The signs were there even before they married. Both on their third marriage, I suspect that niether is committed to *this* one. He's grown his goatee again and I'm sure it will have annoyed Corina who hates it no end. I like it. He's the image of Billy Connolly when he has it. He still has a good head of hair, which used to be dark and curly, but it's now just straggly and grey, still a little too long for my liking.

Foolishly, I had hoped Kooper would come alone. I wanted to explain without Corina having to put in her tuppence worth, and making things worse in the process. I stay at the window while Kooper takes their bags from the boot, and watch them walk miserably to the house. Corina tiptoes across the yard as though the puddles are little cesspools to be avoided on pain of death. I wave, but neither responds.

My son's phone call had caught me by surprise, stunned me actually. Apparently he had come across a letter casting doubt on his heritage. I wasn't prepared for the torrent of fury. Lost for words, I had merely told him to come up to the farm where we could talk face to face. Kooper raved and ranted, demanding an explanation on the spot, but it would take more than a quick phone chat to put the genie back in the bottle, and I refused to discuss it further until he had calmed down. After hanging up, I had almost collapsed, feeling furious with poor Michael. How could he have been so careless? After brooding for an hour or two, I realised that I could only be angry at myself. There is no blame but mine, there never has been. For almost sixty years I have fled from the truth, but now, there can be no more running.

Michael, my husband, died seven weeks ago, just shy of his eightieth birthday and our fifty-ninth wedding anniversary. The doctors said the cause was pneumonia, but throat cancer killed him. A heavy smoker all his life, he had succumbed to the deadly disease like so many of his generation. His final years were not the easiest, but he handled his illness with his usual dignity. Recently we had spent most of our time apart, in order to follow our separate passions. Michael ran our horse stud in Buckinghamshire while I pursued independent interests, including the farm here in Cumbria and my love of landscape painting. He refused to leave the stud so that I could care for him, preferring to hire a full-time nurse so as not to place a burden on me. He had no intention, he said, of allowing me to witness on a daily basis his slow and painful demise. I confess to experiencing more than a little guilt at acceding so readily to his wishes.

Kooper's discovery has now exposed me for what I am: a coward. I've been hiding from the truth for so long now that I had virtually convinced myself of the lie. I thought I would take my secrets to the grave. Perhaps my crimes are too great for true penance, and God has decided I've had it too easy after all. Anyway, I have decided to tell everything. Kooper must know the entire story, no matter what the cost. Stephanie will arrive before lunch and is sure to want the scoop before anyone else. She'll probe Kooper for information, further angering her brother and making it difficult to talk rationally. She's always rubbed him up the wrong way, her bubbling nature fuelling his agitation. I'll need more than a few 'sly grogs' before these days are through.

My farm is called Drover's Elbow – a nostalgic homage to my hidden past – and sits on a rise overlooking a sharp bend in the river. Flanked by high fells, the crystal water meanders over a rocky, trout-filled riverbed through lush green valleys, and spills tamely into the beautiful lake before exiting westwards and eventually out to sea. Blue slate walls, three-feet thick, surround the house. They are covered in lichens and moss, a mottled patina reminiscent of spotted gum trees.

Another shower rushes through the valley, and the peaks have disappeared once more. The forecast, predictably, is for rain all weekend. I'll take a walk alone while they settle in before lunch, to clear my head and prepare for the confrontation to come.

I slip on my wellingtons and a raincoat and leave before Kooper can corner me. I check in at the barn first to see Buttercup (my great-granddaughter named her) who is ready to calve. She's one of five Ayrshires we keep for milking. My eyes adjust to the dark barn and she raises her head, wide-eyed, with a look that says, *I'm just about ready to go, so don't stray too far, Mum.* I stroke her flanks to reassure her and she responds with a snotty snort of thanks. The sweet smell of damp straw and cow dung fills the air and hangs like a curtain. To me, it's not a stench, but a heady fragrance, the aroma of life on a farm.

I'm satisfied that Buttercup still has time before labour. I cross the yard, wanting to make haste while the showers have eased. Cobbles are slick with rain and cow muck, and a stream of brown waste tumbles through the yard to the gutter. Cass and Ben lope over to join me, two border collies in need of a run. Cass has a black-and-white coat and odd-coloured eyes, one blue, the colour of mountain pools, one brown with flecks of gold. She follows me everywhere and rules over Ben and our other dog, Shep, like a tyrant. Poor Ben takes it all in his stride. Shep doesn't want to go out in the rain. He's ensconced in his kennel by the gate, watching our every move.

I climb the stile over the dry-stone wall, pausing to wonder at the vibrant green moss that covers it like throw rugs. I join the footpath that runs all the way down the valley to town, Herdwick sheep scattering as I pass. They watch my progress until they are sure I pose no threat, then return to feed on the lush grass. They are a hardy mountain breed, part of a flock of two hundred. Unlike other farmers who keep mixed flocks, mine are exclusively black-faced Herdwicks, the original mountain breed in this area.

The sky clears again as I reach the National Trust seat overlooking the lake and the mountains beyond; it's a panorama that takes the breath away. The bench has a brass plate and an inscription: *I will lift my eyes unto the hills, from whence cometh my help.* It resonates for me as I look to the mountains for peace. I find solace here in times of trouble. A buzzard winds like a corkscrew high above me, and a curlew, Michael's favourite, takes flight from the golden bracken.

Michael and I were a team, each a complement to the other. We took our dreams and turned them successfully into reality. How could I wish for more? I couldn't. Yet as I bless his memory and our years together, I feel my hidden loss so deep and painful that through all our years of triumph and achievement, not one day has passed without it cutting me like a knife. I will be forever grateful to my husband, though he would chastise me for saying so. You have nothing to be grateful for, he would say.

We were partners. Never once did he look back with regret. For almost sixty years we kept our secret, and now this letter of his. Why would he keep such a thing, a correspondence never sent? Kooper had found it while going through Michael's papers, checking for anything of importance that might need immediate attention. I had been sure he had left little of interest amongst them. Little of interest? Only a bloody time bomb.

Addressed to me, and dated February fourteenth, 1960, the unfinished letter had been unnecessary. Instead, we had met in person, taking the plunge and committing to our lives together. Michael had presumably planned to finish the draft and send it to me, but realising the urgent need to act for his plan to work, he came knocking on my door. I knew nothing of the letter.

My dearest Katherine,

It has been two days since our parting, and already I am missing you badly. I have slept little since disembarking, worried for your wellbeing and distressed over your future. I almost broached the subject while on board, three weeks ago, but I couldn't find the courage to ask. I don't think I have ever met someone as wonderful as you, inside and out. Sorry, that sounds slushy, and I know you are not the slushy type of girl. I'm not one for fancy words, and this all may seem daft to you. I bet you could choose any man you wanted, but correct me if I'm wrong, didn't we find something more than just friendship during the voyage? If I'm out of line, you must say so instantly. I will go on my way and never ask again. But if you feel even a hint of affection for me, then it only makes sense to act quickly.

I had planned to travel home yesterday. My family awaits. I don't know quite how to say this so I will come right to the point. I want to marry you, today, tomorrow, as soon as possible. You have a problem and so do I. Mine is love, yours is the welfare of your child. I don't expect you to reciprocate and love me in return, not yet at least. But one day perhaps. I can offer you loyalty and devotion. Kooper needs a father and a family, I would love him as my own. My plan is that we should marry here in London before travelling home to Bath. I will inform my parents of our meeting during my time in Argentina and of our secret romance. (Secret because I haven't mentioned any girlfriends in my letters home.) As far as they will be concerned, Kooper is the product of our time together. My father may think

And there the letter ends. Little wonder that Kooper is in such a foul mood. I try to imagine how he must feel, but I can only share his devastation at the revelation.

Cass is alert to a huddle of ewes, she pricks her ears and watches with growing impatience. 'Soon, Cass,' I say, thinking about the autumn gathering when we'll bring the sheep from the mountains to the valley for winter. She is one of the best mountain dogs and will work with Shep and the neighbour's dogs over the high ranges. Ben isn't fully trained yet and would do more harm than good. He will stay with me in the valley and wait his turn at future gatherings.

A figure catches my attention, walking up the path towards me. He's wearing one of those green, disposable rain ponchos, over a blue velour tracksuit. He's also wearing white running shoes – spattered in mud – and has a Bluetooth earpiece hanging over his left ear, making him look like a space cadet. He pauses and turns to his struggling companion. She follows at a distance.

'How much further?' asks the young man with a nod of his head to the crag up above.

I follow his line of sight. 'About eight or nine hundred feet. You're not thinking of going up there?'

He gasps and looks to the sky, ignoring my comment. 'It's not stopped raining since we arrived.'

'It tends to do that here. The weather turns very quickly and you're not equipped for the mountains.'

'I hope there's a pub at the top,' he says and marches on regardless.

I sit and wait while his partner makes her way slowly to me. She's carrying an inferior copy of a Gucci handbag and holding a pink umbrella above her head, with black and white cows pictured playing leapfrog. She's walking like she's pooped her knickers. I try not to laugh as she stops before me.

'I tried to tell your friend that the path can be dangerous.'

'He won't listen.'

'You should turn back.'

'Are you from around here?'

I think of what's to come and chuckle, ironically. 'To tell you the truth, I'm not sure where I truly belong.'

She shrugs but doesn't answer and struggles on after her companion. 'Josh! Wait up!'

I watch them disappear over the rise and hope they will see sense and return to safer ground before conditions deteriorate and they end up in trouble. An ominous black cloud turns the land dark once more. The highest peaks have disappeared, and I must head back to the farmhouse before the skies open up. I am surprisingly unafraid, all in all. Perhaps I have always known this day would come.

I return home to a roaring fire. Margery, my live-in housekeeper and friend of twenty-plus years, has made lunch.

Sandwiches, pies and pickles, with cake for dessert. I'm too nervous to think about eating. I take a cup of tea to warm me up.

Drover's Elbow is a large house, added to many times over the years since its first incarnation. It's really too big for me, but I love its homeliness. Windows are small, causing lamps to burn throughout most of the day at this time of year. The warm glow of so many lights and the orange flames of the blazing fire give the room that cosy, nostalgic feel of days long past. Vintage prints cover the walls, and blackened oak beams, decorated with horse brasses are original to the house. The ceilings are low in the lounge, an indication of changing human height since 1612 when the house was built. Kooper is an example at six foot two. His once wiry frame has ballooned so that his belly hangs over his belt like a sack of flour. I suspect he eats far too much fast food and pre-prepared meals, as Corina has no cooking skills whatsoever. Unlike Koop, she is almost emaciated.

I drink tea, avoiding conversation, while Koop picks at the food and Corina settles into an armchair by the fire.

'What anyone sees in a place that's always raining is beyond me,' she says, hugging herself as if she's been out in the rain and is frozen to the bone. I hold my tongue and say nothing in response.

I made it clear that we would not begin until Steph arrives. Murphy's law, she called from the motorway to say she was running late, an accident on the northbound lanes near Shap.

Corina won't take her eyes off me, her gaze is as though it is she I've deceived. She's anxious to get started. Margery hands her a cup of Earl Grey, but I know she'll be thinking about wine. As if she's read my thoughts, she asks if she's allowed to open a bottle of red to go with lunch. I tell her to help herself, and she's discarded her tea and is into the wine rack quicker than a rat up a drainpipe. Whatever Kooper sees in her, it's undoubtedly not her vibrant personality. I think he's attracted to pain; he must be because she's the same as his first wife who was selfish, full of her importance, domineering and manipulative. Every mother's dream of a daughter-in-law. Having said that, Koop's children from his first marriage are a delightful pair, as is my great-granddaughter, Irene. At least something good came from that partnership.

Stephanie arrives like a whirlwind. She spins around the room, shedding greetings along with her coat and scarf, and filling the house instantly with energy and light.

'Oh, would you believe it? I had to duck off at Orton and cut across the back road from there. Hi, Aunty Marge. Then I got stuck behind a blooming tractor. Hello, Corina. Have you changed your hair? It suits you. I thought I'd never get here.' She pecks Koop on the cheek. 'Hey, Koop, you've put on weight again.' Koop doesn't answer but checks his belly.

'Oh, that back road, a tractor pulling hay, a herd crossing from one field to another across the road, then another tractor. I couldn't believe it. Is that another painting, Mum? I do like that one. Francine says she wants you to do one for her.' No one gets a word in edgeways. 'Did you make the pie, Aunty Marge? Looks yummy.'

Steph is everything Kooper is not. Positive by nature, she fails to see the downside of any situation. Younger than him by six years, even so, she has always mothered her brother. There are times I think she's been a better mother than me. It's not that she's more patient, far from it, but she gets things done and drives Kooper forward whether he wants to go or not. She kisses me and gives me a look that says she's here for me, no matter what happens. Done with the greetings, she settles on the arm of my chair and gets right to the point.

'Okay, so what's all the fuss about?'

The room goes silent, and all eyes turn to me. 'I'll make myself scarce,' says Margery, making her way to the door.

'No,' I say. 'You're one of the family, please stay.'

'All sounds pretty serious,' says Steph, a bright smile on her face so that she makes light of the situation. She's like a beacon in the dark. Kooper and Corina respond with grim expressions, as though Steph has said something treasonous.

'Oh, come on, it can't be that bad.'

I pat Steph's hand and take a breath, but before I can speak, Corina opens her mouth, unable to conceal her smirk. 'Michael's not Kooper's dad.'

I could throttle her. I let Corina's outburst slide without comment, close my eyes and count to three, silent in my anger. When I open them, Steph is staring at me, wide-eyed and open-mouthed. 'Mum?'

Kooper chimes in. 'I found a letter in Dad's papers.' He hands the envelope to Steph. She takes out the letter and reads, whispering the words under her breath as she goes. Corina is standing with her arms crossed, her mouth pinched, waiting for Steph to react. Steph drops the letter to her lap and studies me as though she can't comprehend.

I turn to Koop. 'We talked about telling you.' He shakes his head and looks away. 'Please, everyone, sit down,' I say. 'This is going to be a very long day. And Kooper, I'll have one of those red wines too, if you don't mind.'

Kooper complies, though he's sulking. I take a sip and place the glass on the table beside me. When everyone is settled, I begin by telling them of my early years in the London orphanage and my shipment to Australia.

'I was a snip of a child when I left these shores. Skin and bones, there can't have been an ounce of flesh on me. I wasn't fragile though, quite the opposite in fact. And I had my brother, Archie. He made me feel strong, made me feel like I could take on the world. But you can imagine how devastated I was when we were separated on our arrival in Sydney.'

As I speak, my mind drifts back to those early days in Australia, and I'm soon transported to that time long ago. There's still an ache when I talk of Archie. I tell them of Daisy's cruelty, Lachlan's indifference on my arrival and my traumatic introduction to the austere outback life.

'I would never have survived if it were not for Toby and Ellin.' I speak warmly of our friendships, how they saved me from total despair. I recant the suffering Ellin and her family had endured, and wonder aloud if she was ever reunited with her children.

'How could they just take away her children? Surely she had rights,' says Steph.

'That's just how it was. Aboriginals didn't have the same rights.'

'But it was their land.'

'You don't have to tell *me*, Steph.'

I continue with my story as the hours pass and I chronical my childhood, the adventures that nearly killed me. I'm caught up in the memories and realise I'm smiling and laughing over some tales, almost crying over others. Kooper and Corina can't shake their long faces, even when the story is humorous, and there's no sign of empathy when it's not. Koop is irritated and says he wants answers not anecdotes. I can understand his urgency. Steph is absolutely enthralled and keeps interrupting with questions. I resist pressure to skip the details and describe Daisy's illness and her subsequent death, my relief at her passing. But as the spectre of my wedding approaches, I call for a break to compose myself first.

Chapter 32

Tell a story-Kulpa

'*This is ridiculous.*' Kooper stands, and he's even more agitated than before. 'I'm almost sixty years old and never once have I heard you mention that you lived in Australia.'

Steph jumps in, she's two steps ahead as usual. 'What about Argentina? You said you and Dad met in Buenos Aires.'

'We did meet in Argentina, that much is true. But there's so much more to tell before we get to that. Please let me finish my story and then maybe you will understand the need I had for secrecy.'

Darkness has come early. Rain peppers the windows, driven by high winds as the Lakeland storm finally takes hold. Margery stands and announces that she has to see to dinner. She has a roast in the oven and says she is sure everyone will want Yorkshire puddings. 'If I don't get busy,' she says on her way to the door, 'you won't be getting any dinner at all.'

I can't even think of eating, my stomach is in knots.

'You can't stop now,' Kooper demands.

'Well, I need more wine,' says Corina, and everyone rises and takes the opportunity to stretch their legs.

I sigh wearily and tell them we'll continue after dinner, much to Koop's annoyance. He's muttering and has that deep frown etched on his face. I get to my feet in an attempt to escape his ire. 'Margery will need some help in the kitchen.'

Steph pushes me gently back into my chair and says she will help Marge while I gather my thoughts. Corina, as usual, offers no help whatsoever and is already opening another bottle of Margaret River shiraz. I wonder if it occurs to her it's Australian wine and what she thinks of my story so far.

Kooper's face has changed little since arriving. I can see he's angry and I understand why. He wants to get to the nitty-gritty of who is his father. But he needs to know everything if he's to fully grasp my explanation. I'm not sure what he thinks about my tale so far, but he doesn't know the half of it yet. I wonder how he'll cope with the bombshell to come. He's extremely intelligent, but he's always found it hard to deal with emotional things. Perhaps it's my fault; Michael always said I was over-protective. Even as he nears his fifty-ninth birthday, I can't help treating him like a child. He worries about the smallest things, which makes him constantly unhappy. Not that he could ever be happy with Corina on his back 24/7. He wants to run the stud in Buckinghamshire, but I'm not sure it's a good idea. He knows horses, he's grown up with them, but he lacks the intuition needed for buying in bloodstock. And he goes from one business venture to the next, then loses interest. I'd hate to see the stud go the same way. Steph, on the other hand, has a nose for the business of buying and selling animals; she's got her father's instincts. I'd like her to take it on, but I don't want to see Kooper hurt in the process.

The Buckinghamshire stud was Michael's life work, his legacy, and it started with a horse called Ray.

The freighter on which I'd travelled had docked in Buenos Aires after the long voyage from Sydney. Though we'd had a smooth crossing, Kooper must have sensed the ship's motion and complained every step of the way. By the time we hit port in Argentina, I was at my wits' end, a total wreck. We were not allowed to disembark – for our own safety, the captain said – so I spent the time pacing the deck and watching the activity, a welcome relief to the boredom of open sea. Kooper was in my arms, crying inconsolably, when I first spotted Michael. I watched him supervise the loading of a horse into the ship's hold. The commotion seemed to attract everyone with an opinion. Poor Michael, ignoring the advice, waved his arms and shouted orders from the wharf, taking control while amused bystanders looked on. Slung in a purpose-made loading box, the stallion remained calm when hoisted on a crane, much to my surprise, while Michael looked totally stressed by the operation. There was a point when the crane started to sway at a dizzying height above the ship. I thought Michael would have a nervous breakdown, while the horse looked completely unfazed. All these years later, that stallion's bloodline still carries those same laidback traits, until his offspring hit the track of course; there's nothing laid back about them then. I glance at Ray's portrait, hanging above the fireplace. How marvellous the thoroughbred looked in his prime.

'I... I... Michael.' The first words stuttered, as he turned to see me standing against the railing.

'I... I... Katherine,' I mocked, though I was trying to be funny, not unkind.

There was a long pause during which Michael looked stunned. Eventually he closed his mouth and came to his senses. 'Sorry, I meant to say my name is Michael.'

'Yes, I gathered that. I was admiring your horse. It is your horse?'

'It is.' He couldn't take his eyes off me, as though he'd seen a ghost. 'I didn't expect to see another passenger on board. A delightful surprise,' he added quickly. 'We're on our way to England. The horse and me, I mean. But then, you'd know of course that we're going to England. Not that you'd know anything about our plans. I meant that you also travelling would know we were going to England. I'm babbling, aren't I?'

I laughed. 'Just a little. I'm Katherine Bower.'

'Michael Fellows. I think,' he said laughing. 'And who is this little chap?'

Kooper had stopped crying briefly, though his eyes were red and filled with moisture, his nose a snotty mess, and his lip was curled in a pout. He seemed fascinated by our new shipmate, studying Michael's face to determine friend or foe.

'This is Kooper, and I've come to realise that he's been sent by the Devil to deny me sleep and test my patience. He's hardly stopped crying since Sydney and I'm really starting to wonder if he ever will.' To my surprise, Michael took Kooper from my arms and started to rock him. Enthralled, I watched as Koop soon closed his eyes, gave a huge sigh and fell into a peaceful sleep.

The excruciatingly long journey from Buenos Aires to Southampton via Spain gave ample opportunity for Michael and I to become acquainted, spending much of the time below decks, where a special box had been built to house the stallion. We took turns in walking Como El Rayo – or in English, Like Lightning – whose name I quickly shortened to Ray. His enclosure measured just fourteen-feet square, so it was important to keep him moving. Sometimes I would walk the stallion while Michael rocked the baby, or kept him amused with a variety of funny faces. A natural with the boy, I saw the father in him even then. Michael was also an enthusiastic talker, for which I was relieved, for it meant I did not have to spend much time lying about my past. He sensed my reluctance to talk about Australia and didn't press me for details.

'What brought you to Argentina?'

'My father is a horse breeder and trainer. Our family has been in the business of horses for many generations, going back to the sixteenth century in fact. We have a large stable of thoroughbreds on our estate in Somerset, attached to the family home.'

'It sounds very grand.'

'Oh, not really. It's just a business.' Little did I know just how grand it would be. 'I've spent the last year and a half living and working with livestock breeders – experience to make me a man, according to my father – an apprenticeship of sorts. I have to admit, it's been worthwhile, and an amazing adventure. The Gutierrez family who own the stud were wonderful. They took me in as though I was one of their children. There were times I wished I was.'

'The language must have been a challenge.'

'Not really. I speak Spanish, but the dialect *was* tricky at first.'

'You speak Spanish?'

'Oh, I speak seven languages, Spanish is the easiest.'

He then went on to demonstrate his abilities with a thirty-second burst of foreign dialogue.

'Would you like some German?' Another burst of language followed. 'I'm proficient in them all.'

Daisy Stuart would have said he was big-noting; she had no time for braggarts. But I sensed an innocence in his declaration, that it wasn't a boast but a simple statement of fact. He must have read my mind because he apologised profusely, suddenly blushing with embarrassment.

'That sounded so conceited. I didn't mean to brag. Language was part and parcel of my boarding-school tuition.'

'I didn't have much schooling of any kind. But I speak two languages.'

'You do?'

'English and Australian.'

Michael's response was to erupt into a full belly laugh, a little too hearty considering my feeble attempt at humour.

'So where is Mr Bower?' he said, still laughing.

My stomach turned. 'He's dead,' I said sharply.

Michael looked mortified. 'I'm sorry, I didn't realise. That was insensitive of me to raise it.'

The speed of my response had surprised even me. 'No, please, don't be sorry. Of course you didn't realise. How could you have known?'

Michael looked away, embarrassed by his blunder. He didn't press me further; perhaps he saw the rawness of my grief, but days later, he broached the subject again.

'How did he die?'

It took me a long time to answer. Michael waited patiently while I contemplated a response. I wanted to tell him everything, but I knew I could not. 'A shooting accident,' I said eventually. 'I was responsible.'

'I'm sorry.'

'Why? It wasn't *your* fault.' I immediately felt angry at my barbed response. 'I'm sorry, that was uncalled for.'

'It must be hard for you, to know you have lost someone dear and yet feel responsible.'

The corner of my mouth turned in a sad, ironic smile. 'You're a good man, Michael. But can you do something for me?'

'Anything.'

'Then promise me you'll never ask about my past again. I don't want to lie to you.'

Michael took a moment to consider my request, then promised, and that was the last time he spoke of my life in Australia.

Everything happened so fast after we disembarked in Southampton. I can still recall the trepidation I felt on our chaotic arrival in England, the busy port alive with activity, an overwhelming sight, my future uncertain. Michael must have sensed my fear. We had already said our goodbyes when he suddenly insisted on helping me find lodgings.

'Michael, I can't ask you for help, you don't know what you're getting yourself into.'

'You didn't ask, I offered. And anyway, what kind of a man would I be if I left you alone in a strange city with no one to count on? I insist. I've arranged to stay at the Dolphin while I settle Ray into an equine quarantine facility. I'll be here a few days before heading home to Bath.'

Michael was marvellous, chasing around town to find me lodgings while I waited in his posh hotel's lobby drinking tea and feeling special. The Dolphin Hotel was indeed a grand establishment; it gave me a glimpse of Michael's world, though it would soon come crashing around his ears, and all because of me.

I was shocked when he arrived at my lodgings, two days later, and proposed to me on one knee. Initially I refused. I didn't want pity or charity, telling him I was more than capable of taking care of myself and my son. But Michael was insistent, arguing his case passionately while we took endless walks around town, Kooper content in his little world of dreams, oblivious to the decisions that were to be made about his future.

'I can't.'

'It's about your past, isn't it?'

'Don't!'

'I'm not. I don't care about your past. I only care about now, about you and Kooper. What happened to you in Australia is between you and God. I'll never bring it up again, if only you'll give me a chance.'

An ironic smile curled my lip into a sneer. God and I had plenty between us. I looked to the sky, as if for His blessing, and a crow flew by. We were walking on the common and crows were taking flight in numbers from the treetops in a noisy chorus. I thought of the cockies who came to the river gums. Cockies and crows – was this my world turned black and white, inside out?

We married in a registry office in Southampton after a tense fifteen-day wait due to requirements of law. We registered Kooper's birth at the same office before heading to Bath by train, after which all hell broke loose. Michael's father, Lord Grogan Fellows – I had no idea he was a lord until we arrived at the family mansion – left his son in no doubt that nothing short of an annulment would save him from total banishment. I gave Michael every opportunity to change his mind, but he was unshakable, even when his mother turned against him.

'I have no doubt that you will come to your senses,' she said. 'Your father knows what's best for your future. He understands that you are young and that you had to sow some wild oats before settling down, but you shouldn't have brought the crop home with you.'

I overheard their angry confrontation from another room.

'Pay the damn woman and be done with them both,' said Lord Fellows. 'I'm quite sure she'll go quietly once she's some brass in her pocket. You'll see she's easily bought.'

Michael would have none of it. He'd made his choice and nothing would change his mind. I will always remember the hatred on his father's face, directed at me as we drove away for good. Michael never spoke to his father again, abandoning his ancestral home, even as I pleaded for him to reconsider for his own sake.

That year, Michael renounced his peerage and with it, every penny of his inheritance, his sole possession then being the Argentine stallion – his father had wanted no part in the horse. Como El Rayo carried all our hopes for the future, and he didn't let us down. Within two years we bought a small holding west of Buckingham, and Argentine Park would grow to become one of the most highly rated studs in the country.

Chapter 33

Pull out-Ngaathu

Kooper is having one of those arguments with Corina, wherein they shout at each other in whispers. They think they're being discreet. I imagine it's hard to rage in whispers. The spectacle drives me to the kitchen to see if I can do anything to help. Margery and Steph go suddenly quiet as I enter. They've been talking about me.

'Well spit it out,' I say, as they give each other the eye. 'You're shocked and disappointed. Well, you haven't heard the half of it yet.' No one speaks. 'Are you sure I can't do anything to help, Marge?'

'It's all under control,' she says, blushing.

Steph is about to speak when Bill Jackson ducks his head through the back door, saving me from interrogation. He announces that Buttercup is about to give birth. Bill is an apprentice farmhand and works under the supervision of Simon Taylor, my farm manager. But Simon has gone to Scotland for the weekend, leaving Bill alone to deal with the animals. I grab my oilskin coat, don my wellington boots and head to the barn. Steph does the same.

'I had hoped she would wait until Simon got back on Monday,' I say as we dash through the rain. It's a wild night.

Fluorescent bulbs give the barn a cold and eerie glow, the low roof throwing long dark shadows. The stalls are tight, with little room for birthing.

Buttercup is anxious, evidenced by her wide eyes and heavy breathing. She's already laying down, but she's not yet ready to push. Steph kneels beside her and strokes her flanks gently. I tell Bill to go to the house and get himself a warm drink while we wait, and I settle down in the straw next to Steph.

'Kooper's a mess,' Steph says.

'Poor Koop, who can blame him? We almost told him,' I say, looking back over the years. 'He was about ten years old when your father decided he wanted to tell him the truth, about not being his father, but I wouldn't let him. I didn't want anything to take away from their relationship, didn't want Kooper to see Michael in a different light. He was Kooper's dad, that's all I ever wanted him to be, and that's the way I wanted it to stay.'

'So the whole story of you growing up in Argentina was...'

'A lie, I'm afraid. We didn't set out to lie to you, either of you. When we married, we made a pact not to talk about the past. Life had begun anew for both of us and the past held only heartache. It was a naïve concept, but it sounded simple enough at first. In practice it was far from easy. So we agreed to a simple story that would mirror the facts. We would say that I grew up in care. But instead of Australia, we would say it was Argentina, that I grew up in a home in Buenos Aires before meeting Michael as a teenager. Keep it simple, we said. What could go wrong? The trouble was, one untruth led to another, and before long we had woven a web of lies so great... Thankfully, things settled, and by the time we moved to Stoney Stratford, we had learned to push the past into the past where it belonged, and keep it there. Neither you nor Koop showed any interest in my childhood. On the odd occasion when I had to speak of it, the story was an unelaborate lie.'

'You made it so uninteresting, now I know why. I always thought you were ashamed of being an orphan, so I never pressed you for stories. So who is...?'

Bill returns to the barn carrying his mug of tea – he doesn't want to miss anything – and our conversation comes to an abrupt end.

'Have you decided on the stud?' asks Steph, changing the subject.

I look to Bill, but he's gone to a corner of the barn to sit, and he's not listening. 'Not yet,' I say. 'I was hoping we'd be sitting down to discuss that this weekend until Kooper came up with the letter.'

Steph and her husband Kevin have developed a successful business training thoroughbreds. Their daughter, Madison, is a jockey. Racehorses are in the family blood – Kevin's father is a trainer. The team has already provided the racing world with a string of winners, several from our stable. Steph wants to combine the operations, and I agree. Kooper wants to pack up his law practice and take over the stud on his own. I think he wants to prove himself to Corina, who keeps goading him into the idea. I'm totally torn between what's best for the children and for the stud.

Buttercup bellows, a signal that she is now ready to go. I see the water sack appear from her uterus, followed shortly by the calf's heels. 'Shit! She's breech,' I say. 'Bill, go to the house and ask Marge to phone the vet, the number's in my mobile on the kitchen table. Ask her to tell him we have a breech birth.' Bill races off to the house while Steph takes off her coat and prepares for what lies ahead. 'We'll keep her calm for a while and hope John Baxter gets here in time,' I say.

Bill arrives back shortly. 'Mrs Baxter says John is out on a call beyond Braithwaite. She'll give him a hoy and let him know, but doubts he'll be able to help.'

A crack of thunder makes us all jump at once, and Buttercup thrashes. 'Bloody hell!' Steph sighs. 'Go back to the house, Bill. Ask Kooper to come. We may need his strength for this one.'

'I'm strong.'

'I'm sure you are, Bill, but just in case, eh?'

Bill races off once more while Steph takes control. She prepares calving chains and spreads them out ready on the floor of the stall. Done with the chains, she goes to the tap, takes off her shirt and begins to wash, lathering up her arms with soap to the shoulders. This won't be the first time she's helped with a birth.

'Sorry, love,' I say. 'I'm not much help these days.'

Steph laughs. 'Yeah, but if I weren't here you'd be up to your elbows, I bet.' She greases her arms with Vaseline and slides her hand inside to feel for the calf's position. 'It's definitely breech, and it's twisted at a funny angle.' Steph pushes the calf back so that the feet disappear inside the cow once again.'

'Can you feel her front legs?'

Steph struggles. She's as tough as any man, but slightly built. 'I can't get her hock to move up.' She makes another concerted effort. She's now up to her shoulder in the cow. 'It's flexed tight. Hang on, it's moving.' Steph is puffing at the exertion.

'You'll need to keep the fetlock and hock tightly flexed and bring them over the pelvic bone.'

'I know, Mum, just let me concentrate,' she says, a little agitated. 'Got it!'

'Now the other one.' She doesn't answer me, and I get the message.

Bill runs in. 'Koop's on his way,' he says panting. He sees Steph in her bra and blanches. He doesn't know where to look, poor boy.

Kooper appears at last. 'Kooper, wash up and give your sister a hand,' I say.

'It's okay, I've got it,' says Steph. She pulls on the calf's legs until the hooves peep through. 'Chains,' she calls, reaching behind for someone to pass them. Kooper feeds them to her, and Steph attaches them to the calf's legs. Carefully, they pull the calf, Steph making sure no legs are caught inside. With a final effort from Koop, the newborn calf slips into the straw with a slurp, steam rising from its glistening body. Steph removes the birth sack, clears its nose and mouth of fluid, blows up its nose and flicks its ears. The calf takes a breath and raises its head. It's been an effort, but mother and calf look healthy. We drag the calf into a clean stall with fresh straw and watch as Buttercup gets to her feet and follows. She's a good mother and begins to lick the calf clean. A good mother. I look at Kooper, and I wonder if I can say the same.

Chapter 34

Husband-Marli

The next day, we gather again in the lounge so that I can continue. The rain has passed, the mountains are clear, and it looks like a good day ahead, at least as far as the weather is concerned. By the time we had dealt with Buttercup and her calf yesterday evening and had eaten dinner it was far too late to continue where I left off. I retreated to bed before anyone could press me further, much to Kooper's frustration. But I want him to know the whole story, and I need time to explain fully.

Sleep has done little to melt Kooper's frown. He wears it, emblazoned across his forehead, like a badge of honour. Corina looks as if she's about to vomit, and no wonder after the amount of wine she consumed. She'll bounce back by four o'clock, just in time for pre-dinner drinks. Steph takes her place at my side, holding my hand in a show of support. When everyone is ready, I begin where I left off.

'After Daisy's death, everything changed. There was a mood of relief. We had lived with Daisy's illness for so long, it was seen as a blessing when it ended with her passing. Lachlan had been missing from the homestead, unable to cope with her sickness.'

I pictured Lachlan as Ellin begged him to spend more time with Daisy, her condition was grave. He refused, saying he needed to work, and that Daisy would rather be alone when she died. He talked of her death without compassion, or any apparent feelings of regret. Perhaps we all wanted it to end.

'Now that she was gone, it seemed he was always at the house. I saw a new side to him. He was full of good spirits, laughing and joking, his humour infectious. He teased me and horsed around, acting like a clown. It was like a cloud had lifted, a burden shed for the first time in years. When he started making advances, I couldn't help feeling wonderful. I felt flattered by his attention.'

'Mum! You were fifteen!' Steph's outrage is understandable; middle-aged men didn't flirt with fifteen-year-old girls, or shouldn't, and fifteen-year-old girls certainly didn't welcome those advances. 'He was your father.'

'He was never my father,' I snapped.

'Well, you know what I mean. You were in his care and he should have known better. *You* should have known better. What were you thinking?'

Kooper and Corina grimace disapprovingly, as though I had committed some great crime against them personally.

'What was I thinking? I was thinking that for the first time in my life I felt wanted. When he touched me, stroked my hair or brushed my cheek, it made me feel loved. I wanted him to care about me, and when he told me I was lovely, I believed him.'

'But couldn't you see it was wrong?'

'Perhaps.'

'You should have turned tail and run, screamed blue murder and run for help instead of leading him on.' The room goes silent as I look to the floor in shame, searching for words to explain. 'You were a child for God's sake,' Steph says eventually.

'I've asked myself many times why I succumbed so readily to his advances. What made me, a child of fifteen – oh, I was still very much a child, I know that now, you don't have to remind me, Steph – what made me allow a forty-six-year-old man to take such liberties when I should have reacted with disgust and fled? A voice inside my head said as much, but I didn't listen. I can only say in my defence that I was trusting. They were different times, and I knew no better. I wanted to be loved, Steph, was that too much to ask?'

Silence.

'I was a child, yes, and I had until that moment been dominated by this man and his bullying wife. I was vulnerable to the change in him. Suddenly he was nice to me, it made me feel wanted at last. For any of you to judge me, you must first have walked in my shoes.'

Kooper looks out the window. Corina remains indignant, though she can't look me in the eyes. Steph squeezes my hand and apologises for speaking out of turn.

'Lachlan falsified my age. I believe he bribed a Justice of the Peace to ignore the discrepancy, and we married at Broken Hill.'

I go on to describe our wedding day as the images flash through my mind, how I happily made my promises to love, honour and obey, unaware of the ordeal that would follow. It's an even greater ordeal to tell my children of the brutal moments I had long ago banished from my mind. I leave out the worst details, but tell of my wedding night and my misery at the hands of Lachlan, my devastation at his heartless lust, how he left me a broken child.

'Oh, Mum, I'm so sorry.' Steph wraps her arms around me. She's crying buckets, so I kiss her. It should be me crying, me that needs comfort, but I don't. I feel that same cold anger I experienced that morning, as Lachlan drove away, leaving me wretched and changed forever.

Koop clears his throat, but he can't look at me or speak. I know what he's thinking, but he's wrong. I press on with my story, and for a while the sickly feelings of loathing subside as I tell of Lou, our chance meeting, and his time on the station. I'm transported back to see his lazy smile, and a warmth fills my heart. I realise I'm smiling when I describe him, and everyone sees that I love him still. Even after all these years, I can't hide my affection, it's written all over my face when I think of him.

'I knew I loved him from the first time I set eyes on him. He was everything Lachlan was not, and he made it clear that he also had feelings for me. It would have been simpler if I'd up and left with Lou right then, but I didn't, and he went away. That's when the dust storm came through.'

I spend the next hours telling of my fight for survival and my promises to God. I tell of Lou's return, the struggle with my conscience, our inevitable romance and my ultimate betrayal.

'It wasn't betrayal,' says Steph. 'You can't possibly believe that God wanted you to stay loyal to that man, not after what he did?'

'I did at the time, Steph. It was a bargain struck with God, and I failed to live up to my end of it.'

'A bargain with the Devil more like.'

'Steph!'

'Well...'

'When I found I was pregnant, I thought it was a sign.'

'A sign?'

'A sign that God had forgiven me. Why else would He give such a gift? Of course, Lachlan thought it was his, and I was too afraid to tell him the truth. Lou and I decided to wait until after the birth, and then planned to run away together. But we could never have foreseen the twist in the tail, and God's cruel justice.'

I press on while I still have the courage to revisit the events that followed. Koop, Steph and Corina listen in stunned silence as I once again live through the ordeal, the trauma and shock. I describe in detail the birth of the twins.

'Your brother's name is Robin. He died shortly after being born. He was like a premature baby, too weak to survive.' Koop is silent. 'Ellin was trying to hide him from Lachlan, but we were too late. Lachlan returned as she was leaving the house and discovered the truth.'

Anxiety builds in me as I describe the attempt to save my child, how I turned my gun on Lachlan and fired, killing him where he stood. I'm wretched when I finish. Lachlan is once again lying dead on the ground, a vivid re-enactment as the scene plays out in my mind. I'm standing over him and the world spins out of control. I can even smell the gun smoke.

Steph's jaw gapes open, her eyes a picture of disbelief as she tries to absorb the revelation, the conclusion: her mother is a killer. Kooper is distraught. He's shaking his head, hands on his ears as if he might shut out the words, unhear my confession. Corina watches everyone else, waiting for a reaction.

Eventually, it's Kooper who breaks the silence. 'You killed my father?'

Steph turns to him. *'Koop, your father?'*

'I... What... I don't get it,' says Kooper. But he's in shock, unable to rationalise.

'God, you're slow,' Corina says. There's contempt in her voice. She's fit to burst when she turns back to me.

'What?' says Koop.

Finally, Corina breaks into a smug smile, laughs, and turns back to her husband. 'For an intelligent person, you're so dumb at times. What did you think, that one baby was Lachlan's and the other one was Lou's?' Kooper doesn't answer. 'You still don't get it do you?' Koop's trying to make sense of it all. *'You're a bloody Aborigine!'* Corina says, choking over her laughter.

Koop's face contorts as the penny drops. Corina reaches out to take his arm, but he shrugs her off and storms out.

'Koop!' I shout, but he's gone.

'Bloody hell, Corina. Was that really called for?' says Steph as she takes my hand and I get to my feet. My knees are like jelly. I brush Steph off and cross the room to Corina. I'm furious at her remark and want to slap her, but I don't.

'I can't imagine you've ever been truly loved,' I say, trying hard to not to lose it. 'or you would never feel the need to hurt the one you should care about most.' Corina just stares at me. 'Your insensitive remark goes right to the heart of it, you see. It says everything about you. It reveals a sad woman behind the make-up and arrogance, the mean spirit you seem always ready to share. My son does indeed have Aboriginal blood, but every drop is worth more than all the ice that runs through *your* veins.'

Corina's lip quivers. She looks to Steph but finds no support there. All she can say is, 'I'm sorry,' as I leave the room.

Chapter 35

Blame-Winpa

By mid-afternoon, the tantrums are over. I've apologised to Corina for my remarks and she, to her credit, has accepted my contrition with good grace, taking responsibility for her part in the unpleasant encounter. Kooper's hurt is far more significant and will take years to heal, if ever, but there is more to my story, and I must continue if there is to be any catharsis.

We decide that we all need fresh air and drive out to a favourite spot by the lake where we can walk for a while and blow out the cobwebs. It's hard to be angry when surrounded by such tranquil beauty. The lake is a mirror and the mountains are clear. I watch an osprey skim the water and take off towards the peaks.

'He should have flown south weeks ago,' I say, but no one is listening.

I walk arm in arm with Steph. She's huddled in close, wrapped in a winter parka, her nose red with the cold. Kooper and Corina follow until we come to a place to sit.

'I can't imagine what you went through,' says Steph. 'You must have been terrified.'

'I was more than terrified, I was in a complete state of shock. They would call it post-traumatic stress these days. If it had been left up to me, I would have confessed everything and would probably have gone to prison. Instead, I listened to Lou and Ellin, and let them guide me. Lou never wavered for one minute, stepping forward without hesitation to protect me, to protect us both, Koop.' I look to Koop but he doesn't react. 'Lou and Ellin concocted a plan and I was too overwhelmed to object. Lou was to say he killed Lachlan who was drunk and out of control. If I'd been thinking more clearly I would never have agreed. But I let him have his way, and Lou went to trial.'

'It's so amazing that Lou stepped forward to take the blame. Don't you think it's amazing, Koop?' says Steph.

Kooper doesn't respond. He's still seething and can't look me in the eyes. I know this is hard on him, and I'll give him all the time he needs. But I hope he can find it in his heart to forgive me. Unstoppable now, I go on through the trial – how, when it seemed that Lou would be convicted, I left my

memories of that day. We made a pact never to discuss it, he never pressed me to tell him, and I never offered. I didn't want to burden him with the knowledge, what he didn't know couldn't hurt him. I wanted to tell him, many times, when I was low and desperate, alone with my thoughts, with my guilt, but I resisted and was glad he never had to face the implications.'

'It was a terrible secret for you to carry alone.'

'It was my penance to bear.'

We say nothing for a long while.

'Do you think he's still alive?' Steph says, at length.

'Who?'

'Mum.'

I sigh. 'You can't leave it alone, can you?'

'Do you want to know if he is?'

If she understood my terror, she would not have to ask. 'I have a feeling I'm not going to have a choice.'

'You never thought of him, never looked back once, curious to see how he was doing after you left?'

'Of course, I thought of him,' I growl. I hesitate, take a breath. 'I'm sorry. Of course I thought of him,' I repeat in a softer voice. I have no right to get angry. 'I've never stopped thinking of him.' Steph looks at me and I know she's wondering how I could think of him and still love Michael. 'It didn't stop me loving your dad, Steph. What I said is true, I loved Michael deeply. But Lou is my first love, my lost love. Robin, my lost child. There's not a day goes by I don't think of them and miss them both, just as I miss Michael now. You have to remember that in those days, Australia might as well have been the planet Mars it was so far away. We had no internet, no social media, television coverage was poor and usually local, and the newspapers rarely covered anything of Australian news here in England, let alone details from an obscure case in the outback. Once I left Australia, I knew nothing of what happened, and it wouldn't have been easy to find out. And even if I had wanted to, I was a wanted person. I would have risked everything.'

Steph squeezes my arm. 'I know, Mum.' We walk on. I know she's troubled.

'What's bothering you?' I ask.

'He went away, Mum. He was convicted.'

I freeze, unable to comprehend for a long moment. 'No,' I say eventually. 'No, that can't be. I confessed. I cleared his name.' Panic has risen in my chest. I'm short of breath.

'Do you need to sit down?' I shake my head, compose myself. 'They convicted him of murder,' she continues. 'Sentenced him to life in prison.' I waver. Steph is quick to say more. 'But his lawyer appealed because Ellin's eyewitness testimony had not been taken fully into account. They reduced his sentence to fifteen years for manslaughter. He served ten years before being released. I'm sorry,' she adds, her voice soft and sympathetic.

I'm dazed, weeping. Steph wipes my eyes and hugs me. But I find little comfort in her embrace.

Chapter 37

Search-Mayanta

We return to the farm where we are warmed by a blazing fire and my shock begins to thaw along with my fingers. Steph wants to show me on her laptop what she's found. Damn you, Google, I inwardly curse. I can't bring myself to look, so Steph relates the story in more detail.

'The page is an extract from *The Barrier Miner,* a local newspaper from Broken Hill. It's dated November third, 1959.'

'I think we were en route to South America then.'

Steph says there is not a lot of information, no mention of my confession, not even a reference to my sudden disappearance. 'The extract from the paper recaps the case in brief and describes the life sentence as a just conclusion to the trial. There's a second reference to the case almost a year later,' says Steph, as her fingers tap the keys and she brings up a similar-looking archived newspaper page. I feel sick.

'Mum, it says that after convicting Lou and giving him a life sentence for murder, the trial was followed eleven months later by an appeal hearing in front of a panel of judges. In a unanimous decision, they quashed the murder conviction after reviewing the evidence. It quotes the leading judge, "It is the view of the appeals court, that Oogoola Holston's actions resulted in the death of Lachlan Stuart, but in our opinion, the crime falls short of murder because we find that Holston didn't intend to kill Mr Stuart. However, we believe that he acted with reckless indifference and a wanton disregard for the victim's life and as such his actions still required a severe sentence." He was ordered to serve a minimum ten years of a fifteen-year sentence, including time already served while awaiting his appeal.'

'Why didn't they take my confession?'

'It could have been worse,' Steph says unconvincingly. 'He could have...' She lets the train of thought go. 'They sent him to Goulburn Prison. I couldn't find anything about his release. I checked electoral rolls as his name's a little unusual. There's nothing in the Broken Hill area that matches. I checked deaths and marriages. Nothing. I tried Facebook, Instagram and other social media, didn't really expect anything, but again I found nothing.'

'You won't find Lou on Facebook, Steph. And if Lou went back to stock work, he would always be on the move. It wouldn't be unusual for him to be unregistered on electoral rolls. He wouldn't own a house, he would live for short periods on stations or in boarding houses and camps. Some drovers worked until they dropped without ever laying down roots, I suspect Lou would be one of them. He'd be seventy-seven now if he's still alive.'

My mind wanders and I try to imagine what he would look like. Would he still be handsome? Surely yes. I start to cry again. I must be getting soft in my old age. But all I can think about is the ten years of Lou's life lost because of me.

'Mum, are you okay?' Steph asks as the clock on the mantle strikes noon. 'Tempus Fugit', say the words on the clock face. I wonder how Lou found the passing of time. 'At his age, Lou obviously won't be driving stock anymore,' she says. 'He would have only been about thirty when released, so chances are he found a partner and had a family. If so, he may well be sitting at home somewhere enjoying his retirement and reminiscing about the good old days with Kate Stuart.'

'Steph!'

'Sorry, that was flippant. But he may well have a family. That's what I hoped for on Facebook. I thought maybe if he had children, or maybe grandchildren, they might be on social media. Older people often have Facebook pages so they can keep in touch with their kids and grandkids.'

'I don't.'

'You don't even own a computer, Mum.'

'I do, I just don't use it.' The thought of Lou having a family gives me hope that he did find happiness. Do I really want to know?

Reluctantly, I give Steph permission to dig further into Lou's life, and she goes about it with her usual zeal, leaving no stone unturned. She's hired the services of an Australian private investigator specialising in finding people who don't want to be found. Dean Ibrahim, a Melbourne man, is good at his job. Within weeks he's located Lou's family clan, scattered in areas north of Adelaide, and north-west along the Darling River. Information comes to us piecemeal, and my anxiety grows with each new bit of the puzzle. I know where the search is heading. Finally, as I expected, Dean has found Lou. He's alive and living in a nursing home in Wilcannia. He does indeed have a family. Now the inevitable question: did I want to make contact?

I'm at the stud in Buckinghamshire. It's the only way I'll get to speak with Kooper. He has maintained his rage and makes me feel it in his curt exchanges of pleasantries. Steph has been busy, of course, priming him so that he is fully aware of events concerning Lou. Corina had him take one of those DNA tests they advertise on the television to trace your ancestry. Apparently, it *is* possible to have twins from two different fathers and she thought he should know for sure. *Such a supportive partner, bless her.* I tell myself to stop sniping and give her the benefit of the doubt, for Koop's sake. Anyway, the results showed Koop shares a good portion of his heritage with the people of Australasia and Melanesia, as well as having some Scandinavian and Welsh blood. While they say it's not absolute proof of his Aboriginal heritage, it's strong enough evidence to support what I knew to be true. He's Lou's son. I had never a doubt.

I called a family meeting. Corina is present, but this time the balance is more in my favour as Steph's delightful husband, Kevin, and my granddaughter, Madison, have joined us. I'm about to surprise them all with a decision I made a few days ago. I'm going to go to Australia to see Lou.

It is two weeks till Christmas. Typically, we would have had plans in place for the festive season, a family gathering at Drover's Elbow is the tradition, but Kooper has procrastinated, and I struggle with the idea of our first Christmas without Michael. I had thought about changing the venue, a new tradition where we might celebrate away somewhere. But the thought of Christmas at all gives me cause to choke up and cry.

'I've spent my life running,' I begin. 'By now you all know my reasons, though they no longer seem justifiable. Over the years I managed to build a convincing web of deceit, lying to everyone, including me, even convincing myself at times that the whole unhappy episode was a product of my imagination, another life, not mine. There are no excuses for what I have done. I told myself it was for Kooper.'

Koop looks as if he's about to object, but I stop him with a halting hand. 'I told myself it was for Kooper,' I repeat, 'but that was unfair to him, only I can shoulder the blame. I did it because I was afraid, and I've been hiding ever since. I should have told you, Koop.' Koop places his face in his hands. 'But now I'm done with hiding and I'm done with lies. You know the truth now, you know everything. If you wish to punish me by not speaking, I understand. If you no longer wish me to be part of your life, you must do as you think best.'

Kooper does not answer, but Steph jumps in.

'Of course he wants you to be part of his life, Mum. If he—'

'Please, Steph, let me finish. I intend to go to Australia.' There's a gasp from Kevin and Steph. Kooper looks astonished. 'I'm going to find Lou and ask his forgiveness.'

'Mum...' Steph wraps herself around me. Madison joins her while the others look on.

'Steph has found Lou in a nursing home, which I'm sure you are all aware of by now. I want to see him while there's still time.'

'Well, I'm coming with you,' says Steph immediately. 'There's no way I'm letting you go all that way alone. Are you sure about this?'

Kooper interrupts, he's incredulous. 'You can't just show up after fifty-odd years and expect him to, what, welcome you with open arms, tell you everything's fine, and he's not mad you left him holding the bag? My God, Mum, how can you even think about going back?'

He's right. I have no reason to think this will change anything or that Lou will want to see me, let alone forgive me, but I must do what I have to do. I've made up my mind.

'I don't expect anything,' I say to Koop, 'but the time is long past. I should have done this years ago. This is not up for negotiation, Koop. I have to go back.'

'Come with us, Koop,' says Steph. 'You have more at stake than anyone. Mum's not the only one that needs to lay ghosts to rest. If you don't go, you'll always be left wondering.'

Koop's eyes are wide, manic almost. 'You're all crazy. You've gone quite mad. What could I possibly get from meeting a man who has never been a father to me? Dad was my dad, no one else. And by dragging up the past, you're destroying his memory.'

'You're the one who dragged it up, Koop. You brought the letter out into the open,' says Steph.

'Steph, please. It's not Kooper's fault. No one is to blame but me. *Haven't I made that clear by now!*' I turn to Kooper. 'Michael was a father to you in every sense of the word except one. Nothing you say will change that fact. He had the good grace to give up the life he knew for you and me, and he never wanted anything in return except our love, and he got it. Michael knew I had a past, it didn't stop him loving me. He knew you had a father, and it didn't stop him loving you and being your dad. I can't change the things I've done, the hurt I've caused you, Koop, but I must do this now and it would give me the strength to complete it if you were by my side.'

Kooper closes his eyes tight, grimaces as a tear squeezes from his lid and rolls down his cheek. I go to him, offer my arms, and he takes them, weeping like a child into my bosom while I stroke his hair.

Chapter 38

Arrive-Parpa

The plane banks steeply as it begins its final descent. I see the ground, the houses and streets, cars like matchbox toys on the busy city highways. The plane levels out, and there, shining in the sun is the city of Sydney with its jewel of a harbour, waterways and headlands. There are boats on the dazzling water, and high-rise buildings reach skywards in a glistening collection of glass and concrete. This is a far cry from the city I left so many years ago. I see the bridge and the white sails of the Opera House – the sun catches them and they sparkle. I'm sitting in the window seat. Steph and Kooper lean over to get a view.

'Wow!' says Steph. 'It's beautiful.'

Even Koop has given way to smiles.

'It didn't look like this when I sailed from here, all those years ago. The Opera House wasn't even built back then, and there were none of these skyscrapers. I don't think I gave its beauty a second thought. To me the place seemed dismal and intimidating. I couldn't wait to leave.'

I remember our departure on the South American freighter. How fearful I was until well out to sea. Kooper has been a different man since we exorcised our demons before Christmas. He and Corina have decided to separate. I'm not surprised, though I'm broken-hearted for Koop yet again. We celebrated the festive season modestly; no one felt particularly joyous, though we did enjoy sharing memories of Christmases past, with Michael always on our minds. In the back of my mind, however, I had other thoughts at play. I tried hard not to reveal my trepidation of our trip, and I suspected that Kooper hid the same fears.

We had debated at length whether we should make contact with Lou and his family beforehand. Steph and Kevin thought we should at least warn the family of our intentions to visit. But in the end Kooper wanted us to arrive unannounced. He reasoned that if we informed them, it would give the family a chance to put us off. And if they put us off, we would forever be left wondering what would have happened if we'd gone. I tried to imagine how I would feel in Lou's position. Would I want him turning up unexpectedly? I had no hesitation in saying that I would, no matter how painful the meeting might be. So it is that we will arrive out of the blue at the nursing home in Wilcannia.

Two days after arriving, refreshed and prepared, we take the morning flight to Broken Hill. The plane is a Dash 8 and thankfully not as small as I imagined. There are about fifty seats but only a dozen passengers on board. I watch the propellers kick into action, and we are soon in the air, though it's noisy and the plane is vibrating like a jackhammer. We've each taken a window seat to take in the view during the two-and-a-half-hour flight. The suburbs and towns quickly give way to bushland, mile after mile of wooded hills and back country. As the trip progresses, habitation becomes less frequent, farms and small towns appear and disappear as the land stretches out before us. After an hour or so, the earth turns red, and even trees become scarce. Every so often I see the dust plume from a solitary vehicle travelling remote roads and tracks, a signature of life in the outback. Dry creek beds spread like fingers across the land and salt pans dot the landscape. I watch the shadow of our plane on the ground below us. This is the land I knew. This is Australia.

'It's so barren,' says Steph. She's fascinated by the scale of this country, even though we have barely been gone from the city an hour. Koop has gone quiet, lost in his thoughts.

At Broken Hill we pick up a Land Cruiser and drive into town, passing under a sign that says: 'Welcome to Broken Hill, where the outback begins'. I see the mine-heads up front. The town is bigger than I remember, but unlike Sydney, little has changed. I see the clock tower and the main street, we cruise down Argent Street and I recall the supply stores and places I knew. The tenants have changed, but the buildings remain the same. I see the courthouse and the police station, and my heart skips a beat, my chest tightens. It looks quaint now, with its stucco façade and colourful coat of arms: a tourist landmark, no doubt. The bronze soldier still stands on his plinth, and I recall my terror beneath his outstretched arm as the angry mob cornered me there. *Pommy bastard! Slut!* We drive on past, and I say nothing.

We pass the Caledonia Hotel, and I remember talk of Lachlan's drunken binge in there one night, and his return to the homestead, Daisy's cursing. 'Go live with your bloody mates!' she screamed, as Lachlan collapsed on the floor and vomited. 'There's not a man worth having between the bloody lot of you.' I remember the pub in Wilcannia where he met his mates at the back door on Sundays for some sly grog and gambling, and the inn on the highway where he fought when he had too much to drink. Daisy had little patience with Lachlan when he was drunk and wasting money, and even less when he came home violent.

We stay the night at a motel in town. I remain in my room and rest while Koop and Steph go out to eat, though the air conditioner is so noisy it's difficult to sleep. On returning, Steph comments on the courthouse.

'Is that where they held the trial?'

'Yes. The lock-up was behind the courthouse. It's been so many years, but the memories are as vivid now as then, I recall every detail. That was the last place I saw Lou as he stood in the courtroom almost sixty years ago. But it's like watching a movie, as though it's someone else's life I'm seeing.'

The next morning we take the Barrier Highway and head for Wilcannia. The highway is sealed with bitumen, unlike the potholed dirt road I knew as a child, dotted with road-kill and mile after mile of nothing but spinifex grass and mulga scrub. Now I feel at home.

'I can't believe you lived here,' says Steph. 'There's nothing here but wide open space.'

'It takes a special breed of person to live here.'

Koop is silent until we hit Wilcannia, two hours from Broken Hill. We drive into town and cross the river, and then we're already driving out of town.

'Blink, and you'd miss it,' says Koop, the first words he's spoken since leaving the motel.

'This was our nearest town. Slightly closer than Broken Hill, but it's still almost two hours of dirt roads to Cutaway Creek. We were very isolated.'

We turn back and stop at the bridge. Sadly, I recall dear Toby. This was where he died.

'It's a funny-looking bridge,' says Steph.

'This is the Darling River. The bridge raises to allow boats to pass under.'

'Boats! But there's hardly any water, just mud and slime,' Steph says.

'There used to be water, sometimes it was full. I told you how it flooded once. Toby used to bring me here to show me the paddle boats passing under the bridge on their way down the river. We'd sit right over there and watch the bridge go up and down. I remember one boat called *Marion,* and thought it strange to give a boat a girl's name. We tied our horses under those very trees. Toby would tell me stories from when he was a boy, fishing in the river for golden perch and yabbies. He'd be sad to see the river like this now.'

We locate the nursing home – a fibro cottage with an extension built on the back, like a portable school classroom. There's a sign outside that reads, 'Opal Palliative Care Unit'. My heart sinks.

'Nobody said anything about palliative care,' says Steph.

I'm angry we didn't know beforehand. 'This is a mistake,' I say, panicking.

We're parked outside, staring at the building, when a woman appears through the front door, followed by a man who is laughing. The woman is Indigenous, maybe thirty-five to forty years old, round-faced with a jolly appearance. The middle-aged man has silver hair and looks like a young Bill Clinton. They pause on the threshold and look to our vehicle, the woman raises her hand to shield her eyes from the sun. It's midday and hot. She's curious, waves and comes down to the street.

'Can I help you, folks?' she says smiling.

I suddenly want to give an excuse and leave.

Steph lowers the window. 'Hi,' she says. 'We're looking for the resident of a nursing home here in town, Lou Holston. This was the address we were given.'

The woman sees me in the back seat. 'This is a palliative care facility, not a nursing home. Are you sure it's Lou that you're looking for?'

The man is standing on the steps watching. Kooper looks as anxious as me as the man comes down to join us.

'These folks are looking for Lou.'

'I'm Doctor Walsh,' says the man. 'Lou is one of my patients.'

'This is my mum,' says Steph. 'She's an old friend of Lou's. We're here from England, and my mum wants to say hello.'

The doctor's face softens, but the woman frowns. 'This is Lisa Chalmers, she's Lou's niece,' the man says.

There's no going back now, so I get out of the vehicle. Steph and Kooper follow my lead.

I offer my hand to Lisa. 'I'm Katherine Fellows.' I'm trembling when she shakes my hand. 'Perhaps we could talk somewhere private.'

Chapter 39

Meet-Pinta

We walk a couple of blocks to a rural supplies yard where Lisa is the administration manager. She shows us into a small office and offers tea and coffee before settling down to talk. The office is cramped for space and has all the indications of a hectic schedule, a desk loaded with files and paperwork, a computer, and there's a printer balanced on a pile of books in the corner of the room. There are schedules and timetables, photos of local customers, and children's artwork displayed on the walls, some of it quite good. There are certificates awarded for local business excellence and thanks for sponsoring community events. The office is hot and has no air conditioning.

'How do you know my uncle?' is Lisa's first question as she squeezes behind her desk. I'm finding it hard to know where to begin.

'Lisa, this is difficult for me and, to be honest, I don't know where to start. Lou and I were... close. I said we were old friends, but we were more than that.' Lisa doesn't respond. I can't read her face. 'I'm talking way back before... before any of you three were born.' Kooper shifts uncomfortably and looks away.

Lisa smiles and raises her eyebrows and points a finger in the air as if she's suddenly had an idea. 'I'm sorry, what did you say your name was again?'

'Katherine, Katherine Fellows. Lou would know me by a previous name—'

Lisa cuts me off with a choked laugh. Her mouth drops open, and her eyes are wide and astonished. 'You're Kate. Oh my Lord, you're Kate!'

I don't know how to respond. Lisa knows who I am and my heart's pounding again. Steph and Koop are watching me, waiting, but I'm dumbstruck. Lisa breaks the silence.

'You're really Kate Stuart? I can't believe it.' She chuckles. 'Papa Lou told us so much about you, I feel as though I know you.'

'Papa Lou?'

'Everyone knows him as Papa Lou. My, my, after all these years and here you are.'

'Here I am. We didn't know Lou was in palliative care, that's a shock.'

Lisa sighs. 'Papa Lou is in the final stages of liver failure. He's in care so that they can manage his condition, make him as comfortable as possible, but he's past all treatments for his illness now. He's made his peace and is in good spirits.' Lisa pauses. 'Can I ask, if you didn't know about Lou's condition, why now after all these years?'

I explain the discovery of a letter that led to our decision to come from England, but I'm cautious and don't go into detail, I have no idea how much Lisa and her family know about the past.

'Papa Lou has children who must decide if it's in his interests to see you. They may well say it's too much for him at this stage, that it might upset him. I'll talk to them first and let you know.'

I tell her we understand and we leave Lisa with a phone number and go before too many awkward questions can be asked. The drive back to Broken Hill is a silent one. When Steph's mobile phone buzzes that evening, it's Lisa to say that she's spoken to the family and they have given permission for a visit. It's Saturday tomorrow, and Lou's close kin will be at the hospice for most of the day, taking turns to sit at his bedside. Lisa says that Lou will be told of my visit beforehand

and I should prepare myself if he decides at the last minute that he doesn't want to see me. I'm trembling again.

For the second night in a row, I do not sleep. I lie awake and relive my time at Cutaway Creek. When we emerge from the motel, there's a thick veil of fog, and the air is chilled.

'It's freezing,' says Steph. 'More like England than Australia.'

'It gets cold at night, even in the summer,' I say. 'Don't worry, you'll be wishing for a cold morning fog later in the day.'

'The forecast is forty-two degrees and sunny,' Koop chips in.

He drives, and we make the most of an early start. There's not much traffic, but when a road train suddenly looms up out of the mist, almost clipping our car, it frightens the hell out of us.

'Did you see that!' says Koop. 'It must have been thirty or forty metres long.'

'Imagine it driving around the Lake District,' says Steph.

Koop is rattled by the close encounter for twenty minutes after. The sun is fast burning off the fog now, and we see the vast open plains of scrub.

'Oh, look, look, kangaroos!' Steph is excited to see a mob of ten or fifteen eastern greys staggered across the road.

When we arrive in Wilcannia, it's still only 9.40. We find a little café and order coffee and toasted sandwiches. My appetite is low, but I feel the need for sustenance before my ordeal, and it's looking more and more like an ordeal. But

I'm getting used to the constant nervous reactions, stomach churns and heart palpitations. We take our time, killing the minutes until our 10.30 appointment. The café is a cosy cottage full of charm, and I imagine tourists stopping in for tea and scones on their way through the outback.

Lisa meets us at the hospice and introduces us to Kirstie, Lou's daughter. I wonder what Kooper thinks of his half-sister as he shakes her hand. She takes after Lisa in her manner, bright and friendly, if not a little cautious. She's petite and lean, has high, well-defined cheek bones and a sparkle in her eyes that betrays her love for life. She says she's spoken to Lou, and he's prepared to see me. I'm not sure I can say the same, now the time has come, and we enter the care unit. There's a medicinal smell inside, accompanied by the fragrant aroma of a large frangipani that stands outside an open window. The cottage is bright and clean, and a nurse greets us at a front desk where we are invited to sign in. It's decided that I will go in alone at first. I'm quaking.

Tentatively, I enter the room. My breathing is heavy. Lou is sitting up in bed amongst white sheets and propped against pillows. There's a drip line leading to his arm, an oxygen line strapped under his nose. He opens his eyes as I enter. I smile, and so does he. I step closer, shocked to see him aged, though I could not have expected any different. His irises are the same deep-water green, but there's a heavy yellow tinge to the whites, and they're bloodshot with a maze of thin red veins. He's clean-shaven and his hair is a shock of white, a little wild.

His weathered skin is profoundly wrinkled and has sunspots, his mouth looks dry and chapped.

'Hello, Kate,' he says, his voice low and soft.

There's a gulf between us I dare not cross. I'm afraid of what I will find. 'Hello, Lou.' It's all I can manage as I choke up and tears cloud my eyes. I reach out and take his hand in both of mine. He takes me in, and I watch his gaze following the features of my face. He's probably thinking how old and weary I look. 'It's been a long time,' I say eventually, my voice barely audible.

'I'm afraid I'm not in the best shape.' His smile is warm, his voice like feathers. 'I knew you'd come one day.'

I can no longer control my tears. I start to sob and all the weeks of distress and fear threaten to explode. 'Oh, Lou, I'm so sorry. I—'

He squeezes my hand, but he's weak. 'Sorry for what? You have nothing to be sorry for,' he whispers. A tear drops from his cheek to the bedsheet.

'I do, I do,' I say sharply. 'I should never have left you to... Why didn't they believe my confession? Why...?' I'm distraught already, and angry that I am. I had wanted so much to be strong. 'I never knew. I never knew, otherwise I would have... Oh, Lou, I'm so sorry.'

'Hey, hey,' he says, 'that's all in the past. It's how I wanted it.'

'But my letter, my confession to the prosecutor...'

'He never received it, Kate. Ellin brought it to me, and I told her to burn it. They never read your confession. The important thing was that you and the boy were safe. I made the call, I didn't want it any other way. Besides,' he says. 'I was out in no time.'

'Ten years!'

There's a long pause. 'How have you been, Kate?'

I laugh and blow my nose. 'For the last sixty years, you mean?' I wipe the tears from my face and sniff. 'I've been luckier than I had a right to be.' I hesitate. 'Kooper is outside.'

Lou's smile widens. 'Little Kuparr,' he says.

'We spell it K-o-o-p-e-r,' I say. 'In England, they spell it with a C. Koop always had to correct people and eventually he started to introduce himself as Kooper with a K.' I chuckle, though it comes out like a croak. 'There's a funny family story from when he signed up for a Saturday chess club and he came home wearing a name badge that read: Cooper Witherkay.'

Lou laughs, but it's an effort, and he starts to cough. I fetch him a glass of water from the side table. When he's settled, I say, 'I met your daughter, Kirstie, she's lovely. Lisa too.'

'Yeah, I'm blessed to have them around. When Lisa told me you were here, she said you were very posh.'

'Posh?' I laugh.

'She said you talked posh like the Queen.'

I realise I'm not the Kate who left all those years ago, and must appear so to Lou as he tries to come to terms with the old woman he sees before him now. Michael was raised within aristocratic circles, he had that air of the privately educated English gentry. No doubt some of him has rubbed off on me over the years.

'Well, I know I've lost my Aussie twang, but I don't think I'm posh, and I'm certainly no Queen. I suppose Daisy Stuart would have said I'd crawled up my own arse.'

Lou smiles. 'Yeah, Daisy was known for her colourful way of expressing her opinions.'

We chuckle at the memories. I find it funny how when I think of Daisy now it's with a measure of fondness. Time has mellowed the image of the tyrant who made my childhood hell.

'Lisa is Ellin's granddaughter. Ellin died back in 1998. Same year my wife passed away.'

'I'm sorry,' I say.

'Yeah, me too.' Lou sighs. 'They was good people, them both.'

'Lisa says you also have a son.'

No sooner have I said this than I hear a gentle knock on the door. I turn. Kooper stands in the doorway and beside him is a broad-shouldered Indigenous man. He's wearing a business shirt and a green striped tie, I assume he's a doctor. I begin to speak, about to introduce Koop to Lou when I glance at the man and freeze. A shiver runs down my neck and it feels as though the world has shifted plates beneath the earth's crust. I take a long look at the smiling man, his eyes, the way he curls his lip. I'm dizzy, breathless, I can't speak. The air is thick between us, a chasm that threatens to pull me in and swallow me. I step forward, come right up before him, raise my hand and touch his cheek.

'Dear God, please. This can't be,' I whisper. 'Oh, dear God, please don't do this to me, not this.' I stagger, can't breathe. I gasp like I'm in agony, turn to Lou, back again. 'No, no, no. I can't... Lou?' I cry out. I don't recognise my voice, it's like the wail of a grieving wolf, howling at the moon.

It takes me a moment to understand where I am and what has happened. I've had a dizzy spell and I'm sitting in a chair being attended to by the nurse. I look to Kooper, fresh panic. I see Lou, then look to the man who now stands beside his bed, concerned, watching me recover.

Lou speaks. 'This here's Robin,' he says. 'Go and say hi to your mama, boy.'

Chapter 40

Grieve-Wayu

I'm exhausted by the time we reach our motel. Koop and Steph want to go out to eat, but I just can't find the energy or the motivation to join them. I'm feeling a little out of sorts, but I don't want to tell them. I encourage them to go, telling them I'm happy to make myself a cup of tea and have an early night. They're both in a great mood as they leave, and it's gratifying to see them so positive after what has transpired.

They've not long left when my heart begins to race, my hands are clammy. I'm sitting on the bed. It's suddenly silent. The room closes in around me, and I'm alone at last with my thoughts. Like everyone else, I had come away from the hospice on a high, smiles galore. My son was alive, a miracle.

I couldn't be happier. I had been dazed in the bedlam that followed the revelation, but the mood was joyous, everyone talking over one another in a battle to share their thoughts. A real reunion. It went on like that throughout the afternoon, while I tried to take it all in. Only later as we were driving back to Broken Hill, did I had start to feel uneasy. I sat in silence while Koop and Steph rattled on cheerfully about the day, but their voices were distant to me. I could not stop thinking of Robin and the years we had missed, the loss I now felt anew.

I think it's only now hitting me, the reality of what's happened. There's a growing feeling of discontent, a nagging voice that says I've been aggrieved. I'm conflicted between what I have found and what I have lost. I tell myself that it's futile to think about what might have been, it's now that counts, yet I can't help brooding on the years that have passed. I sit alone and contemplate, simmering under the weight. A sickly surge turns my stomach and a headache so intense makes me screw my eyes tight at the pain. Fifty-nine years. My insides churn. I think of the moments we should have shared, the joy we might have had if we had all been together, and I flush with anger at my years of ignorance. The time has gone, can never be reclaimed. I know I should be grateful, having found my dear son, I should be overjoyed, and I am, truly I am, yet I also feel so empty and bereaved, it's almost too much to bear. I dwell on the thought. My lip quivers. The grief is building in me, my eyes filling with tears. I start to sob. Over these last few months, these bloody emotions of mine have been stretched from pillar to post. I don't know when it will end. My chest heaves in convulsive jolts, the sound almost mechanical, as if a motor were trying to turn over, spluttering and coughing in an effort to start. My mouth twists in agony, I begin to wail. The floodgates open and I can't stop the flow.

I don't know how long I've been weeping, when there's a tap on the door, so delicate I can hardly hear it above my mournful cries. I'm in no condition to answer. My bawling continues unabated. The door to my unit cracks open. There's a woman peeking through the gap, she's come to see what's wrong, but still I can't stop. She steps inside, tentative steps, and closes the door behind her. Of Asian appearance, she has high cheek bones and soft pale skin, Japanese I think, though my tears are clouding my view. She has her hands clasped like she's praying, concerned for my welfare. I attempt to speak, to assure her that I'm okay, but I can't find my voice and there's only a groan escapes my lips. The woman approaches and sits at my side. She's older than I first thought, in her 60s perhaps. The lines of her face are softened by make-up, her eyes full of compassion. Her presence makes me feel worse somehow and I howl even more. She doesn't speak. She raises her hands and I slump into her open arms, fall against her breast where I wail and weep like a child. And there we sit, this stranger and I, as I pour out my heartbreak.

Ten minutes pass, and finally I'm spent. I slowly stop weeping, regaining my composure as the woman relaxes her hold on me. She releases me and smiles, a sympathetic smile that warms my heart.

'Thank you.' I blow my nose, breathe deep and sigh.

The woman stands, bows serenely and walks to the door. I want to thank her properly, to explain my distress and apologise for causing her to be concerned. I'm about to speak when she turns.

'Watashi wa anata ga heiwa o mitsukeru koto o negatte imasu.'

I don't understand the words, but her compassion is clear. I'm moved by her kindness, and manage a sad smile in return. She bows once more and leaves, closing the door gently behind her.

I sleep like a baby.

The following morning, we are leaving the motel unit when I pause, my attention drawn to a family of six who are packing into their SUV rental. They are speaking excitedly in Japanese. The father is busy organising their luggage into the rear hatch, while the mother sees to three young children as they squabble over seats. I assume it's the grandmother, the woman who sees me across the parking lot, our gaze meeting in a silent affirmation of our encounter last evening. The moment hangs between us, then she bows her head imperceptibly. I do the same and smile my appreciation. A hint of affection curls her lips, then she breaks eye contact and climbs in beside the children. Neither Steph nor Koop have noticed the exchange. I have no grounds for my whimsical notion, but it occurs to me that the kindness of this stranger was born out of her own personal loss, that she knew what I suffered because she'd suffered too. Perhaps she was on her own journey of redemption, a similar quest in the name of lost love.

We meet Robin and Kirstie for breakfast at a nearby café. Customers fill the tables, and there's a steady stream at the takeaway counter. Bacon sandwiches and pulled-pork rolls appear to top the order list, while fried eggs and hash browns sizzle on the hotplate. The flat white coffees smell delicious, and a young barista expertly serves up one after the other to waiting customers, brilliantly clad in fluorescent work wear and steel-toed boots. Breakfast on the run as they make their way to work at the mines.

'How's Papa Lou?' asks Steph above the noisy clatter.

'I spoke to Lisa this morning, and she said he slept well considering. I'm not sure how much he was taking in as the day went on,' says Kirstie.

'He's not the only one,' I say, but I'm only half joking.

'He doesn't have a lot of strength and yesterday would have taken a toll on anyone,' Kirstie continues. 'He's a happy man though, I'll say that much.'

Robin has Lou's eyes, and there's a twist in his mouth that's uncannily like his father's. I look at my two sons and wonder how they could differ so much in appearance. As if he's read my mind, Robin says to Koop:

'It's like looking in the mirror. The two of us could swap places and no one would know.' Everyone laughs. Robin has obviously inherited his father's sense of humour.

'We should do that,' says Koop, 'see who notices first.'

There's more chuckles and it's good to see everyone smiling and getting along. Robin is a fine-looking man. Like the rest of the family, he has inherited Lou's easy-going nature. He's outgoing, confident and instantly likeable. It has taken me a while to get over the shock, an understatement for my reaction, but my unrestrained outpouring of sorrow last evening has somehow cleansed me. Tears flowed, lots of tears, as I struggled to come to terms with the loss of so many years. But I cannot change what's passed, and I don't want to waste whatever time I have left, embittered and miserable, yearning over what can never be returned to me. Oddly, Kooper seems to have taken the news easily, as though he has received the missing piece of his puzzle. He can't take his eyes off his twin brother.

Yesterday, I relived the moments after their birth, every detail replayed in my mind. Robin was so tiny and weak, like a premature baby, clinging to life by a thread. Whisked away by Ellin, and later by Mary, there was no chance to form a bond with him. He was barely alive when Ellin told me his only chance at life lay in the hands of an Aunty Martha, a traditional healer I had never even met. In my confusion I let him go, unable to cope with the trauma unfolding around me. Then Ellin informed me of his death; it was all such a blur, I never stood a chance. I should be angry at Ellin, but I can't find it in my heart to condemn her actions. She did it, Lou assures me, to protect both Kooper and me, and at his insistence. When she asked me to name my dead child, she must have known he would survive and expected that we would be reunited.

'It must have been hard for you while your father was in prison.' I instantly regret my words, they sound so inadequate. Of course it was hard, and Lou would never have been locked away if it wasn't for me. My feelings of guilt are overwhelming, but I don't want to start crying again, so I fiddle in my bag as a distraction, then blow my nose and say that it's allergies.

'Mary raised me early on,' Robin says as I settle. 'She did her best, cared for me like I was her own. Her intentions were good, but Mary was a deeply troubled woman. She'd lost three kids to the welfare mob and I think she found it difficult to cope with that knowledge. She wasn't about to let me go the same way, so she stuck to me like shit to a blanket. Sorry.'

I snicker at the apology. 'I've heard worse. You never met Daisy Stuart.' I can't help grinning when I think of her cursing. 'You were taken into care?'

'Not for long. They came for us in 1961 and took us to the mission. Mary told them I was her son and they knew no different. They were used to her turning up with a new kid in tow. It wasn't long before Mary started running again. She never got too far, but she always took me with her. She hated the mission. They closed it when I was two years old. We moved about after that and things took a turn for the worse.

Mary started drinking. I was left alone a lot of the time, had no structure to my life.'

There's a lump in my throat. 'I'm so sorry,' is all I can say.

'Don't be. It was a long time ago. Aunty Ellin intervened and took me under her wing, and Mary left with a fella to Adelaide. By the time Papa came out, Ellin had me on a good track. I was studying hard, reading and writing at a high level and spending less time with kids who had no interest in learning. When Papa came home and took charge, he struggled at first. He couldn't find work and became depressed. Then he met Angela, Kirstie's mum. They married soon after. They had Kirstie the following year and I suddenly had a real family.'

I'm choking up, thinking of my poor son's disjointed childhood, and regretting that I wasn't there for him. The thought of him taken away to live on a mission turns me quite sick. I think of my childhood, the orphanage and my dispatch to Australia – children should not have to go through such things, and I of all people should have kept Robin safe.

'There was a short spell where I got in with the wrong crowd. But Papa was determined to set me straight. He had seen enough of kids who took the wrong path and ended up in Goulburn Prison. He made sure I went back to school and did my homework and stuff. And Angela wouldn't put up with any nonsense. She took me aside and said I had to take control of my life or I'd end up a stereotype. I got what she meant. If I wanted to live life on an equal footing to the whitefellas, she said, I had to stop living up to their expectations and do something with my life. She was very blunt when it came to doing things for yourself. The next thing I knew I was enjoying school again, not only that, I was good at learning. I went to college and followed that with a masters degree and a PhD at Adelaide University, where I studied law.'

'Isn't it weird that we both became lawyers?' says Kooper. He's all smiles.

'It's pretty cool actually,' says Steph. 'Maybe there was a psychic connection.'

'Papa tried to find you,' says Robin, changing the subject. 'But he had no idea where you'd gone. He spent time searching cities like Adelaide, Melbourne and Sydney, but he found no clue to your whereabouts. He wondered if you'd gone to England, and if it wasn't for me, I think he would have gone to look.'

'I don't think he could have found me there, even if he had tried.'

'I'm sure he wouldn't have,' Robin continues. 'I've been to England many times and made enquiries, but do you know how many Stuarts there are in the UK? And anyway, we didn't know whether you had changed your name or not.'

'You've been to England?'

The thought of him being so near without me knowing sends shivers down my spine. I imagine us passing in the street, strangers unnoticed in the mist of anonymity. What if I'd caught his eyes? Would I have known? Would I have recognised him? I know I would have.

Robin explains that he's travelled all over the world as a consultant and lobbyist for Indigenous repatriation. 'I'm just part of a larger team working to repatriate the remains of our ancestors. Do you know there's over six hundred sets of human remains in England alone?'

'I don't understand,' says Koop. 'Where are they?'

'They're held by museums, scientific organisations and private collections. Our work is painstakingly slow, but it's important to our people. I handle some of the legal issues and lobby governments and collectors to return the remains to Australia. Papa was the one who got me interested in the work. He was obsessed by the thought of our ancestor's bones decorating houses in Europe and America. He calls them Black Bones. Apparently, there was a man who wandered the country collecting Aboriginal remains for collectors around the world. His name was—'

'George Black,' I say before he can finish.

'That's right, George Black. How did you know?'

'Lou told me the story many years ago and the name must have stuck with me. I didn't believe him at first. I thought he was making it up.'

My mind drifts back to that fateful night by the fire. I see Lou laughing and dancing in the flickering glow of the flames. I see smiles turn to sadness as he told the tales of white invaders, his people's bones, scattered in the dirt, only for the graves to be desecrated for curiosity and greed. I remember his lack of malice, his generous attitude to my white heritage.

'I don't hate no one me,' he said when I asked him how he felt about whitefellas.

It's no wonder I remember that night; it was a night that changed everything, when we danced beneath that starry sky. There were more than just sparks in the air that night. It seems like yesterday, and I can almost hear the crackle of the fire, the smell of hardwood burning bright. I recall the gentle brush of his lips on my skin as we nestled in his bed, wrapped in love and blankets. Yes, that night changed everything; it changed me forever.

'Mum, are you listening?' I snap out of my reverie. 'Robin was just saying how Lou had nightmares about that bastard.'

Robin laughs. 'Papa was sure Black had him marked down for collection. We used to laugh about it when we were kids. I'd come up behind him, dig him in the ribs, make him jump and say, "I'm George Black and I've come for ya bones." Papa would pretend to be cross and say it was no joke, he'd come for me one day. He was right, of course, it's not funny. Our people are stored in jars and cardboard boxes all over the world.'

We settle into an easy conversation about Robin's childhood and compare his milestones with Koop's. Robin tells of his wife Tania and twin daughters, Cassidy and Karla, both married and living in Melbourne, where Cassidy is pregnant with my second great-granddaughter.

'Twins. They must run in the family.'

'Yeah,' says Robin; 'in more ways than one. Tania is also a twin, so there's plenty of twin genes to go around.'

'Do you know if it's possible to visit Cutaway Creek?' I ask, changing the subject.

'Whatever happened to the station?' Steph cuts in. 'Mum abandoned it, but she never sold it, would she still own it, or did it pass to the government?'

Robin smiles, and so does Kirstie. I can see they know the answer to Steph's enquiry. 'No, I'm afraid your mum...' Robin hesitates. '*Our* mum,' he says, 'no longer has any rights to the property and neither does the state.'

'Then who?' says Steph.

'Well, actually, Papa owns it, though we're in the process of transferring ownership to the trust.'

'The trust?'

'Papa's trust. Cutaway Creek lay vacant for years. When Mary left for Adelaide, Ellin took me to live on the station in her old camp. When Papa came out of prison, he joined us there, but we didn't stay long. When he realised that the homestead was still abandoned, Papa moved us in. Nobody stopped us. Years of heavy drought and neglect had left the entire station in a dilapidated state of disrepair. So Papa went about fixing it up. After a while, it just seemed like home. We kept thinking someone would come along and move us out, but it never happened. We were still living there when I went to law school. And during my studies, I learned about adverse possession.'

'Adverse possession?' Steph cuts in.

Kooper speaks before Robin can answer. 'Like squatter's rights in the UK,' he says. 'If a property has been abandoned and squatters move in and stay for a certain number of years, and the owner doesn't show up or contest the ownership, the squatters can gain ownership.' Koop looks to Robin for confirmation. 'Is that right?'

'Basically, yes. In this case, we were the squatters. We had already been living at the station for fifteen years when I eventually applied for Papa to get title. I made sure we met all the requirements before we applied to have it legalised, and the next thing you know, Papa was a landowner.' Robin looks at me. 'Sorry,' he says, realising the implications.

'Sorry? Don't be sorry,' I say. 'It's great. In fact, it's fantastic. I thought it would have gone to the Crown. But when you say Papa's Trust, what is that?'

'Well, when Papa was in prison, he saw kids come through, barely turned adult, too many of our mob in proportion to other inmates. It was always the same story, they came from poor communities where there was no work and no support. It made a big impression on Papa. When he came out, he struggled to find work. By then, most of the stations only hired young men with bikes and four-wheel drives.'

'No more horses,' I say, with more than a hint of nostalgia.

'Less and less. As time went on, the bigger stations started using helicopters for mustering. Papa and his kind were a dying breed. When we moved into the homestead, Papa decided to farm it.'

'Sheep?'

'A few. He couldn't work the station like the old days, like when you were here. The pastures were virtually useless after years of neglect and drought. But we kept enough livestock to feed us through the year, sell just enough to cover our needs.'

My mind reaches back to the musters of old, the thriving station with its annual gatherings of unique characters, animal and human. Despite my traumas, I can't help but see them as the good days of my youth.

'You were telling us about the trust,' says Koop.

'Yes, sorry. Three years ago, Papa came to me with an idea. He said he was sick and tired of seeing kids getting into trouble because they had nothing to do. "Why can't we have them here, teach them some life skills?" he said. I started looking into government grants and we began making plans for an adventure camp, where we could provide mentors and councillors for those who need guidance. Papa thought it could be a kind of way station for troubled kids, a safe place for those whose parents were struggling to cope, or just a place where kids could take a holiday and learn about the bush, survival skills and stuff.'

'Sounds great.'

'It was a good idea, but a lot of work to get off the ground. It took endless paperwork for different agencies and a lot of hustling bureaucrats, but we made it. We were awarded our funding and now the project's been up and running for almost four years.'

'And how's it going?' asks Steph.

'It's going well. Our hope is to return the place to a full working sheep station, using traditional skills and methods, proving permanent jobs for the community and even more opportunities for kids who need help.'

'Horses?' I ask.

'Horses,' says Kirstie.

'Yeh, we definitely have horses. We want the kids to have an authentic experience.' Robin is speaking with such passion and I'm so proud that he's turned out to be such an articulate and well educated man. He and Kirstie go on to explain the work of the trust in detail, and I watch as Koop gets into the conversation enthusiastically. Before my eyes, I see their friendship unfolding like a flower in the sun.

Chapter 41

Return-Thika

At the advice of the doctor, we leave Lou to rest for the day. The emotional strain has taken its toll, and the doctor feels Lou needs some quiet time on his own to recover. It's an opportunity to take a ride out to the station. I'm excited to see the place now. There will be mixed emotions, of course, I'll be confronting some old ghosts, but Robin and Kirstie are keen to show us what the trust has achieved, and I'm bursting to see for myself.

Robin drives his vehicle, Koop riding alongside him. Kirstie joins Steph and me in the Land Cruiser, and we follow behind. Steph drives, and we hang back a kilometre or so, to avoid the dust from Robin's vehicle. I can taste the dust and feel the grit on my teeth; it's like old times. As we drive, Kirstie explains her role in the trust. She is a trained social worker. She shares the same enthusiasm for the work as Robin. After a while, we settle into silence, and I take in the familiar landscape; it's food for my senses.

We turn off the road and into the station. A five-bar gate is off its hinges and lies rotting against the fence line, instead there's a cattle grid, which we rumble over, and I notice a rusty old mail box, perched on a post, but it's so dilapidated it's incapable of holding mail. I recall riding down on Tuesdays and Fridays to pick up the mail. Kirstie notices me looking.

'They no longer deliver mail out of town, haven't done for many years. We have a box at the post office.'

'I'd like a pound for every time I rode down to find it empty. We never had much in the way of correspondence,' I say with nostalgia.

I have no trepidation as we approach the homestead. The trauma that had built up in me for months has finally dissipated, and I'm feeling quite exhilarated at the prospect of our visit. I see the bore, but there's a new windmill to pump the water, and black sails have given way to shiny aluminium. There's also a new water tank sitting high in the air, bigger than the old one and made of plastic instead of galvanised tin. The homestead comes entirely into view, and I'm smiling. I never thought I would be so happy to see the place again. We come to a stop behind Robin and wait until the dust settles before climbing out. I'm immediately transported back to the first time I set foot in this yard. I recall the towering figure of Father Donahue, looking down on me, his enormous hand wrapped around mine. I see Daisy Stuart standing on the verandah, and Lachlan by her side. It's a vision that still stirs fear in me. I push their faces from my mind and take in the familiar buildings. Little has changed, though some of the structures have seen better days. There's a new roof on the homestead, but it still looks like a cat wearing a hat to me.

There's a young boy high up on the ladder to the water tank. He's watching our arrival with interest. He catches my eye and smiles, which lights his face. The boy hangs upside down to impress me. We're greeted with handshakes and a welcome by a young man in his early thirties, and a woman the same age. There are several young children gathered in a circle by the paddock. A young girl is standing in the middle telling a story. We hear them all laugh at something she says to amuse them. Laughter was not a regular occurrence when the Stuarts lived here. They laugh again, and I can't help smiling.

'Those kids are here for a summer camp,' says Kirstie. 'They're from a community on the outskirts of Adelaide. Dale is going to take them for art classes later. Dale is one of our team leaders.'

I turn and see Kooper and Robin on their way to the woolshed. Robin is animated, and Kooper is grinning like a Cheshire cat. I start to dwell on the time they have missed together; how I would have loved to watch them grow side by side. I wonder what kind of brothers they would have been.

Robin has become a rock of a man, broad-shouldered and square-jawed, and he walks like he knows his place in the world and is confident in that knowledge. How far he has come from that tiny flightless bird.

'Katherine?'

Kirstie brings me back from my thoughts. 'I'm sorry, I was watching the two of them together and...'

'I can't imagine how you must have felt when you discovered he was alive.'

I see the compassion on her face and hug her. 'There's so much to come to terms with, I'm trying to take it slowly.'

The boys have disappeared inside the woolshed. I remember its construction and how the station came alive with workers who came to help from all over the country. I recall Lou, sitting on the ridge, singing aloud while workers around him howled like dogs to put him off tune. And I recall him looking down to me and saying, 'Don't *you* start howling too, Kate. A man needs some support from his audience.'

'Is that a football pitch I see in the paddock? Never had one of them in my day,' I say, trying to distract myself from the weight of the past, now pressing on my chest.

Kirstie laughs. 'Yeah, it's part of the program here. Football – that's Aussie rules football – is pretty popular amongst Aboriginal kids. We try to get professional teams to support us by sending coaches and players to give clinics. They also donate kits and such.'

'Sounds great.'

'Yeah, it is, but sometimes I think we're just scratching the surface, these kids need so much more. Our communities need investment so our kids can have a future. And don't get me started on government support.'

'I'm ashamed to say that I'm ignorant when it comes to modern day Australia. I guess I avoided it over the years, afraid of dragging up my secrets with any mention of the place. But I do understand your frustration, I've read a lot about the local mobs during the last few months. It's hard to imagine that after all these years you're still struggling to find a voice.'

'There's plenty of good people fighting the fight. Probably more now than ever before. But there's growing anger and frustration amongst some at being constantly ignored on important issues.'

I think of the prejudice that was rife when I met Lou. Listening to Kirstie tell her stories, not a lot has changed. We walk around the stables, and I see more children under instruction.

'Half of these children would have been taken away to the missions when I was a girl. When I heard Robin had had suffered the same fate, I wanted to find someone responsible and punch them on the nose. But then I suppose that would have to be me getting clobbered. I was responsible, no one else.'

'Oh, Kate. You can't blame yourself, you didn't know.'

'I should have.' We're silent for a while. I'm fuming again. It's going to take an effort for me to get over these reactions, to stop feeling anger and guilt at every new comment, but I'll try not to let it cloud the positives in our reunion. 'It's hard to imagine such a cruel government policy that could separate families.'

'You know, Kate, there are those who would have those times back in a flash.'

When we meet up with Kooper and Robin, back at the homestead, they are discussing much the same subject.

'Who's the acrobat?' I ask, looking up to the water tank.

'That's Jarli,' says Robin. 'He finds it difficult to engage with the other kids. His parents are both in custody, and he's been in foster care on and off since he was born. He's a smart kid, but keeps himself to himself, despite our best efforts.'

I leave the others to go inside and I wander casually to the base of the ladder. Jarli has been watching me like a hawk since our arrival. 'Sure is hot,' I say, without looking up. Jarli doesn't answer. 'I am so thirsty, where oh where would I find water?' Still, Jarli is silent. 'I bet if I looked hard enough I could find water, maybe even a water tank.' Jarli giggles. 'Did I hear someone laughing at me?' Jarli giggles again. I look up and feign fright. 'Goodness me! I didn't see you up there.' Jarli is beaming down on me. His eyes are jewels, his smile like snow. 'You know, I used to climb that ladder. I was about your age too. I used to climb and swing and imagine I was atop a ship's mast, looking out to sea. Can you see any ships?' Jarli shakes his head. 'Do you think I could climb up there with you?' Jarli nods.

I can't believe I'm doing this. Slowly, I ascend the ladder, one careful step at a time. I'm still pretty fit, but I know this is stupid. I reach the top and Jarli shifts over so that I can hoist myself alongside him on the platform. I'm puffing more from nerves than exertion. We hang our legs over the edge and kick them back and forth in the air.

'How old are you, Jarli?'

'Eleven,' he says. 'How old are you?'

I chuckle. 'Oh, way past eleven. But when I was still small like you, I sat in this very spot. Do you see those trees out there by the creek?' Jarli nods. 'That's Mr Churchill and his wife and daughters.' Jarli covers his mouth with his hand to stifle a laugh. 'You don't believe me? Mr Churchill sees everything, just like we can see everything from here. He sees you and all the kids and watches over them to keep them safe like he did with me. If you look closely, you can see his face. Do you see it there beneath that big old branch?' Jarli squints. 'Do you see?'

'I see it,' he says and points excitedly. 'There are the eyes, there's the mouth, and his nose is all funny and twisted.'

'That's right. And he's waving his arms at you, can you see?' Jarli nods and waves back.

We sit without speaking for a while until Jarli breaks the silence. 'My pop's a policeman.'

'Is that right? Do you like policemen?'

Jarli thinks for a moment. 'No,' he shakes his head. 'My pop's not a policeman.'

'Okay,' I say cautiously. 'But policemen are nice people, aren't they? They try to help us when we need them or when we're in trouble.'

'They took my pop away.'

I'm immediately out of my depth, worried about saying the wrong thing. 'Do you worry about your pop?' Jarli nods. 'My pop went away too. I was even smaller than you. I worried about where he had gone, but I had people to look after me, just like you.'

'Where did he go?'

Suddenly I was a child again, frightened and confused. 'He had important things to do,' I say. But there's a lingering resentment in my voice, even after all these years. He abandoned Archie and me, no matter how Sister Josephine justified his actions. 'Grown men don't take care of little girls,' she said. But was I any better, had I not followed in my father's footsteps? I see Robin, still wet from birth, my tiny bird abandoned by me, and my stomach rolls.

Jarli puts his hand in mine. 'Don't cry,' he says.

'What in God's name are you doing up there? Are you crazy?' Steph and the others are in the yard looking up at us. 'Mum, you're going to hurt yourself, please come down.'

I look at Jarli and we both place a hand on our mouths and giggle.

Chapter 42

Remember-Yuri-pa

All the children and staff gather under a shade structure to greet us, and Kirstie conducts a welcome to country ceremony. Kooper hasn't quite grasped the importance of it yet, but this is *his* country. To me, it feels like a welcome home.

Lunch is a noisy affair. Some of the older kids attend to the barbeques, while the rest join us at picnic tables, where we are served up snags on bread buns with onions. The sausage smell is enough to stir even my poor appetite. I watch everyone enjoying the food, and though it's simple fare, it seems like a feast to me. I've made a new friend in Jarli. He sits at my side and asks me to help him pick the onions out of his hotdog bun.

The other children are chattering enthusiastically, stuffing their faces with food a drink and laughing as they eat. There's a little girl sitting opposite me and her face is covered in ketchup. I take a napkin and wipe her mouth. She giggles.

When we've finished eating, Dale puts on a tune for the kids to dance to. One of the boys follows this by giving us a solo singing performance over the PA system, a hip-hop song by an Aboriginal artist. He's really good. The boy tells us he wants to be a professional singer like his idol, and by the sound of his voice, I think he might just make it. The entertainment isn't over. Kirstie's team are determined to show us their full repertoire of performing arts. For the first time in months I feel so relaxed I could almost sing too. Almost. My voice has never matched my love for good music. Kirstie says that they'll finish with traditional dancing. I immediately think of Lou, dancing around the fire, his body taught and lean, his movements full of meaning and expression. How marvellous he looked as I watched him perform.

Steph and Koop are coerced into joining the group, but their moves look more like they're doing the chicken dance, much to the delight and laughter of everyone watching.

The kids go back to their activities. I show Koop where I slept after arriving from England. My outhouse is now a storage shed, but to me it's still my first bedroom. I show him a line on the door frame where I marked the waterline from the flood. Koop can't believe that I lived in the dark shed and wonders what kind of people would keep me there. In the homestead,

I show him the bedroom where he and Robin were born, the kitchen where I toiled at the rugged old Aga stove. I hear the distant creak of its door on old hinges, the clang of steel when it closed. It still dominates the kitchen, though there's a fine-looking electric appliance that looks almost new at its side. I turn and see Koop staring out of the window. The land is a brilliant ochre with a blueish shimmer where the scrub forms a band and is absorbed into the horizon.

'Do you think it's possible to feel someone who's not there?' Koop says. His gaze is fixed on the landscape, as if he's looking into the past.

'You mean like when someone has died?'

'Remember I told you once, when I was still in junior school, that I thought someone was following me?'

'Yes, I do remember. You had us worried sick. We even had the police involved. We spent months watching everyone with suspicion, anyone who gave you so much as a sideways glance.'

'I think I've always known about Robin,' he says, his faraway eyes, searching the scene for a glimpse of his past. 'Subconsciously knew he existed.' He turns. 'I think my whole life has been spent waiting for this moment, knowing it would come. I felt him all this time.'

'Toby once told me that Aboriginals believe that the space between things, time and distance, are constant, that everything exists at once in the Dreaming. It makes perfect sense that you felt a connection with Robin, that he's always been with you, that you've been connected to him and to the land here.'

There's a long silence as Koop contemplates. 'Would you have come back sooner if you had known about Robin?'

'I would never have left, no matter what the consequences.'

As we come back to the yard, Koop doesn't realise, but we stop at the spot where Lachlan died. It's a memory I'll take to the grave, but I say nothing as Robin re-joins us. He puts his arm across Koop's shoulder, and we walk to the stable, chatting like we've never been apart. I'm impressed to see that the station has so many horses. I stroke the head of a friendly mare.

'We could go for a ride out to the river if you'd like,' says Robin.

'Oh, I don't ride anymore. There comes a time in life when we have to accept our age and leave these things to the young.'

'Like climbing water towers?'

'Yes, and I nearly broke my neck getting down.' We all laugh. 'I stopped riding a few years ago after a horse kicked me and broke my hip. I had steel pins in for months. We only have racehorses, and they're too much of a horse for an old girl to handle.'

'We could hook you up with gentle Jenny,' says Robin. 'How about you, Koop, fancy a ride?'

Koop declines and I get the feeling he's keen for me to spend some time alone with Robin. He heads back to the others.

Jenny is indeed a beautiful mare, and she's as gentle as her nickname suggests. We saddle up and lope out, side by side towards the creek. Robin has none of his father's style, but he's obviously comfortable in the saddle.

'How's it feel?' he asks.

'It feels great, actually. I do miss riding.'

I tell him about Jack, how he gave me a whole new lease on life, gave me a friend when I had none, how he had died so tragically while trying to carry me to safety.

It's swelteringly hot, and the earth looks as inhospitable as it ever did; dry and dusty, there's nothing to call fodder in the ground. 'I'd forgotten how harsh this land was, tucked away in my rainy Lakeland hideaway.'

'It's the worst it's been for years.'

There are a couple of ewes snacking on a struggling saltbush, trying desperately to find sustenance in its withered leaves. The Australian merino is such a different animal to my Herdwick breed, but each is bred for the extremes of climate. They're such tough creatures. I tell Robin about our farm, and he listens with great interest, asking questions about my life, about Michael and the stud.

When we arrive at the creek, it looks much the same as it always did, but it's bone dry after months of drought. Mr Churchill smiles a welcome when he sees me. There's a tyre swing hanging from a branch. One of his limbs is broken and lies across the bank and into the creek bed. He's getting old like me. We dismount, and I take Robin to a spot beneath the old man, kneeling to touch the ground. This was where Ellin buried the boys' placenta, though I don't say this.

'I would have found you,' I say. 'If I'd known, I would have found you no matter what.'

Robin kneels and grasps my hand. 'I know, Mum,' he says, and my heart melts at him calling me that. I'm choked up and want to weep yet again. I've never been a crier, just the opposite, yet that's all I seem to have done lately. 'Papa told me everything,' he continues. 'First through Ellin, when Papa was still in prison. He had her tell me the truth from the off. When he came out, he sat me down and told me in his own words, told me the whole story, everything. He loved you dearly and was determined for me to know who you were, and that you hadn't abandoned me. He blamed himself for your leaving. It might seem a little weird now, but even after he married Angela, we talked about you like you were going to show up any day. Angela was great about it. She never once gave the impression she was jealous or anything like that. She was pretty special.'

'She sounds gracious. I'm so glad you had her to count on, to watch over you as you grew.' Even as I bless her name, there's a twinge of what can only be envy in my heart. This wonderful woman gave my son so much love, and yet I can only wish it had been me instead of her.

'We talked about you all the time. Papa wanted me to know you like he did, but he didn't have a photograph so he would describe you in detail. He swore we would be reunited one day. He was right.'

'And how did the reality stack up?'

'He did a good job, but it would be hard for anyone to live up to the perfect image I had in my head.'

I blush and change the subject. 'We passed over the river, it's in a sorry state.'

'The Baaka's dying. We've had several big fish kills and there'll be more to come.'

'I read about that. It's terrible.'

'The government says it's just the effects of the drought. They won't admit that it's bad management. Too much water being drained off for irrigation, it's not sustainable. To us, the Darling River is our lifeblood, our people are named after the river. But we don't get a say in how its managed.'

'It must be infuriating.'

'It's more than that. It's tragic.'

Silence lingers for a while. I'm thinking of all the injustices suffered by Indigenous people the world over. It makes me so angry.

'Will you be coming back to England, for the repatriation work, I mean?'

'I'm sure I will. It's a long and painful process and usually requires tons of negotiation. There's a lot more willingness to return remains now than there used to be, but there are still those who don't understand the significance of returning our ancestors to country.'

'It's a disgrace, it really is.'

'Nobody cares. It's just one more insult to our culture. What gets me more than anything is how the remains have often been treated, sitting on shelves in dusty basements, or worse, in boxes alongside stuffed animals. We received some a year or so back, returned from a private collection in America. They arrived unceremoniously in a shabby cardboard box, covered in dust. We found several skulls in the shipment, but one of them had been turned into an ashtray and, by the look of it, very well used. I was livid.'

I'm still stewing on Robin's tales when we return to the station, where Koop and Steph are trying to play Aussie rules football with the kids in the paddock. I say trying because Koop thinks it's Premier League and is kicking the ball around the field chased by dozens of screaming kids. I can't get over the transformation in his mood, and can't remember when I last saw him so alive and happy. I'm happy too, of course, but there are so many conflicts pulling me apart. While I rejoice over Robin, I don't know how much time Lou has left. I was heartbroken to discover his condition. These unexpected circumstances have changed everything, and created a new struggle with my conscience. I'd made a decision before coming to Australia that I told no one about. Now I'm not so sure it was a good one.

Chapter 43

We two-Ngaliwa

We plan the following day so that I visit Lou on my own for the morning. Koop and Robin will join us after lunch, while Steph will spend the day with Kirstie at the station. Lou is sitting up and looks bright and re-energised after the trauma of the previous visit. I wonder whose shock was the greater – his at seeing me, or mine for discovering my son alive and well. It's incredible to me that such shattering revelations could already be behind us. Such is our ease together we might never have been apart. A new monitoring system has been hooked up to Lou since my last visit. The colourful display shows a constant readout of various vital signs. A little red heart pulses on the screen, and I imagine Lou's beating its slow rhythm inside his chest to the same tempo. There's an IV attached to a cannula in his arm and he's got a button to administer pain relief. An oxygen line leads to his nose to supplement his airflow. Lou watches me checking everything out.

'I can get high whenever I want now,' he says, smiling. 'It's like I'm my own private drug dealer.'

I laugh, but seeing the bells and whistles brings home the reality of his condition. 'Maybe you can give me some of your medication while the nurse is not looking.'

He chuckles, but it's an effort. I lean in close to kiss his forehead, and smell his skin and the freshly laundered cotton beneath his head, and I want to cry. I breathe deeply to maintain control, sit in the chair beside him and hold his hand.

'We've a bit to catch up on,' he says.

'Just a bit.' We sit quietly for a moment, and I remind myself not to get emotional for Lou's sake. He asks me to tell him about England and what happened after I left Cutaway Creek. 'Wow, you don't want much,' I say, making light of the prospect. 'Where would I start?'

'Start at the beginning, I've got nothing urgent planned.'

I smile; he deserves to know everything. 'Life has been good to me, Lou, more than I deserve.' He listens silently as I tell him of my time in Sydney, Alonso and the voyage to South America. I describe my chance encounter with Michael on the voyage to England, his proposal and how he gave up everything for Kooper and me. 'He would have been Lord Michael Fellows if he hadn't thrown it all away for us.'

'He sounds like a terrific person.'

'He was.'

'You were lucky to find a husband so quickly.'

'I'll admit that I accepted Michael's proposal in haste, out of a sense of fear I suppose.'

'I didn't mean...'

'No, you're right, it *was* quick. I was terrified that the authorities were chasing me. I constantly looked over my shoulder, imagined them on my trail, law enforcement officers tracking me to England. Sounds daft now, knowing what I do. But I thought it wouldn't be long before they knocked on the door and arrested me, took my baby and shipped me back to face trial. How could I have known what you had done for me?

'I had funds enough. Lachlan had a stash of cash in a box in the attic, but I spent half of that getting to England. I knew it wouldn't last long, then how would I care for my baby? So it was a question of survival, and I did what I had to. I needed security for Kooper, so in a small registry office, I became Michael's wife. Only when we arrived at his family's stately home did I realise what I had signed up for. *Talk about financial security*. Michael had said little about the family's wealth or position. I understood later that this was not out of modesty but apprehension, that he knew what the reaction would be to his marriage and didn't want to paint a picture of a life we would never enjoy together.'

'You didn't get on with his folks?'

'Not exactly. I remember well the look on Lady Fellows' face when Michael introduced her to his new bride and young son. It was like something evil had climbed out of the gutter and crawled into her home. Lord Fellows, on the other hand, could not take his eyes off me, as though he saw right through to my soul and knew everything. I half expected him to accuse me of murder right there and then.'

'They should have known what a catch their son made.'

'I don't know about that, but they should have put his feelings first and given him a chance at least. They saved their admonitions for private, but I heard their angry voices taking Michael to task. I knew I would never be happy with such a weight of disapproval hanging over us. Had Michael not walked us away for good, my future and that of Kooper would surely have taken a different path. I couldn't have lived with the pressure of his family. Wealth or no wealth.'

'You'd have made a great Lady Fellows.'

'Because I'm posh, right? Well as Daisy would say, they could stick it up their bloody arses.'

We laugh at the thought, and I wipe a tear from Lou's eye. 'Go on,' he says.

'We leased a smallholding near the city of Bath. It had a stable for Ray and ample land to build a paddock and exercise ring. Michael had enough reserves to begin the enterprise without help from his father. He was a born entrepreneur, and Ray had an impressive set of papers. We soon had our first cover, and the Argentine Park Stud was up and running.'

Lou is listening intently. 'It must have been exciting for you.'

'I'm rattling on, aren't I?'

'Please, I want to hear everything.'

'Really?'

'Really.'

'The big breakthrough came with Dance Lightly,' I continue, 'a mare sired by the great Canadian stallion, Northern Dancer. Ray covered her in August, and the foal was a stallion called La Chacarera. He went on to win some high-profile races, including Royal Ascot and the St Leger. He had an amazing career.'

My mind leaps back to the winner's enclosure after victory in the Gold Cup, and our subsequent introduction to Queen Elizabeth and the Duke. She chatted to Michael for several minutes, though I have no idea what she said; I was so overawed by the occasion. My only thought was that I hoped Michael's parents were watching his triumph.

'Once retired to stud,' I continue, without mentioning the Queen. I was already sounding too grandiose. 'La Chacarera joined Ray to make Argentine Park one of the country's leading studs. By the time we purchased the stable in Buckinghamshire, our name was widely known. With a growing list of successes, we boasted waiting times of up to two years for covers.'

'Impressive,' says Lou.

'We took the name, Argentine Park, with us when we went to Buckinghamshire, having purchased the stud farm with a huge mortgage. At the time it was no small risk. But life was moving in the right direction, and we were confident of success. The stud is set on eighty-five acres of post-and-rail paddocks.'

'Eighty-five acres? That's *huge!*'

I saw Lou grinning. 'You're pulling my leg.'

'Me?'

'I know it's not Cutaway Creek Station, but in England it's big enough.'

'I'm kidding. Sorry, go on.'

'You always were a joker, it's one of the things that drew me to you.' There's an awkward moment of silence as I remember him, a young man, laughing and joking. I dwell briefly on our lost youth and feel a lump in my throat, heaviness in my heart. I try to hide my grief. 'Anyway,' I say eventually, 'we have a red-brick house, barns and stables with thirty-six boxes, everything we ever dreamed it could be. Mature trees surround the property now, trees we planted ourselves as saplings. A quaint village called Stoney Stratford sits only five minutes down the road. It's idyllic England in many ways.'

'How did Koop take to English country life?'

'Great at first. He was a happy young child. He seemed destined to follow in our footsteps because he loved horses. That was until he went to grammar school and suddenly lost interest. At twelve he caught a viral infection which saw him hospitalised for a month. He suffered from chronic fatigue for over two years, and was never the same after that. He became moody and withdrawn. We thought at first it was just the teenage blues. But we constantly had to fight to keep him from depression and it worried us no end. Things improved as Steph grew older. It's hard to keep a straight face when your sister is all smiles and laughter. She followed him everywhere, and when I look back now, I think she saved his life in many ways.'

'Steph is lovely,' says Lou.

'Yes, she is. I don't know how I would have coped with all this without her.'

'Tell me about the farm.'

'It's as far from Cutaway Creek as you could imagine. It rains almost every day, the highest rainfall in England, actually. And we have four distinct seasons that I look forward to every year. The Lake District is so beautiful, it takes poets to describe it. There are mountains and lakes, rivers and waterfalls, and charming villages made of local green slate.'

'You named the farm Drover's Elbow.'

I laugh. 'I did. It seemed appropriate at the time, given that it sits on the elbow of the river, though it's a far cry from the original. Michael had his stud, and I was happy, living and working alongside him as we built up the business. But after a holiday in Keswick one year – that's the nearest town to where we live on the farm – I fell in love with the Lakes and yearned for a place of our own there. We found the farm up for sale, though it hadn't been worked for years, the owners had run it as a bed and breakfast and campsite. We decided to renovate the farmhouse, and then gradually reintroduced livestock. We divided our time between Argentine Park and Drover's, but as the farm responsibilities grew, it became more than a hobby farm. I focused on the farm operations and Michael the stud. We were both happy with the situation and the compromises we made to achieve it.'

I think of the time Michael and I spent apart, sometimes weeks without seeing each other. It was a little strained at first, but he knew how much the farm meant to me and I would never have expected him to turn his back on the stud.

'It must have been a solid marriage to live apart for so much of the time.'

'Yes it was, but Michael had always been a workaholic and by that time in our lives, it just didn't seem like a big deal.'

'How about Kooper? If not the horses, where do his interests lie?'

Lou has a coughing fit, and a nurse comes to check on him. I can see he's in pain, but he hasn't administered any medication. I think he wants to keep his mind clear while we talk.

The nurse retreats, and I continue. 'Kooper was not an outgoing child. I know it was only my imagination, but I sometimes felt that he was aware of his missing twin, that it weighed on his mind somehow and contributed to his depression. It's uncanny that he confirmed as much to me only yesterday. It seems he's been feeling his brother's presence all his life, but he never knew what it was until now. He never told me this before. Anyway, when Steph came along, he turned out to be a good older brother. But as his sister grew, her personality dominated. She was everything he wasn't, right from the beginning. She would chatter on endlessly, and Koop would say she was giving him an earache.'

Lou chuckles. 'We have a few like that in our mob.'

'Don't get me wrong, he loves her like crazy. But sometimes she just overpowers him. She made friends easily, and he just retreated. But he was a thoughtful boy, and academically, very clever. While Steph spent every spare minute at the stud and with the horses, Koop studied. I still can't get over he and Robin both ending up lawyers. Who would have thought? They must have been studying at the exact same moment, each at the other end of the world.'

Lou nods in agreement. 'Robin was the same. He showed no real interest in the land, he wanted knowledge and took every opportunity to get it. Everyone thought he was a troublemaker, and he did get into trouble, went right off the rails for a time, but who could blame him when his papa was nowhere to be seen.'

'Or his mother,' I say, guilt stabbing me in the gut.

'I'm sorry, I didn't mean...' Lou presses his button and releases some medicine at last. I wait while he composes himself. 'I didn't mean to make you feel bad, Kate. You had no way of knowing he was alive. I was the one responsible for him, and I made that decision.'

'But you had no right to leave me out of that decision,' I say, with too much recrimination.

'I wish I could change that, Kate, change the way it worked out. If I'd realised I wouldn't be able to find you, I'd have done things differently. I was only trying to protect you and both the boys. It was the only way I knew how.' He closes his eyes, and I regret my rebuke. I squeeze his hand in both of mine, raise it to my mouth and kiss him.

'Ellin gave Mr Tupper your letter and asked him to pass it on to me. When I read it... When I read it, I decided there and then that I would have it destroyed. Tupper said you had up and gone. I was so relieved that you wouldn't be able to fight me on it.'

'I would never have gone if I'd known you would destroy the confession.'

Lou's face softens. 'I thought I had a good chance of beating the charge. I was wrong as it turned out. Tupper turned tail and headed back to the city, and a lawyer from Parkes took my case to the appeal. I was lucky I didn't get life. They sent me to Goulburn to serve my time. That was a shit of a place,' he says, sighing.

'I can't imagine how terrible.'

'Mary took Robin to a traditional healer, a Ngangkari woman who tended him until he was strong enough. It was touch and go for a while. But Robin was a fighter, Kate, a real fighter. He pulled through, came on in leaps and bounds. I wanted him to know you, everything about you. I wrote letters about you, told him how I would find you as soon as I got out and that we would all be together. Then I heard the Protection Board had taken him to the mission. I was devastated. Mary stuck with him and they thought she was his mother, but you know Mary, she wasn't the strongest of women. Her heart was there but she was a restless soul, she'd spent most of her life in and out of missions, losing her children to the Protection Board, it left her a mess. When Ellin said Mary had started drinking, we knew we had to get Robin away. The mission was closed and it wasn't long before Mary took off with a fella from Adelaide, leaving Robin with Ellin and we lost touch with her soon after.'

'I should have been there for him.'

Lou doesn't reply.

'I spent years looking for you,' he says eventually.

'Robin told me. What a mess I made of things.'

'We both had a hand in it, Kate.'

How many times have I relived those final days? The terror, the panic when I feared for my sons more than my life. I know now how traumatised I was, how confused and alone I must have been to let Robin go.

'When Steph was fifteen, we went to a school sports day,' I say, reflecting back. 'All her classmates were there, all of a similar age, fourteen, fifteen. I watched them chasing around the park, acting daft like kids do, teasing the boys and lighting up the day with the innocent smiles of youth, laughing and giggling, ordinary children enjoying life as they should. I imagined what it would be like if she had to marry a man more than three times her age, endure the abuse, the cruelty, the trauma of that awful wedding day. I tried to imagine her giving birth, dealing with Lachlan's death. I wondered how she would cope. The prospect was horrifying. We were so young, Lou, so young, you and I.'

'That's why you can never blame yourself for what happened,' Lou says with a squeeze of my hand.

I know Lou is right, I could never have been entirely responsible for my decisions and the course of my life – I was no more than a child at the time. These are not my excuses, nothing can absolve me for what I did, for my role leading up to that day and the decisions that followed, but these are the facts. Perhaps I can finally forgive myself, now that I know Lou has forgiven me. I have been punished with the loss of years, years watching Robin grow, watching my sons grow up together. There's only an empty ache where those memories should rest. It's a void that can never be filled. But is it punishment enough?

'Tell me about your wife.'

'Angela. She was a shrimp,' he says fondly. 'only five foot two, but she was a formidable woman. Independent and opinionated, that was Angela.' Lou chuckles as he reflects on her memory. 'She was a Gundungurra woman, born and bred on the mission at La Perouse – that's over Sydney way, on the coast. She was visiting relatives when we met and we just hit it off. She was passionate about Indigenous issues and was determined to get the schooling she missed out on as a girl. She said she wanted to go to university one day, and she did, though she was fifty by the time she earned a scholarship. She did five years of study then worked in Aboriginal health, and became very politically motivated. A lot of Robin and Kirstie's views come from Ange. She taught them never to kowtow to anyone and to be proud of their heritage. She was a fiery one alright.'

'She sounds perfect.'

'Oh, I don't imagine she would describe herself as perfect, but she had great pride in who she was, and she instilled that in the kids. She had emerged from the mission a determined woman. She had a strong sense of right and wrong, and somehow, she managed to have faith in God, even though she questioned where He was when she needed him as a child.'

'I know just how she felt.'

'What about your god? Did you patch things up with him?'

'Oh, we still have our battles.' I think of my struggle with faith; it has never really ended. 'There were dark times, Lou, when I too thought God had abandoned me. I can't pretend there weren't. Sometimes my loss seemed too much to bear, my guilt too heavy to carry. But as time passed, the pain was not so raw, and the more I immersed myself in the family and the business, the less time I had to dwell on my role in Lachlan's death, on the loss of you and Robin. Time was a healer, and there's no disputing the good fortune that blessed me. But I never did go back to church, I felt I'd gone beyond that concept, the whole House of the Lord thing. It wasn't that I'd lost faith completely, or blamed God for what had happened, more that I found God elsewhere, everywhere, a constant companion, though we argued a lot.' I chuckle and wonder if God's listening in.

'So, are you at peace now, Kate?'

'I thought I was until recently. We still had the occasional cross word, God and me, but I was content. I have to admit I was devastated when Koop found the letter – I thought God had pulled the plug on our relationship yet again. I thought I would lose everything. I should have had more faith. Look at where it's brought us.' I pause and sigh. 'I still grieve our lost years, though I'm grateful for these moments we have now.'

'I'm sorry you suffered.'

We are silent with our thoughts as I pluck up the courage to speak. 'There's something else I need to tell you,' I say at length. I'm hesitant, but I can't keep it inside any longer. 'I came here intent on turning myself in.'

Lou looks astonished. 'I must be losing my hearing as well as my liver, because I swear you said, *turn yourself in.*' His face goes through a random range of expressions, confused by what he's heard. 'Are Kooper and Stephanie aware of this?'

'No. It's a decision I made before we left England. They don't know anything about it.'

Now he looks annoyed. 'You don't need any of my drugs, Kate, you've been smoking something wacky already.' There's no humour in his comment.

'Just hear me out,' I say. He sighs and rolls his eyes. 'When I heard you had been convicted, I knew I had to clear your name. I decided to come and face up to you, and face up to my crime, to the law. You've shouldered the blame all these years while I hid like a coward. I decided I had to put that right.'

Lou shakes his head, he's getting upset and is struggling to compose himself. I can see on the monitor that his heart rate has risen.

'Kate,' he says eventually. 'Look at me. I want you to look me in the eyes, because I'm only going to say this once. You're a fool!' Now I'm taken aback. 'A damn fool for even thinking it. If I was stronger, I'd put an end to this nonsense right now. I'd march you straight back to that airport and pack you off to England, before you can do anything so stupid. How can you be so inconsiderate?'

'But—'

'No buts, Kate. Just shut up for a minute and listen. *We*, understand? *We* were responsible for what happened to Lachlan, not you, not me, *we*, because of our actions together. And I served *our* time – *our* time, Kate. I wanted it that way so our boys could have a future, so they wouldn't end up like all the other kids and taken away from us for ever. I served our time. That was the price I paid, so don't make that for nothing because you want to be some kind of martyr. Don't make those years count for nothing, Kate. We've suffered enough from the decisions we made. Lachlan would have killed our sons, killed us too probably, and though we didn't want him dead, he brought it on himself and you did what you did to save us. And another thing, if that god of yours has more to say about it, let him talk to me. I'll be seeing him soon enough and I'll tell him a thing or two.' Lou stews on the subject for several long moments. 'Does that put an end to it, Kate?' he says emphatically.

What can I say after that? I have been well and truly told and I'm compelled to see the sense in his argument. I'm ashamed to say I'm relieved. I smile, kiss his hand and nod my compliance. I let Lou calm down in silence, watching the monitor as his heart rate slows back to normal and he begins to relax. I understand his anger, and I'll abide by his wishes. He's right; I'll wait for God to have the last word when our time comes, until then I'm going to embrace every minute.

'We both did what we thought was the best,' I say eventually.

Lou nods and sighs. 'There were times I wished it had never happened the way it did. Many times I wanted to turn the clock back, rewrite history and have our chance again. But now I know our fate was a blessing for us both.'

'A blessing?'

'You had Michael in your life, I had Angela. You have Steph, I got Kirstie. We have two grown boys to be proud of, grandchildren and great-grandchildren coming out of our ears. What more could we want? I wouldn't change anything now, and neither would you. Our sacrifice made the world a better place, and for that, I will forever be thankful.'

I lean over and kiss Lou's cheek. 'Through all these years I've loved you, everything you say reminds me why.'

'You were never far from my mind, Kate. When I knew I was dying, I was afraid.'

I squeeze his hand. 'Oh, Lou, I'm so sorry.'

'Not afraid of dying,' he says quickly. 'And don't you start feeling sorry for me either. I made my peace with dying long ago. I was going to say I was afraid because I thought I wouldn't see you in time. I knew you would come, Kate, never doubted it for a minute. I've always known. But I started to think maybe you'd get here too late.'

I'm choking up and struggling to stay strong. 'Well, I made it,' is all I can say without breaking down completely.

Lou looks exhausted. 'That you did, Kate. That you did.'

Chapter 44

Spirit-Kulypa

Lou passes peacefully two days later, serene and content, with his extended family by his side. We have spent our treasured time telling the tales of our lives, enjoying the adventures of children and adults alike, stories from both sides of the world. We've cried tears of sadness and of joy; we've broken each other's hearts, and healed them with love, forgiveness and compassion. When it became apparent that Lou was losing his battle, the room filled with family members from every corner of the state. Aunts, uncles, nephews and nieces, they came with friends, elders and infants, to see him on his way. When Lou could no longer join in the telling of stories, he had listened with pride, I could see it in his eyes. And just as Lisa had finished a hilarious anecdote about

Robin's first date, and we had all roared with laughter, Lou gave a final sigh and slipped into the Dreaming.

We are driving across the outback. The heat is relentless. I watch the miles and miles of dry land go by, with its straw-coloured grasses, salt bush and mulga. A mob of red kangaroos matches our speed briefly, before peeling away to safety. In my mind's eye I'm riding Jack, Lou at my side on Smokey. We're galloping, racing each other to the ridge. Young and fearless, we hoot and holler above the thunder of hooves.

The four-wheel drive slides to a stop near the creek, and we step out into the heat of the day. There's a breeze but the air is like a hairdryer on our faces. A brown snake slithers from sight. The land is a vivid mix of red, yellow and orange. I look to the sky and see a thin veil of cloud, high in the stratosphere, otherwise, it's blue. Koop and Steph are in awe of the expanse.

'How big is that sky,' says Steph.

We are silent for a while, as if to speak would shatter our reverence. Robin is carrying a cardboard cylinder with flowers printed on the outside. It looks as though it could carry a bottle of wine, a gift pack, but it holds Lou's ashes. 'It's a scatter-pack,' said the man at the crematorium, when Koop and Robin went to collect their father's remains. We had expected something more dignified, a little wooden casket or an urn perhaps. Lou would have thought it ironic, having ended up in a cardboard box after all his fretting. But it won't be for long and I'm sure he would have seen the funny side of the travesty.

I lead the way, and with the help of Robin, we clamber over the worn rocks to the top of Yalta Maku, following the footsteps of those who had gone before over thousands of years. At the summit we absorb the powerful moment and acknowledge the unique spirituality of this special place. Kirstie and Robin have left their families at home. They have paid their respects during a memorial service at the crematorium chapel, and a celebration at the community hall in Wilcannia where they conducted the sorry business with songs and stories. This moment is shared only by the five of us.

For a moment, I am transported back. Lou is at my side, takes my hand, places it on the rock surface and covers it with his. 'Do you feel it?' he asks.

'Feel what?'

'Close your eyes. Think of nothing but your hand on the stone, on the land beneath your palm. Now, let yourself connect.' He waits in silence. 'Do you feel it now?' he says eventually.

I concentrate, and soon I'm filled with awareness. My heart races. 'I feel it,' I say.

'That's country,' says Lou. 'That's my place, that's me.'

I snap out of my trance. The others are looking to the horizon, taking in the isolation. I think of Lou and his spiritual connection to the land. I wonder wistfully if he used it somehow to bring us here before he died, conjured up

Michael's letter and had it drop into Kooper's hands. Perhaps he conspired with Michael through the Dreaming to have us share his final days.

This is the land of my childhood, my youth. I stayed eight short years in Australia, only a few weeks of which I spent with Lou. Yet the impact on my life has been profound. How could we have imagined that our brief encounter could last a lifetime, that after all these years we would rediscover a bond so strong and unbreakable, it would span all space and time? I see Robin and Kooper, side by side, brothers. I've never seen Kooper so content, so at peace. He came to me this morning and said, 'I'm home, Mum, this is where I belong.' I wonder how life will play out from now and into the future, but there is time enough before we have to make decisions. Steph and Kirstie have become the best of friends; there's enough energy between them to build nations. I don't know what will happen next; I only know that we are one and nothing can ever break us apart again.

The time comes, and we make our way gingerly to ground level, my old limbs are not as agile as my mind.

Blood red earth. The intensity of the colour is emphasised by long black shadows thrown forth by the rocks, like sentinels, they watch over our gathering. I imagine spirits within these standing monoliths, Lou's ancestors waiting patiently to finally take him into the Dreaming. It takes me a while to identify the place, but I'm sure it's the right spot. We stand in a semi-circle, silently contemplating. I think about the bones by the dry creek to the east, and those scattered about the vast land, the story of life repeated infinitely. In the end, we're all just bones in the dirt; the names are different, but the bones are the same. I see our footprints in the dust, they will soon be blown away and disappear with the wind. The memories will remain for a while until they too join the Dreaming. There's a tear in my eye again, but it's not for Lou, it's for myself.

I had wanted to say something profound, but the right words elude me. Robin opens the tube and offers it to me. I reach in, take a handful of ashes, and kneel. I scrape a hollow in the earth, plant a kiss on his remains and scatter his ashes in the ground. Everyone does the same before Robin empties the cylinder completely, the remaining contents caught on the breeze and sailing into the sun.

I hear Lou's voice. 'I am the earth; the earth is me.'

Until we meet again, dear Lou, together in the Dreaming.

[End]

ACKNOWLEDGEMENTS

I would like to acknowledge the traditional owners of Australia, and pay respect to the Aboriginal Elders, past, present and future, who hold the traditions, memories and the culture of Indigenous Australia. In particular, I acknowledge the indigenous people of the Baaka (Darling) River, where this novel is partially set.

Black Bones, Red Earth is a work of fiction, but certain characters and events have been inspired by true stories. I have tried where possible to stay faithful to history and geography, otherwise I have used my imagination.

I am deeply indebted to Aunty Val (Velma) Mulcahy, Aunty Bev (Beverly) Lane and Aunty Annie Warren, Gundungurra Elders, for allowing me to sit and yarn, week after week, during the writing of this novel. Thanks especially to Aunty

Val for her stories, and for educating me on the history of her people and the Aboriginal culture, which allowed me to tell this tale with some measure of authenticity. This novel pays respect to the stolen generation and the trauma they suffered due to separation from their families.

Indigenous language used in the story has come mainly from the Paakantyi dialects, however, due to the origins of certain characters, some words might originate from other regions of Australia. Among the resources of particular help while writing this novel: Jeremy Beckett's journal, *George Dutton's Country: Portrait of an Aboriginal Drover,* Bruce Pascoe's *Dark Emu,* Rachel Perkins' documentary series *First Australians,* Paul Daley's essay *Restless Indigenous Remains,* Luise A. Hercus' *Paakantyi Dictionary,* Jens Korff, Creative Spirits, Gordon Briscoe's *Racial Folly,* Jeremy Beckett and Luise A. Hercus' *Two Rainbow Serpents Travelling,* Douglas J. McDonald for his help on DNA testing.

Thank you Christine Fletcher and Mary Cunnane for sending my work in the right direction. Readers: Des Lewis, Anthony Lee, Mary Hughes and (Gundungurra Elder) Aunty Bev (Beverly Lane). My wonderful editor, Lauren Finger, for her diligent work and assistance. And finally, thank you to all my family and friends for your undying encouragement, love, and support – Lee Richie.

ABOUT THE AUTHOR

Lee Richie is the Australian author of *Black Bones, Red Earth.*

Lee was born and grew up in Liverpool, England, where he married and fathered three sons. Lee and his family emigrated to Canada in 1982 where they spent ten years, before moving to Australia. After years in international management, Lee has swapped spreadsheets for manuscripts and is now writing full-time from his home in the Southern Highlands of New South Wales, Australia.

Lee is also the author of the young adult novel, *Alexander Bottom & the Dreamweaver's Daughter,* which was well-received by readers worldwide.

www.leerichie.com

www.ingramcontent.com/pod-product-compliance
Lightning Source LLC
Chambersburg PA
CBHW021953130726
47903CB00014B/1120
9780648256434